THORNS

HISTORICAL MYSTERIES COLLECTION

BARBARA GASKELL DENVIL

Copyright © 2024 by Barbara Gaskell Denvil
All Rights Reserved, no part of this book may be
Reproduced without prior permission of the author
except in the case of brief quotations and reviews

Cover design by
It' A Wrap

Also By
Barbara Gaskell Denvil

Historical Mysteries Collection

Blessop's Wife

The Summer of Discontent

Vespers

The Flame Eater

Satin Cinnabar

Sumerford's Autumn

The Western Gate

The Deception of Consequences

Cornucopia

(An Historical Fantasy series)

The Corn

The Mill

The Dunes

Stars And A Wind Trilogy

A White Horizon

The Wind From The North

The Singing Star

The Omnibus Edition

Mysteries of another sort

Between

The Games People Play

(A serial Killer Trilogy)

If When

Ashes From Ashes

Daisy Chains

Time Travel Mysteries

Future Tense

The Barometer Sequence

Fair Weather

Dark Weather

NOTES FROM THE AUTHOR

Just a few words to anyone reading this book.

The background to the plot, the events of England in 1485, are correct within the boundaries of known and accepted history. The same events have been interpreted differently by other authors, but since there is no poof in either direction, I have kept with my own judgement, all of which is entirely possible, probable and logical.

I have used modern language throughout, including words unknown in that period, and a manner of speech which most people of that time would not even have understood. I consider this also logical. Their own fashions of language at that time would be barely understandable to us now, and I have no wish to drive my readers crazy with medieval wordage.

Therefore, I hope you will forgive any colloquial conversations which may seem out of context. I assure you, you could hardly enjoy any accurate medieval manner of speaking, unless you are an academic historian.

Another issue may be in English and American spelling. We

share the same language more or less but have chosen to spell so many words differently. I am English and this novel is set in the English medieval period, so I have kept to the English spelling. I hope this doesn't cause any problems.

    I simply hope you enjoy my book.

CHAPTER ONE

It was the twelfth chime of the church bells which woke her at midnight on Christmas Day, to find her husband lying dead beside her.

Impenetrable fear echoed as the fading chime of the bell turned in her head.

The man, who an hour past, had been in her arms, warming her body from the chill of the room, now lay cold and rigid at her side and froze the sheet where the heat from earlier only echoed, as did the church clock, and as did the fear in her heart.

Illiana knew. Yet hoping, whispering, "My love? Do you hear me? Please tell me." No answer followed, The sour smell of vomit lay close across both linen and feathers. Easing herself from the eiderdown, she bent over, but she knew it was not sleep. It was death. Not a dream, but a nightmare.

Downstairs, the halls darkened, a hundred candles sizzled into melted wax or their flames were snuffed as the pages, so tired now, wandered the hall, the gallery and the corridors, watched by the steward as they neglected sleeping dogs and doused any spitting cinders still alive in the inglenooks. Grey Friars had chimed the final goodnight to a long and festive day, yet now the celebration rang its permission for weary servants to crawl at last to their beds.

As shutters were finally lifted downstairs, upstairs the shutters clanked as the new countess staggered to the window and pulled them down. In the glint of light as a full moon pierced the gloom, she saw the vomit on her husband's chin. He lay on his back and around him, smothering the open lips and dripping to his naked chest below, was the partially digested food of his earlier feasting. The smell was strong, sickly-sweet and vile. as Illiana tried to breathe.

She shouted as she cried. "Please Benedict, you can't leave me." Her sobbing was now louder than her words, "you've had no blessing. You don't deserve to suffer in purgatory. I beg you to come back." She stroked the pale hair from his forehead. It was slick with sweat and his eyes were shut. Benedict had drunk more wine than she had ever seen him drink before. It had been his celebration, not only for the holy day but for his own anniversary, one month of happiness wed to his second wife.

She desperately hoped, he had died of pleasure and delight.

Shivering, Illiana flung on her bedrobe, reached for the bell hanging beside the bedcurtains, and swung it in panic, calling for help. Then waiting silently for the steward to answer the call, her own thoughts pushed deeper. She imagined the ragged gargle of his throat gasping, no breath coming, only splutter and vomit, and the final desperation of the man dying beside her as she slept, unaware of the misery. She collapsed in sobs.

The steward had recognised the urgency of the call, thundered up the stairs and into the earl's bedchamber, then shrank back as the bilious stench told its own tale.

Manders stared back at Illiana. He stuttered. "My lady, the earl is, - no longer alive."

"I know." Her face shone wet in the moonlight.

Taking an unlit candle from the table, Iliana lifted the flint and lit it. She held the flickering flame high as she returned to the bed and looked down at the unmoving body there beneath the velvet covers. The stench hung heavy over the dead man, rising gradually to fill the claustrophobic chamber, its intricately painted beams holding up the vaulted ceiling and its collection of spiders too high to reach and sweep away. The wide bedstead lay safe from falling insects beneath the tessellated tester, yet could not protect the room from death.

Manders bent, then dared to say, "My lady, I am deeply sorry. This is terrible. Ask whatever you wish. At first prayers, I will contact the bishop of Grey Friars and arrange the blessing and the funeral. I'll send a page for his lordship's doctor immediately." His grey hair in his eyes, Manders stared, worried, then turned towards the doorway, but looked back. "My lady, shall I inform your mother?"

"Not now. Let her sleep." Illiana wanted no inevitable accusations, nor orders of what to do next. As the steward hurried past, she returned to her tears, already missing the husband she had barely known.

After years of rarely seeing this man, the Earl of Birstall, her master, she had discovered that seeing him as her husband was so very different. From a distance, he had smiled at her. From his own bed, as her husband, he had cared for her. He had told her he loved her. She had kissed him in return and let him teach her what being a wife involved.

There had followed a month of gentle understanding, a wagon-full of new clothes, jewellery which shone and sparkled in the candlelight, and even a maid to help dress her and arrange her hair. The maid invariably sat on the bedside rug and giggled, endlessly chatting, since this was the friend she had known for years. They had been servants together and Illiana had known Sabine since they had both been just skinny children.

Now on the evening of Christmas Day, having nearly learned to love the earl, everything had surged backwards against the tide, her hopeful dreams sinking again into the muddy banks of brown sludge.

As Manders sent a page running for the doctor. the church bell rang again, one chime echoing, and so a new day had begun. In London's unlit streets, the night was still young but already the riverbank was crisp with frost. Deeper along the lanes and the cobbled streets, the day's smoke from five hundred chimneys hung low in a rusty cloud that hid the stars yet smelled sour, no wind gusted to sweep the smoke clean of their embers. Beneath the low mist, folk hurried home after their celebrations, delighted by the best day of the year, or staggering, cupshotten, trying to remember the way home. Heads down, men pulled up their cotes and unbuttoned their codpieces, pissing into the gutters, into the river further south, or simply against whatever wall was close.

Doctor Sutton arrived almost immediately and was thankfully sober, he quickly glanced at the bed, drew in his breath and without hesitation, he spoke to Illiana. "My lady, I'd recommend you wait downstairs. There's naught you'll be wanting to see here."

"I'll turn my back," soft voiced. "But I need to know what has happened. I have to know that it – wasn't – me." There had been the dream before she woke. "I mean," and she was stuttering, "I know it wasn't me, but if I rolled on top of him or threw out my arm in my sleep –"

"I can tell you now, my lady, there's little to say." The doctor's voice was efficient and without sympathy. "His lordship died quickly and without pain. He was still asleep, or would have known to roll over and clear his throat. But he choked, my lady, and the vomit fell back along the throat to block the lungs. No doubt a large quantity of Burgundy. I'm sorry to say this is no rare occurrence on nights after celebrations."

Illiana nodded. She was breathing more deeply herself. "I know what he drank. So, it must be as you say, sir."

Doctor Sutton pulled back the covers over the large man, but made no attempt to move or cleanse him. Manders showed the doctor out as Illiana stayed beside the mullioned window. "My lady, it is yourself who suffers now. I'll have the bed warmed in one of the spare chambers, and send in your maid. Meanwhile I'll call for Farther Joshua to bless his lordship, and he will arrange for the funeral."

"Yes. Please wake Sabine and ask her to come. And tell my mother in the morning." Sabine, the only friend she'd ever had before her marriage, would help a lot. She sat again beside the body, and stared down at him. Benedict's cheeks fell hollow. This time she cried for herself. She saw herself once more as a penniless brat. A future without the lord as her husband.

Yet perhaps the absurdity of her marriage had always been fated to dissolve. Her father, the dashing Spaniard, had once been chief groom. Though dead as her husband, she could barely remember much of him except his laugh. He had always laughed. When she had tripped, he had laughed. The grooms joking had made him laugh. The escape of a fox captured by one of the hounds had made him laugh. Falling over his own bootlaces and smashing his head on the cobbles, had made him laugh as he washed off the blood. When Pappa died, she was sure he had been laughing. But perhaps the heart attack had been stronger than his good humour. The laugh had presumably doubled him over, then abruptly he would have slumped in silence.

As daughter of the head groom and senior housekeeper of the grand palace of Lord Benedict, Earl of Latymer, just outside the parish of Grey Friars, Illiana had been a servant, but treated without contempt. Fatherless at the age of eleven years, she had been given a broom, a mop and a small brush, and her mother, weeping after the death of Diego, had trained her to clean the manor kitchens. At first Mama, spoke little Spanish, but once her daughter was learning perfect Spanish from her father, mama joined in, and learned a great deal more. Before Diego's death, they had been speaking perfect Spanish as well as English. Even once a widow, as housekeeper, mother and daughter had lived in comfort.

At the age of nineteen, menial comfort had changed to luxury when the lord himself noticed, courted and finally asked to marry her. They had married on the open doorstep to Christ Church, Grey Friars, and it had been her twentieth birthday. Benedict, Earl Latymer, had turned sixty-two shortly before Illiana had spoken with him. At first, barely knowing him, she had refused the offer, not to his face but to her mother.

"He could be my grandpapa."

"Since you have no grandpapa, you might as well take this one, foolish girl. You'll be a countess. Just think about it. We could never have dreamed – never even thought of such a thing. An earl falls for his housekeeper's daughter. And you know about the wealth. You certainly don't deserve such grandeur, but you should be on your knees kissing his feet in gratitude."

"But I don't love him and I never could."

"You'll do as you're told, look after him, forget your broom. Accept being a lady instead of a brat."

"You actually believe this? Lord Benedict wants me as a wife? The only thing he ever says to me is, '*Well done, child.*' And now he wants to marry me? I don't believe a word of it."

"Stupid girl. He spoke to me himself."

Illiana had dropped the broom handle and leaned back against the wall. "Mama I can't marry an earl. I don't know how to be a countess. I'd bring him shame. Besides, I've never – well, you know I've never. My first time with an old, old man is such a strange idea. He's sixty- one Mama."

Her mother's eyes narrowed. "Age has nothing to do with it, stupid girl. Once you learn how to be rich and titled, hopefully you will have learned a little more intelligence."

And yet Lord Benedict had proved as sweet as roast figs and she had learned to like and admire him within the first few days.

She was astonished, flattered, and attracted to the idea of

access to luxury for the first time in her life. Yet an earl three times her age could surely be terrifying. Within the first week, delight had replaced fear. Benedict was a kind man, a handsome man, a delightful and loving man. With no children from his first marriage, he had long been a patient widower. Now, urgently, he was infatuated and dreamed of being presented with sons. Even the first night of their bedding had not been the fierce imposition Illianaa had expected. Her new lord had been careful not to hurt her.

Now those memories were sweet. The stark present was not sweet at all.

Above the bed, the spiders and the silently drifting smoke from the dying fire within the grate, now only a smoulder of ash and embers, were all that moved. Illiana stared down at the devastating change in her life. She wished her husband a soft goodbye, thanked him for everything he had done for her, and hoped he would find a quick entrance to the halls of Paradise beyond purgatory, even though, through no fault of his own, there had been no visit from priest or bishop and had never heard the calming words of his Last Rights.

CHAPTER TWO

In the spare bedchamber hastily prepared, Sabine was waiting. Illiana rushed into Sabine's embrace and laid her head on her friend's shoulder. "So, you know what happened?"

Cuddling back, Sabine said, "The entire household knows now. Even when you buy a new hat, the entire household gossips about whether they like it or not. So when this sort of ghastly nightmare happens – well, there's no one asleep now. I'd wager the gossip has already reached the city centre."

"The priest's coming, so we can hide in here. It's not really hiding of course, but I don't want to see dear Benedict carted away. At least he'll get the blessing after all. He deserves Paradise."

"It's going to be hard to talk about anything else."

Illiana slumped back onto the newly made bed, its counterpane spread smooth with one small square bump showing near the end where a hot brick still lay, warming the sheets. The little fire was recent, and the logs were not yet fully alight. Only the crackle interrupted their soft voices.

"I suppose that's true. I'll miss him. He was so kind and so thoughtful." Illiana lay back, her tousled curls on the bolster. She closed her eyes. "But, what happens next? I've been a simple maid mopping floors, and wife for such a short time. Now I'll have to grow up and look after myself."

Yet Illiana's thoughts were elsewhere. "Benedict's heir is his younger brother. Him and that horrid sister Beatrice don't like me, and Olivia, well, she's his wife, she only does what she's told without a single thought of her own. Actually, I can see them secretly seething when they have to meet me. So they aren't going to let me stay here. I'm supposed to be a countess, I can't just go back to cleaning kitchens. Can I? That wouldn't be fair to Benedict and besides, I'd hate it, but the new earl isn't going to give me money, is he?"

"Then perhaps start collecting every bit of silver and gold and anything else valuable. It's not really stealing, is it. At the moment it's actually all yours. If we're chucked out and have to live in a hut somewhere, we ought to gather some comfy stuff or things to sell. I'll help." Sabine stood beside the bed, gazing at her friend.

She shook her head. "I thought I was rich. I wanted to find you a rich husband too, once I was settled. We'd have been comfortable friends. I should've been quicker, but I don't know anyone else, not even Benedict's friends or family. Can I be a dowager when I'm still so young?"

Sabine didn't know. "We'll have to ask someone. Don't you want to visit your mother?"

"Later when she wakes."

"Why wait?"

"You know she doesn't like me." Illiana managed the first smile of the evening. "A month ago there was all the rush and panic of the wedding when I hardly knew him, so I was a coward then too. I still am, I suppose."

"I saw you shivering." Sabine sniggered. "All those gorgeous clothes and underneath the satin your knees were shaking."

"Of course I was scared. I had no idea what to expect." Illiana sat up abruptly and stared at her friend. "But that was November. I'd just got used to everything – somethings not yet – and now this. He was so nice. He really was. I'll miss him. I do already."

"You couldn't have been in love with any one that quickly. It was just that amazing change in your life. I thought you were such a lucky monster. Now, of course, you're horribly unlucky. So, when we collect what money we can, we go away together."

Illiana managed another smile and her dimples peeped. "I love the idea, but what about our parents?"

Since the wedding her mother was no longer the housekeeper, she had her own grand bedchamber and received an allowance five times larger than her previous salary. Nicholas Farrier, Sabines father, however, continued as groom, now the chief since Diego's death years before.

"My dad loves the stables. I reckon he loves horses more than me." The subject was sufficiently perplexing and entirely boring, to inspire an immediate relapse into sleep.

It was dawn when Nicholas hauled himself from the straw in the stables, saddled two of the horses, as ordered, and then watched Manders and his assistant ride into the pale pink of the rising sun.

The locals were waking, many already marching off to work, their wives emptying the chamber pots from the windows and into the gutters below. The gates were opening, the barrows of fruit trundling down to the markets, and the stalls set up, awnings erected in case it rained.

Now the day after Christmas, St. Stephen's Day, the sky seemed as though swept clear in the night, but no one trusted a December day not to end in rain or perhaps snow.

Christ's Church on the road to Newgate, and attached to the Grey Friars Monastery, was no grand cathedral, it stood small beneath its layered tower, quietly absorbing the religious fervour of the monks and their chanting. For that, Lord Benedict, Earl Latymer, had always loved it and had often taken mass there when Sunday seemed too beautiful for him to remain in his own chapel. Loving a place of religious beauty had never been as difficult as loving a woman.

His previous experience had convinced him that neither love nor passion existed. Seeing, gradually adoring, and finally marrying Illiana, the girl had taught him something he had never previously believed, that love was not a concept, but could actually exist. Their month as husband and wife had taught him not only love, but also the amazement of happiness. A brief lesson, however.

Illiana hoped that he now lay in the glory of the heavens, where one far distant day she intended to join him. He was to be buried in the church he admired, his coffin crossing the great pillared entrance where he had wed just thirty-nine days before.

The morning following his death, both Illiana and her mother washed and dressed the body carefully in the clothes he had worn on his wedding day. Illiana touched her husband with care, sorrow and sweet memories. Her mother was efficient, practical and unemotional.

"Such a careless passing," she muttered, although more to herself than to her trembling daughter. "What did he think he was doing, leaving us without resources? Utterly selfish."

Each morning the entire household attended the private chapel, taking Mass and praying for the soul of their lord. The hustle, bustle and gossip thrived. Illiana, however, ate little and spent most of her days in bed, quietly crying, and wondering if she had turned into the fool her mother frequently called her.

Five days later, on the thirty-first of December, after the strict period of gloom from closed shutters, whispering and walking softly, tiptoes up the stairs, and every person dressed in the dark clothes supplied by the countess, Manders returned, accompanied by the new earl and both his wife and elder sister.

The new arrivals were loud and demanding. They accepted the rules of mourning yet before any other announcement, ordered a feast and minstrels to celebrate rather than commiserate. The new earl did not resemble his older brother. As Benedict had been strident, wide shouldered, tall, and imposing. Unlike Benedict, Benjamin expected all around him to be partially deaf and therefore shouted constantly. Full face, especially on the rare attempts at a small smile, this was a handsome if imperious gentleman. In profile, however, his appearance diminished. His nose was tiny, flat, but wide nostrils flared while his mouth slanted downwards, and his chin protruded a considerable amount beyond his lower lip.

"The funeral will be tomorrow," he announced. "The first day of January. Everyone is to attend. By the afternoon I shall organise the running of the staff to my own wishes, and I demand the retirement and disappearance of the Dowager within the two days following the funeral at the latest."

Illiana heard and blushed but had expected it already. Half her clothes were packed ready, a gold candlestick ensconced, a silver bowl wrapped within her slippers.

Having announced his orders without the bother of addressing Illiana in person, Benjamin Latymer, Earl of Birstall, marched through her home and demanded the changes he desired.

Two more days only, and the grand bedchamber would no longer offer slumber to Illiana, since she would no longer be resident. The bedding would be changed immediately after, candles would surround the room, and the garderobe would be emptied and cleaned. The smaller bedchamber next door would now be that of his wife Olivia, a quiet woman. Illiana only ever heard her whisper *Of course.* His sister Beatrice could claim the smallest bedchamber that overlooked nothing more interesting than rooftops.

"My lord," Illiana was standing, waiting for whatever might be worst, and now bowed her head, "as my dear late husband spoke of you several times, I shall be only too delighted to leave."

Slowly the glints of light blue beneath their heavy lids settled on her. "If you wish," he told her, "you might remain here in different lodgings. The kitchen where I believe you slept before your absurd pretence of marriage."

Illiana smiled. "Thank you, my lord, for corroborating what my husband said of you. I shall now retire to my bedchamber. I trust you will take temporary accommodation on the upper floor. Or you may wish to stay at the Red Partridge beside the church. I shall also inform the bishop, whom I know well and who will conduct the funeral, that I shall be present and demand the chair of the widow. Before the funeral, however, I shall ask my late lord's lawyer to read the final Will and Testament in our presence. After which I shall retire and leave you to your inevitable complaints."

It was as the new earl dozed on the settle after midday dinner that the lawyer arrived.

Illiana followed Manders as he answered the door bell. Timothy Proze marched immediately to the grand Hall, unfolding the two papers after he had unrolled the scroll.

Her back to the great Inglenook fire, Illiana stood before Benjamin could grab the chance, and she raised her chin. Benjamin open his eyes and gulped.

"I welcome my new brother, my new sister, and my sister-in-law to my late husband's home. I also welcome my late lord's lawyer, Timothy Proze, who will now read my husband's will and testament before we eat."

No platters yet spread across the table, although jugs of wine topped the linen tablecloth. Every cup brimmed with the Burgundy. The tiny flicker of beeswax candles reflected in the deep crimson. Lawyer Proze emptied his silver cup, passed by Manders, before speaking.

"As the lawyer of Lord Benedict Latymer, the late earl, I hold, in his own handwriting, his detailed wishes for the last will and testament he intended to have made legal and indisputable. I can swear on the Holy Bible that his lordship wrote this in my presence. It was given to me to script in full legal terms and pass the church courts as incontestable, but as his lordship was not expected to expire for some considerable time, this paper is not yet reproduced in the required terms. However, I have checked both with the bishop and with the church court, and since this is provable as his lordship's final intentions, with myself as witness, with his steward, Michael Manders, also present and therefore unarguably a second witness, it must be accepted as legally the one and only last will and testament of Lord Benedict Latymer, second Earl of Birstall."

The new earl hauled himself into a more conscious position on the settle, and clasped his hands over his paunch. His wife had disappeared into the shadows. The lawyer looked smug. Manders stood by the door feeling important, the late earl's little sister sat huddled without expression, and Illiana's mother sat straight, her arguments prepared. Illiana stood, unmoving.

Pushing against the back of the settle, the new earl scowled. His forehead remained unfurrowed but the lower half of his face puckered into dislike. "No need for that. He can't choose his own heir. I'm already the Earl and the property's mine, the decisions are mine and his decisions mean nothing. Everything now belongs to me."

Proze bowed with a twitch of condescension. "My lord, as lawyer for royalty, as well as for the elite, my knowledge of the law never comes under criticism, so kindly reserve your doubts until I have explained the earl's wishes. They are brief and cannot be questioned."

"Get on with it man," mumbled the sister, knowing she was unlikely to gain anything at all.

"My apologies, Lady Beatrice," Proze bowed again and held the scroll, unrolled, before the candle. "I shall begin. Written by Lord Benedict, Earl of Birstall, this day the eighteenth of November in the Year of our Lord, 1482, being my personal and twice witnessed final will and testament. Since my heir remains my younger brother, Benjamin, he will inherit the title and all property which has originally been inherited by myself from our father Bartholomew Latymer, awarded by His Royal Majesty after the battle of Tewksbury. This specifically covers Bartholomew Latymer's house in London, the manor of Latymer and Denton in Suffolk, and the village of Birstall, all of which accompanies the title of earl. Also included are all goods and chattels within those two mansions and their grounds. The income from the Suffolk properties which covers three farms and one village, are also part of the Latymer inheritance." The lawyer now paused, looking first directly at the earl, naturally smiling at the list of his new wealth, but then turned his gaze to Illiana, and his own smile was wide. He continued, "All other properties and personal items owned personally by myself, will be bequeathed to my betrothed and legal wife, the Lady Illiana Latymer, Countess of Birstall. This includes the majority of the contents of the Latymer house, the house in Muggle Lane at present leased to the church, and the manor and village in Devonshire, known as Benedict House, the Village of Benedict's bridge, and all income and items contained there. I also bequeath the sum of two thousand pounds to be paid annually to my wife Illiana, from the income of the title of Birstall. Two horses from my Latymer stables shall be hers, the litter which I have already presented to her, and the title of the Dowager Countess which shall be hers by right for life. I also bequeath to her my wedding ring, my gold chain of office, and my three other personal finger rings. Should I remember any other properties in my ownership or other situations, I hold the right to add these to my testament before my death."

There followed a startled pause.

Wondering if she could encourage an honest faint, Illiana stood unmoving. Her mother squeaked and closed her eyes. The new earl stared and his mouth hung open. It was his sister Beatrice who bounced to her feet, one black satin outer sleeve slapping against her wine cup and spilling the contents. The Burgundy puddled the tablecloth and dripped against her black satin skirts.

"No mention of me, I see." She spat, yelling, high pitched. "And this kitchen scrubber who had no right to wed the earl. I call it illegal and must be proclaimed invalid. How can she gain so much after such an improper marriage of less than two months? How do we know the marriage was even consummated? I challenge the whole vile thing."

"Consummation," Proze answered, his smile a declaration of freezing sarcasm, "cannot be within your province to challenge, my lady. And the marriage itself, having been announced and blessed by the Bishop of Ludgate and Fleet himself, is beyond doubt. The last testament which I have read has been signed and sealed by the late earl, signed and announced valid by the bishop, signed and witnessed by myself and by the earl's steward Michael Manders. My lady, should you wish to contest this declaration on legal grounds, you will need to speak with another lawyer. However, I can advise you that there is no conceivable manner in which these words can be proved unacceptable."

He sat with a flourish. Manders bowed, strode to the great doors beyond the dining table, and clapped at those waiting in the corridor. "Begin serving."

Now seated, Illiana watched, although virtually unseeing, as the steam and rich aromas of platters swept beneath her nose. She had hoped for some indulgence from a man who seemed to have loved her. The great gold and diamond ring denoting their marriage, perhaps. Some other personal items. Even a purse to help her begin a new life. The forthcoming shower of riches, however, which she had not even yet known existed, was unimaginable and already she had forgotten all details except the incredible extent of such generosity.

Benedict, of course, had never liked either his brother or sister.

With a gulp of relief, Illiana nodded, smiling. "So, my lord, you have inherited a great deal but not the wealth within my late husband's freedom to give as he wished. However, since you have taken it upon yourself to – let us say – retire me – from my home, I trust that you will take it upon yourself to provide the necessary indulgences due to the church regarding the funeral. Remembering, naturally, that your lordship's great generosity, or lack of it, will be made fully public by the church," she declared as she swept from the hall.

Cuddled within her soon to be lost bedchamber, Illiana and her friend Sabine attempted the mental challenge of counting what had been gained.

"Well, he was a very rich man."

"Now I am rich too. I haven't seen the Muggle house but I knew it existed, it's up by Cripplegate. Benedict would never have bought a slum, now would he! So it's rented out to the church and I bet they pay well. As for everything else, oh Sabine darling, I didn't even know he had another house in the country. Where is Devon? And certainly more money than I could even count."

"Two thousand pounds a year. I don't think I ever saw a pound, let alone thousands. I can't count that far. We could buy the whole world, and this Benedict house in Devon and the income there?"

"I never even heard of it. It's the new little house in Muggle Lane we'll see first. You and me, Sabine, and I suppose my mother, if we can stop the church paying rent, we'll actually live there. Not a long trip, but an exciting one."

"But we might have to share it with priests. They definitely wouldn't want us there. I think Devon would be better, wherever it is."

The door crashed open. "That," declared Illiana's mother, "will be a journey to remember. A journey to thrill and fortune." Quite suddenly Bertha liked her daughter a good deal more than previously.

. . .

It was the funeral which demanded several hour's preparation on the following morning, the chaos punctured only by whispers. Sabine wore a dust hemmed tunic as Illiana, needed help to dress.

"You're wearing that? No. You have to come too, Sabbs. And take anything you want of mine to wear. Something black, I've got more than enough."

Illiana pointed to the black folds hanging from the garderobe peg. She already wore black, but the gown she wanted was beautiful rather than sorrowful. "I'm not going to risk that man treating me like a serving maid."

"Nothing wrong with serving maids," sniffed Sabine, since she still officially was one.

"That man won't think so."

Over her head and falling neatly to her shoulders, the gown was as light as ashes, it's low silver trimmed neckline flat against the white frills of her shift beneath. Illiana lifted her arm. "Sabs, can you tie the ribbons tightly, more than usual. Poor Benedict isn't going to see me."

"I love this dress. So much silk. Silver embroidered cuffs, neck, and hem, double skirts but so light. If it wasn't black, I'd love it more." Sabine fussed.

"I like it being black. My garters are black too. Stockings – black. And guess what colour my shoes are, almost as black as my hair."

"Your hair shines most of all."

"I love my Spanish colouring, but you're all soft yellow and that's much prettier. More fashionable."

The funeral was slow as the carriage trundled along. First behind rode the new earl, as yet unable to claim inheritance until his brother lay deep beneath the ground. The elaborate coffin perched high on the deep sided barrow, the two horses slow, their tails and manes plaited, their backs covered in black damask. Then the new countess and the earl's elder sister rode slowly and carefully, reigns held tight. Behind them, Illiana rode within the litter, its curtains pulled. The entire household followed in silence, walking, heads lowered, four abreast, keeping pace with the hooves of the horses on the cobbles.

There was no sunshine but the morning was galloping past. London's gates had been unlocked some hours previously, while the traders, with barrows piled, rumbled and clattered through the foreign market, filling its spaces as soon as the gates clanged loud and swung wide. As sheep and geese were herded in from the ice puddled slopes of the countryside, they stared around at the city sights never before known to them.

The local sheriff finished his breakfast, slurped down the rest of his ale, buckled his belt and strode out into the familiar lanes and the winter wind. He stopped abruptly as the funeral procession passed, removed his hat and bowed before moving on. A horizon of smoke was already puffing its rank clouds of rust coloured dirt from the endless towers of brick chimneys, low clouds of bleak grey merging. The flickering of tiny candle flames appeared in windows behind oil cloth and shaved bone, while wives tied their aprons, brushed down the creases, and hurried out with buckets to the great tubs outside, collecting what rainwater remained to carry back into the kitchen for cooking and washing.

The chanting of prayer echoed from the doors of the monastery. The Bishop of Ludgate and Fleet, in the full glory of ecclesiastical costume, stood at the open doorway of Christ Church, the priest behind him.

As the funeral procession stopped at the church entrance, so Manders and five other men of the household stepped forwards and carried the coffin on their shoulders and up the aisle to the alter. Here they rested the coffin.

Lord Benedict Latymer Earl of Birstall, was buried with ritual and song beneath the tiles of the side chapel, its great coloured window having once been donated by the earl himself, his coffin now covered by the stone that announced both his life and his death. The shuffle of mourners stood back in the aisle, their heads bowed, muttering the Prayer of the Holy Lord in Latin. Illiana neither recognised nor knew any of them, but stood between her mother and Sabine, trying extremely hard not to cry.

CHAPTER THREE

Once back home, there was a late dinner. The new earl took central place, and his small sister sat beside him, his quiet wife on the other side. Neither had attended their brother's recent wedding, of which they had heartily disapproved. Seeing Illiana had not changed their minds. A dishwashing harlot, when discovered as beautiful, was simply seen as more of a harlot.

Illiana sat at the end of the table, her black silks gleaming now in the candlelight as they had in the hundred candles lighting the church. The mystical chant which had started the funeral still echoed in Illiana's mind and she felt Benedict smile at her. She smiled back. Fully aware that this would be her penultimate, perhaps even her last, meal at her husband's mansion, Illiana had already practised what she intended to say. She hoped Benedict would approve.

The good food smelled rich and steam continued to rise. The piled platters had been carried in and placed central, the pages had then hurried to serve, the new earl the priority, followed by the dowager countess, unusually young for a dowager, and looking perhaps more like a hungry fifteen year old. She clutched her silver cup and drank, watched her mother over the brim of the cup and with a movement virtually invisible, she shook her head. Illiana had told her mother not to question anything yet. Later there would be time.

Pointing to whatever they wished, each was served, their cups refilled, and were interrupted only by the clank and clatter of platters, spoons and knives, jugs and cups, and the rustle of long sleeves. Illiana ate little and drank too much. But she waited until she saw the platters removed and those of the second course were brought in. Then she pushed back her small chair, and raised her cup.

Benjamin, Beatrice and Olivia all stared in suspicion, Lawyer Proze and the Bishop of Ludgate and Fleet both wiped their fingers on the napkins over their shoulders, raised their cups and smiled, but her mother carefully looked down.

The three cups of wine had been drunk for courage, telling herself, "I am a widow. I am a countess. I am not to be treated as the kitchen scrubber that I was. I must learn to be as Benedict wished me to be."

She spoke clearly. "I drink to my late husband," Illiana said, and did so. "He was a man of courage and kindness, and was much loved and admired by his highness, King Edward. When the first earl sadly died, God rest his soul, Benedict inherited the title, and was promised greater rewards, although it seems he also inherited his father's sad fate of dying too young. I pray to our Lord to pass my late husband the blessings he so righteously deserves. However, being without children, the honour of Earl of Birstall will be passed to his brother. But I wish to emphasise and announce once more that the great heroism my late husband displayed made him an honoured friend to the king, and that cannot be passed on as there is no heir to such valour."

The dismissive reference to his heirdom had stayed illusive but the new earl's eyes squinted as Benjamin pushed away his empty platter, lifted his cup, and spoke in a rush. "Yes, I drink to my brother, although I despise his choice of female. You think your marriage legal?" He turned to face the lawyer. "Absurd. You can say whatever you wish, sir, but I'm telling you that slum brat shall not inherit a farthing."

Beatrice, with a sniff into her cup, added, "And she and that pompous mother of hers are leaving here tomorrow. I'll make sure of that."

Looking up, Illiana bit her tongue and smiled. "I doubt you know any grain of sand regarding the legality of my marriage, nor the details of my own family, or do you wish to prove the truth of your personal valour now, sufficient to attack his lordship the bishop and accuse him of lies regarding the earl's second marriage?"

His mouth was full of lamb filled dumpling, but Proze stood, swallowed, and managed to speak with clarity. "I admit to being surprised at your words, my lord. I assure you that not one word of your brother's last testament can be legally challenged. Nor are there any properties, finances nor even items which have hereby been bequeathed to the dowager countess which should rightfully belong to the heir to the title."

"And what's been said as yours, Benjamin," spat his sister, "might be the legal minimum. But it's still a fortune. And me? I don't get a handkerchief. Not a pair of stockings. Not even a spoon's worth of lavender." The steam rising, she slammed down her spoon into the rich slices of venison on her platter. The gravy spun to her fingers and the neck of her gown. She seemed unconcerned and wiped her fingers on the napkin over her shoulder. "But I tell you one thing, I'll be staying here in a better bedchamber, once the trollop's gone. And you are obliged to clothe me and feed me until I marry myself."

"Which might take some years," smiled her brother. "I've been married twice and don't miss the first, I was glad enough when she died. You, at an age I dare not repeat, have never married at all. Nor ever will, unless you find some poor creature who wants a witch for a wife."

Her voice almost disappeared. "You know the man I loved. And he was killed in the duel."

"Loving anyone is the act of a fool." It was his silent wife who blushed.

Quickly, the bishop interrupted, standing and raising his own cup. "I drink to our Father in heaven and pray He will take the second Earl of Birstall into His bosom, rewarding his good deeds practised during life on this earth." It was a short and friendly speech but silenced all others at the table.

The serving of the second course continued, and Illiana tried to eat little and drink more. She was silent again. Now, the wine still tightly clasped, her spoon and knife discarded, Illiana tried to imagine what Benedict might say, if he watched her from above. '*I never meant to leave you, my dearest. But take no notice of my brother, nor of my sister. I have often told you what I thought of them.*'

Her own imagination supplied the words. The brightness of his laugh didn't shine from the prime place at the table. No warm hand reached to her elbow, helping her rise. No chuckle when he asked if she had eaten enough of the apple tart and the peaks of cream. No assurance that she could drink as much as she ever wished, and indeed should enjoy the absolute freedom to act as she desired. No gentle kiss on her cheek when they both rose, and he whispered that he would see her at the stables if she wished to ride out with him.

So now she ate quietly, said nothing to the new heir or her sisters-in-law, nor even to the lawyer. There was time for her to eat enough to quieten her hunger, and she had drunk enough to soothe her timidity.

The funeral hung in a smog of dark memory across the hall's great beams, a threat slit with the flicker of candles. The afternoon dragged as the deepening grey of evening slipped over the outside of the windows. Illiana chewed, drank, and kept her eyes low.

When she glimpsed twilight, she knew she would soon have the excuse of exhaustion and could creep up to bed. There she would miss Benedict even more profoundly, but instead of sleeping, or even thinking, she would finish packing. Sabine would help her, while packing her own small bag. It would be early the next morning that she could conclude the escape.

Twilight inched into deeper blackness and the page lit her fire in the bedchamber. Heat swirled up as the flames rose. Her fingers thawed, her toes drew warmth from the rug, but the bed was empty and no muscled arms stretched out to grasp her.

She was not, however, alone. Her mother had the great wooden chest already half filled with gowns, capes, woollen underskirts, linen shifts and shoes of black, grey and blue.

"Mother, do I need that much? I already have what I need in that bag."

"You have what I chose," Bertha grumbled. "You've had a good twenty years to learn obedience. It's time you were used to the idea. Besides, I'm leaving no expensive clothing behind for either of those two obnoxious women."

Sabine was collecting whatever seemed attractive, yet was without the Latymer coat of arms carved or painted, which would have proved it was part of those items belonging to the title. There were silver candlesticks and a golden frame, although the led backed mirror within the frame was broken. Gazing sadly at the rich patterned counterpane, Illiana collected her combs, potted aloe vera and herbal tonics, rose water and the graver.

"Do you think they'd miss the counterpane?" she whispered to her mother. Benedict's testament had stated clearly that many of the contents here, were indeed hers by right. However, the new earl, as Illiana was quite sure, would object to anything she took apart from her clothes. He might even object to that.

It was Sabine who whispered back, "No one will know who it belongs to. There's no embroidered coat of arms. Take the blankets too. Take everything. The bolster, the pillows, those nice white sheets. Pappa is down in the stables, preparing two litters and four horses for early in the morning. Yes, don't bother telling me that's more than the testament specified but if anyone dares challenge it, you can call me as a witness."

"I wish I could take my bed as well – I mean, no – I don't know what I mean. I can't take anything this big."

"But we can sneak some of the things from downstairs."

Sabine led the careful tip toe down the wide stairs to the ground floor where the great hall spread to the front. Creeping and silent left them almost unseen and it was as they reached the final four steps that they stopped, seeing shadows and hearing Manders open the front doors, pulling them open for the two shadows to leave.

Illiana stared. The first shadow was very tall and dressed as a noble gentleman. His fine wide shoulders tapered down into slim darkness. But for a moment she saw the moving profile, quickly disappearing as he pulled on his feathered hat over black hair and turned again to leave. Manders bowed low and the echo of his voice, although blurred from the distance, murmured, "Thank you, my lord. Thank you on behalf of this household."

The taller shadow nodded and marched out into the equal blackness of the night. But as he left, Illiana saw the flash of eyes beneath lowered lids, and was puzzled. Someone of considerable standing had visited, and then left, had stayed only moments, and had then departed without ceremony. A friend of the new earl, she supposed, and yet had not acted as any friend, momentarily entering and leaving without wine, or even called good wishes.

Manders stayed one moment at the door, now closed, and seemed to be mumbling to himself.

Illiana grabbed Sabine's shoulder. "Not now," she whispered. "I'm not going to be seen pilfering more candlesticks. It doesn't matter. I have to speak to the wretched earl in the morning before we leave. Now it's bedtime. You sleep with me, Sabs, our last comfy night of luxury."

She slept badly and had expected nothing better.

What became better, was the morning, as she sat for her final breakfast. The table was already fully occupied except for the new countess, who as yet Illiana barely knew. She felt she knew her brother and sister-in-law only too well. Now, she decided she had not known them at all, for as she sat, Benjamin, barely rising in acknowledgement, nodded, his napkin remaining across his shoulder, saying, "My lady, I'm pleased you have joined us. I wish to tell you that I have somewhat changed my mind over night."

Illiana raised her eyebrows and took up her own napkin. This man had never before addressed her as a lady. "In what manner, sir?"

The new earl cleared his throat, frog-like. "I believe I have somewhat misunderstood you, my lady, and have used words I should not have used. I was under a sad misapprehension. Forgive me. I will not now be questioning my brother's last testament, nor do I wish you and your lady mother to leave here so abruptly. I beg you to stay until you yourself wish to retire elsewhere. To one of your other establishments, perhaps." He was staring down at his platter of thin sliced ham, and did not raise his eyes to Illiana. He then muttered his following words. "Naturally, continuing to live here under my protection and in all the luxury you have become accustomed to, although no longer in the lord's chamber which must become my own, you may choose to donate your allowance of two thousand pound each year back to myself. But we shall speak of that another time." And very quickly he bent his head to his ham and beer.

For a glazed eyed moment, Illiana would have liked to throw her platter at him, but did not. She sat, puzzling out both Benjamin's thoughts and her own. Being prepared and ready to leave, she neither wanted to stay nor needed to stay. She, her mother, her friend Sabine and Sabine's father, however, would be transferring to a home she had never seen, had never heard of, and did not know whether it might be an unfurnished and bed-less palace, or a hut suitable only for goats. She had seen Muggle Street, leading to the Northern Gate at Cripplgate, and knew it to be busy, noisy and persistently crammed with sheep, oxen and cattle entering London on their way to the Shambles. Besides, the house, still rented to the church, might be locked.

Travelling south to the manor in Devon would need considerably more organisation. She had no idea where that was either.

Sitting straight, she stared across at the top of the earl's head. She said quietly, "I thank you, my lord. I accept your offer that I remain here for the time being. As for other matters, they can be discussed when the time allows. And what bedchamber do you suggest I occupy?"

"Humph," answered the earl, ignoring the scowl from his adjacent sister, "your lady mother's present bedchamber, in which she is welcome to remain, leads to the rear of the first storey, and as no doubt you know, from there a short passage leads to the east wing. That holds one bedchamber to each storey, complete with garderobe naturally. It may have been originally meant as the lady's wing. The window looks out across the grounds at the back. I would gladly allot that wing to yourself, my lady, with space for your maid, and your dear mother close by."

He still avoided Illiana's direct gaze, but he was no longer shouting.

With an irritation of having to admit and accept this vile man's sudden generosity, Illiana spoke with unwilling politeness, "I accept, my lord. That space will be most acceptable. I shall have both my maid and Manders arrange that this morning. Yes, acceptable. I mean to say, thank you, I accept."

Beatrice interrupted, though spoke only to her brother. "Fool that you are. You want that trollop here permanently, sharing our table? You give the slut a better bedchamber than I have myself? Lady's quarters indeed. Hadn't you noticed that I'm a lady too, and one of quality? If you think you'll get a split penny from her, then you're quite lunar crazed."

"I shall speak to you later, Beatrice," Benjamin told her directly, his face flushed as he returned to his beer cup.

Illiana, eating very little, knew her thoughts jumbled. She was already packed sufficiently for the expected move away, to now be changed to a simple move into the East Wing, and at least now had the pleasure of knowing she would be denying it to both Benjamin's wife and sister, even while losing the bed so thick with memory-perfumes. Now the existing staff would manage all the humping and bumping and as dowager countess, she would barely lift a toe. Staying at the house which had been the only home she had ever known, was without doubt a pleasure in spite of those who would now also be staying there. It would also prolong her ability to claim freedom, the power of her title, and the ability to speak whatever and whenever she wished. Yet it threatened her with leading a life of continuous anger.

No one would have the ability to take her yearly allowance from her. She would remain wealthy without having to refurnish a new house. She said softly, "As the dowager countess, my lord, I thank you." She tossed down her napkin, stood, and left the hall, aiming for her waiting mother and maid, having an amazing new change of plans to tell them, yet without being able to explain the motive. The new bedchamber, as she already knew, was welcoming and three pages, Manders and Sabine helped her unpack everything she had packed before.

Bertha smiled. "I shall remain in my own chamber, with no need to pack or repack. Very proper." She seemed less surprised than Illiana had expected.

"I'll sleep on your pallet bed," Sabine grinned. She was, with Illiana's help, remaking the bed and topping it with the much-loved old counterpane across the new eiderdown.

"Forget pallets on the floor. You can sleep right here beside me," Illiana said. "What on earth do you think made that damned man change his mind?"

"He's after your grand inheritance," said Bertha quickly. "But he won't get it. Don't you dare give him a farthing, stupid girl."

"I've no intention of it."

"In the meantime, I shall go down to the stables and inform Nicholas."

"I'll tell Papa myself," said Sabine. "He'll be hugging me, so happy."

"And I'll need a new bolster and maybe new pillows." Illiana poked at the threadbare and flat linen clumps at the top of her new bed. "After dinner, Sabs, do you want to go to market? We have the money to buy whatever we want."

CHAPTER FOUR

It was after a large but stilted and speechless midday dinner, that Illiana managed to corner the steward alone.

"Manders, one moment. I need to ask you something."

"My lady?" He bowed as always.

"There was a late-night visitor yesterday, but I think he only stayed moments. A tall gentleman accompanied by a short one. A page, or something perhaps. Did he only see Lord Benjamin? Can you please tell me who that gentleman was?'

The steward looked uncomfortable. "My lady, the gentleman, previously unknown to his lordship, is the Earl of Cleeves eldest son, and heir, Viscount Charles. He spoke only briefly to Lord Benjamin, and naturally, I was not present to overhear the conversation."

Since this meant entirely nothing to Iliana, she thanked the steward and prepared to travel to market with her maid. This she had done many, many times in the past, yet never before as a countess.

The new life started with a new storm.

Sabine, already waiting, called, "You sure you want to go. It's pouring."

"I used to walk in the rain all the time. I could take a horse, but it's not far."

"You used to walk in the rain because you didn't know how to ride." Sabine grinned.

"I can ride now. Sort of well enough." Illiana said, looking suddenly weepy. Well, in the rain, no one would know she was crying. "But horses can't squeeze between all those stalls. Just put your hood up." Her own hooded cloak was somewhat more cosy and well lined than Sabine's but she'd forgotten that. Now she silently reminded herself she should buy her friend a new one. She was, after all, now a rich countess. As she pulled on her gloves, she was also in possession of Benedict's large brown leather purse, which was now strapped to her belt within the thick red oilcloth. Sabine watched her. "Yes, alright," Illiana conceded, "I have Benedict's purse. It's not stealing. He always said I could help myself if I wanted something, and I'm sure he wouldn't want me to sleep without pillows." She sniffed. "Even if I'm without *him*. And then my allowance starts anyway."

Her boots did not squelch and did not slip. Sabine's did both. Illiana nodded to herself. That was clearly something else she should have bought Sabine already.

The foreign market was the gathering of stalls further north, before the conduit encouraged the endless queues of folk, clinking their buckets. Stalls of winter fruit, piled with apples, berries and plums, pears and quinces, smelled rich and made every shopper thirsty. Those selling candles and firelighters were central, keeping their smells of stale tallow far from that of roots and fruit. The ovens of freshly made bread stood near the entrance, and that was a perfume no one avoided, but there were three or four butchers and the drip of blood was avoided by some. There were nowhere near as many butchers as kept to the Shambles, but the abattoirs outside the city wall sometimes set up stalls in the market to sell their own produce.

There was invariably a tooth puller and he, with his pliers waving on high, also stood in pools of blood, but anyone with a murderous pain splitting his gums would not complain of blood in his own mouth. The knife sharpener trundled his barrow and wheel, walked the stalls, calling his business, taking the open way past other stalls to where stood those for the wealthy, selling poppets for children, stuffed with wool and wearing tiny painted eyes. Also painted pebbles for playing marbles, even the carved beauty of chess pieces ready for a more adult game, and Scarapini tarot cards, ready for the great gamble and winners of fortune.

Noise scrambled every ear as the stall-holders shouted their wares, the screams of those losing their teeth was abrupt but frequent, and children squealed as they played. As blood, leaf, muscle and hoof fell to the gutters, the market also swarmed with starving dogs, hopeful goats, the beggars from Bedlam and others without home or fire.

The sound which pounded the loudest was the shriek and holler of the crowds watching the dog fights, followed by the cock fights, each attracting the betting of every man watching, pushing and bellowing as he called his bet.

Preparing and then arriving had taken considerable time. Now the rain was a scatter of windswept silver droplets, an afterthought left over from the night's storm. The cobbles were slippery but the sun banished the grey clouds and the puddles reflected the golden sheen.

Beneath their windswept shelters, stalls overflowed with parsnips and onions, turnips, cabbage, peas, carrots and beams. Although they were shielded by the awning above, another sheen of fresh rain glistened across the bright fresh colours.

"All that shouting and barking is horrible." Illiana turned, looking towards the raised surrounds of the blood smeared pit.

Sabine hopped on one small foot, and her smile was excited. "I could afford to bet," she said softly and carefully, as though expecting to be criticised and stopped. "I used to look at those fights when I was younger. Horrible, but I couldn't stop watching. It was like being caught on a hook."

"So, you're a sardine, fished and dangled on horsehair."

"True," Sabine giggled. "So just for a celebration, shall I do it? I could choose a dog or a cockerel. The very first time in my life I can afford it. Honestly, it would be a real thrill. What should I bet? Thrupence? More? I'd feel so special. So rich."

"Do what you like," Illiana told her. "That's what I'm doing – for the very first time in my life. Doing what I like. I wasn't married long enough to feel I could do that, when my mother kept telling me to obey Benedict. Now I'm a rich countess. I feel like a duchess. Perhaps even a princess."

Sabine's giggle was always infectious. "So, I can gamble and watch horrible fights and do whatever I want."

"Sabs, you've always had funny ideas. But blood, and pain? It makes me sick just thinking about it. Like I said, do what you want even when you shouldn't want it. Aren't you freezing? I've got a fur-lined cape and I'm still cold." Illiana pulled it tight. "It's still January, after all."

"Excitement warms me up." Her giggle turned into a snort.

"Go and watch that sickening animal fight – but I'm not coming with you," Illiana sniffed. "I hate those fights. My father took me to a cock fight once when I was little, and it made me sick. You go and bet a shilling and I'll tell you that you deserved to lose when you come back penniless. I'm going to buy the woolly gloves we saw back near the gates."

"When I win, I'll buy you some more and me too. Red for me, green for you." Sabine pulled her purse from its strap and opened it, peering inside. "I've got two shillings. Wow- shall I?"

"Do whatever you like, and stop being daft," Illiana told her. "Go and give the second shilling to one of the beggars. Look at that poor woman sitting in the gutter. I'll give you the shilling back afterwards."

The two waved at each other as they walked in the opposite directions, Sabine towards the raised plinth where men crowded, sitting, standing, climbing, and all staring down into the pit where the two dogs entered, barking in fury but held tight on the leash by their owners. Neither was a full breed, but both were a similar size, teeth protruding, striving one towards the other.

Sabine reached over the heads of the sitting crowd. "I'll bet a shilling on the white dog with the black ears."

"He's mine, lady. Jammy Chops I calls him. A good bet, he is, and has won before. But you sure about a whole shilling?"

"Yes. Can't anyone afford to go a whole shilling on the black one?"

"Brownie's mine," a man larger than the others, clapped his hands for attention. "I'll bet you. I can afford a shilling, and reckon I'll end with two o' them." He was smiling. Sabine disliked his smile, and hoped she'd win.

Five rows of stalls separated the dog fight from those shopping. Taking only a moment to buy the two pairs of gloves she fell for, the red and the green, Illiana wandered the lanes, and sheltered under the striped awnings when the frozen drizzle spangled the cobbles. She hoped that Sabine would catch her up before it poured once again, and soaked everything. Still aware of the clamour from the fight-pit, she moved to the outer ring and bought the clutches of herbs that she loved, elder, parsley, lovage, and caraway seeds. Then she wandered back in the direction of the fighting pit, hoping that whatever fight there had been, it would now be over. She could hear the squabbling but the cheers seemed done as each man counted his winnings or complained of his loss.

Illiana was sure she heard Sabine's voice amongst others. "Look, look, I won. Four backed me and I have a whole four shillings. I'm rich as a - ," Sabine looked around and hugged her. "I'm rich as a book printer. Look. Four shillings. Three shillings profit. And I gave my first shilling to an old lady with a beard sitting beside the apple stall."

"You're a saint." Illiana replied mocking, though with an affectionate smile.

The victor held his small white dog in his arms, kissing it's crumbled nose. Blood streaked its haunches, sticky and dark now. It's tongue licked at it's owner's fingers. "My little angel," mumbled the man. "Third time, eh?"

A large man with a twisted face, two deep scars running across his nose and cheeks, was holding a quivering scrap of fat black fur. The legs dangled between his fingers. His eyes were wet.

Looking flushed and deeply guilty, Sabine faced the man. "Browny's not gone, look mister. Maybe it's his way out of the fights, but you can try and look after him and get medicines or salves or something. Here." And she thrust the palm full of golden coins towards him. But, clutching his small dying dog, he had no free hand to grasp the money.

"He's alive, honestly he is. Hurry and take him to a doctor. This will pay for all of it." She turned, "Illiana, please, have you got a handkerchief?"

Illiana was avoiding both men and both dogs, but handed over her large linen handkerchief. Sabine grabbed it, first thrust it towards the crying man, then managed the solution herself, tying the linen around Browny's neck. The man breathed, "Bless you, lady."

"Quick, to the doctor."

The man was dressed in rags, his bare feet thick in blood, mud and frost. "He done it, I hears his breath. Come on, little one."

"Well, he may not have enough for new clothes," Sabine sighed, "but he's got enough for medicines and bandages and a doctor for the dog."

"If he doesn't run off and spend it all on beer and wine," Illiana sniffed. "He certainly didn't look like a man used to winning a fortune on his beloved dog. And with four shillings, he could buy some shoes as well."

"Nice hopes," Illiana said. "Just don't go to any more of those horrid fights." And she thrust the new warm gloves into her friend's empty hands.

~

FEBRUARY AWOKE to sunshine which glittered over the wet cobbles. As usual, there had been rain in the night but now a golden dawn promised better weather.

In her newly adored bedchamber, Illiana sat with Sabine and Bertha, although a little squashed, on the well cushioned settle, interested only in the small fire blazing before the with a crackle of tree bark already sprinkled over the previous night's ashes. The waiting logs sat, stored dry in the inglenook corner, ready for the page to start the upstairs duties.

"We'll have an early Spring," Bertha said, while well snuggled. "Sunshine will bring the warm days and we won't even need a fire."

Yet, the clear dry sky ushered in a new burst of winter. Over the following days, a frost rimed the frame of every mullion in crisp white. The fire in the generous inglenook was continuously lit, and the flames soared, discovering the twigs beneath the coal, and the coal beneath the coke, with an eventual rush to the chimney, although that was too straight to block all the smoke. This swirled dark haze quickly fell back down to its inception. Then wine was poured, pewter Latymer cups overflowing.

Candles were set ready in every room, the new beds were erected and hung with heavy curtains and the testers that would hopefully keep lice, spiders, mice and dust from those sleeping below, were quickly upended and cleaned with breathless squeaks from the maids. Cleaning filled the mornings. Wine and chatter filled the evenings as Sabine, having pulled the settle so close to the fire that her cheeks looked scorched, sat next to Bertha, but Illiana sat on the floor opposite the fire, cuddled onto her new Turkey rug which she had bought only three days previously.

"A dowager countess does not sit on the floor like a new page."

"Sorry, mother, but I like it."

"Your garderobe needs cleaning too," Bertha also sniffed to her daughter. "The privy is frozen at the bottom."

"Mother, that's the weather. The maids can't stop the cold."

"I'd sooner call for that long handled toasting spike," Sabine sighed. "This fire is gorgeous." She was already holding her palms towards the grate. "The idea of toasted bread – well, soaking up honey, butter perhaps. They'll have plenty of fresh baked loaves down in the kitchens."

"Ring the bell, Sabs. Call for bread and the toasting fork. And call for your father too."

"He doesn't feel the cold." Another giggle. "He's more interested in making sure the horses don't catch colds."

OUTSIDE UNDER THE constant control of Nicholas the chief groom, the horses were scrubbed down and fed, settled in their stables in semi-warmth, with bales of straw and oil cloth jackets across their quivering backs.

Winter continued, everyone sitting snug, gazing into the fire, enjoying the conversations, discussions and arguments until finally sleep was the ultimate decision. Olivia was less often present.

Bitter days offered little else apart from Mass on Sunday mornings, which was the one and only day during which Illiana saw the new countess beside her husband Benjamin Latymer and his sister.

"Olivia, and do you mind if I call you that, my lady? These are cold days. Yet I rarely see you in the hall close to the great fire.

Would you accompany me this evening? Surely, we have a great deal to speak of with each other?"

The new countess smiled, although hesitant. "Oh, dear, I am a little shy perhaps." Olivia seemed to cringe and Illiana noticed the tiny cut on one lip, and the small bruise on the woman's left cheek bone.

"I confess to getting a trifle listless sometimes," Illiana said more softly. "I should be glad of your company, should you ever feel the same."

"I'll, thank you, and indeed, I shall," Olivia twittered, but had clamped her right hand over the bruise. She would, Illiana now realised, not wish to have her small injuries noticed, nor be recognised as an abused wife.

Illiana once again cursed Benjamin under her breath.

THE DELICIOUS EXCITEMENT and the riding lessons, the outings to the Gold Row and to the other grand places, Guild Halls, Cathedrals and aqueducts in London City, had all finished as Benedict's loving company had disappeared. Without chaperone, it was only the foreign market where Illiana felt safe to wander with Sabine.

February's frosty sunshine reflected over the skins of fresh leeks, cauliflower, lettuce and carrots. Folk gathered up armfuls, paid the slightly higher prices, then followed the scent of fresh baked bread. The cheat lay ready for sale in large rolls of light brown, while small loaves of white manchet demanded a much higher price, but smelt even better, and offered a good crust for soaking in soup.

The breads oven stood by the entrance to the marketplace and many brought their own tubs, paying the smaller price of cooking their own dough. Beside the oven, two aproned women stood, calling, "Do your own, my friends, but our cheat is as tasty as manchet. Breathe in the perfume, of our manchet too. Rye or barley, we do it best."

Those men not permitting their wives out alone, pushed past quickly, collecting whatever their wives had told them to buy. Oysters, fresh and cheap. The last of the berries, the first of the new spices. Women shopped in groups, laughing, joking, pointing out absurdities, while solitary servants overloaded themselves and staggered, hurrying home.

Giggling, Sabine nodded. "Yes, passing on the orders. You see what's best value and you judge it all better than me. You can guess where I'm going."

Illiana guessed. "You won last time, but you'll lose today. Besides," and she pulled a face, "don't you remember how upsetting it was with that little black dog about to die. All the blood. It was horrible."

"Oh dear." Sabine stopped, staring at her feet. "Yes. I was almost in tears."

"I know why you want the excitement and everyone cheering and all the fun of getting it right. Gambling is addictive so be careful, but it's up to you. Do what you like."

Hesitating, then shaking her head, Sabine mumbled, "I'll promise this is the last time. Does that sound alright? I'm still the giddy child I want to be. You've grown up but I don't want to."

"When I was little," Illiana frowned, "I still never wanted to bet on dogs dying but I know lots do it."

Raising both eyebrows, and staring at Illiana, Sabine looked hopeful. "Just one last go, and I'll only bet sixpence. I won't look at the loser, and if I win anything I'll give it to that same old woman sitting in the gutter. With sixpence she can buy a big meat pie."

"It's not up to me to say," Illiana smiled. "I'm not your boss."

"You are actually."

She started to walk away, but called back, "Do what you want, but making this the last time sounds good to me."

Illiana watched as Sabine disappeared into the crowds. The fighting pit was near the back of the market past the Smithy, and Illiana walked in the opposite direction.

THORNS

The market sizzled on good days, the wonderful smells fighting with the stench near the leather stall and others, the shouting of the sellers and the laughing and bustling of the crowds. It was an atmosphere she had loved, yet now, finally, as the judgement of price against quality bored her, she felt little interest in what she would buy since there was nothing she needed or wanted.

Illiana wandered aimlessly. Staring at more capes, she turned away as the seamstress eagerly began to barter prices. The cobbler held up more boots, but Illiana shook her head. She decided that once Sabine returned from the blood and squeal of fighting dogs, she would never bother trudging down to the market ever again.

COLD DAYS BECAME COLD WEEKS.

It was when her mother's interminable whines and complaints tired her, that Illiana, carefully alone, re-introduced herself to the solar, although ready to leave immediately should it be already occupied by those she wished to avoid. The fire was lit, the window shutters open to sun and rain, frost and the rattle of the wind, but the settle and three chairs seemed unoccupied. This day not only was Olivia absent, but so was everyone else.

Illiana sank down on the one cushioned chair, high backed and close to the fire and closed her eyes in relief. The timid hiccup startled her and she looked around, expecting to see a scared hound seeking warm shelter. Instead she saw the pink flushed face of her new sister-in-law. Olivia had blended into the shadowed settle, dressed in the same unpattened dark blue as the cushions. For a brief moment the two women watched each other. Then, still flushed, Olivia scrambled to her feet and the countess apologised to the dowager countess.

"My lady, I'm truly sorry. Forgive me."

Illiana sat forwards. "What on earth for, Olivia?"

"Being here." Olivia hovered. "I mean, I've done nothing, but I'm sure you don't want me here."

Although she hadn't, Illiana immediately shook her head. "Gracious, you're as welcome here as I am, my lady." She paused, then said, "Are you escaping your husband?'

Olivia's gasp turned. "I – well, my lady, I dare not answer that but Benjamin and my – dear – sister-in-law, they have taken the litter to St. Paul's. I declined. Not that I was invited."

"I loved my husband even though Benedict was many years older than me." It abruptly felt unwise to talk about herself. "But not all arranged marriages are successful. Do you have family nearby? No friends to visit?"

The soft blue shadow shook it's head. "My lord has forbidden me to associate with my own family. They live at some distance, some miles past the marshes in Kent, near Hever Manor. It is more than a year since I saw my mother there."

Illiana blinked. "You have the right to invite them here. Feasting, for Easter perhaps. Or perhaps I might invite them for you."

The shaken head, dark in a deep blue cap held by black pins, her hair invisible beneath, repeated. Olivia's voice quivered. "My lady, that's a great kindness. However, they would not accept. There's contempt, even hatred. You see, Benjamin expected a larger dowry but my pappa is not so wealthy, and I am a younger sister, so he refused, but only after seeing me married. Now I can't visit – I see no one."

"Well, you can see me," said Illiana at once. "This is the perfect place, perfect timing, and we must meet every day and become friends."

Olivia's smile burst the shadow, but she remained furtive and nervous, while Illiana rediscovered a measure of happiness.

Until the interruption.

CHAPTER FIVE

The Ides of March, the fifteenth of the month, brought a dread of another sort. Drizzle had darkened most of the day and now early evening brought a greater sustained darkness. The household had already gathered in the Hall, but the dinner bell had not yet called.

"My lady," Manders opened the door to the solar where once again Illiana and Olivia sat by the inglenook, backs shivering in the draft, fronts burning in the golden reflections of the flames, "Master Farrier wishes a private word."

Clearly, he addressed Illiana, and she saw Nicholas, Sabine's father, standing, waiting, behind the steward. Olivia shrank back but Illiana stood and darted forwards. "Nicholas, is something wrong?"

"Proper wrong, lady. Tis my little one." He was tall, taller than tall and almost as wide. He towered over Manders, who had stepped back. Sabine's father and only living parent, was rarely seen beyond the stables. But now his wide pale eyes were water logged. "Tis my Sabine, lady. Went to market though never said why. That were eight of the bell this morning. Tis almost eight of the bell this afternoon. She's not home. I been searching, my lady, but Sabs ain't at the market no more. She ain't no where." The huge man bent and sobbed.

"Manders," she called to him, "please, my cape, gloves and boots." Then facing back to Nicholas, she asked quickly, "You've searched the market? It'll be closing now but the fighting pit will still be open and I'd wager that's where she went. I'll check there now. Have you walked the back streets? The shops?"

Looming, his hair dripping less than his eyes, Nicholas Farrier nodded. "Reckon I've walked London. I walked the Thames banks three times each way. Done as far as the Tower, then far as Ludgate, but I ain't gone through no gates yet. Why would my little one go outta London now? Surely she's still within them walls."

Two pages brought the outdoor clothes Illiana had demanded, and she turned to Olivia, who sat very still, staring and clutching her fingers. "Would you come with me, my lady?" Olivia shivered, shaking her head. Again, Illiana turned to the groom. "Nicholas, I'm sure Sabine would never wish to leave you. We'll search together. I expect you'll see more if you ride, but I'll stay on foot. Hurry, the gates will close soon."

From the length of Cheapside, cutting north to Bishopsgate, Illiana approached the entrance to the Foreign Market, and hurried inside before a loud declaration of it being closed to the public. Almost every stall had shut, those smaller already carted away. Shutters pulled up, and the narrow walks littered with lettuce leaves and crumbled crumbs. The stray dog packs had moved in, but the fighting dogs were being carried from the pit, though the crowds had not yet entirely left their arguments over winnings and losing, cheating and shouting.

Wrapped tight, fur lining over her small headdress and hem to her boots, Illiana used the power of nobility and asked the only question she needed answered. "A young woman, yellow curls over her shoulders, the prettiest young woman. She loved the fights and may have bet a shilling, but someone took her. Who saw her? Who saw her led away?"

A short man leaned on a broom handle, "Reckon I saw a pretty lass a good handful o' hours long gone. She lost her pennies but I ain't seen her since."

Illiana handed out her gloved palm, two silver pennies shining. "Did anyone approach her? Where was she heading when she left the pit?"

A larger hand reached over her shoulder, and took the pennies in a sudden grasp. "I'll not risk saying too much," whispering, "But I saw a red cape pulled away, two of them villains, them Delgado's, and I seen 'em afore, so tis well nigh for certain. I'll say no more." As Illiana reached out to question him, he had gone, merging with the crowd.

From her purse, she held up another penny. It shone as the guards walked past, swinging their lanterns. "Who else saw something? Anything at all to do with the blonde girl in the red cloak. Who are these bad folk, called Delgardo's?"

The crowd swarmed, shouting again, yelling and bustling around the pit. "I got five bob for little Miss Scarlet."

Suddenly, "Yes, I saw her. Two big fellows talked to her. I saw her shake them curls, but off she went, walking between them. Big fellows and chatting in foreign. Up that way, towards the Wall. I reckon they went to the Bishopsgate."

It made no sense. "Sabine doesn't speak anything other than English. Did she try to get away?"

"No idea, missus. I'm mighty busy today." He moved away without claiming his penny.

Standing, staring, Illiana wondered whether this might be a lie, simply mischief or spiteful, malicious or stupid. Sabine would not walk off with strangers. If it happened at all, then the men were surely friends. Family, or staff from the house, grooms she'd known, or scullery boys. Even so, to disappear without a word to her father, did not fit character or sense.

Continuing to wander, she asked others, stall holders packing up near the pit, women still shopping who looked friendly enough to reply. Eventually it was a child who helped. A small boy, shuffling after a woman who headed for the closing gates, stopped and said, "Yes, well, sort of yes, lady. She were being dragged off. Walking, that is, but them men had her arms. She were yelling. I told my mum but she didn't see naught cos she were chatting with my aunty."

"Thank you," and Illiana stuffed three pennies into the child's hand and approached the mother.

"I heard some yells," the woman smiled, "but I only saw two large lads, striding off to the Bishopsgate or maybe the Aldgate, and no way was I going to grab at one of them."

A young man pushed past. "You give me sixpence, lady, and I reckon I saw them."

"Tell me first, and if I believe you I'll give you what you ask.

"Hours and hours gone," he gabbled in a hurry. "Afore dinner, it was. I saw her cos she wagered on me dad's pup, and she lost. Then up comes two big gents wiv right funny voices. I know what they says too, I listened cos they was funny. *"We's lost, little hija, you shows us the way to the wall and reckon I'll give you more than the coins you just lost."* She were proper pleased and said yes. Off she went. I heard her yelling a moment later but I dunno what fer."

"You heard one say the word *hija* ?"

The boy nodded. "Sounded like that."

"Spanish." Illiana wanted to cry, and gave the boy a silver shilling and he ran.

She stood very still, refused to cry and felt extremely sick.

The crowds had faded and no other man or child came towards her, offering information. In the echoes of the now deserted market cobbles, avoiding the starving, scrounging dogs, Illiana walked quickly towards the way into the wider roads beyond.

The gates had not yet slammed shut. Immediately outside, she stood at the smithy. The Smith was busy building up the second forge. He was using the bellows too, busy increasing flame to the charcoal, and Illiana couldn't interrupt. When the forge was too hot for the smith to stand too close, she called, "Master Smith, I hate to bother you but this is urgent. Can you help?"

The man turned. He wore only a sleeveless vest over skin tight hose, and the muscles beneath and beyond were pouring sweat. His body glowed in the fire's reflection. Illiana felt suddenly shy and looked down

"Depends what you're after, mistress. There's the best nails in the whole guild on show there, and it's arrows will be next."

Illiana shook her head, the hood of her cape bounced and the dark fur hid her eyes. "I've been told my friend was taken away. Really dragged away. She was here at the market this morning, and now she's gone. The man who told me said Delgardo. You work close to the market. Do you know that word?"

Staring, he stopped work, rubbing his hands across the remains of his shirt. "Tis a word the whole world knows, mistress." He paused, then lowered his voice. "Tis possible some idiot from Bedlam wanted to frighten you. It's a name to frighten anyone. Spanish pirates, they are."

Illiana felt the freeze of fear down her spine, and the tears forming again behind her eyes. "So, they'd abduct a young girl? They'd be arrested surely. I have to go to the sheriff."

"My lady, I shall help, if I can. You speak of the Delgardo's?"

At first the sudden interruption scared and then annoyed her, but the man who spoke, heavily fur caped, and unusually tall, looked down at her. His hat, wide brimmed, wore a small embroidered coat of arms and around his neck, glinting as the cape swung, was a royal collar, rich golden scrolled links and a hanging centre of sun, star and rose. She bit her lip.

· · ·

THE SMITH HAD AGAIN TAKEN up the bellows.

Illiana gazed instead at the man now watching her. "Do you know me, sir?"

His smile was a tiny twitch at one corner of his mouth. "Not yet, my lady, but once you explain, since I know a good deal of the Delgardo pirates, I shall help as I can."

Immediately she told the stranger her story. "Would pirates steal my friend? She's – my maid."

"As his highness's Marshall, my lady, I know a good deal concerning the scum who attempt to invade this country. Let me introduce myself, lady. I am Charles, Viscount Valdar, and I work as marshal for King Edward. My experience has frequently included encounters with pirates, Spanish, Moors, French and English. The Delgado's are a mob of sailors and robbers from Spain, sometimes attracting new blood and swelling in number, but rarely dare enter this far into the country."

Looking, silently hoping, even praying, Illiana abruptly found the man's eyes had transfixed her into their depths. Shaking herself back together. "Lord Charles," and even the name sounded strangely familiar. "What will they do with her?" Illiana's voice was barely audible.

"Once the pirates have enough captives, they'll sail back to Spain and sell them as slaves." Viscount Charles was not quite as tall as Sabine's father, but only a finger's width less. In the darkening gloom of evening, his eyes were deeply intense and seemed black.

"These are pirates, then." Illiana was shivering, although the wind had calmed. "I can hire a ship or pay for a passage. Where should I go?" Yet both his unusual height and the gentleman's name reverberated in Illiana's mind. She had heard it somewhere before.

The Viscount regarded Illiana as though he had not previously realised she was entirely insane. Through the increasing night's gloom, his eyes were unblinking. "Madam, you aspire to something you cannot do. You would more likely be taken prisoner yourself. I know who you are and I know your life has been somewhat challenging recently, but what you speak of is beyond your capabilities. Spain at this time does not simply accept slaves and the hare'ems of the Moors, it is also practising a religious tyranny which tortures and kills." He raised one dark eyebrow. "It will be difficult, but I assure you, my lady, you must accept the loss of your maid."

She stared back. "I will not, sir." She shrugged, turning away. "I shall remember your advice, my lord, but your opinion does not rule my own."

Illiana paused as he spoke again. "My own responsibility is to annihilate the cruelty of these pirates, my lady," he said softly. "Should I discover your maid, I will return her to you."

As Illiana began to thank him she realised that he had gone. His retinue had been waiting, he had re-joined them, mounted, and had ridden off with the clatter, chink and thunder of hooves that always announced royalty within the city.

Now she was alone, but not one thread of her determination had wavered. Waiting, as previously arranged, for Nicholas to join her, she re-swallowed the last hour's words and actions. Clearly the danger needed careful attention, but Sabine's rescue would be the prime aim, and only drowning, she decided, could stop her.

Never having sailed before, never even having seen the sea, the beach, a sea port or any thing beyond the great river, Illiana now needed advice of a far more practical nature. The fear which had ravaged her initially at Sabine's disappearance, and which had increased as she heard of pirates, now doubled again as she realised what a dread-full task this promised to be.

Leaning against the closed gates, trying to bring back the enthusiasm, she heard a breathless question. "I pray – I pray so over and again, lady, you got an answer?" Bustling, panting, Nicholas marched up from the Cheaps. "Bin up, bin down, lady. I found naught." He held the reigns as the horse stood placid beside him.

It would be so sweet, Illiana thought, to mimic a horse and not to care as long as food kept coming. She told Nicholas her news, and finally, "I'm going to find a ship that will take me to Spain. You are free to come, or not, as you wish. If you want to travel with me, I will naturally pay whatever expenses arise. I will not return without Sabine. I promise."

The head groom almost collapsed to his knees. The news was horrific and yet now the race to find his daughter seemed somehow miraculous.

"Lady, sure I'll come. Protect your ladyship, I will, with life and limb and whatever else you be wanting. Just bless you, and tell me whatever you wants."

"I wants," said Illiana, "I mean, I want us to leave as soon as possible. I have to delay long enough to pack a bag and draw the coins I'll need. Hopefully we can leave tomorrow morning, but have you any idea where we find a ship to Spain? What part of Spain, how big is it?"

"There be ports all along the river, lady, I'll take you home for the packing, then I'll walk the banks and see what boat will take us." He patted the horse's saddle. "You ride, lady. T'will be quicker."

IT WAS INDEED MUCH QUICKER, and on arriving home, immediately she called for her mother's made, and told her what she needed packed. Almost smiling, she reminded herself that she had packed laboriously after abruptly becoming a widow, expecting to be hustled off to a shack in Muggle Lane rented by the church. Then, just as abruptly, she had unpacked, and now, she was needing to pack again.

She rang for Manders. Her cape and gloves were flung to the rug near the fire to dry off, yet a rain drop still clung to her nose.

"Manders. I'm hopelessly ignorant. Tell me how and where I may rent a berth on some sort of ship going to Spain."

The pause halted finally with a gulp. "My lady, is this for some other passenger, may I ask, or is the intention to travel yourself?"

"Myself, and Nicholas will look after me. I need a ship tomorrow, if possible, I need my funds in coin, and I need to know where to aim for in Spain, to chase the Delgado's."

For a moment she thought Manders was about to faint. Instead, he tottered, straightened, and bowed. "My lady, we need to speak."

CHAPTER SIX

"My lady, this news is terrible indeed. I am shocked and distressed and will do whatever I can to help," Manders seemed to shrink, before forcing himself straight once more. "Yes, I have heard of the Delgado pirates, and they are horrible and I believe they occupy the southern coast of the Spanish and Moorish lands, but I will discover more within the hour, if your ladyship can wait. Forgive me, I must add, and I must beg you, my lady, you must not travel yourself, even with your groom. Master Farrier is a strong and clever man, madam, but he is no soldier. Yet you speak of terrible danger."

Smiling and thanking him, Illiana did not bother to repeat her own plans. "I beg you to find out as quickly as you can, and as much as you can, concerning Spain and the Delgado's. That would be so immensely helpful. I will be up until late, Manders, and if possible, I shall leave tomorrow morning."

Manders marched off in gloom and flurry while Illiana searched out both Olivia and her mother. Olivia was a quick visit.

"You are quite mad and so courageous, my dear," she told Illiana, while trembling in spite of the fire which had scorched her nose into three blisters. "I can get money, indeed I shall, but I cannot see any other way to help. I simply wish you'd send a sheriff or a page or anyone but yourself."

"The coins would help enormously," she told her new faltering friend. Her mother gave the opposite advice in almost every way.

"Stupid girl. You certainly don't have the brains to see through such a venture. Simply get all the money you can, and pack for emergencies. I shall come with you, naturally. Otherwise, you will most certainly drown or land in Constantinople or somewhere equally crazy. You know yourself absolutely incapable, so you will need an intelligent companion. So come on, girl. Get moving. No time to waste."

This was an unexpected shock, and although Illiana was not immediately sure whether she was delighted or horrified with this news, she obediently returned to her bedchamber and asked for three more items to be packed, having reconsidered possible emergencies. She then clutched up her cloak and gloves from where the maid had politely taken them from the floor and folded them on a chair, and left the house without anyone seeing her.

No horse was needed since the sheriff's office was simply one street north and one more east, and she was well aware that his office would be closing in moments.

Illiana's dramatic appearance startled even the flames, as she found the sheriff chewing smoked bacon and slurping from a cup of beer. Bursting through the door, she frightened him as much as she was frightened herself. Stepping back in a hurry from the pan over the fire, the sheriff stared at the grandly dressed stranger.

Grandly dressed females never walked alone. They never marched alone into his office, and especially just minutes before he intended locking up. He stuttered as Illiana interrupted him, in some detail, with the disaster which had occurred earlier that day.

He was no help. "I've never heard of them."

"As the law-keeper in this area," Illiana looked stern, "surely you should know what I refer to, sir. I was told that everyone knows about them. Surely you - ?"

The sheriff swallowed his mouthful and grunted. "Well, of course I've heard of them, but they don't come to London. There's not a single man of law would let them in."

"Yet they have indeed been let in. Or at least, not kept out. My friend has been dragged off, sir, and I demand help even if it is only advice and information. She was seen at the foreign market this morning, surrounded by the Delgados."

"Here?" The sheriff flinched again and sat, indicating the opposite facing stool. "My lady, I've heard about taking slaves to Spain and other places too, but right here? I thought it was just on the coast especially while all the men were out on fishing boats."

Illiana sat. "It seems few noticed and those that did were too frightened."

He scowled. "We get pirates from France and pirates from Africa and Greece and Turkey as well as Spain. When the ships sail into port, the young ones run. Slaves make good money I reckon. If tis the Delgardos, you'd best forget your friend for she won't be coming back."

Now glaring and leaning forwards towards him, Illiana gritted her teeth, saying, "Your lack of interest is quite shocking sir. I had expected more help than that. Now at least tell me what you know of their destination, where they sail from and sail to, and where I arrange to sail for Spain myself."

Staring back, the sheriff managed, "I'm – mighty sorry – but tis naught I can do, my lady. Far as I know, the Delgados, being the worst known, they'll be off to the estuary." Illiana's knees seemed to have melted and she grabbed the stool where she sat, as though expecting to fall, as the sheriff grumbled on. "If folks say they saw them, then must be true. Other pirates don't come up into London. They'd be proper scared of anything and everything. Tis only them Delgardos would risk that, grab what they want and laugh about it. Would have their caravel at some spot downstream, not risking the customs exploring what they had – then off to Grays in the estuary."

"So I can check if they've passed through one of the gates? Which? Bishopsgate?"

"From the market, yes indeed, Bishopsgate. But tis closed now."

"There'll still be a guard," Illiana insisted. "Then what? Is their own ship waiting at Gray's?"

"Reckon so. First a wherry to Grays and then set sail. They wouldn't hang around once they've got what they want." The sheriff stood, although hesitant. "Good luck finding what you want, lady, but now tis time for lockup."

Walking alone and in the darkness all the way to Bishopsgate now would be extremely unwise and Illiana returned home. She then hurried to the stables. There Nicholas stood outside, well wrapped, his bag-pack already at his side. He was immediately eager as he saw the dowager countess. "My lady, I'm right glad to see you. I been all around, and got some ideas for the morning." He was bowing repeatedly.

"Did you check at Bishopsgate before they shut?"

"I did, my lady." Even the giant now seemed exhausted and leaned back against the wooden wall that enclosed the courtyard and stables. "She were seen, though kept mute so weren't stopped. Then gatekeeper, he reckoned the bastards – excuse my language, lady – stuffed rags in her mouth so the lass couldn't speak and would have threatened him too no doubt. At least the truth be proved and I knows where to go."

Beneath the enforced straight back and raised chin, steady voice and determination, Illiana felt sick, faint and bewildered. Her head whirled and made her dizzy. "So, it seems the Delgardos had a ship waiting on the estuary. They have to avoid customs, so it's all planned, and, according to tides, they may have left already."

Now her voice was unsteady again. "Nicholas, do you think we should leave tonight?"

It was not the groom's voice that answered her, it was her mother's.

"We need a good night's sleep. If they've sailed already, we can't overtake them anyway. At least I speak Spanish, and so do you, stupid girl, although rather badly and no doubt you've forgotten half of it. So we leave in the morning, as soon as the gates open."

Nicholas, since it was his daughter for whom they searched, had the courage to speak again, although softly. "My lady, tis as you say and I thank you from my heart. If I can add, tis not likely of help to follow them pirates far as the sea ports. Just past the Bridge, the docks south of St. Katherine's, there's caravels will dock there, and the lighters and wherries what will bring the cargo beneath the Bridge. Then they sets sail again. Some to France, some far as Italy. There's expected tomorrow a caravel what will return to Seville. Reckon that's the ship we needs. Tis for trade, but reckon they has a cabin or two. Unloads at dawn and will sail off on the next high tide."

Bertha smiled and Illiana smiled wider, feeling suddenly excited, drowning out fear and bilious doubt.

"Nicholas, you're a saint and a genius. So we set off tomorrow morning at dawn. No matter if the gates are still closed. We go by the river."

WHO SLEPT well that night was never discussed, though more of the household saw them off than the number of travellers themselves. Six pages carried three packed bags, Olivia, still in her bedrobe, kissed Illiana's cheek and promised to pray for her safe return, Manders bowed and held open the double doors, Floss, the assistant cook, presented an armful of food for the journey including two flasks of wine, a scullery boy packaged the food in folded unbleached linen, while two pages and Bertha's maid helped both ladies tuck themselves within their fur lined cloaks, and their leather gloves, lined in wool.

Beatrice remained hidden in bed and was definitely not missed, yet a hurried appearance from Lord Benjamin nodded a polite goodbye, although he did not seem to have the faintest understanding of what had inspired Illiana's departure. She did not explain.

"I shall be returning soon," she assured him, carefully ignoring the two skinny ankles and unwashed toes protruding beneath his badly fitting bedrobe. She was surprised to have seen him at all, and still could not even guess why the man she loathed and who clearly loathed her, had so abruptly altered his opinion and now even appeared friendly.

Outside Nicholas Farrier was already waiting, also well snuggled in lather and fur, with three horses, two well saddled, and the third leading a small sheltered litter.

The baggage was also hauled into the litter, and an assistant groom of dubious age, hopped to the front, ready both to drive the litter, and finally to lead all back to Latymer House, once the dowager countess, her mother and her chief groom had boarded their passage to Spain.

"We's ready," he said briskly, helping Illiana mount while Manders helped Bertha climb into the litter, "Right, we's away."

With the gates soon to open, they headed south and east into Thames Street and along the banks with their first glimmer of sprouting daisies, towards the Bridge, and beyond to Wool Wharf, and the great docks where sea going carvels and caravels headed out to France and beyond.

It was chilly with a haze of early drizzle. The river was busy. Oars clanked and splashed, the wherry boats headed in all directions, their owners shouting and waving. On land the merchants were swarming, as shoppers and workers pushed past, some towards the Tower but most heading north.

The Wool Warf was pounding, the two wide quays taking three vessels each, and the cranes swinging, every man yelling, as the huge cartons of unwoven wool were crashed onto the decks. Captains yelled to their crews, even louder than the crane drivers, and the loaders and carters were too busy and breathless to shout at all. The bustle was difficult to pass, and passengers kept back from the quays until the cranes moved away, and then it was their turn to push and seethe.

Nicholas told his young groom to wait as the two women tottered to the cobbles. "You'll help the ladies on deck, carry the baggage, and see the ship sail afore you rides back home," he told the boy Eown. "The ships ain't loaded yet and next high tide don't come till after sunset, mayhaps eight of the evening. You got a long wait, lad, though you'll be well paid for it."

First it was Nicholas, nodding to his companions, who strode off to check on the *caravele Los Valientes*, hopefully, already in the process of filling the holds.

Illiana stood alone, back from cranes and running sailors, safe from the stink of unwashed wool, only recently stored on the farms outside the city walls, and from as far away as Gloucestershire. The wind was cold in her face and she wrapped her gloved hands around her waist, holding the cloak tight. The noise shattered her thoughts, but she was no longer frightened. Never having seen a caravel before, a ship with masts too high to sail beneath London's great stone bridge and its busy hub, houses and carts, Illiana was awed by the ships anchored here, those out from the quays still awaiting the pilot boats and the customs officers to board and check.

Never having seen an ocean wave, let alone sailed one, Illiana was fascinated and banished the fearful doubts. She wondered how a ship might be kept warm and doubted that the rooms could have fires, since wooden hulls were the only protection from the danger of the high seas. And if the wind was freezing here in port, she could guess what it might be like once out on the waves.

The sun was rising yet bore no discernible warmth, but the ships all had their sails down, oars out ready on those at anchor, but invisible on those bobbing on their ropes along the quays.

She saw no ship's names, but knew there was time. There would be endless time. Even a fast caravel with a strong wind blowing from the west, would take four long weeks to sail from London to the Middle Sea and onwards to the Spanish port of Seville.

Then, everything would be more difficult still.

Illiana turned, Nicholas was shouting over the mill.

"My lady, we got our listings fixed and tis paid an'all. Two cabins fer the price o' one, since tis not yet called an easy crossing. We waits for Los Valientes, but she won't be sailing till evening, once the sun goes down. We can board at six of the evening, but no supper to be had that first night. Will you come to the inn here, lady, and we can take an early dinner and sit out the day."

Following him at once, Illiana beckoned to her mother and slipped her arm to Bertha's elbow. Bertha pulled away. "I'm coming, stupid girl. Do you suppose it's only you can be hungry?'

THE SMALL INN was crammed with those rushing food and gulping their drinks. Everyone was in a hurry. The talk was a permanent fervour. The continuous buzz allowed Nicholas to speak without being overheard by anyone except his two lady companions. "Right, now, tis two cabins, but ain't got no idea what they's like. I doesn't mind, not a wit, whether you would like one each, or be together. I's happy sleeping with the crew, be it up or down. I'll learn more about the sailing business. We'll not be seeing them Delgardos on route as they left last night, and we's not leaving till gone eight this evening. I done ordered food, but 'afraid there ain't much choice. T'will be ham and bread likely to be stale, and I gets beer while you gets wine. Tis Spanish wine arrives here in bloody big crates – excuse my language – so tis Spanish wine we'll be getting."

Illiana followed this information with only one ear. Now comfortable and warm, expecting food and wine without interest in the quality, she was remembering the home she already desperately missed.

Here in the public room of the inn, the smells swamped, fried food and beer, unwashed bodies and sour breath. Hardly unusual. Yet as the door smashed open and new customers entered, the reek of wool sacks, rank drips of wine from stored crates, the metal against wood scraping of the cranes, and beneath it all, the permanent drift of brine and rats.

Illiana missed the house and her bedchamber of luxury. She missed Benedict, his strong arms, his whispers of love and his promises of life together. She felt a moment of misery. That might have been her own house, living as a countess, passing her days with a man as kind as she ever could have wished. The promise of eternal delight had lasted just thirty one days, and delight had abruptly turned to misery.

Having lost Benedict, having lost her home which she had known since birth although her bedchambers had certainly changed, now she had lost safety and comfort, and most wretched of all, she had lost her friend Sabine, that friendship now replaced with the horror of what might be happening to an innocent girl snatched by pirates.

She snapped back once the food and wine arrived, which seemed overcooked but smelled glorious, and Illiana reminded herself of excitement and the escape from the new lord, and the inevitable months of dreary boredom that would now swirl into months of adventure. Dangerous adventure, but boredom be damned.

"She's coming in," someone called from outside, poking his head around the inn's doorway, bring in the rush of fresh wind and rank smells. "Tis the Valientes."

. . .

Los Valientes, had been moored close to the small quay, and had rolled on its anchor, accepting the tide that swept in from the estuary further out, its three masts tall against the sky, but its sails flat now, ready for reassembling as soon as it was out with tide once more. A small rowing boat was now, heavily roped, pulling it in to the docks. The carrack swung against the quay, heavier ropes were thrown, and its hull was pulled tight against the cement. Where three vessels had previously been held, now there was space only for two, and the cranes began to clatter and roll.

A vast number of wine barrels were gradually unloaded, hauled to port, and stacked. The scurry of the crew still onboard was fast and disciplined.

"It will be a long time before she's ready to embark," someone said into Illiana's ear. "But you's one o' them passengers, ain't you, lady?"

"If this is the right ship," Illiana turned. "And I'm fairly sure it is. It's very large."

"She's one o' the biggest," the sailor nodded before wandering off.

Nicholas stood at Illiana's back, watching the carrack brought in, the flourish on deck with the first unloading. An opening on deck, planks upended, was surrounded by the crew, each tugging on ropes as the cargo was slowly brought up from the hold, huge boxes, packages and bundles drawn up onto deck where the crane could reach them, hauling them onto solid land. Smaller loads were carried and then rolled down the gang plank to the dock. Most of the cargo, however, consisted of enormous wine casks and the barrels themselves, which needed the largest crane.

Everything moved, swinging and creaking, while gulls swept and called overhead, the weight of each load thumping as it landed, and the crew grunting as they struggled. Wood slammed against cement, groaned as planks wheezed against plant, metal slapped, the wind whistled where rigging remained and water rolled like a cupshotten sailor.

Illiana eyed the Passarella as it was lowered. "Is that how we climb onboard? It looks like a promise of a very cold bath."

From behind her, Nickolas laughed. "Reckon tis easy enough. Only a few folk drown."

She hadn't actually been joking. "I'd sooner be lifted on by the crane."

Nicholas snorted as the crane ropes swung and cargo thudded, some upended. "I'll be helping you and your mother, both, I promise, lady. Perhaps a push from behind."

The clang and crash of unloading continued, and then the same as bales of untreated wool were loaded onboard, and pushed down the hole on deck and into the hold.

Gradually twilight misted around them as the gulls quietened and flew to their nests, some perching on both the ship's mizzen mast and the main mast, beneath which the rigging lay carefully coiled. Others settled on the forecastle where the captain, unapproachable, now stood staring back out to sea.

More excited than Illiana, in spite of having more to fear regarding his daughter, Nicholas braced against the wind and grinned, stuffing the ticket behind his belt.

"There's some as speak English and there's some as don't," another passing sailor informed them. "Tis a Spanish ship and a trading vessel what carries passengers. This be a mighty different craft."

Nicholas interrupted. "Them bastards – forgive the language, lady – won't never have a ship like this. More like them others, them caravels we seen afore, far smaller. Lighter too, and faster. Well armed, I reckon. T'will arrive four or more days afore us, but we got no choice. In Seville we'll find the buggers and catch my Sabs back to safe arms."

Illiana ignored the passing cackle. "Are we sure they'll be in Seville?"

Nicholas glowered into the wind. "Or Cadiz or Almaria by force o' bad weather, but Seville I hopes."

Bertha snorted. "They'll never escape us, those nasty pirates. No buona fortuna for them." She shook her head and pushed back towards the ale house inn with a beckoning wave at her daughter, but Illiana stayed where she was.

Nicholas was wondering how many travellers usually died at sea. Illiana walked to the edge of the quay, away from the two cranes. Once again the voice of her hopeful imagination whispered in her head, of the adventure to come.

Now, gradually only a faint rush of ripples slapped the carrack's hull, tied fast by ropes thicker than those for hanging pirates, and the wooden planks preserved under black pitch.

The shouting grew louder, and a sudden rush of wind reeked of colder and stronger brine. Illiana felt her eyes water, and wandered back to join her mother. Their litter she could still see tethered back at the entrance to the docks, but the boy groom stood beside the horse, scratching her mane, the baggage by his feet. Illiana sank down beside her mother, and ordered another small cup of cheap wine.

Bertha introduced the elderly man, well bearded, who sat opposite. "A very interesting gentleman," Bertha said. "Allan Miller, this is my daughter Illiana. This gentleman is a regular traveller."

"Aye," the man pulled at his greying beard. "These ships are for trading and little else," he explained. "Goods on a carrack pile up mighty well, them deep holds can carry good stores and this carrack surely is half the size of some others. So tis grain, fruit, wheat and salt we gets from Spain, and wine casks too. English wine is good stuff and cheaper, but tis a bit too sweet for my taste. Working here I get to try wines from Italy, Spain and Brittany. French is too pricey but no doubt tis worth it, and we fill those ships with wool, leather and ale."

"And passengers," Illiana suggested.

"Not as trade," the man sniggered. "But the captain here on this Carrack, well tis Godwin Nape, and he'll made sure you travel well."

"The pirates who trade their captive passengers?" Illiana asked. "What about them? I'm sure you've heard of the Delgado's?"

The man leaned forwards and lowered his voice. "None here, lass. Can't face the customs nor the pilots and don't need no cranes. They keeps out on the coast. Never met one and never want to, but them Delgardo's, they sails a caravel, *La Brava*, as is known, too sleek and fast and never caught, and has three cannons on deck."

"*La Brava*," Illiana repeated. "We hope to catch her moored in Seville."

CHAPTER SEVEN

The light was ebbing, the sun had faded and the encroaching night's darkness gloamed more deeply. The distant church bell had chimed six times, faint behind the clouds.

"Ready to go onboard, ladies? Two cabins reserved, and the gen'elman to sleep on deck or wiv the crew in them bilges."

The passarella, a plank already laid for boarding, was frequently used by a running and jumping crew, yet the slant was considerable

Bertha and her impatient daughter were both guided by Nicholas, and a small boy leading them upwards. Then standing on deck, they gazed in amazement at what now surrounded them. The loading had finished but now the crew swept out the bilges, the deck and the rigging while the captain shouted and told them to get a move on.

There was no place for fascinated passengers, and quickly they were shown the two tiny cabins where they would spend the next month.

"Around thirty days most likely. Depends on weather and little else. We don't expect a fast journey in mid winter, but it has happened more than once if the winds blow in the proper direction. Your food, twice a day, with ale for waking, will be brought down to you here, but you can come up on deck when you wants. Just don't expect a greeting from the crew."

This was the small boy, seemingly little more than ten years of age, who had led them onboard and down the wooden steps at the rear, where the cabins faced each other over a tiny unlit corridor. it was some time before they spoke with anyone else.

Both cabins held two beds, each clamped to the floorboards, each as narrow as a napkin, barely wide enough for one sleeper, and only if glued during rough seas. The first cabin was low ceilinged, had no window, a small table between the beds was hooked to the floor and the wall behind, and two stools, three legged, just fitted at the opposite corners without being crashed over when the door opened. A horn enclosed lantern swung from the beams and the candle within, was large enough, only if it was rarely lit. A chamber pot sat beneath one bed, and was not screwed to the floor. Illiana bleakly imagined, once full, what would happen to that bed pan if the sea grew rough.

The second cabin was even smaller with one bed sitting on top of the other, screwed tight but with barely space to squeeze between. There was a cask, one stool and one bed pan.

"Yours," Bertha pointed and nodded to Nicholas. "Illiana and I will share the larger."

His duty done, the boy scampered off, calling out, "No time for supper tonight but I'll bring the beer in the morning, lest we already sunk."

On deck, now moving towards the gunnels, the captain roared over the wind. "Back to the oars. Heading out."

Once again the rattle, clank and thump increased, as oars were pulled up and shoved through their slots, hitting the flat water as the dock worker untied the ropes from the buoys, then hauled back onboard by others on deck.

As the ship finally left the dock and the captain took the tiller, and with a sudden left tipped lurch, everything began to roll. The wind whistled like a gale, tugging at caps, capes and rigging, the oars were stored flat once more and the crew rushed to raise the sails. As energetic as the wind, the rich smell of brine sprang fresher and stronger, and the stink of the untreated wool from the hold sank back, outclassed.

In the cabins, everyone yelped and then apologised to whoever was listening.

Lurching from side to side, the empty chamber pots slipped, and the baggage rolled, only their weight discouraging their destruction. Nicholas discovered the two small wedges beneath the beds where the chamber pots could be secured.

"Right," Bertha croaked, "I need to ask if there's a privy."

"Over the side for men, nothing for women," Illiana shook her head. "Female passengers must be rare." She smiled and stood, both her arms out to test her own bAllance. "And I assume we empty the chamber pots over the side and spill them on the way."

"Then I shall inform Nicholas that it's his responsibility, and not ours. At least we had maids to do that at home."

"Remembering that sometimes that maid was me, but at least our floors didn't roll and lurch. Perhaps now we're facing even a month of misery," Illiana said. Immediately the floor beneath her tipped, abruptly, she lost the balance she had been practising and tumbled to the bed. The rolling of the ship seemed excessive. "I suppose this is horribly normal."

The reek of the salty brine became overpowering. Dirt, sweat and dribbles of water swept past the doorway and filled the cabin. Bertha doubled over, retching. Illiana gulped, holding her stomach. "I've heard of people being sea-sick. I think that's going to be me as well. Or will we get accustomed?"

"We won't," Bertha reclaimed her breath, gasping. "I have no intention of leaving this room until we arrive in Spain."

The night was calm except for an hour of wind which drove the ship forward and the exhaustion of the day brought sleep deep enough to stay dreamless.

With sudden calm, the morning brought a bright blue sea of wavelets and a sky bright with golden sunshine. Illiana tiptoed from the cabin, carefully closed the door behind her without even a click, and peeped through the tiny window.

"It's beautiful," Illiana whispered to herself, peering at the blue and golden calm. "Even though it's only March."

The voice behind her interrupted. "We've sailed southeast," Nicholas muttered. "I reckon the south east is another world."

Creeping as though escaping from the depths, they climbed downstairs, peeping through the window as they passed. And so they arrived on deck and gazed at a wonderland they could never have imagined. Wet, slippery, the wooden slats of the deck were drying in the sunshine and a golden sparkle fizzled in the warmth.

Gazing in all directions, finally the carrack's geography settled, seeming simple, as the light explored every corner and flung reflections, almost as lucid as the truth above, into the water below. The sky was a blue pale enough to appear heavenly, enriching the huge circular sun which sat only a mast's height above the flat yet rippled blue horizon.

The rear of the deck rose like a wooden tenement, four levels towering upwards, the highest seemingly an additional small deck, the poop deck, adorned with a mast, its sail billowing forwards with the sweep of salty wind raging from behind. Their cabins, Nicholas said, pointing, were on the lower level, four wooden steps up. What was above them, perhaps other cabins for captain and principal officers, they could not know. The levels also led down, possibly as far as the cargo hold.

A considerable walk ahead, which they did not yet risk, stood the main mast, two sails, huge and bulging, bright white in the sun and gulping at the wind that blew them. High above even the sails, a small basket of wood sat attached to the mast, only reached by the soaring sweep of rigging, the taught rise of robe vibrating only as the wind gusted.

Beyond this at the ship's bow, another three levels had been built, leaning forwards in the direction the ship must sail, and as though peering optimistically ahead. On the deck over these, the third mast, smaller but rich with sail, stood proud, and prouder still, from the top tip flew the Spanish flag, it's colours vivid.

A bustling crew was already at work, and Illiana, sheltered by Nicholas, kept back. Men climbed the rigging, called to each other, swept salt from the planks beneath them, peered over the sides and yelled back. The words were Spanish, yet accents disguised more than half.

"I don't understand much." At first Illiana whispered but the shouts drowned out her voice, and the rush of wind drowned the rest. She began to shout as well. "I sort of speak Spanish though I suppose I've forgotten a lot."

"Reckon what these fellows says," Nicholas said, "won't be o' much interest. Tis a flat sea. Tis not leaking. Stuff like that." Illiana smiled. She stood carefully, legs apart, leaning back when the lurches shook her. Nicholas, heavier and more stable with out much effort, did the same, his bulk steady behind her while still holding her, a large hand on each shoulder. He remained unmoving until, reassured she was also steady, he then said, "Roll with it, little one. But gentle. Just a little sway, like you is listening to slow music for a mighty slow dance."

She moved as told and felt the vile lurch of her stomach ease away. A sensation of utter safety held her tight.

The sky was so huge, it seemed to have absorbed everything she had ever known, encompassing a heaven so enormous as though perhaps the entire world had doubled and more. Studded across the gigantic blue expanse of the sea, were a thousand tiny dazzling diamonds, as light caught the tips of minute ripples, and a pale sweep of hazy impossibility above and behind, suggested an infinity she could not believe.

She whispered, "No end? Water for ever?" and made the mistake of clutching the ledge topping the gunnels, looking directly down. An even less expected and almost greater beauty shone back at her as she gazed at a million reflections. Then she doubled over, released the gunwales and was sick again directly into the glory of the sea.

"Mustn't never look down," Nicholas grinned at her, wiping her mouth with his own sleeve. "Look up or forwards."

"Why," she mumbled, "should my disgusting stomach care where I look?"

"Ballance," again he held her, steadying her. "But there be more worth on a ship than looking fer fish and sea serpents."

Yet she wondered how much more difficult it might be in a storm and high waves. She said, "I love it, but should I -well, my mother will wake soon."

Still now supporting her back, Nicholas bent and muttered in a conspiratorial wheeze. "Gotta tell you, lady, summit not too bad but I reckon you orta know. Back in the market, searching for my poor little lass, there was a stall selling matchlocks. It were your money, so I gotta tell you, well, yes, I bought 'em. Two. Aucubas."

"Matchlocks? Guns?" Illiana was startled. "And you know what to do with them?"

He nodded, smiling. "Used one before. Back in the battles. Then had one to guard the stables when the losers came scrabbling. They ain't easy, 'specially loading, but I know what I'm doing." His smiled grew. "Later, when there's time and peace and all that, I'll show you. It ain't too hard to hold and point, and pulled the little trigger. Loading, well that's down to me."

Staring back, Illiana also smiled. Puzzled fear merged with excitement. "They have great big, long spouts, don't they?" she spluttered. "I saw one once."

"Muzzles, lady, not spouts." Nicholas sniggered softly. "Yep, you need two hands to hold it, unless you lays the muzzle across a table or some fellow's shoulder, but it ain't as hard as you might think. If I can do it, anyone can."

Bertha was already awake, and as Illiana entered, the cabin boy was close behind with two wooden mugs of ale. Illiana took both cups and handed one to her mother.

"Mamma, please come up on deck. Only four little steps. It's windy, but only from behind, and the air is so fresh. It smells of salt but it feels invigorating. There's beauty in every blink."

Hiccupping and sipping, Bertha was still wrapped tight within the blankets and looked slightly green. "Definitely not. I feel sick." And was, retching over her top blanket.

Illiana gradually learned to love her cabin, its tiny embrace, its dark warmth and comfort, and even the partial privacy. She had known far worse beds and now even adored the roll of the night, soothing and leading to sweet dreams. Bertha struggled with nausea and lay sleeping, her stomach scrunched beneath her knees for every night and half each day.

Eyes tight shut, Bertha also dreamed of her long gone husband swimming through the placid water, coming from Spain to accompany her back to his homeland. She told no one of these dreams, and meanwhile Nicholas felt no such problem and strode the decks, wherever he was permitted.

The days grew longer and the continuous glare of sunshine on water became monotonous, each day dragging and indistinguishable, so forcing a boredom more pleasant, but, equally as inescapable as sweeping kitchen floors. Twice, briefly, the slick black divided tail of some monstrous animal swept from the deep water around them. Illiana thought this glorious but her mother shaded her eyes and repeated the stories of dragons.

Small enough to call fish, fat and leaping, little gleaming wet creatures jumped from the gentle waves, and, as if dancing, repeated, bringing a white froth on every ripple.

. . .

It was early, the sunshine not yet triumphant, when Illiana saw the captain at the tiller. The crew, either busy or still asleep, did not approach her, and uninterrupted, Illiana climbed the steps to the quarter deck at the prow. Neither a tall nor an impressive man, she approached him without hesitation.

"Por favor, senor," speaking in Spanish, "may I ask you some questions?"

The man turned and smiled. "You ask, senorita," he said, "and we shall see what I answer."

His accent was strong and disguised some words, but Illiana found that she remembered the long gone lessons from her father. She also smiled. "I was told we arrive in Seville. Before us, a day before, or even two days, from a dock at Grays, another ship sailed off. I know the name of the ship and I do know the name of the men in charge. Can I ask more?"

The captain seemed puzzled. "And why would you know that, lady? You' may not even known my own name which is Garcia Rozangia and I am pleased to meet my lady passenger, but ships sailing from Grays are those evading customs, a caravele no doubt, and likely the captain is not a man any woman wants to know."

Illiana nodded more eagerly than the captain had expected. "The pirate Delgardo."

"Lady, you travel on a Spanish ship and a trading vessel as carries passengers. What you ask after be a mighty different craft." Captain Rezangia frowned. "Indeed, lady, tis no doubt Gomez Delgardo, and best never see him long as you live."

"I understand," Illiana told him. "But those pirates stole my friend. She's in terrible danger. I have to get her back. Rescue her."

"That be sad," the man nodded. "But the Los Valientos won't be chasing no pirates, no chance. When you arrives in Seville, you'll find her docked, I reckon, less she docks in Almaria or Cadiz, forced by bad weather. Elvira Brava, she's smaller and faster than the Carrack here, and better armed. You say she left a day or more before us, then she'll dock four days or five before."

Although disappointed, Illiana wasn't surprised. "I never expected you to chase a pirate ship. I just want to know how I find my friend."

"We have cannons," he told her. "But I'll use them only in defence and never attack. You must travel from port to Granada, lady. That's where them evil monsters does their business."

The ship stopped briefly in France, once again unloading, then loading again. The cabin boy, too small for the heaving weights, bustled the English group down to the cabins. "You be in the way and break yer legs if you stays up on deck," he told Illiana.

Stamping and hauling brought the same noises she remembered from before. "More loading," she asked. "more passengers?"

The boy shook his head. "This be a trading vessel, lady. From England we carries wool, and woollen cloth with ale, beer, well tanned leather, mighty fine pewter and the best ironworks in the world. Tis all onboard and now we sells half in France. Back comes wine, flax and fruit. All for the market in Spain. Spain be the best. Wine and Jerez, spices, fruit, and copper. We even sometimes brings back mirrors and silk, paper, sugar and treacle from Italy. Tis a mighty good business. So's a few passengers might as well get a look in."

"I'm learning a lot." She smiled.

The boy's chest swelled. "Goods on a well built ship pile up mighty well, our holds carry good stores even tho' we surely is half the size o' some., we does mighty well. Trade wiv Spain and France and our pretty island an'all." Clearly the boy himself was English although he spoke it poorly, and probably spoke poor Spanish too.

"And how long do we have to stay in the French port?"

"A couple o' hours," said the boy. "You just keeps out the way till the tide comes in and we goes out."

It was the ideal moment for learning the skill of the matchlock, and for that hour Illiana sat in Nicholas's cabin, learning to balance and point the long steel muzzle, heavy but not as heavy as the buckets she'd once been accustomed to carrying every day, while also pulling the trigger, and preferably without falling over. As yet unloaded, gun practice seemed safe enough and even amazing. This was certainly a skill Illiana had never dreamed of mastering.

"Not that you've mastered naught," Nicholas added. "But you ain't as bad as I'd reckoned."

"Wonderful praise," and she felt like a hero.

THE STORM ARRIVED four days later.

Early April had carried a spring as sweet as an English summer. While the little group sat on deck, the old wood bleached by sun and now feeling like the hot bricks used in England to warm a Cold bed, each basked, drinking sunshine and the bright sparkle of the water.

No woman dared show her unprotected body and not even ankles were permitted such freedom, for a lady speaking through chapped lips and smiling from tanned skin, was no lady at all. Nicholas, however, risked rolling down his hose, and was rolling up his sleeves as quickly. The heat was like drinking balm, but the stop was sudden.

Well covered and shaded by wide brimmed hats, the women could only crouch.

"What's that?" Illiana pointed out to sea.

"Nothing, ignorant child." Her mother squinted into the thick mist across the distant horizon. "An early night. A fog. Spain may have such interesting weather. We've no way of knowing."

"Then I'm not ignorant," Illiana sighed. "None of us know."

"Tis a storm rolling in," shouted the cabin boy from where he had been sitting in the crow's-nest, high on the midden mast, sharpening his knife with a stone. He jumped up, pointed and shouted again. "Captain, tis a mighty nasty storm just an hour north west."

The crew moved at once. From the snoozing pleasure of little to do, they leapt into action, firstly to the rigging and the limp sail, hanging slack in the heat.

"Downstairs. Back to yer cabins," someone shouted at Nicholas.

"Seems there's bad weather on the way," he nodded, helping Bertha to her feet.

"After being so hot and so calm," Illiana said, already on her feet and half way to the steps, "now so sudden."

Several of the crew were surrounding the masts, untying the rigging at the base of each one, then climbing up, hand over knee, flattening the sails tight, each rolled around and safe against the coming wind.

"Ain't no wind. Tis a gale," a second voice shouted from high on the mizzen mast.

Once no sail flapped nor spread, each without even a pocket to tempt gale nor hurricane, the crew scrambled to the gunnels, ready to bale. The captain stayed at the tiller, and the three passengers were safe in their cabins.

The storm was sprung by lightening and following the explosion was immediate thunder. The sun disappeared. It was midday but cast deep night on everything once visible. Then the wind caught one side of the rising decks and the ship rolled like a barrel, forced to swing so abruptly and so fiercely, it seemed to slap against the waves as though about to capsize. Waves swamped every deck, sluicing halfway up the main mast and soaking the wrapped sail.

Illiana, her mother, and even Nicholas, having kept together, unsure and unaccustomed, stayed close in one cabin. Abruptly they tumbled from bed to floor and remained there, catching their breath. The ship continued to roll like an apple ripe from its tree.

"How many die at sea?" Bertha whispered.

"Dunno," Nicholas answered her, "but tis only a storm. Back at home we moans and complain and hurries indoors. Tis the same thing here, I reckon, but the floor is a fair mile less trusty." He sat cross legged on the bed. "I ain't never known someone die from a nasty big noise." He grinned but now it was too dark for anyone to see their own fingers.

Illiana whispered. "It must surely happen a lot. We get lots of storms, don't we, on land. So it has to be the same at sea." The slap of the waves against the ship's sides was a sound as thunderous as the thunder, and the ship vibrated as though shivering, as terrified as the shivering passengers.

"So go and play with the monsters," Bertha snapped. "Stupid child. I'd guess the sea serpents get belly aches in this weather."

"If they have bellies," Nicholas said. "Fishes surely don't."

"They all eat," suggested Illiana. "Food has to go somewhere. They come clean from the kitchens to the platters, but they must have started with food in their middles."

The distraction did not cancel the thunder, and only gradually after the second explosion, did Bertha climb back to the bed.

Salt water had leaked from deck to steps, steps to passage, and from there it seeped beneath every door to every cabin, but the rolling had gentled, no thunder echoed now, only the whistle of the wind. The storm was already in slow decline. It had lasted less than half of one hour, but it seemed everything was drenched.

The cabin boy's voice, bright as ever, penetrated. "You folks all safe?" he asked, and pushed open their door. Everyone still sat huddled and the boy sniggered. "It were short enough," he told them. "Tis usual enough this time o' year and it weren't bad. Can be mighty worse. Just the leakage. Twill dry soon enough."

A little later, when the golden burst of sunshine oozed down the steps to the cabins, everyone risked climbing back to the deck. Where brine had washed down from the storm, some still slopped, yet the deck had dried and was steaming.

The ship, two rows of men still at the oars, accepted the waves that still slapped at its sides. The great sails remained flat to the masts, clamped against the wind. The storm had ebbed and the sunshine was regal, yet the crew continued to row until the ocean sagged lower than the bow wave.

Finally the waves slackened, and only a faint rush of ripples chased over the water as the crew secured the oars at their feet beneath the benches, then ran to the three masts, unfurling the sails, replaced and tightened the rigging, and some began to sweep the deck free of dried salt.

"It is another world," Illiana said in a whisper. "It's another world to yesterday. It's – well – it's a wonderland."

"I reckon it is, every new day," Nicholas nodded. His eyes reflected the sun. 'But," and he abruptly turned away, "we ain't here for the fun of it."

Illiana gulped. Whereas her mother complained, drooping, and losing appetite, she was adoring an adventure which seemed to have grown her from widow to queen. She had almost forgotten, Sabine might be trapped in terrible conditions, being raped, being whipped, or even, and, she looked down, being killed.

The following day dawned sweet once more, and after Illiana had taken the stale bread slicked in lamb fat with the taste of strong dripping along the edges, and drunk her first ale of the day, she wandered up again on deck. The glorious weather was no surprise, but the surprise came with seeing her mother sitting small on one of the rowing benches, silent, content, and watching the crew.

Bertha had been the least active of the group during the entire journey and now seeing her seemed curious to Illiana. She walked over. Accustomed now to the roll of the ship, she walked with the same roll, then sat beside her mother, who squinted into the sun. "You have a reason for following me?"

Illiana, who never expected gentle remarks from her mother, although sometimes still wished for them, smiled. "No. I only just saw you, Mamma. It's nice seeing you in the sun. Most of the time you stay in our cabin."

Bertha answered without smiling. "You understand nothing, stupid girl. You simply wander, and enjoy yourself, which is selfish as usual. I have been working harder than I ever did in the kitchens. Listening and learning. Have you ever tried such a pastime, while you just pretend to be a superior countess? So off you go and leave me in peace."

Illiana, as usual over the years, made little sense of her mother's remarks, and did as she was told. Her mother's proclaimed hard work made no sense. With little interest, she left Bertha alone.

The days stretched, seemingly eating more hours coughed up by the waves, than had been as usual on land. Each was beautiful, but there was little to discuss and everyone now listened to the strident crew rather than to each other. It had seemed such a long month as March sailed into April, and even April was approaching its end when a thin dark line, too distant to seem exciting, appeared on the horizon.

CHAPTER EIGHT

When first the Spanish coast sat sweet on the horizon, it seemed little more than a far and pointless line, marking the end of the sea and the beginning of the sky. Yet there was wind in the sails, and it was blowing in the right direction. The thin stripe of distant land grew close and darker, more defined, and finally thicker. Watching patiently, as the carrack neared its home, and when the land became visible as such, even Bertha felt the excitement.

Two long yet eager hours later, with the crew more rushed, hectic and noisy than was even usual, though still far from the visible quay, the crew dropped anchor and the ship lay almost still, bobbing without direction, the sails now tight folded around the foot of each mast and the wind ignored, its power reduced to caps blowing and the brine slapping the ship's sides.

"It's Spain. We're here. Arrived."

"Tis Spain indeed. But we ain't arrived," shouted the cabin boy from the other side of the deck. "Tis Sanlucar, but we got two days more up the river afore we reach Seville."

From the small coastal port of Sanlucar, they sailed the great

Guadalquivir , a river as vast as another ocean. Still the ship's sides creaked, the hull rolled and fresh water waves slapped up to the gunnels.

Now the scenery changed, river banks both sides, even glimpses of buildings, tiny villages and folk pushing barrows beneath the golden sunshine.

It was three mornings later when the crew bustled again, tightening the rigging, half the men at the oars, others hauling open the trapdoors in the deck leading down to the holds, and preparing, finally, to land.

Illiana's heart was thumping so loudly, she was surprised that only she could hear it.

"Baggage," she called, heading back to the cabin, but Nicholas was already rummaging, and Bertha, flopped on her bed, was complaining that she was tired of everything she possessed and had no wish to pack.

For some time the boat rocked as it waited for permission to pull into shore, and the crew were hoisting up the parcels from the hold, as the captain shouted his orders from the forecastle. The goods were stacked on deck, ready for the crane to lift. Then a tiny boat, rowed by one man, sailed to the side and the one man shouted up.

"Customs coming onboard."

The three passengers, now clustered together in the principal cabin, heard the commotion with fascination and impatience.

"You gotta wait," the cabin boy shouted, pushing the door open one inch. "Unloading first, and t'will take some time, unloading takes a good couple o' hours. But after that, there won't be no loading, and you can leave, t'will still be midday. I'll call when time is right. Don't come up yet or you'll get tangled up with them wool bales and be carted off by the cranes."

"We gotter wait for the tide?" Nicholas yelled. At that moment, the sea seemed virtually flat.

They heard the cabin boy laughing. "We're in the great river now, mate. There ain't no tide. Tis peace or tis storm, That's all."

The first stop, and the pound of unloading and then loading, which had taken place in France, many weeks past, had been an interesting but mysterious slam, smash, vibration and echo, while no passengers were permitted on deck to witness the pandemonium. The risk would have likely been getting pushed off ship and into the sea.

Now, although obligatory, waiting was the initial order, the excitement blossomed. Momentary imprisonment perhaps, but finally they had arrived at their destination.

Once the customs officer had finished his inspection, which included peeping at the passengers huddled in the shadows, the crew once more took to the oars, the anchor had been raised, and before them in glittering sun bleached colour, was the vast port of Seville. It was the pilot boat which then hauled them in to the dock, the crew packed away benches and oars, and ropes were flung, caught, the crew leapt, and the gunnels cracked against stone.

The shouting increased, the crane squeaked and trundled, and the woollen bundles brought from England, some with their rough straw and flax sides splitting, were swung from deck to the docks, where porters and carts were lined ready to collect. Then the additional cargo picked up in France was delivered to those prepared on land.

As the calamity faded and the world seemed almost peaceful beyond their cabin walls, once again the cabin boy's call accompanied three sharp knocks on their door. "Time's come. Bring yer bags."

Thumping the few steps to deck, now Illiana, her mother and Nicholas pushed out into the startling brilliance of sheer blinding sunshine. They wore the fur lined cloaks of their initial arrival, boots to conquer rain, mud and freeze, gloves, mittens for Bertha, and little hats cramped beneath their hoods. Now steam instead of rain greeted them.

The deck was free of packages, the holds empty, but crew still clattered, cleaning every visible wooden plank of salt and dirt, bringing down all rigging and carefully carrying the folded sails from deck to hold. The captain still shouted, the cabin boy still ran, and the passarella led once more down a steep slope to shore.

Risking the fall, everyone had previously hated that gang plank but now, cloaks flying, they hurried down, Nicholas grabbing up all baggage, and soon stood grinning on the quay. The water which almost still surrounded them, still dazzled, but now the water was still and there was no scent of brine. Nicholas led the way from quay to port, dumped the bags back to ground, and stood triumphant.

"We's here. Now real life starts." Illiana had thought him the only one speaking no Spanish, but evidently he had mastered a little during the previous month. As he waved a hand at one of the waiting porters, and informed him, in broken but accurate dialect, that a litter and two horses were required, and first an inn where they could change into lighter clothes and relax over some decent food and drink before setting off.

""Which is not to say," indeed said in adequate Spanish, "that we knows where to go. Now, what about a little help from the locals that surely know everything going on around here. We're chasing those wicked pirates. Where do they go?"

The porter, although summoning the required litter and horses, looked nervous. I'll not speak of pirates, my lord. They head for the Moorish palaces, but there's trouble there too, with the foreign lords pushed out. If you go first to the city and into an inn, plenty being easy to find, sir, there'll be plenty to help."

"Umm," said Nicholas.

Illiana stepped forwards. "Then we need a guide."

Bertha interrupted. "I shall arrange what is necessary, and turned to the dithering porter. "We need only a litter, the driver and his horses, who will take us to a suitable hospice or inn within Seville."

And so it happened.

They left the indigenous, invigorating and infectious buzz of the port, and sank back on the cushions as the echoes faded, the sunshine increased, the smell of brine diminished and fresh hot air blew in.

Once again an unknown world stretched before them, excitingly and shiningly endless. Against the vivid blue sky, scuffed hills rolled into a bright distance. Beyond the hills, the sky was empty except for the sun, but below clustered small stone houses, great soaring churches, narrow roads of beaten earth winding and interlacing, but few folk moving. A man, bent, held the reigns and led his donkey, as bent as its owner. A woman walked barefoot to the church and further into the shadows.

The docks had been a raucous bustle, but, at first the city seemed sweet, calm and lime washed. Long winding lanes were of beaten earth instead of cobbles, and the houses either side were bleached white, low, a little ramshackle, but peacefully shaded by trees and their fluttering spring leaves budding and blossoming in the sunshine.

Quickly the squash of poor living quarters also passed, now buildings soared, white stone gleamed and windows, pushed wide, led to iron sided balconies. Some seemed more like palaces, and a church as vast as any dream of a cathedral, stood proud, although partially still under construction.

Yet as they approached the huge open Plaza Espana, suddenly, as the litter's driver reigned in his horses and stopped as the horses snorted and reared, frightened, there was an abrupt stink of filth and bulging black smoke, a rising darkness and unexpected terror high over the rooftops. The bliss of heat, beauty and anticipation ceased, as though banished, and the billowing stench became stronger.

Bertha shrieked and pushed closer to Nicholas, while Illiana pulled wider the already open curtains, and called to their driver. "What is it?"

"Can't go no further," the driver said, speaking in a panic. "I'm backing off. You want the rooms to rent, then you pay me, take your bags and walk to the next corner. Be quick and best not to look beyond."

The change seemed alarming, but without any understanding of what might happen in Seville or any other part of Spain, Nicholas helped Bertha dismount, Illiana paid the driver, with an additional coin of thanks, and grabbing up their bags, all three plodded forwards as directed.

The sun beat down but so did an even greater heat without the sun's golden light, nor the delicious scents of blossom and happiness.

The Albergue de la Belleza, palatial and beautiful, spread it white stone walls high and wide and the grand entrance, doors open, ushered them in. A tall liveried man beneath thick black hair, bowed and Collected the baggage. Within moments they stood in their own bedchamber, an annex leading to a palate bed next to the garderobe, where Nicholas accepted his place as the servant. The principal bed was four posted and wide enough to sleep six, if they accepted an enforced cuddle.

The view from window showed them what was bringing clouds of dark smoke and the foul trail of death.

Neither close, yet not far enough, within the square beyond and below, three burning masses of flame and smoke burst, standing separate and tall like ship masts, each set alight while surrounded by bulging straw, twigs and dried leaves, watched by crowds of people, intent but not too close, their expressions hidden in smut, flying cinders and smoke. Wind gusted flame and soot as the vaporous darkness swirled higher. The violence of spit, crackle and hiss faded into the spires of flame. The figures, however, could still clearly be seen. Three men had been tied there, hands chained to the wood, feet amongst the leaves. And now those figures remained as the fire ripped upwards and into the clothes, then the flesh and hair, the eyes and the minds of those condemned to burn whilst still alive. Now their hairless and featureless heads hung, empty eyes hidden behind the hunger of blazing flame, the bodies blackened as they fell in tumbling pieces and blew out in cinders. The screams were now silent and the men were dead.

Before them but standing at a distance safe from discomfort, a priest stood, his hands together as he prayed. Two other men stood at his side, holding rakes and pikes, but as yet unneeded, for the fires ebbed. The stench was of burning flesh, the destruction of brains and bones, the turning of a man into sparks and ashes, twisting within the misery and murder.

Nodding, the priest, two assistants behind him, marched out through the crowds, pushing their way with scowls and elbows when those standing there refused to move. Then the two guards left, holding up their pikes, and this time the crowds moved quickly aside.

The fading torture dumbed into crackle. The charred embers remained on their pyres.

Bertha fell back onto the bed, silent in shock. Illiana stood staring as though paralysed. Nicholas pulled her away and closed the huge window of glass doors, shutting off access to the balcony beyond. He shook his head, guttural and bilious. "No. Tis a torture to watch such evil torture." He lunged back, blocking the window.

Illiana whispered. "What does it mean?"

Nicholas found it hard to speak. "I heard of summit. Long ago, yes, in Portugal I heard, something in France but afore I was born. Don't reckon English folk took little notice." He shook his head, now almost violently. "Never come to us, thank the Lord. Tis the church, but I don't reckon true nor sanctioned. Must punish heresy, they says."

"Sixty, seventy, terrible long years ago, the Lollards were burned alive in England. That was heresy and the church condoned it. No, they ordered it." Illiana stumbled over her words.

Nicholas, muttering, "Perhaps them Lollards were bad folk."

"I was taught our god loved us." Illiana heaved and clutched her throat. At first on the tipping swell of the ocean, she had been sick and had vomited for a day. Then she had become accustomed, but now she was as bilious or more, and rushed to the garderobe. When she reappeared, her face was grey and without any light in her eyes. "I just pray never to see anything like that again. Perhaps we shouldn't stay in Seville. We have to ride to Granada, and there can't be any burning there. Everybody is Muslim. It's only our kind Christian church that burns people alive."

"I thought I was hungry," Nicholas muttered. "Now if I sees a single crumb, I reckon I'd be as sick as I feel now. I still smells that disgusting stink."

"It'll be dinner served soon," Bertha looked up, her face tear stained and white. "I'll eat nothing, and can't watch others eat."

"We won't eat, but we should drink," gulped Illiana. "I'll call for wine and beer to be brought to our room. I'll never sleep unless I drink first, and as much as I can."

"We got no litter now," Nicholas nodded, equally pale faced. "So I buys horses in the morning and we rides fer Granada."

They had seen little but smelled more, and although those who died had been strangers, they screamed in agony and begged for mercy through the dreams of Illiana, Bertha and Nicholas that night.

T HE MORNING, blindingly hot and bakingly dry, was not cooled by breezes, yet this was, without speaking, a relief to all three. A wind might carry ash, and ash might be what was left of three men, now gone.

Although wanting to get far away, the group rode slowly at first, tired from sleepless hours and hungry from the inability to eat.

Then they crossed the Guadal Cuvier river, finding a bridge

beyond the city, eager to escape without guide. The new litter rattled and squeaked as its wheels found the holes in the narrow streets, and the horses stumbled, then trotted on. Nicholas rode beside the litter, speaking sometimes to Bertha who sat within. Illiana also rode, and although almost fluent in Spanish, said nothing, even as Nicholas stopped folk he saw passing, bending to ask directions when he could. She felt herself aflame with a sickening fear previously unknown. She watched little except the tail and rump of the horse ahead. Her mind retraced the horror she could not forget.

They rode the bridge and then the rolling hills, the path of beaten earth leading them without steep rises or sudden drops. The weather remained wearily hot. A slight breeze cooled them as they rode to the crests of the rambling hillsides, yet the sun still blasted nearly as infernal as the fire. From England, they were unaccustomed to such a ferocious Spring.

It was now the first days of May, but they saw no spring English daisies, ramsoms, anenomies, cow parsley nor Nedombines, Instead, they saw everything that was unknown to them. They stared at leaf and brilliant pink flowers clambering over walls, seeming to eat the trees as they climbed. They saw great fields of vines spreading across the valleys, and only Nicholas said he recognised what he called a palm tree, unknown to anyone else. Then for some miles there were fig trees, although the fruit was not ripe, and orange, lemon and lime trees, recognisable by the fruits England imported from Spain.

As they watched the countryside, passing the huge open spaces and unrecognisable growth, the misery turned gradually to wonder but no one spoke at first. When they saw the tiny village increasing in size around them, Nicholas looked back at Illiana, saying, "We should eat whether wanted or not, and we need to find a place to sleep. It's not dark yet, but we's all bloody exhausted."

They were riding a gentle slope and above them on the left,

was a wall of stones, rigid as a blockage against tumbles and slides of higher land. Into this rock were caves dug by hand, some closed by wooden doors, others left open to tunnels within. . Further along the road they followed, cottages sat amongst the fruiting trees and vines sweeping across fences blocking the tumble downwards.

The village was surprising, pretty, warm under the first flecks of dusk, and absolutely quiet. Nicholas chose a door at random, a cottage deeply thatched but covered in a twist of flowering beauty. It took sometime for anyone to answer. Then, as the door opened slowly, hesitantly, the dusk blew away and the sky was abruptly dark. "No twilight, in Spain, it seems," he grumbled. "One minute tis day and the next tis night."

Illiana faced the small man who peered from the opening crack. Together they spoke Spanish, although, quickly realising that he spoke to foreigners, the small man explained far more than he had been asked.

The tiny cottage door was still open, as he spoke in a mumbled hurry. "These folk won't help others lest they are robbed or killed. There's wicked gangs and robbers, they tramp the south here in Andalusia, hiding at day, attacking the poor and rich alike. There's even more danger now, it only takes gossip against you, and that brings the inquisitors around to arrest you at once. Folk doesn't go out any more, and will call down from the windows if they see someone they know walking past with a tray of stuff to sell. We sit in our homes and pray for salvation. But seeing you folk well dressed and from across the sea, I'll follow my priest's sermons and invite you in. You can eat, and can sleep, but I confess, I've little food to offer."

"I'll always pay for everything," Illiana told him, "as long as I have something to pay with." And, smiling, she handed the man a handful of Spanish coins.

The small man, his back a little bent beneath his smock, stood staring at his open palm, whispering, "No, lady, tis too much."

Illiana shook her head. "It's not too much for eating and sleeping, and three of us, all hungry. Horses too, as hungry as us. I'm no longer poor, but I can remember how wretched being poor really was." She waved a hand at the man, then leaned down from her saddle, closing his palm around the silver coins.

Having dismounted, leaving the litter parked at the cottage door, and now with the man's advice, they took each horse to a back yard, walled by the hillside, where the grass was short, baked brown, and hay was scattered. Loosely tethered, first the horses ate and then rested. For some time, Nicholas stayed to calm and reassure then, then he joined the others in the cottage. The day had been long.

Within the cottage, the small wife was lighting a candle, and was startled as her visitors crowded around her. Her husband immediately opened his hand and her smile grew at once. She took one coin from his palm, dashed from the open door, running immediately to the next cottage. Meanwhile the man Indicated the three stools sitting around the central fire, and the linen covered bundle of straw along one wall. Illiana thought this must be their bed. There were no stairs, but a large bucket of water stood at the other wall. As everyone sat wherever they could, the wife returned with an armful of packages.

"We'll eat well," the wife smiled. She knelt by the tiny spluttering fire built on the floor of beaten earth, and began to gather pots for her cooking. "Tis like at last the Lord God's holy mercy. This evening we shall have full bellies and talk of neither torture nor starvation."

"Me," the husband pointed to himself, "Pedro." Then he pointed to the woman. "Luzia." Everyone introduced themselves, and described their relationship. The food was hot, there was clean water, and for some hours of laughter and discussion the conversation continued with limited understanding yet absolute enjoyment.

Luzia, having no platters, used stale bread to hold hot food, and the guests used only their own knives and fingers to eat what they truly found delicious. Cups were large and wooden, however, and drinking was as much a pleasure. Yet it was Luzia, finally, who spluttered and hung her head.

"Cowards we all are now," she admitted. "Our church doesn't love us now and we have no protection from the gangs. Sometimes the thieves come to the door and just tell us to hand over everything we have. They tell us if we fight back or refuse them, then they'll tell the priests that we're heretics."

"Then off to the cells we go," Pedro muttered. "And we know full well what comes next."

Luzia stared up. "I live in a thorn bush," She muttered. "If I sit very still and don't move, then I feel safe. I'm surrounded by thorns and they threaten death. I dare not move even to talk to the priest, for a dozen long thorns will dig into my flesh. We no longer die of the life we called normal. The new life wants us dead far quicker and will bring even more pain."

Yet it was finally the absurd pleasure which wiped away the flaming deaths they had witnessed, and for that night they slept well, although Nicholas and the two owners of the cottage slept only on the ground.

CHAPTER NINE

They woke late. The host and hostess were already out, but returned quickly with fresh bread and milk. It was also then that the necessary questions were asked, and the humour and comfort disappeared.

"Sir, you spoke of gangs and thieves. You've heard of the Delgardos."

The wife leaned forwards from the stool where she sat between Illiana and Bertha. "This is the danger, sir, the fear that is ruining our lives. We fear the gangs who rampage and attack us, but we also fear the law, for the church spoke of love yet now it hates us. It wants us all cooked until dead. We get the courage to face the church, or at least we try. But still come the gangs. The Delgardo's is a name we know, for they're the worst, but they live far from here and nearer Granada. But there's plenty of other gangs we fear just the same."

Pedro nodded to his wife, and continued the explanation. To those living so close, the nightmare had become torture. "I've not seen them, but we hear the stories. The Delgado's," He said, "have almost a village of their own, houses large and small, women kept, then bargains made with the remaining Islamic rulers. There's palaces and towns, but they were all built by Muslims, and they took slaves too, bought and paid for, often from the Delgardos. Now there's war there, down in the valleys, started with armies from the King and Queen to get the Muslims out. Though it ain't the Muslims we're terrified of. Some are friends. Good folk. The gangs are Spanish like us and the church wants pain."

"So the Delgardos are dead?" Bertha hoped.

Luzia shook her head. "Not at all. The war is just starting and the Palace Alhambra still takes no notice and still buys women for their hareem. It frightens people and the Spanish don't go there unless they're paid to fight. They don't frighten me. They want young and beautiful girls, not little old crones like me, but I'll go nowhere near, risk or no. Now," she sighed, "there's what the priests call the inquisition. There's nowhere safe right along our Southern coast. Where Andalusia was once our paradise, now it is our tragic nightmare. Now we lock all our doors and never travel beyond our village if we can help it. We're not only terrified of the Delgardos, and there are other gangs and robbers too, but worst of all, the church which once gave us hope and promises, now slaughters us and is worse than the war. It's like I said. You live in a thorn bush, you can't turn neither one way nor the other, you escape the thorns one side, you're speared by the thorns on the other."

As Iliana left the following morning, and before she mounted, she pushed more coins into Luzia's hand. "Please don't say no. You had the courage to take us in and you looked after us so well. I do hope this will bring some security."

With a brilliant blue sky and a blazing sun, the heat grew. In the valleys it seemed suffocating but as they rode the gentle hills, a fresher warmth bathed them. The horses tired quickly when the slopes became more challenging and rolling hillsides turned to mountain sides, first to climb, and then to descend. Ditches were scrubby and the earth seemed more like tired sand. Everything echoed the dry heat. At one point the pathway faded, the track was ragged and seemed dangerous, but as the crossing pointed downward, they followed the direction even when a clear road no longer existed.

Within the next valley, the hillsides cradled another village. The barren heights softened and a grassy dip was sweet with wild flowers as the way became marked and easy once again. Even the grass was green, sweet with the memory of winter's rain. Each morning early, the birds sang, chattering, diving. Then the day's heat grew and even the birds found some shelter in the thicker trees.

The horses plodded, the litter rattled, and everyone yawned, hats pulled low over watery eyes. It was the third day in another village where they finally stopped, the horses drooping. Bought in Seville, each horse had been described as trained over difficult terrain. The riders, however, were not experienced. Although Nicholas had worked close to horses all his life, he had rarely needed to ride for such distances. But after those three sweat filled days, forced to sleep beneath the trees, the next village brought them luck, for a tiny inn sat solid, half a mile before the houses clustered. Nicholas fed the animals, spoke to them, reassured them, and paid for them to be watered and scrubbed down.

Bertha and Illiana tumbled past the open doorway and collapsed at the long table. An equally long bench either side offered the space they needed, and immediately they ordered clean water and wine. The rich smell of food drifted from the kitchens at the back. Bertha bent over the table, her forehead to the unpolished wood. "I've hardly moved all day, stuck in that litter. It bumps and rocks, sliding and tipping. I'm tired enough to sleep here and now."

"I think it's more exhausting," Illiana answered, "cramped in a lumpy bumpy litter than it is on horseback."

"Just see if there are bedchambers free for sleeping," Bertha sniffed.

"You didn't call me a stupid girl," Illiana pointed out. "Are you sure you were speaking to me?"

Bertha glared, but Nicholas, not yet sitting, smiled down at them all. "I done paid and we got two rooms, being all there is. One for all men. One for women. I hope your bed's proper big, not like them skimpy cabins."

Should there be a number of women needing an overnight bed, Illiana knew, invariably being both tallest and slimmest, she would either be squashed in the middle, be pushed over the edge in the night, or be required to sleep at the opposite end with sweaty feet poking their toes to her chest. She simply hoped that she and her mother would be the only guests. The food was good. That helped.

"Sometimes," Nicholas said, leaning back against the high Spanish stone behind the bench, "I feels a mighty weight in my head, being as I know tis guilt. Tis because of me, and my girl Sabine, we done seen them horrors o' torture, not even them bloody Delgardos, but from church and state. Now the misery o' riding for miles an' miles without no protection from the heat."

"We've all come for Sabine," Illiana murmured. "You haven't dragged us. We absolutely will rescue Sabine. Only that matters."

"You've not dragged us anywhere," Bertha sat straight. "I accuse only these unknown Delgardos, whoever they are, and I came because I speak Spanish. I knew I could help."

Illiana brightened. It was rare that she admired her mother. She smiled widely but received no smile back. "It's been depressing," she nodded. "Not the excitement I confess I wanted, but we love Sabine. We wanted to come. I won't leave until she's in your arms."

Nicholas sniffed. "You both is saints, real and true."

Illiana was eating but now abruptly looked up. "No saint. Not ever," she said, her voice a little broken. "I think I've always been a docile daughter, a tame wife, an obedient servant. A *yes dear, no sir,* sort of person. Now I decided I was going to be a new-born tempest. At least I remember most of my Spanish. But the worst of all -,"

"I know," Bertha said more loudly. "I know exactly what you did, but I won't talk about that and certainly not here." She raised her hand, as though forcing silence. "Let us concentrate on the future and not on the past. I shall never forget what I know happened, but I am also determined for better turns of the great Wheel of Fortune. I sat on that horrid rolling deck listening to the crew speaking Spanish for hours, for days. I know I speak it better than all of them."

Having no idea what she might have done, simply staring back, Illiana gulped and obeyed the command. Slowly, she returned to the platter, the tortilla, and her napkin. Nicholas, equally confused, escaped, marching off to refill his cup. Bertha stared back at her daughter. Finally Illiana mumbled, "three days, more, that's all, and we'll be in the Muslim Palace and we'll find Sabine. Then we can go home."

Bertha sniffed. "Nicholas says he won't leave until he's killed every one of the Delgardos."

It was a night of sweating and restless dreams. Illiana slept badly and woke badly. She had a headache. Yet Bertha woke smiling, stretched, opened the shutters and pointed to the rising sun. Illiana blinked as the dawning brilliance hurt her still pounding headache, and she turned away.

"You had your hands clenched all night," her mother told her. "I saw you. I heard you too. You kept grunting. So, it's hardly surprising if you have a headache. It's your own fault."

No other women had joined them in the female bedchamber. The inn was empty apart from the three newcomers. The area around them, the empty hills and clamped shut valleys, welcomed no visitors. Accustomed to her mother, she said nothing and once dressed, followed her to the dining chamber, it's one long table and benches.

"I need food first," she said, sinking to the bench. "I'll get no willow bark out here." She wondered, once again in silence, what Sabine was suffering at that same moment, and was convinced, almost knew, that it would be something far worse.

While Illiana felt ill, thinking only of Sabine, her mother was thinking of something quite different. Spain had reignited memories, the glitter of the language she had initially thought so strange when she first met her husband, and then gradually learned to understand, and then to speak. It was why she had come. No other reason. Sabine had been a charming child, a nice girl, but it was Diego she had come for. To see the land where he had grown, to see the people he might once have seen himself, and to hear the language that brought back the sweetness.

Those sweet memories, visualising again how she had loved being loved and had loved back, which had seemed sublime. Immediately the best faded into the worst, Diego dead, the blood drying.

Bertha, without knowledge yet with the insistence of instinct, knew what had happened and had never forgotten.

Since Nicholas was still absent, Bertha believed she could now speak to her daughter without being overheard, always previously an impossibility in the earl's home, and so prepared a more significant speech, long and to the point, something she had resisted but now felt she should explain with vehemence.

The interruption therefore, was entirely unexpected. The shadow loomed over the table, and both Illiana and Bertha looked up, but the shadow was not Nicholas. The shadow smiled yet this was simply a small tuck, almost invisible, at the corner of the closed mouth.

"I am impressed, my lady," said Lord Charles, the bow simply a nod of his head. "I had not expected you to prove the courage you claimed. So, I now acknowledge the bravery I failed to initially acknowledge.

"What the devil!" Illiana stuttered with significantly less diplomacy. "It's you."

Tall, dark and clothed in the same black and gold livery but no longer wearing the royal collar and insignia of England, Viscount Charles extended his smile just a fraction. "Not officially designated as a devil yet, my lady, simply a humble viscount, and I am here on the king's demand."

He remained standing, his legs long and slim although muscled, and outlined in tight silk hose, gleaming as black as his hair. Straight and unmoving, he appeared to be waiting for some reply. Bertha found her voice.

"My lord, we have not previously met, but I see you know my daughter. Welcome to Spain. That is, we are here on unusual business. You say you are here on royal business?"

"Yes, and yet not, my lady." The faint smile turned to faint frown. "I am here on his highness's business and on his orders. However, I no longer obey the late King Edward, but his official Protector of the Realm, Duke of Gloucester."

They were wondering whether they spoke different languages. "There isn't a protector of any realm," Iliana said. "What happened to the king?"

"I believe you have missed the recent developments," said the unmoving shadow. "His highness, King Edward, sadly died in early April. The heir has not yet been crowned and indeed, there are difficulties regarding this. There have been outrageous attempts to grab power and cause uprisings. Dear England, sits sadly never less peaceful. Meanwhile I obey Richard of Gloucester, the official Protector and Defender, the Constable of all England, and the duke now thankfully and legally enforcing control over the disturbing threat of dangerous chaos."

"Oh, bother," Illiana sighed.

The shadowed smile widened, risking a shadowed grin. His eyes reflected the candle flame but the inferred chuckle remained silent. "My lady," the deep voice slowed, "a great deal has swept through our country since your ship sailed. After the king's tragic death, caused evidently by his heart's difficulty accepting his body's unusual growth and his majesty's recent appetite. Then followed by the queen's Woodville family initiating a variety of attempts to take over the country. One by one these were thwarted by the Duke of Gloucester, already proclaimed Lord Protector of the entire realm in his late majesty's last will and testament. The country's prisons, dungeons and locked doors are now under renewed importance.'

"You mean," Illiana sat rigid and shocked, "the king died and those horrid Woodvilles tried a rebellion?"

"I believe I inferred something of the sort," smiled Lord Charles.

Bertha hiccupped. "Heavens. Sad to lose our king, God rest his soul. I have heard that he ate too many lampreys. No sooner than we left the country – but my lord, I should say, please join us. May I – have the honour, as it is, - of inviting you to breakfast with us? You certainly appear to be the bearer of unexpected tidings."

It was not entirely clear whether the faint noise was a snort or a chuckle, but the viscount pulled out the stool at the head of the long table and sat, stretching his legs. "I thank you, madam," he said, "but I breakfasted several hours past. Nor can I stay long, since my men are outside by the stables, brushing and watering the horses. Your groom, Nicholas Farrier, I believe, is kindly assisting." The inn's owner rushed to the table as he saw the new liveried customer, and Lord Charles ordered a cup of Rioja in brisk Spanish, and then turned back to his audience. "I assume, since I must deduce you are here to follow the Delgardo pirate family, you are therefore travelling to Granada?"

"How do you know absolutely everything?" Illiana demanded.

Again, the viscount chuckled. "I am here on the orders of His Highness, the late King Edward, Lord God rest his soul. However, I have more recent news from every spy and traveller, trader and cut-throat who sails between England, France and Spain. I receive news faster than the wind would blow it."

Both Illiana and Bertha were staring, barely blinking. Finally,

Illiana mumbled, "What is the king's business that you're on – doing – here for?" And she continued staring.

The viscount's chuckle was now audible. The wine he had ordered was delivered, and he lifted the cup, still smiling. "Sadly, royal business is rarely open for discussion, my lady." He drank, then smiled over the brim. "The Delgardos, however, are surely more open for explanation. Perhaps I should explain that I have some advice which might help you. I cannot help you directly, since I and my men travel in the opposite direction and have no other option. But just three miles from here within the Valley of Bubion, entered only by a pathway of steep dissuasion, is where the Delgardo family live, and it should be avoided at all costs. Take another road. Do not go near that place. You would not find your friend, your groom would be killed immediately and you would be taken as slaves."

She was now white faced, but Illiana said, "You seem to know a great deal about those pirates, my lord."

"I do." The viscount finished his wine. "And they know my name as well as I know theirs. I would simply suggest that you avoid that area, and should any of that wolf pack intercept you, give my name, and insist that you travel with my protection."

"But you won't be with us," Bertha complained. "You said so."

"Sadly, I cannot," he said, tossing his empty cup to the table, pushing back the stool, and standing. "My royal orders allow me no alternatives. But," and as he turned to leave, he looked back briefly, "you will probably find the girl you search for somewhere within the Palace of Alhambra, but be equally careful there, since Islam does not always love Christianity, and the Spanish State also wars with Granada's elite." Now he paused. "I imagine it probable we will meet again in the near future." The viscount nodded, replaced his hat, and marched from the ale and dining chamber.

Illiana watched the fading darkness of the shadow. Nicholas's cheerful bustle overcame the following silence.

Illiana's relief welcomed him. "We know. You've been helping some English men. A troop on some sort of mission. What happened?"

Having wiped his hands on his hose, Nicholas sat on the discarded stool and eyed the empty wine cup. "I must admit," he said through the grin, "I bin working hard with them men, and I's mighty hungry. Mighty thirsty too. Tis time for breakfast?"

"You worked with a remarkable company, I think," Illiana said while Bertha waved at the owner, asking for the third breakfast to be served.

"Surely did," Nicholas agreed. "Didn't expect no English. Was nice to speak me own language again. Mighty interesting too."

"You mean they actually told you what they were up to?" Illiana was surprised.

"Well," he started with a slurp of ale, "not as how they said naught of orders and such. King's business, I gather, but t'was the inquisition as they talked of. Seeing them, ten and more in them smart black doublets and them sleeves all full o' gold trim, right next to our horses, their own mighty fine stallions was fed and watered, and right busy they looked. So, I says as how there weren't naught on horses I didn't know, and would be glad to help."

"So, you did."

"At the blink, so sure, what they let me, and enjoyed it."

"So, with the moments of pleasure over," said Illiana, looking away, "we need to get back to business. We still have a long way to go."

"We do, and we does," Nicholas agreed, mouth full. "But with caution. Them fighters was saying as how the Spanish king and queen want the whole country to be theirs, and will dominate. Sending off them Jews and them Muslims what own the south. His Holiness the Pope ain't happy and says how the inquisition goes above and beyond. I reckon tis what them English fighters come here for."

"If they stop poor people being burned while still alive, that would be wonderful, but they can't stop it. How can they?"

"Not our problem, stupid girl," Bertha cut in. "Get your cloak. It's time to go."

Outside the heat neither diminished nor increased. "Just boiled up and stuffy," said Nicholas "Best if it rains, but reckon it won't."

The heat was rarely silent. It seemed to crack and sizzle around them. Their own horses neighed and grunted as they trudged. Bird song sprang, clamouring when the trees reached high, yet more common was the rustle and scratch of the small animals they heard but did not see. Once they saw an eagle overhead, huge wings spread, almost unmoving as the raptor watched below as they watched it above

It was after several hours when they heard something a little different, more erratic, less tentative, and it was below the banks that something rustled. The scrubby bush was high here, and thick with thorns and the thrust of tiny animals, wild and hungry. The horses backed, then reared, then Illiana's horse snorted and began to gallop. Most of their weapons were still packaged in Ned's saddle bag but the shorter knives lay parcelled in the litter, flat on the packages of clothes. Quickly, Nicholas had his and the litter's horse under control, also closing on the litter to calm the horse that pulled it and call to Bertha sitting within. "Nothing bad as yet, but must catch t'other," and turned to race after Illiana. But the danger they had sensed, the warnings of danger they had heard and the fear they felt themselves was vibrant now. Even Bertha grabbed a knife.

It was while Illiana was some distance ahead, attempting to slow and calm her frightened mount, that the three men crawled from their hiding place beneath the canopy of leaf and thorn. They held swords out before them and walked forwards. Nicholas held out his own sword. "Some ragged gang, eh?" he demanded. "And what do you want of us? You try to hurt us, and I kills the lot of you afore you remembers yer own names."

The first man laughed. He was short, very wide shouldered and muscled like an ox and his laugh resembled a low pitched crackle. Over both impressive shoulders he wore a baldrick, each carrying a sword of different design. Beneath the excess of steel, the short man wore the clothes of a king. His hair was long, uncombed and rich but unwashed black.

Behind, standing considerably taller, two other men were equally well armed, equally muscled, black hair in their eyes, but it was the short leader who roared as though calling his troops into battle. Now he held a sword in each hand, one long, the other curved, both reflecting the sun. "I'll introduce you," he yelled in perfect English, arms upstretched, "to the man about to kill you all. I am the king of kings, Juan Delgado. My brothers stand with me, and we dislike strangers in our lands."

Although clearly outnumbered, Nicholas gripped the solid wooden hilt of his sword and stood waiting. He was not as muscled as the men he now faced, but he had defended himself well enough in the past. Those facing him seemed somehow absurd with their flashing steel, their wide legged stance and their tessellated clothes. Sudden, flamboyant, more show than activity.

Then from directly behind, Nicholas felt the weight of metal resting on both his own shoulders, and knew at once what this meant. He did not dare turn and dislodge what obviously Illiana had found, unwrapped, and knew how to use. Almost at once the explosion deafened him. The emphasis of crashing sound and vibration shook him and the stink of sulphur was almost as disgusting as the smoke now shrouding his face.

Illiana, still mounted, came forwards, both long barrelled guns still raised and pointing now at the leader. Clearly the metal barrels were heavy, for her arms were supported by both elbows steady on her knees and the horse was guided only by her ankles in the stirrups. Her eyes were squinting as though the shot she had fired had shunted backwards, even though fired forwards

One of the other men lay, choking and cursing, on the ground, the other brother staggering while bending over him. Seeing the bright metal scimitar reach fast towards his neck, Nicholas swallowed and kicked out, at the same moment twisting. He grabbed the short man's hair as he passed, wrenching. The gang leader was unprepared and rolled as he fell.

Instead, the following explosion hissed into the second brother's face. Illiana had never seen the utter bloody destruction a human head ever before, and she found it as sickening as the burning in Seville. Worse, in fact, since this time she had caused it. The gun steamed. The trigger was hot to hold and the barrel was lost in dirty smoke. She clutched at the reigns, leaned across her horse's neck, and dropped both heavy metal guns to the scrub, by her horse's hooves.

The brother still reeling in pain, now stumbling to his knees, crawled to the dead body beside him. The leader abandoned Nicholas, and leapt at Illiana, screaming in Spanish.

Now outnumbered with one brother dead and the other badly wounded, the short leader abandoned wisdom and thrust his sword at Illiana's horse, trying to haul her from the saddle by her ankle. At the same moment Nicholas thrust his own sword into the wretches' back, his hat already caught in the scrubby thorns.

Bleeding, the man rolled again, panting, scrambled up and kicked again at Illiana, but she had managed to kneel, feeling the boot only against her foot, as she rushed to Nicholas. With his help, she re-mounted.

After firing the second time, Illiana had known she could reload neither, so abandoned the matchlock guns. The new fangled weapons were heavy and difficult to balance, but after firing, they were even more difficult to hold as they vibrated, burned, and stank. Nor did she have the sulphur, or the knowledge, to make the weapons work a second time.

Nicholas, still on his feet, had already snatched up both guns, although had no possibility of now re-loading either. However, pointing one at the short leader of the pirates, he shouted in

English, "I've guns. Two, I got. You even ever heard o' them, have you? Like cannons, they is, only safe to hold." The guns he held did not look safe, as both still vibrated from the previous explosions, and Nicholas's hand vibrated even more. The smoke, however, was clearing. "I'll shoot you with both of them if you try anything. You've got a dead brother, and maybe a dying one. Get the hell out before you're dead as well."

The pirate's mouth spat froth and for a moment he stood unmoving, hands clenched and his body trembling in uncontrollable fury. Then his living brother called in Spanish, "Detente ahora. Vien aqui."

The call was clearly urgent. Again, the furious man spat, shook recognition into his head, and stamped across the dull earth to where one brother lay and the other sat.

Nicholas was now up and mounted and immediately led the litter's horse from danger, on and up the path, his other arm outstretched to Illiana, now unarmed, as she rode even closer behind. Both long barrelled metal guns, clanking and pounding, were immediately chucked into the litter between the curtains, as Bertha eyed the smoking crash and cowered back, teeth chattering.

They spurred their horses into a weary gallop and left the one dead and two wounded men well behind them. Although remaining untouched by any sword, Nicholas was glaring, panicked, forcing the horses onwards and upwards. It was some time before he permitted the race to slow, and eventually to stop. He still clutched Illiana's reigns, now calling across, soothing both horse and rider.

"You're safe, little one. Safe with me and so are all of us." He pointed. Between rocks, a sliver of water sped downhill, glittering fresh in the sunlight. Desperate, the horses drank, heads firmly bent as they lapped and slurped, while somehow regaining breath. As they had slowed, Bertha was peering between the heavy curtains, expecting more attacks. She waved a knife in one hand but did not leap from the litter.

Nicholas gazed down at Illiana. Her face was still smudged in rank smoke and he saw the blood on her fingers. She shook her head. "I'm alright. But when I grabbed those triggers and pulled, I felt like I was being exploded too. One of those guns seemed to backfire, but I'm not badly hurt. Just shaken."

She was helped from the saddle, Nicholas bent and filled his cask from the spinning cold water slide, and first gave it to Illiana. She drank, gulping and then sipping before handing it back. Nicholas refilled it and gave it to Bertha. Finally, he drank the water himself.

"Two guns is gonner come in handy wherever we goes," he nodded. "I can reload 'em when there be time, but only the armies got any idea how to do it fast and use them things on the move."

Illiana was staring into space. "Did I really *kill* someone?"

"No," Nicholas was adamant. "T'was the gunn as did it, and I reckon you saved my life. Bloody brave, it were. I reckon you was brilliant, Lady. I taught you what to do, but I never sat and let you do it. That courage were all your own."

Now kneeling and rinsing the bloody fingers in the stream, she remained blank. Finally she whispered, "Were they expensive? Just smoke and shivers of fire and ashes and shreds of metal. I never want to hold one again and I never – ever – possibly could kill a man again.".

"They sit amongst the knives and swords here in the litter," Bertha called. "Horrid, nasty things. Just scorched steel, and smelly."

"But saved my life," Nicholas said again. "Known to backfire sometimes, they does, and you needs training. Well, none o' us bin proper trained. If I can't shove in the next loading, it don't matter. I'll just bang the muzzle over some Delgardo nose. Real heavy, them guns is."

Close to tumbling from her saddle as she tried to remount, Illiana hung to her horses' neck, her hands covered in the froth that had blown from its mouth. Nicholas controlled both himself and his horse. Without thinking, now Bertha dashed from the wobble of the litter and collapsed, breathless, on the sandy ground.

Sitting slumped, she stared up. "Are you sure we're safe? How can you know?" Bertha sounded gruff. "I don't feel safe, not at all. I want another drink, my throat's parched. Wine would be better but I suppose we don't have any. So are you sure we're safe here? Or are we still in danger?" It was hard to talk and Bertha sounded increasingly shrill.

"We ain't really safe," Nicholas muttered at last. "That bastard swine has a dead brother now and a wounded one to worry over but he's a fool and a proper demon too. I reckon there's others around, but I also reckons them fools weren't no Delgado's. Some other gabble pretending. They wasn't clever enough fer Delgado's, but we needs to keep travelling." He helped Bertha back into the litter, and there she crouched in one corner where a small cushion insulated against the bumping and sliding beneath.

She was crying, although not for her daughter. The tears were invisible but she felt them like ice and could hardly open her eyes. She was crying at herself. She remembered who she'd been once, passionately in love with a man of amazing abilities, who had waited patiently for five hours without eating or drinking, sitting outside the room where she was giving birth, then had rushed in to kiss her and love her before even seeing the child, having heard her own screaming from the pain of childbirth.

He had been clever, and kept them well protected, money increasing. At first, she had not needed to work, only to look after her pretty child and breast feed. Diego had worked long hours, covering for the double upkeep. Life had been hard yet had seemed endlessly sweet. Now she remembered how she had adored him, and how she had been a strident and courageous woman, confident and clever. Without a husband to inspire her, she swore silently at herself, she was a coward. Once again life was hard. She should never have come and decided it was no wonder Diego had left this land.

When Diego had died, she had died too. The sweet, loving and appreciative woman had crept away and the bitter old hag, the cowardice only partially hidden, had moved in.

"Now," sighed Bertha, once more peering out from the curtains, "I imagine it is high time we found a place to sleep for ourselves, and not out here thanks very much. Too near those Delgardos, whoever they were."

"We need to keep riding," Nicholas said. "A titchy moment for the horses, then off we go again. Downhill, like you said, and find a village."

"Downhill?" Illiana queried, catching her breath. "Not the valley we were told about, where the Delgardoes live?"

There were no names written and no sign posts. "Bloody no way," Nicholas insisted. "We's gone far too far ahead than that, and this pathway ain't as steep as the Delgardo path is said to be."

"Then I trust you're right," Illiana muttered, though not as positive as she claimed. Although this extended their journey, they had little choice. The pathway into the valley was neither steep nor broken and within a swelling mass of beauty, a busy inn waited.

"Snug," Nicholas pointed. It was. Beneath a flowering chaos of bougainvillea, too thick across one window to see anything beyond or behind, splayed a huge wooden building. With a race of exhaustion, they grabbed their baggage and even Nicholas left the inn's groom to stable and care for the horses.

The porter nodded and held up three fingers. Nicholas contradicted with two fingers, and nodding, the porter, four of their packages in his arms, led them upstairs. The bliss of collapsing on a neat cool bed was what each one had dreamed about for many long miles.

Eventually they ate at a table outside, the thick red bougainvillea like a hanging curtain behind them. The lowering sun tinged the platters and bathed in the mugs of wine, each reflection like a greeting. Fish sat large on beds of warm wheat, softened by sauces of black pepper, sliced onion and a soup like gravy which tasted of wine. Sausages were heaped on the second platter, and a third which swam with whipped eggs surrounding pastry crackers. The heat smelled of far more than sunshine and even Illiana was hungry.

Rich drifting perfumes of food replaced the rancid memory of dark smoke, soot and raging sulphur. There was time to relax, raise cups of wine, talk softly of the present and the future, and forget misery, forcing it to sink away with the sun up behind the hills.

CHAPTER TEN

"My lord," Degal Gardener appeared at his Marshall's elbow, "his lordship the archbishop is ready, and has agreed."

"Reluctantly?" Charles asked, turning.

"Hard to say, my lord." Degal nodded, smiling. "His holiness has one of those faces, which we've all seen so many times before, where expression cannot find any unlocked entrance. The eyes too cold – the mouth incapable of moving."

"You describe him perfectly," Charles said, his own smile Barely noticeable. "I shall find this marble statue and finish our business here."

His holiness, Iñigo Manrique de Lara, stood, his arms crossed before him, each hand tucked neatly and invisibly into the opposite sleeve. Both Charles and Degal bowed, although not with noticeable solemnity.

Charles spoke perfect Spanish, saying, "Your holiness, I thank you for accepting my request. I am sure you have already been fully informed of my mission."

The Andalusian Archbishop nodded. "Si." There was, indeed, a lack of any facial expression. The pale brown eyes remained glass.

"I therefore have little more to say, sir," Charles nodded. "You are aware, my lord, of the instructions and encouragement from their highnesses, monarchs of this glorious country, and from his holiness the Pope, Sixtus the fourth, having authorized the holy office of the inquisition to which you are bound." Charles paused before continuing, "Since I am also sure you are aware, his holiness the pope wishes the severity of the great church's actions to be kept merciful, when possible. I have been asked, by his highness, king of England, to emphasize this wish, while sending his dutiful appreciation of your great work. While entirely obedient to his holiness Sixtus IV, no inquisition has been authorised in England, nor will be."

Clearly the entire speech was repeated by rote.

The archbishop squinted, nodded, and murmured, "I need no reminders from your king, sir. My duty is in Spain and my own wishes are, without exception, transferred to the Spanish courts. The Holy Catholic Church does not authorise any form of punishment as such, sir, as you must know. It is the courts who take matters further when heresy is suspected."

Charles chuckled, the sound soft yet exaggerated within the echoes of the cathedral.

"Your holiness, I fully and entirely understand. I am equally sure that you fully and entirely understand. My last message, directly from his highness of England, is that you hold no jurisdiction whatsoever, over any English citizen. Simply a small reminder, my lord. I trust you understand?"

The archbishop's face remained blank, eyes frost. "I understand more than you appear to realise, sir." he said. "You are now fully and entirely excused."

Charles bowed briefly, turned and left the cathedral with Degal following. Charles crossed himself, but did not retire accompanied by the honoured respect of stepping backwards. Nor did he speak again until outside in the blinding sunshine. His men were waiting for him, crowding around.

Degal spoke first. "Unflinching as always, our courageous leader," and bowed majestically to Charles, who laughed.

"Simple enough, my friend. I obey orders, as the archbishop also does." He re-buckled his diagonal sword belt once more, retrieving his other sword and dagger from the man he had passed them to before entering the cathedral. "And yes, he got the point. I doubt I've seen brown ice quite so prominent before, but our kingly Edward needed the point made, no English souls ever to be taken by this wretched inquisition. The point was recognised in that brown ice.."

The horses had remained stabled at the hotel where the small force had claimed comfort within Seville. It stood not far from the cathedral, nor distant from the Plaza where the dark remains of three fires had only recently been cleared. A faint smoky tinge of the smell hung in the breeze, baked by the unclouded sun.

Most of the men retired to the stables themselves, but the viscount slumped at the small table, four stools beside an empty fire grate.

Degal watched his leader, and beside him sat the troop's second-in-command, Allan Reed. Charles leaned back against the unplastered stone wall.

"Here on duty, as we all are," he sighed, "indeed but I also have my own interests."

Allan raised an eyebrow. "I'll gladly come or stay, as you tell me. You know that, my lord."

"Good. I'll need you." Charles looked up. "And you, Degal. I may also call for Roland. The four of us should be enough. We'll ride tomorrow morning for Granada."

Degal grinned, abruptly delighted. "We can enjoy the company of the Delgardo mob? A charming idea, my friend. Or simply the Muslim chief?"

"Both," Charles said, his eyes now on the table where his wine cup sat.

"Then we need Faramond too," Allan said. "He's best with the bow and best with his knuckles. Not for setting against Abdallah Muhammad, I hasten to tell you before you all laugh at me. No, but to send against the Delgardos. It's them we need to kill off."

"The sultan is the man I intend speaking with," Charles replied, "and Delgardo is the one I intend killing."

"The sultan?" Degal smiled, as usual. "Boabdil, we call him. Not that I ever met the man. I've heard said, though, that he's a tyrant."

"I imagine that depends on your religious beliefs," Charles said. "But I need to speak to him. So," he grinned abruptly, "we leave our own country of chaos, and travel to another country of even more hideous chaos."

"So one day we return to a peaceful summer island with a small boy sitting the throne. Long live King Edward V."

Now Charles was no longer smiling, but said softly, "From the little I know, I believe there will be no child king, but a fair and just king of great loyalty and intelligence. It is early as yet, so we shall see."

Refusing the expense of taking a private bedchamber in the city hotel, Charles shared with both Allan and Degal, but as they snored, he lay awake a little longer, decided, planned, and finally dreamed.

Lying naked and sweating beneath the one linen sheet, at some distance from Allan, whose body heat smothered the sheet beneath them both, Charles pondered the situation at the home he had left when sailing to Spain, and included the more recent news he had received by messenger, concerning not his own father, in whom he had no interest whatsoever, but in the condition of the realm and its possible king.

Since his boyhood, Charles had worked for the crown. Now it

seemed as though the crown might collapse. That would affect him greatly, but also the whole land.

There had been gossip. It was said that the children of the late king, the Lord God rest his soul, had been proved bastards. The clandestine and long unannounced, had not, it was now muttered, been the first of such secret hand fastings. It had simply been his highness King Edward's favourite device to secretly marry the female he fancied, but who pretended virtuosity and refused to hop into his bed,to persuade the women into his lascivious embrace. That kept them subservient and willing for as long as he could be bothered. Once bored, he would desert them and find another. The woman, abandoned, could not and would not dare, prove that an unworthy and private marriage had taken place.

Elizabeth Woodville, however, had been less easily tricked. She was more devious herself. After two months of secrecy while she gradually came to realise that her wedding would probably never be admitted by the king, and herself now unwanted, she had abruptly announced carrying the king's child. He had other bastard children, but now the new wife proclaimed herself ready to prove her own wedding. Edward had relented. She was extremely beautiful after all. The pregnancy proved false, but the marriage was announced legal.

The Lady Eleanor Talbot, daughter to the Earl of Shrewsbury, had now died. She had, however, still been very much alive during the bigamous wedding to the Woodville wife. Yet now the earl himself, and others of the great families of Talbot and Butler, travelled to London in grand force, and presented themselves to Richard, Duke of Gloucester, the Constable of all England, and Protector and Defender of the realm, announcing that the Lady Eleanor had been legally wed to his highness at the time of his bigamous marriage to Elizabeth Woodville. Thus, her children were, without argument, illegitimate. The Prince Edward, already announced Edward V, could be no king at all.

The grand Duchess of Norfolk, sister of the late Lady Eleanor, now spoke at the three estates of government, Nobles, Church and Commons, and cited all she knew herself, also adding the name of Bishop Stillington who, she said, had stood witness during the wedding itself.

The Bishop of Bath and Wells, a man of considerable importance within the realm, now stood tall and claimed this to be the truth. He had indeed stood witness at the marriage of his highness to the Lady Eleanor.

Presumably Edward, perhaps on his death-bed, had confessed this to Elizabeth. It had therefore been the initiation of the Woodville family's attempt to take over all power in England and crown Edward before he could be pronounced a bastard.

The proof roared loud. Few, except those who would benefit from Woodville power, could deny the absolute. There were also uprisings of those who disputed the facts, and of those who knew such truths. Executions were inevitable.

"S<small>HIT</small>," Charles said to himself as his two companions slept, and he pushed the crumpled message beneath the bed beside the chamber pot.

His own duties, not yet finished, would preceed any return to London where he would doubtless be called upon, as Marshall, to aid the completion of whatever plans were now in force by hand of the Protector.

It did not hinder other dreams, and it was easy to discard the weight of duty, present, past and future, and instead dream of sweeter things. Yet those sweeter things, Charles informed himself more than once, should be kept more secret even than the first marriage of the late king.

"We cannot leave Spain until our orders have been fulfilled," Charles told his troop the following morning. "Within the month, King and queen, Ferdinand and Isabella, will settle in Seville and take up their combined headquarters there. Once settled, I shall be obliged to attend on them, announce the final summary of my mission from the English monarchy, and then be free to leave. That means we can't leave now, yet staying carried some risk of simply waiting. Instead, I intend visiting Granada, since I have agendas of my own, and of making some interesting plans to annihilate the Delgardo gang."

Allan Reed waved his enthusiasm, shouting, "I have volunteered to accompany our leader, and so has Degal. We hope Master Roland will join us, and perhaps Framon Smith, our bowyer triumphant. But who else wants to come? Not obligatory, since this is a decision only of our leader. Who wants to rest in the straw with the horses, and who wants to come with us?"

The reply was loud and eager. Every man cheered, and surrounded Charles. Some cheered for the lord. Others, less subservient, clapped Charles on the back and roared their choices.

"You want us left here fer weeks, naught to do, just sniffing dung and daily cupshotten?"

"Lord Charles, what a treat, sleeping with them horses and mucking out the straw. Long as you bring us Spanish wine and all them squawking birds, roast and honey glazed, I'll follow you to Hell and back."

Charles, grinning, said, "You think I'll starve you, Michael?"

"You drink from the same barrell, we knows tis the best."

"Can I not swill the cheap rubbish like the rest of you?"

"My Lord, I wouldna know the difference."

Charles wondered how much he would recognise himself, but laughed, saying, "Then we leave within the hour and ride to Granada, with deviations to the Delgardo valley on the way."

"Now, I wonders why our sweet Marshall might want such a new game for the filling in of time," Faramon Smith grinned at Ulric, the guard riding beside him. "You reckon it could be that pretty female he met up with, what rode east when we road west?"

Ulric, descendant of the Northeners who once occupied half of England, shook blond hair from his blue eyes and cackled. "The pretty lass what went to Granada, looking fer another lass previous took by them Delgardos? Wot gives you that brave idea, my friend? Mayhaps something to do with us now riding east to Granada with a little visit to them Delgardos along the way?"

THE HEAT CONTINUED and bird song was penetrating, although the birds were rarely seen as they clustered in the high trees, or flew even higher into the sun's blinding sparkle. As loud as bird song was the continuous buzz of the insects, with midges and the later awakening mosquitoes soon prominent.

The sweat of fifteen mounted men accompanied their clatter and thump, and few spoke during the long days. They cantered only when they saw the glitter of water ahead, for the horses needed a slow walk in such weather over so many rough miles. It was therefore while in the saddle, that Charles silently admitted only to himself, the inner motive for this additional journey.

The warmth of desire, overtaking even the warmth of sun on his back, and the shadow of his desire not to desire, exhausted Charles over the endless seeming scrub, but powered his aim.

Illiana's face sat close behind his eyes, his imagination sweeping her body, her waist small and tight beneath his arm, the warmth of her burning his thoughts, the curve of her hips and his own fingers brushing against her breast. He knew exactly who she was in some detail, and knew equally that she did not, and never would, belong to him. He knew, as vibrantly, that his so recently and unexpectedly discovered passion would never be satisfied, but that ignoring it when no other activity could occupy his thoughts, would hurt neither himself, nor her.

Back in England, it seemed life would be endowed only by chaos, bloodshed and hatred. As was Spain. What a loving world he had been born into. Not that he enjoyed any interesting moments of shooting from his mother's womb, a shame perhaps, but nor did he remember her miserable death only one day afterwards. The lack of memory was in that case extremely welcome.

The virtual lack of memory of his father, had never bothered him either. The Earl of Cleeves, a man he had possibly seen once or twice during his nursery years, was indeed the noble gentleman who had sired him. Yet either because of the death of his wife, or simply because any interest in his tiresome young heir felt utterly irrelevant, the earl preferred hunting, falconry, feasting with royalty at Westminster or attending Mass at the Abbey. He travelled to France for jousts, which he claimed always to win, or visited young women on his estates, who presumably dared not refuse to entertain him.

Long years passed when the young Charles forgot entirely that he had ever had a Papa, until abruptly the tall man would appear, demand to know if his son and heir was in good health and under strict discipline, and then disappear again.

The child would ask," Who was that?"

One of his many nurses or tutors would answer, "Your beloved Papa, my lord, the earl."

"Oh – him," the child would answer, and return to his studying.

Memories of the first woman he had ever met, who excited him, were of considerably more interest. At the age of twenty eight years, living occasionally at his ancestral home in The Strand, of such enormous size that he had several times been lost within it while young, he had enjoyed the company of many women, both peasant and noble. The tingle of excitement had been common enough, delightful enough, and educational enough over the years, but never once had he dreamed of the same woman who was sharing his bed.

Now he dreamed of one who would never share his bed at all, and much as he enjoyed the dreams, he teased himself, laughed at himself, and wondered how a man of considerable experience could remain such an innocent fool.

Instead, he chose to listen to Allan and Degal, riding close, who now shared an intermittent conversation. It was Allan who said first, "They say the Alhambra is mighty grand."

"Unique, I heard."

"I'll be glad to see it, perhaps." Allan snorted. "But tis the Delgardos I want to see, and want to charge, and want to kill, one by one."

"Or two by two," Degl sniggered.

"I've heard enough stories of the bastards in England," Allan continued, "Some young girl, perhaps a pretty ten years daughter of the local miller, and there she is waving goodbye to her uncle off fishing for the day, up at dawn on a calm sea, when behind her two ruffians speak a foreign language and grab her, hands over her mouth, dragging her into the alleys behind the wharf. Then rape, and off to another ship of men armed and ready to rape again and again. She jumps into the Narrow Sea, or lies sobbing in the bilges. Sold, after weeks at sea, to some Islamic sultan for his harem. Or maybe just to scrub the kitchen floors, and be raped by the chef."

"Sounds as if you've been in some harem yourself," Degal frowned.

"You know how many girls are taken from our coasts and markets every year by pirates and gangs?" Allan insisted. "Ten – fifteen – or more. Makes me think – if it was ever a young daughter of mine – what I'd do."

"Most," Degal added, "just shout and curse and say prayers for the poor child, and forget it. They have to concentrate on the daughters left to them."

"Reckon I'll kill a Delgardo for every father left weeping," said Allan. "And if we don't see none of the filthy gang, I'll go looking."

"You'll not find enough buggers to slaughter."

"T'will be more interesting searching them out and doing them in, than just sitting in the bloody saddle waiting while our bored viscount politely tells these Spanish idiots not to grab any English folks in their burning pyres."

CHAPTER ELEVEN

The Moorish Palace Alhambra gazed out from its peaks, staring down across the Islamic realm of Granada, once land of the Moors, which spread to the southern edges of Spain. This land of power and beauty was now, said King Ferdinand and his queen Isabella, the rightful property of the Spanish crown, and both Moors and Jews should leave and return to wherever they previously belonged. Unless, a tempting alternative, they converted to Christianity and the Roman Catholic faith.

The palace towered beyond the mass of thick greenery that grew over the hill tops. The stone shone like candle flame in the glare of sunshine. High walls surrounded turrets, and a faint gurgle of splashing water echoed beyond. Illiana, Bertha and Nicholas stared, fascinated. It had taken many hot long days to reach their destination, but now it seemed they had arrived in a new world.

"Is it a palace to admire or to fear?' Bertha said, gazing from the litter's open curtains. "We still don't know what we'll be facing."

"We'll be facing Muslims," Illiana mumbled. "But I'm not sure what that really means, except they'll be foreign."

"Everyone's foreign," Nicholas muttered. "So, these Spanish are fighting Muslims because they's foreign, but Spanish is foreign too. Tis a strange country o' strange foreigners."

"I don't pretend to understand," Illiana nodded. "The whole place belonged to the Moors, didn't it? But now it's all ordered to suddenly join a different church. Muslims aren't Jews and the Jews aren't Islamic, yet it seems both are foreign. So, is it the church or being foreign that matters?"

"We don't have to understand, stupid child." Bertha now waggled one finger. "We're here to find an innocent girl who's English and shouldn't be here at all."

The procession plodded down the valley path and then took the way climbing upwards. They could see the tall buildings high above, some silhouetted against the blue sky, others brightly coloured. They were not so far away, but the way was up. This slope was steeper than previous hills, and Illiana, frightened of falling backwards from the saddle, leaned forwards, her cheek almost to the horse's mane.

"Lady, don't be leaning forwards," Nicholas called to her. "You reckons it gives the poor thing ballance, but just makes his neck and front legs a bloody sight harder to lift. No, best not lean back neither. Please lady, just sit straight."

It was Bertha, shouting from the litter, who had enjoyed Nicholas's correction. "Do as you're told, stupid girl. You claim to have learned riding, but clearly you've learned no skill at all."

Sitting straight as advised, Illiana ignored her mother, who had never sat a horse nor even a goat. "It's a hard time now in Spain," she said, speaking to Nicholas. "Thank the Lord it's not happening in our own country, but here it's getting worse. A hundred years gone, the church burned heretics in England too, but not any more. Actually there probably aren't any heretics around now, but here it's all fighting, killing, burning."

"Every bugger kills every bugger in this place" Nicholas added. "Kings, queens, gangs, pirates, armies, and now the church, but here we is, and my pretty Sabs not able to protect naught."

Bertha shouted, "So we find Sabina, we rescue her, and we rescue ourselves from this wicked place as soon as we can."

The Alhambra remained silhouetted until the sun had set. No twilight warned that the day was tired, was leaving, the night coming. Abruptly the wild colours lighting the sky, sprang like magic, and orange sank to dark grey, then into an endless black. The diamond stars, little more than pin pricks in black velvet, seemed even more beautiful than the blazing sun. Lights sprang from the palace windows, and it seemed the stars were intimidated, and their lights faded. It was as the moon shine shimmered on the horizon , promising the rise of the final miracle, that the small party stopped, exhausted, and looked up and around them. Now the moon spangled the sky with a silver halo, and the high metal gates of the palace caught the reflection and devoured it.

Her voice hushed, Illiana asked Nicholas, "Is it too late to knock on doors? If so, we sleep out here, and shelter against the wall?

"Seeing as we doesn't knows aught o' this mighty place, late nor early," Nicholas shook his head, "I reckons we moves down them banks. There be hundreds o' buildings down there. Look. Ti's more than a village, tis a mighty grand town. We'll find an inn."

"Do the Moors have inns?" Illiana shivered, looking down over the opposite hill to that which they had recently climbed. "I've heard they don't drink beer nor wine."

The only visible gate had no obvious method of opening from the outside. Now Nicholas began to ride slowly around the palace outskirts. It was vast. Some considerable time later, he returned. Illiana had stayed by the gate, peering through its bars. In the darkness she could see little but thought there was water.

"Tis fair beautiful," Nicholas was saying. "But I ain't found no way in."

Illiana still gazed through the high gateway. "Nothing like our castles inside," she whispered to herself. "Of course, there's all this stone and walls and towers, which is like other castles, but there's a garden. A lake or a fountain or something even more unusual. Something catches the moonlight."

"But we can't get in." Bertha had climbed from the litter.

"Unless we jump the wall."

"Stupid child. It's best if you simply keep quiet."

Away from the moon's rising majesty, the stars still glittered. Ignoring her mother, Illiana murmured, "Do angels light candles? Is it another God sitting here over a palace? Surely, it's the same God with a different name in a different language."

Nicholas grinned at her. "Only one God, they says, but tis every name different in every country. Now, lady, listen. There be summit I seen on t'other side. A huge door stands in the wall with guards outside. Five o' them in long white coats. I bowed and in English o'course, asked, all official, fer us to visit, but no bugger understood me. So, we all goes together to that bloody tight shut doorway and you asks in Spanish to meet their king. Or, we goes down the hill, stay overnight somewhere easier in town."

"I'm not sure," Illiana smiled. "If I say we go down to the town first, and wait to come back here in the morning with advice from the people, would you think me a coward?"

"No, I reckon you be mighty sensible."

"Then we go and find an inn or a family to let us sleep there."

Even Bertha sighed in relief.

The ride down the rock strewn slope was short, without difficulty, yet as buildings became more crowded and more varied, none of the company could recognise where they might be accepted. No inn, no tavern, no welcoming hospice and not even a cosy and average house appeared as the obvious place to stay. A glimpse of water glittering with moonlight peeped between the trees, and the road curved, and in the last slope to the valley, the houses became smaller, white and beautiful in the moonlight.

"No palaces no more, thank the Lord, whatever they calls Him here," Nicholas muttered. "Tis mighty late. We needs to knock on any door where folk might help."

He slipped from the saddle, took two exhausted steps and tapped timidly on the wide carved doorway of the nearest building. It was the house opposite where the door swung open and an elderly man regarded them with deep suspicion. He wore a turban, white linen, over a long white gown, leather belted. This puzzled Nicholas, who bowed.

Although he integrated the few words of Spanish he had leaned on the ship's journey, Nicholas's accent sometimes made his English more understandable.

"Sir," he said, straightening, "as folk arrived from England, we is proper ignorant of Islam, so we begs forgiveness if any mistakes sounds proper bad. But," he waved an explanatory hand, "we is here for a right serious reason, urgent to us, so we wants to approach them as lives in the palace. Yet we doesn't know, as it were, how to gain entry." He tried to look apologetic, not an expression he managed at all well, "Being as how tis late and our ladies is tired."

The man thought a moment, then stepped aside. He spoke in English although his words were hesitant. "Home has space. Sleep. You eat?"

"When tis possible," Nicholas said.

Illiana kept silent. Muslims, she had been told, will not speak to women. But to Nicholas, she whispered, "Ask him if he wants to speak to females in Spanish."

Bertha once again climbed from the litter, and seemed dutifully humble. Her Spanish was elaborately polite. "Sir, forgive me, but as we are English, our groom speaks only his own language. We would be immensely grateful if we might rest here for the night, and explain our mission, while asking for your kind advice."

The interior was unlike the houses of England and even of those in the villages they had crossed in Andalusia. An open courtyard stood centre, and around this, rooms were spacious although some doors clearly were not for opening. Doors, both open and closed, were of decorated metal. Following their new host into one large room, they saw it only furnished on both sides of the floor and over vast patterned tiles, with thick woven and tapestry cushions in vivid colours. Here, they realised, they were expected to sit.

Bertha decided she would never be able to get up again, but dutifully sat and found herself comfortable.

"I am," said their host, "name of Halil. Now food?"

It was later when they talked and accepted the lessons of the area, the religion and the unexpected. Often Illiana translated for Nicholas. Halil accepted this yet did not look at her when she spoke, nor when he replied. He sat quietly and permanently smiled, remaining barefoot while not expecting anyone else to kick off their boots.

"I reckons," Nicholas said while grinning, "our handsome host be enjoying our ignorance. Tis an evening o' surprises both fer him and fer us."

At which Halil, clearly understanding, chuckled, spreading his arms. "Indeed. Surprise."

When food was brought, laid on trays and platters across the long space between the sides of piled cushions, it seemed strange at first, to half sit and half stretch, then simply reach out to choose whatever seemed attractive from the vast variety on the floor.

Adaptation was slow, but the food was appreciated and however strange the method, this was delicious. Vast quantities of fruit lay on the platters, roots of types never seen before, fish, rice and spices. Saffron, already known in England but rare and extremely expensive, here seemed to adorn every plate. Without the appearance of knives or spoons, the three guests ate with their fingers and didn't complain.

One room at a considerable distance was then offered to the women for sleep, and the beds were blankets rolled on the floor. The men's bedchamber was more comfortable, more grand and peered out from high windows.

Nicholas said, "At home we does it the other way around, but this is the way I like," and thanked the servant who showed him to the doorway. Illiana and Bertha, not accustomed to long discussions, now talked themselves into exhaustion. They could, they supposed, sleep late the following morning.

Amongst the groans, complaints and approval, questions and yawns, Bertha had said, "We're not going to be allowed into the main palace, are we? I thought our own people were haughty enough about wives and other women, men being the only ones able to fight on the battlefield. These Moorish people seem to think women are too daft to escape the kitchen."

"I think their kitchens are principally male too."

"Humph," snorted Bertha. "Women are probably kept in the privy."

Illiana shrugged. "Perhaps we're so beautiful and so precious, no man can risk his women being stolen away." She paused, the humour now flat. "Like Sabine."

"Well, Sabine's not here, is she," Bertha snorted again. "And if every woman is locked up in secret, how do we ever find her? It's those vile Delgardos we need to question, not the Muslims who wouldn't even look at us."

"There's Nicholas, and he wants Sabine back even more than I do."

"Naturally, but he's not going to be the best at intelligent interrogation." Bertha's snorts were now frequent.

Illiana sighed. "I think he's clever. He's knowledgeable, and he's so, so kind. Just because he's a groom, doesn't mean he's an idiot. I used to be a maid with a broom."

"Exactly," snorted her mother.

"Possibly." Illiana risked agreeing with her mother. "Probably I am stupid, but I know enough to think we're just going to waste time wandering around palaces here. They're magnificent, I'd wager every one of them is beautiful. Meanwhile Sabine could be suffering torture."

"Or shut up in a hareem, which means you think she's precious and protected."

"Would any of these magnificent princes, or emirs or sultans, ever need to buy slaves from the Delgardos."

"As I have said before," Bertha pointed out, "we need to stop eating off the floor and gazing at palaces. We need to find the pirates."

"So we need to ask this emir about the Delgardos, get whatever information we can, and then ride out to search for them." Illiana sniffed. "Not that I want to see those beasts. I just want to see Sabine."

No window offered dramatic scenes of the night sky, nor of the houses leading up the slopes, nor further down into the valley. Bedchambers, it seemed, especially those for females, were of the utmost privacy and as no person was permitted to look in, so no woman was permitted to look out.

When finally they slept from complete exhaustion, they remained in uninterrupted black silence, and did not wake until a hesitant knock on the door was accompanied by a careful whisper.

The sweet peep of new vision, the blue horizon and the rich pink of exuberance also remained invisible as Nicholas, tentative, tapped on the door.

"Tis late, ladies" It was Nicholas's voice. "There be a breakfast to love, with bread and buckets o' amazing fruit, and there's a lot to ask this helpful fellow, him and his servants too. Trouble is," his voice rose a little, "there ain't not one fellow what understands a bloody word I says."

Emir Halil sat cross legged, the platters of fruit spread before him, and beside him sat a much older gentleman in a long white gown and deep blue turban. His beard was white, long, thick, and impressive, yet his hair remained unseen. Halil spoke first.

"My uncle," and he clasped the older man's shoulder. The rest of the conversation, which included the uncle to a considerable extent, was in both Arabic and Spanish. The uncle spoke only

Arabic and Halil translated into Spanish. Illiana then translated into English for Nicholas. This delayed both questions and answers, yet after the boredom of lagging time, the information proved important.

"We are well aware of the Spanish ruffians of the family Delgardo. There are other gangs. We have seen faces come, leave, and come again a hundred times. Whether they bring slaves from other countries, women for sale, or precious metals and stones, not every emir is interested. We know many more legal and acceptable methods of trade," they were told. "These degenerates, although none are Muslim, stay close and do business here. The entirety of Granada was once vast and larger than the Christian lands of Spain. There were, and still are Jews too. Once we mixed, traded, and built ships and dined together, but now the Spanish king and queen want the whole of the country under Christian rule."

"And it seems they've got most of it back already," Bertha ventured, although immediately Halil and his uncle looked down.

"There are troops on our borders. They bargain, but if bargaining resolves nothing and they do not get the results they want, then they fight. The Jews often agree to convert to Christian beliefs, while praying secretly in their own tradition, but if caught, it is said they commit heresy. They are killed. We do not convert, nor pretend to. Gradually we surrender. We vacate our homes, where we have lived in relative peace for generations. We sail back across the Middle Sea to our original countries in Africa, but we hate to leave so much behind. Do the Christians destroy the beauty we leave?"

"We've not bin here long enough to know," Nicholas said. "Be bloody daft if they does."

"I have no idea," Bertha sniffed. "And do Jews take girls and buy slaves?"

"The Jews take only one wife, but can take slaves from the pirates," Halil continued. "However, there are more than two hundred homes here, both vast, and small. You cannot search every one, and where the women are kept locked away, you would never find your friend even had she been taken there."

Illiana risked speaking once more. "My lord, we thank you deeply and with our hearts, although our hearts are Christian," she said. "But we aren't here to understand such Spanish political differences. Then of course, without understanding, we have no way of knowing which is right, nor which is wrong. A church that tortures and burns frightens me, and if there are whole armies of Spanish moving in down south, then that's the last thing we want to see. No wars and no inquisitions, and so we leave, with, once again, great thanks for your help." And although no one was looking at her, she scrambled up and curtseyed.

MANY HOURS HAD PASSED and the conversation had been lengthy. This was not only because of the double translation, but also the considerable detail of the discussion.

It was later that afternoon when Illiana, her mother, Nicholas and their newly energetic horses finally left the home of the young emir, and travelled even further south.

The ride through the town was neither challenging nor helpful. No one strode the sun kissed streets. As buildings became more crowded and more varied, still nothing seemed open, busy, nor recognisable as a place where the company might be accepted. No inn, no tavern, no welcoming hospice and not even a cosy and average house appeared as the obvious place to stay. They saw no stalls, no shops, no folk sitting outside at tables in the sunshine, raising their cups to drink the wine's bright reflections. A severe and sun beaten silence was unfriendly. The beauty around their clattering horses was profound, but did not wish the strangers to admit their tiny and unwanted invasion.

Slowed by the bump and rattle of the litter, the twists of narrow streets, and the barriers of high stone walls, the day's afternoon dragged and without food nor a place to buy it, they rode into a sudden night. A glimpse of water glittering with moonlight, peeped between the trees as the roads curved, and in the last slope within the valley, the walls of every building stood white and beautiful in the moonlight.

"Well, we surely knows we ain't wanted here," Nicholas muttered from the saddle. "But at least we learned summint."

"We know nothing," Illiana replied, "except that we'll resolve even less until we find the Delgardos."

"I'll fight them buggers with all my might," Nicholas said at once. "But reckon t'will be the most dangerous day of all."

"If it's just the three of us. I'll fight but I can't imagine any Delgardo pirate collapsing at my feet. He'd laugh, and knock me out and take me prisoner."

"Not if you use them guns again. I've cleaned and re-armed both them clever little devils, and you knows where they's kept in my saddle bags. Safer now, I reckon, than in the litter."

They camped on the river banks, warm and comfortable as the clear gurgle of the water span its reflections. The nights were not cold, and their blankets and cushions were always kept in the litter for Bertha's comfort. Nicholas released the horses, keeping them tethered but close enough to the river for them to drink and graze at will. The litter, quickly unattached, sat cosy, curtains closed, and both Bertha and Illiana slept tucked within, while Nicholas cheerfully stretched under the leaves of the almond tree, one blanket enough, and snored as the stars watched down. Whether it was a Christian God, a Muslim Allah, or the same God who ruled them all, they did not care, but loved the fresh warmth of the night and the memories of the elegance and charm they had seen, with the peaceful glory of nature in a foreign land.

The delight of what they saw, the excitement of what they might see and the fascination of what they had never expected to see, merged with the fear of never finding Sabine or of finding her dead, and now, even worse was the haunting terror of the inquisition.

Having achieved no more than a hot and sticky doze, and now waking while the moon still shone silver, Illiana crawled from the litter without waking her mother, crept to the river, and sat there. There was too much baggage bustling into her mind, and she could not sleep longer. Hopeful excitement remained, yet little of the bustle she envisaged was pleasant.

CHAPTER TWELVE

Taking the lower road and following the sweetly generous sweep of the Guadalquivir River, Charles and his troop of English guards camped that night, as usual, on the banks. Their horses grazed, drank and slept, warm in the Spanish moonlight. Travelling so frequently across the long miles from one city to another, following the progress of Spanish royalty, or heading once more for the site of the holy inquisitions' tribunals, this was not the time for the expense of inns, hostels or grand invitations to the ancient monuments or palaces.

The nights were mild and the grass soft after long hot days, and the river offered water, fresh and clean, for both horses and men.

Having crossed the low trailing boundaries of the Delgado Village without being attacked, or even seeing anyone except for a woman filling a bucket with water, they had kept riding, as Charles continued his interest in discovering Illiana's small group. Now, watching the endless diamond glitter of stars both above, and within the river's slow tranquillity below, Charles wandered, thinking not of the woman he followed, but of the chaos in England which he had unknowingly left to gather behind him.

Another of the spies known to Charles, indeed, a pair of young Spanish brothers, had spoken quietly with him that very morning.

Murmuring, as though with strangers, "Tis a great deal that has been happening, my lord. We had an arranged meeting with our father two days past, and he told us the strife in England is ongoing. What has happened may be a relief to some, sir, and this is exceedingly important."

The meeting had lasted some time, a great deal more had been said, almost the possibility of solutions. Charles had truly experienced relief, but nothing could yet be described as final.

Official messages from England sometimes took more than a month to arrive, and although greater news, arranged and carried by spies, was considerably faster, no information could ever be considered immediate.

One courier might say such a situation had occurred. Three days later a different rider might call, explaining that the situation had not occurred after all, for it had been interrupted by battle and death. No travelling missive could swear to the immediate truth.

It was June now, the day of Justin the Martyr, and while Charles bent and drank from the river, a half mile downstream Illiana was crouched, clearing her mind of the infiltration of thoughts she wanted gone.

"I am, as my mother knows," she told herself, "a fool and an idiot. I thought I was bound for learning once I could claim the title of countess, but poor Benedict, I hardly think of him now. He was so kind. However, now my mind swims between my saddle, poor dear Sabine, and my own future."

A tinge of silver in the water at her feet, gave the moon's reflection a halo. Her own horse, nudging the back of her neck, startled her.

"Since I'll never know my future until it happens, why think of it? As a very young girl, my father played with me, taught me his language, threw tucked balls of muddy grass for me to catch, then laughed when I missed them, and took me to church every Sunday. Then he died. I didn't understand death then, but I missed him. I became a little 'yes' girl. *Yes Mamma. Yes, immediately, my Lord. No sir, I always do as I'm told.* Just a polite servant, taught how to sweep, how to scrape dirt from boots, and how to address my betters, and every person I met was my better, until I married the earl."

Illiana laughed at herself. She had tried to find the courage Benedict had taught her, as the horror of Sabine's disappearance made that courage imperative. "Where is she now? Where's my courage now? Am I just too stupid to know where to go and what to do? Mother doesn't help. Knowing how foolish I am, should she not take over the directions, and lead us to the right places? Nicholas tries, but he knows nothing of Spain. My mother should know more."

If her imagined courage did not exist, then she wondered how she might search for it and ignite it. Otherwise, if she should lay on the dew spangled shrubs along the river banks, close her eyes in terror, and never find either Sabine, or herself.

A FEW STEPS beyond the half mile upstream, Charles kicked at the pebbles and tumbled his thoughts around the last message from England, and the warnings.

There was sand and a little dewy scrub on his livery, but he bent to drink from the river and stood again with his black silk knees turning brown and green.

Every country, including England, had its dangers. Yet now the small risk of danger had turned, here in Spain, to murderous chaos. The Spanish royal army hounded the boarders of Moorish Granada, threatening, killing but also bargaining, while demanding the expulsion of all Muslims and Jews. Even those whose ancestors who had lived there for hundreds of years, who had built their palaces, created the miracle of drainage. irrigation and of bringing drinking water to dry establishments and had helped enrich Spain itself, were threatened.

Whether the priority was, as they claimed, the need to rejoin in a wholly Christian land, or whether it was simply for enjoying the power and pleasure of ruling over the entire country, was not clear.

Muslims would rarely convert to Christianity. Many jews, however, more pragmatic, cheerfully converted yet continued to practise their own faith in private. When discovered, the church stepped in. They were accused of heresy. They were then burned alive at the stake, as were others who had been accused of other heretical crimes, and so Spain shivered beneath the beating sunshine.

England shivered under a very different threat.

It was normal for any heir to the throne, still juvenile, to be governed by his mother's family once his father died. It happened almost as tradition, and getting such power under control could be slow and tedious. Yet although after the sad death of Edward IV, the new king was just twelve years of age, he was virtually swallowed by the Woodville family which rushed to grab power to such an extent that it bordered on panic.

They accompanied the prince to London with such an enormous armed guard of several thousand, it seemed they feared he would be grabbed by witches. They pushed for the coronation to take place so quickly there would barely be time to cook a pheasant for the feast. They also arranged for the prince to carefully avoid the actual place where the travelling Duke of Gloucester, the official Protector, had already arranged to meet them.

Richard, Duke of Gloucester had his own spies and knew of the charade. He was no fool, having lived through nearly thirty years of conspiracies, contrived by idiots and by masters of manipulation, the duke understood all those who practised such devices. He had overcome in the past as he did now, taking control of the young prince himself, using his own small guard and dismissing the enormous Woodville troops, and proceeded to London with the young prince kept safe, comfortable and amused.

Half the Woodville clan, including the queen, promptly grabbed all the royal property they could and rushed into Westminster sanctuary, where the queen and her direct family, daughters and servants, took up residence in Cheyenygate Mansion, previously inhabited by the Abbot. Uncle Edward Woodville had already set sail with ten thousand pounds of stolen treasure.

Richard promptly arrested those Woodvilles who had purposefully kept the new young king from being present at the arranged meeting place. Clearly the Woodville pack knew of a secret which threatened their imminent joy of power, should any one discover it.

The secret was indeed discovered. The Talbot family, Earls of Shrewsbury and entitled in many ways over the years, were an important part of the English nobility. John Talbot, the first earl, had been father to his beautiful daughter Eleanor, although the lady had since died. Her younger sister Elizabeth, Duchess of Norfolk, now arrived at court in the company of Robert Stillington, Bishop of Bath and Wells. They had a considerable amount to say and their proven story was both fascinating and disastrous.

Concerning such amazing and essential developments, information had three times been sent by messenger to Charles, Marshall of the specific troop sent abroad by orders of the late king. He now knew the entire story.

Charles already knew the dangers which were turning the country he called his own, and which he loved, into a land of chaos and danger almost akin to that of the changing Spanish peninsular. Indeed, the two sons of the late king, now occupying the royal quarters at the Tower of London, were abruptly announced illegitimate and no longer able to inherit the right to the throne.

The final message from England had enlarged the situation.

The full details, accompanied by those vital witnesses to the secret marriage of King Edward IV to Lady Eleanor Talbot, which had made the king's later marriage to Elizabeth Woodville entirely improper and bigamous, were now presented to the Council of Government, Nobility, Church and Commons, although some of the members had already left London for their own homes. Titulus Regius was confirmed and Richard of Gloucester was announced as the rightful heir to the throne.

The Woodville dilemma, apparent to all, but which had previously seemed without reason, now announced the motive within the nation's confusion. Indeed, the English had previously remained ignorant, but clearly Elizabeth Woodville had been told, perhaps on her husband's deathbed.

The abrupt Woodville behaviour, including panic and uprisings immediately after King Edward's death, was now understood. As was their determination to have Prince Edward crowned as quickly as possible. Once crowned and anointed by God, he could no longer have been pronounced illegitimate. Long live the King. However, it was Richard, the late king's youngest son, who was now the rightful heir and the date of his coronation was set.

What Richard thought of these unexpected catastrophies, was unknown. He might be horrified, Charles wondered, or delighted. The duke had a reputation of immense loyalty and justice, intelligence and religious devotion. A good king then. Yet the English chaos continued. A plot to reinstate the twelve year old prince, was uncovered, the perpetrator, Hastings, was executed and others within the plot were immediately arrested. Uprisings, it seemed, continued.

Charles sighed. The new king, Richard, should he ever reach coronation, would no doubt be entirely confused and ready for a possible Apocalypse. Charles decided that chaos had never before been quite so chaotic, and since he worked for the English crown, and his future also rested upon it, the chaos would not only embrace him but probably destroy him.

Meanwhile Spain celebrated the uncovering of heresy and burned the heretics alive in public. England caught perpetrators of treachery and executed them in public. Both countries raged in their confusion, one belief crashing against another.

The chuckle of the water beside him was a peaceful contrast and Charles sat, reflecting on what he knew, and what he did not yet know. Doubtless the Duke of Gloucester would be King Richard within weeks and Charles would return home to a home entirely reconstructed. Hope for stability instead of destruction, remained. What his barely recognisable father, Earl of Cleeves, was doing, floated unknown to him as always. Charles had not the faintest idea what side his father had chosen, whether he had ignored the entire situation or instead joined the chaos. And Charles did not really care. His own loyalty to Richard was already clear enough.

He wandered again. Behind him, just a little inland, the camp was quiet. He still saw the pale wisps of smoke rising from the ashes of the abandoned cooking fire, twisting like thin grey wings against the blackness above. Leaving this behind him, he walked downstream, where he knew that his exclamations and occasional chuckles would not be heard by any of his men.

Instead, he heard something quite distinct, someone crying, soft but echoing misery, and so was himself interrupted. Not wishing to embarrass a miserable stranger, he turned again. Then he paused. The miserable stranger, almost certainly female, might need help. To ignore another's misery was a judgement sometimes difficult to justify. The woman might conceivably be facing a monster leaping at her from the river. Turning once more, he moved towards the sound, and then recognised the situation more distinctly still.

Chaos, he decided, might occasionally bring a more satisfactory solution than expected. Illiana heard footsteps, told herself to stop being a fool, and looked up. Bright dark eyes, meeting the same, stared, realising that neither person, so suddenly startled, could imagine what to say.

Then Charles said, little more than a murmur, "It seems I have interrupted a private moment, madam."

"It seems," Illiana retorted, embarrassed, "that you take an interest in matters that are clearly none of your business."

Charles stepped back and bowed. His dark eyes whirled with something she had not yet managed to fathom, but this time, although he was dutifully polite, she sensed a tone of amusement.

He told her, "I accept the rebuke, my lady. As niece to the Baron Oswey, and now Dowager Countess, and as a woman whose courage I admire, clearly, I owe you an apology. I had simply hoped that I might be capable of helping during moments of distress."

Half the statement seemed kind. The other half was utterly confusing, particularly since the name Oswey meant nothing to her. Nor was there any way that a virtual stranger could help when her misery concerned her lack of confidence, her floundering sense of purpose, and personal doubts.

Muttering, "I'm not sure – I mean, well! Clearly you don't really know who I am, and actually, I don't really know who you are either. I thought you were going in the opposite direction. But since you're here, unless you're about to leave, then you could always help find Sabine."

With no desire to delve deeper, Charles stood straight and smiled. The smile, although his usual, tucked only vaguely at both corners of his mouth. "My lady, that is precisely why I and my men have returned, having completed my duty in Seville. I have only a number of days before I am obliged to fulfil other tasks, but in the meantime, I would gladly help. I offer my full co-operation in whatever you ask of me. I had supposed that I and my men would take at least one of the Delgardos into custody for questioning. Their village is certainly close."

Illiana hadn't known that either. "Go on then," she said. Then realised that the entire situation was becoming absurd, and she began to laugh. "Sorry," she hiccupped. "I ought to be thanking you. I was feeling sorry for myself and was sniffing away, thinking no one could hear me. My mother and Sabine's father are just a little way up there under the trees. Hopefully asleep. I just sort of crept away. We'd all love your help with Sabine, truly we would."

"In which case," Charles relaxed, "you have it. My men are not far upriver. I'll escort you there, it would be safer with a troop of guards so close." He raised an eyebrow. "May I wake your mother and the groom?"

"Oh! Yes please."

Illiana led this odd acquaintance up the sloping bank to the distant line of trees and pointed to the sycamore branches and their busy shade. "My mother's in the litter. I don't really want to wake them, but we'd be safer coming where -," And she stopped.

The blankets and heavy cloaks lay heaped but strangely flat. The litter stood, yet its curtains were open and partially ripped. Nothing moved except the grazing horses, untethered and wandering. Charles marched forwards, bending over the empty bedding. He pulled up one of the cloaks, and dropped it immediately. His expression, with the stars glitter barely lighting the rich darkness, was impossible to see. Illiana remained unmoving, bleak, horrified and wordless.

Striding back to her, Charles took her arm and led her away.

"There are two possibilities, and both are difficult to understand," he told her, still walking and bringing her forcefully with him. "Either your mother and groom needed refreshment or were searching for you, and have gone elsewhere." He did not add that without their cloaks, this would be absurd. Nor did he mention the blood he had seen, wet and fresh. "Or they have been taken by someone. Perhaps the Delgardos. Therefore, my dear, I am taking you to my troop, where you will remain guarded by my men. The rest of us will march to the village and uncover whatever has occurred. When I return, and I assure you, I shall most certainly return, I'll bring your belongings, litter and horses with me."

"Then I'm coming with you," Illiana insisted.

"To purposefully increase your own danger, and to distract my men from discovering your mother?"

His voice was neither soft nor understanding. Illiana shivered. "I suppose you're right. I'm sorry. I'll do whatever you say."

Having little choice, Illiana now sat by the cooking fire's smoking embers, where sparks of warmth welcomed her. Charles woke his men.

"Wake," he called. His voice loud and imperious. "No time for sleeping. This lady is the countess of Birstall, her companions have been taken. Since that Delgado gang stay not far from here, I intend marching on them first. Meanwhile, the lady must claim safety here. Therefore, get yourselves ready to approach the village with me, a mile perhaps, though I cannot be sure of distance. Dougal and Sam, You'll stay and guard this lady with your lives, until I return. That will take time, no doubt." He turned to Illiana, "You, however, my dear, should sleep if you can. You will be entirely safe and there is a considerable weight of blankets available. Help yourself. If you sleep, it will be a huge benefit to all of us by the morning."

"But to know what happened?"

"Once I return with specific explanations, hopefully accompanied by your mother and groom, you will know it. Until then, lying awake in worry and misery is pointless, and also a considerable handicap."

Within a rumble of men grabbing their weapons, the snorting of horses waking and quickly resaddled, then the thunder of hooves, so the scramble of darker shadows within shadows faded. Illiana shivered.

"Sit close to the fire, my lady," Dougal said, bringing several blankets bundled in his arms. "I'll build up the fire a little." He bent, making the bed for her to lie on, and then added a heap of small twigs to the embers. The blaze was tiny, but sufficient. It had not been a cold night but now heat dithered beneath the stars.

Obedient to the uniformed man helping her, Illiana lay, surprisingly comfortably but with thoughts of disaster and fear. One minute she had been absorbed only with her own stupidity, and then the interruption by the man reminding her there was more to life than herself, and finally by yet another disaster. Within moments, she slept and did not dream.

Charles and his twelve men rode upwards from the riverbanks to the valley where the crags and rising pathway wound into richer darkness.

The path stretched and bent, skirting the dips within the sandy scrub, then through trees, first occasional palms, then clusters of sycamore and birch, bush and weed, where the fluster of the hiding wildlife delved deeper into the undergrowth. It was two miles of slow progress up, and then steeply down into the long valley's sanctum.

From a shallow path, an abrupt and narrow rise became a crag, and the party looked down at the spread of village immediately below. Tiny houses, pale stone peeping from bougainvillea, flat rooves of wood and slate poking without chimney nor thatch, and no sign of life, all lay in peaceful silence, just below them. Beyond, on the flat shadowed green behind the village, goats curled and horses grazed or slept. Cottage windows were shuttered, doors tightly closed. A well had been dug, standing in a paved square. Not even the echoes of snoring broke the peace. Charles knew this was the Delgardo village, and led his men down the steep rocky sides of stone into the first entrance of beaten earth, dry as sand, which approached the largest of the houses towering at the village entrance.

Its door, double and copper bared, faced him as Charles rode forwards, did not dismount, but from the height of the horse's pale back, kicked five times at the rattling wood. The immediate panic within now echoed with the slam, clank, and footsteps of arousal.

He waited, then kicked again and shouted. "In the name of English royalty," he roared. "Open as commanded."

The door opened, as commanded. A pale face peeped out, dark eyebrows beneath a bald head, and beside him, peering beneath his arm, a dark woman, her brown skin wrinkled and tired.

She mumbled to the armpit beside her. "¿Un extraño? ¿Una horda de extraños??"

The bald man straightened. "You say you be English," the man shouted, furious. "Then you got no right here. Fuera de juego."

Peering down at him, an expression of ice, Charles now also spoke Spanish, "I come in the name of my king," he spat. "And with the authority of your King Ferdinand. You attempt to evade me or deny me, and you will be imprisoned. No doubt you should already be in the dungeons, as should your leaders. I ask only one question, and you will answer it. Where are the English couple, recently dragged here? Where exactly are they now?"

Both the small man and tiny woman at the doorway stared, blank. "Tis the home of Gomez Delgardo," finally the man said. "The great leader living here. Our captain who no one denies for fear of life. If he was here, you'd all be dead within the first breeze, you stupid fools. You don't talk of kings when looking into the face of a Delgardo. There's not one of our men here tonight. Went sailing a week back. You'll not find one here."

Charles dismounted, handing the reigns to Allan Reed, directly behind him. "Then I shall have proof. Search this house," he said, and called three of the others to follow him. Pushing past the couple at the doorway, Charles marched inside.

It was dark, shutters lifted over the empty window openings, but two stubby candles lay on a shelf and Charles took these, lighting both with his own flint, then passed one flaring flame to Allan, keeping the other.

The house was large although without beauty. Stairs twisted to open spaces beneath the shadow of the roof, where clothes piled the dust across planked floors. Kitchens spread across the ground floor, cushions tipped, settles faced one to the other, stools stood or lay, a squalid mess of objects and belongings littered every space. Beneath the roof were separate bedchambers, some neater than others, beds unmade, sheets and blankets strewn. Although the space was large, no other person seemed present.

Charles finally faced the elderly man and the little woman. "You attend to this house in your master's absence.?"

Both nodded. The woman said, "Si, sí, señor. Claro."

"Then you make a remarkably bad job of it," Charles said, eyes lowered. "Where else might these prisoners be?"

"Look wherever you wish," the man answered, shuffling bare feet on the boards. "If such a thing did happen here, then tis only this house would have prisoners. There is no possibility of others, I'll not be helping so fuera de juego."

Charles slammed his fist against other doors, and the noise had woken most retainers. He pushed in without invitation but found every house either empty, or at least empty of Bertha and Nicholas, without sign of any disturbance, blood or confusion. He did not bother to search every house since there were a hundred or more, but soon shook his head and without apology marched from the village, slamming the last door behind him.

"There's not a wretched damned pirate present, let alone any captives. It seems the entire gang are once again at sea." Charles kicked the final door shut, and stamped back to his men.

They stood again outside the leader's home, watched discreetly by the old couple at the gap in the doorway. Allan said, "So tell us, sir, where have these people been taken?"

"I don't know," Charles told him, mounting at once. "I only know where they have *not* been taken. Now I suspect the Spanish army, those previously threatening the Alhambra and the Moorish palaces. If a troop of soldiers rode from there, and back towards Seville, saw strangers sleeping in the wild, I doubt they'd have ignored them. I believe we'll find them in the crypts of Seville, or near enough."

"Tis a long ride, my lord, and if we don't know what dungeon? Nor what church? Nor what town?"

The men waited. "We collect the litter and horses on the way back to the campsite," Charles eventually said. "We eat, regain energy, then ride for Cordoba."

"Sorry, my lord, but you're saying Seville?"

"I'm saying Cordoba."

Charles, now settled in the saddle, was riding south once more, leaving the cluttered valley and turning back towards the sleeping swell of the river and the campsite they had left more than three hours before.

Allan rode close. "We expected Seville, but Cordoba's a good deal north. You've decided on that?"

"You think me crazed?" Now Charles chuckled, barely heard, but said, "I know every detail of what was going on in Seville. They awaited their kings, but they told me of the army holding the South of Granada. Those men were due to be relieved, each unit staying two months, eventually returned to their camps, soldiers on foot, without exception, returning to Cordoba. Those who arrested folk sleeping peacefully on the ground near the river bank would only have been foot soldiers. Mounted troops would have ridden north."

"Then, sadly, we ride to Cordoba."

Suddenly, Charles was laughing. "Now I am back on my own designated business, obeying Royal orders indeed." Riding fast, the brim of his hat low over his eyes, he spoke to Allan at his side, but also to himself. "My duty is to help the English folk trapped here in Spain, and in any manner unjustly suffering from the Inquisition. This is most definitely what we face now, and our duty is more than clear."

Illiana was awake since hours had passed, and was sitting, impatient, both excited and terrified, by her two polite guards. She jumped up when she heard the tired thunder of the horses. Then she ran to face their leader.

Charles dismounted, stroked his stallion's mottled cream and brown silk neck, and nodded to Degal who marched over, taking the reigns. Charles gazed down at Illiana, her hair, loose, unpinned and uncombed, was black and curled below her shoulders. He smiled, although only to himself.

"I have no news, neither good nor bad," he told her. "Good perhaps, since now I know that the Delgardos did not take your mother nor your groom, but bad, since we cannot be sure where or by whom. I now believe we should ride to Cordoba. Not a quick nor easy ride, I am sorry to tell you, but I believe we shall find your people there, held either by the army or the church. Under such circumstances, they will not be dead, but inevitably imprisoned." He watched, and quickly read her expression and the words hidden in her eyes. "You've no need to accompany us. I can leave you both safe and comfortable, and return as quickly as I may."

Illiana was now vehement. "I'm coming. I'll never be left, not now, never again." She stared up at him. "I promise I'll try not to be in the way. I'm not the best rider, but not the worst either. I'll keep to whatever pace, and I won't complain."

The tuck at the corner of his mouth twitched. The rumble of chaos both in England and in Spain, now seemed to have embraced and combined.

Charles, while watching the disciplined order of his men as they prepared, was thinking instead of the young woman he had intended to help, now knowing the help would be considerably more complicated, and indeed prolonged. Not that he doubted the outcome. It was his mission, to remove any of his own people from the Spanish turmoil. It also would donate him greater time in which to see the woman as naked in truth as he already saw her in his mind.

Finally, he said, "We eat first, water the horses, and I talk to the men. We'll leave for Cordoba in an hour. So, you eat with us, and you leave with us."

CHAPTER THIRTEEN

The Andalusian city of Cordoba glittered in the late morning sun, the golden blaze directly above them as they rode the narrow, twisting lanes, every man and one woman tired, the woman now ready to collapse.

Charles rode directly to the Cathedral of Our Lady of the Assumption. The glory of the building, more dazzling in Islamic style beauty, seemed wonderful to all the men gazing upwards, but less to Illiana. She had drifted from the leader's side and now rode between two of the troop, both keeping a tight and careful pace, more interested in keeping her protected than in their own normal positions within the troop.

Heat reflected from each passing wall of white stone. It buried itself in the dry earth, transforming the ground beneath hoof and foot into a burning oven. From the huge openness above it beamed without distraction. Now it was only heat that Illiana knew. From below it blazed. From above it blazed, and from every side it blazed again. Her cloak was thrown off across her knees and the high neck of her shift hung in damp resignation, while over this the long crimson gown, once expensive kermes died silk, the coolest she owned, fell moist and limp over her legs. Her tiny neat headdress of little more than pearls, still left her head pounding, and her hair sweat-damp. She gripped the reigns with the only energy she had remaining, afraid that if she dared sit relaxed, then she would slip and fall.

No movement rustled as they passed. No eyes peeped from the wooden shuttered windows. Houses seemed vacant, utterly silent, acknowledging neither life nor emotion. No bird sang nor wing fluttered. Whether the city hid from the heat, or from the inquisition, no one knew. Illiana guessed it would be both, but her own thoughts could not drift beyond heat ravaged exhaustion.

When the horses were stopped, heads down, Charles, Allan and Degal dismounted and entered the open doors of the cathedral, while the others sat waiting. Charles came first to Illiana. She stared down. It felt like days, perhaps weeks, since she had seen him. Longer since she had heard him. Now he reached up both arms, helping her dismount, almost tumbling. He was gazing back at her and she felt herself drawn into the shadowed tunnels behind his eyes.

He told her, "We are here, little one, and will now discover the truth." She felt his support as his hand was strong beneath her elbow, and he led her within the sudden cool relief of the huge building before them.

At first the great patterned tiles echoed beneath her riding boots, now eight clacking warnings of arrival. The priests appeared more quietly, heads bowed, shadowed within their robes. One stepped forward, and Charles faced him, bowed, straightened, and spoke in Spanish without any local dialect.

"My lord father," Charles spoke as the lord himself, "as the royal marshal of the English Lord Protector, I travel in Spain to relieve your Holy Mission of the Inquisition, already I believe under duress, of the additional duty examining English subjects, over which this country has no jurisdiction. I am sure you understand me, sir. Yet two of my company, while sleeping, have been taken and almost certainly brought to this great city. One male, Nicholas Farrier, and one female, Lady Bertha Oswy, must be returned to my protection without delay, as I trust you understand, sir."

Although puzzled at the name given to her mother, who was surely the plain Mistress Caravidio, Illiana remained carefully silent, but saw the priest's acknowledgement, even while she found standing difficult. The coolness within the marble and tiles, all golden sun removed, helped her breathing, yet she longed to collapse.

The priest was frowning as though irritated. "Sir Marshall, I accept the Right of your royal mission. I have been informed that a peasant of English heritage, who speaks none of our language, is being held without jurisdiction. He was, however, in the company of a widow known to have committed heresy and sins of the flesh. This woman must face the tribunal and will not be released. I direct you, sir, to travel to the Alcazar and relate to the guards as I have informed you. You are naturally welcome to return here, my lord, should you discover further difficulties." He stepped back abruptly, turned, and followed the other priest into the shadows from where they had first appeared.

Outside once more under the heaving heat, Charles again supported Illiana, holding both her arms. "You'll have your groom safe within moments, little one." He spoke quietly, his expression gentler than was normal. "There is some difficulty regarding your mother. Can you give any reason for the priest's unforgiving explanation?"

Illiana shook her head. "I don't understand a word. No, I don't mean the language. I mean the idea of my mother, my father was Spanish. Does that mean they think Mamma comes under their dreadful law?"

"Sadly," and speaking more quietly still, "the wife takes on the obligations of her husband. As yet, she has barely met anyone, let alone had the opportunity to be classified as heretical. Can you explain any of this?"

She thought she'd be sick. "No. My mother's a good woman. She obeys the church and goes to Mass more often than I ever did, and no one here knows her."

Charles helped her mount, regain the reigns, and settle herself on the saddle. His immediate sympathy for a young woman who attracted him, was now combined with a new sparkling interest. "I have a place arranged for us to stay in safety, Illiana. My dear, I shall take you there now, and you'll be protected while you rest. Hopefully you can sleep. My assistants and I will retrieve your groom and attempt to have your mother released. Worry about nothing, and fear nothing." His voice raised a little, but his eyes still remained fixed to hers. "There is no danger while I am here. My men will guard you with their lives."

THE LONG LOW wooden shed-like barracks sometimes housing the Spanish guards of Cordoba, welcomed them. Clearly Charles and his troop were expected and no others appeared. Illiana was immediately shown to a tiny dark room, its bed the only furniture apart from a wall held brazier, a hand-held fan lying on the minute table, and the bed pan snuggled beneath the raised mattress. "Stay here and rest, water will be brought," Charles told her briefly, "and sleep until I return."

She was left. The silent space, although enclosed, being dark and seeming cool, enveloped her and within minutes, as though obedient, Illiana was deeply asleep.

Having no method of knowing the time, nor for knowing what time had passed, Illiana woke to the same silence and the same darkness, but a tiny wooden cup and a large wooden jug both stood on the table top and both were brimming with clean water. Twisting around, she sat upright and drank, then drank again, and finally lay back.

She was asleep when Nicholas tapped on the low door, and whispered her name. Excitement pushed out exhaustion, her voice was hoarse as she called him in, and although he hurried to kneel beside her bed, she flung both arms around his neck.

"Oh, Nicholas, thank the Lord." She paused then, releasing him. "My mother?"

Now Nicholas sat on the bare earthen floor. In spite of the darkness, Illiana could see the flicker of tears in his eyes. "Lady, tis a mystery, and a bad one. I'll not dither thither nor lie, for we needs to know how to get your lady back. Me not understanding Spanish apart from them si and no and por favor stuff, makes it mighty hard fer me to know what happened. Tis the lord in livery what knows the details. Them soldiers all come clankling and snorting as we woke and I were glad simply to see you wasn't with us and I reckoned t'was a hope you stayed safe. Them soldiers poked and prodded and then started shouting. One got angry. Hauled the lady from the litter they did, grabbed us, tied on horseback indeed, and rode fer miles upon miles. I slept, I confess, under the scorch and them long hours and locked up in a pokey dungeon. Now I's just mighty happy to know you safe."

He slumped, relief overcoming misery. Illiana whispered again, "My mother didn't come back with you? So, where's Charles?"

"Done gone again," Nicholas told her. "I ain't even seen yer lady mum, nor knows where she be, but I reckon tis your captain has gone to get her."

"Is it later? Should you eat?

"I ain't hungry," his voice was more of a moan. "You wants food, lady, then I fetches it, but I can't eat not a crumb."

"Nor me," Illiana told him. "We both need sleep. You have a bed?" Nicholas nodded, and very slowly, returned to it.

Within a dreaming misery, Illiana fell asleep in her own sweat.

Although with no idea whether it was morning, Illiana woke ravenous. She rolled from the bed, opened the door, and peered around. From the far end of the corridor there was a window brightly lit, and the shuffle and voices of men. Trying to neaten her hair without mirror or comb, she followed both light and noise, and was immediately facing a large room of tables and talking men, eating, fingers without napkins, from huge platters.

At once Charles was beside her. "I'm delighted you slept well, little one. So did your groom Nicholas. After imprisonment, freedom always brings deep sleep. I have a good deal to tell you. Come and join us for breaking fast."

There was water, there was wine, there was cut ham, curds and whey in vast bowls, spoons in a heap, dark bread in larger heaps, tiny plates of marmalade, and sliced fruit, although of a sort unknown to Illiana. Across the table, she faced Charles, Degal and Allan. Charles, marmalade on his thumb, leaned over towards her, helping her choose from the platters, and he filled two cups, one with water and one with wine.

When he spoke, it was no whisper. "Eat up, little one, while I explain what you need to know," he said, as once again she felt trapped in the darkness of his eyes. "The tribunal refuses to release your mother. I have threatened, and repeated threats, but as yet I've not discovered the means to have your mother released. I've been unable to see her. However, I can insist on your right to visit her and speak with her. She's held beneath the House of the Tribunal, attached to the Alcazar. The inquisitor here, a Dominican lawyer, informed me that your mother is the bigamous wife of a Spanish criminal known to them, and thus she is held here by Right of the Papal Bull."

In panic, although she was more concentrated on food than thoughts of her mother, Illiana looked up in amazement and swallowed her first sip of wine. The water was finished. She gulped and blinked. "Bigamous? But I'm sure Mamma never wed another man. She was besotted with my father. Yes, he was Spanish, but they lived in England. You know my home, I saw you once. You know I was Benedict's legal wife. I'm the dowager countess. How can my mother be arrested?"

"It is precisely that," Charles said, refilling her cup from the water pitcher, "which I need to know."

"You seem to know strange names for her."

Charles raised one dark eyebrow. "Did she never tell you? I had an idea that she kept her birthright private, since her father disowned her on marriage. So presumably, you're unaware that your mother was the third daughter of the Baron Oswey. She became affianced to the baron's chief groom, and he disowned his daughter immediately. Your grandfather is dead now, God rest his soul, and your mother's brother is the baron, but when I discussed this with him, he showed little interest in discovering his sister's situation. However, she still holds the Right of relationship, as you do, little one."

Illiana shivered. "You've got us muddled. None of that's true. It sounds ridiculous, and anyway, it has nothing to do with Spain and my father."

He was smiling, the twitch at the side of his mouth more pronounced, as he stood. "I return to those dungeons within the hour," he said. "Know yourself a lady, my dear. Perhaps also the daughter of a Spanish criminal, whether bigamous or otherwise, I have no idea. Stay safe and rest. The gardens beyond the barracks are safe ground, and my men know to look after you. I may be gone some hours, but I'll speak to you directly on return." He pointed over her head. "Your groom sits with my men at the far end of the room. He knows more now since I've spoken with him. Once I have permission for your mother to see you," I'll come directly to take you to her."

With no further need for food or wine, Illiana felt more bewildered than she had the day before, or the day before that. Perhaps even another day, long gone. Travelling now seemed endless and she could no longer count the days. Yet her only reason for any day's travel, now seemed virtually but sadly forgotten.

However, she refused to forget. "And Sabine?"

"I apologise for my increasing ignorance," Charles said, still smiling, "no one here admits knowing of her, and denies her presence at the Alcazar. We are surrounded by the invisible knots of mystery, my dear." He paused, then spoke again without the smile. "I must inform you, little one, that within this week, I shall be forced to return to Seville, but we'll discuss that later, hopefully having already discovered other more satisfactory answers."

Watching him leave, Illiana shivered again. She knew nothing. She did not even know who her mother was, nor who she was herself. The slim dark figure leaving, striding between the long tables as every man waved, bowed or cheered, gave her a strange sense of safety, yet without understanding. She understood less than when arriving in Spain, and that had seemed strange enough. She had Nicholas and her mother beside her, but most of all, she had known her own confidence. Now she knew neither confidence nor courage, and stared around, searching for Nicholas.

He came to her. "I reckons," he said, noticing her empty cups and the cream of whey on her lips, "we walks together now in the grounds, lady, and I tells you the sprinkling more of what I knows."

The grounds were roughly sloped but the hills remained, bleached under the distant sun, in the far blurred dazzle. There was no river, but a small clump of tall palm trees offered a smattering of shade and here Illiana and Nicholas sat on the tangle of weed and grass within the shadows.

"Don't be worried," Illiana said quickly. "I've got to try and make sense of something. I'm sorry we're no closer to Sabine, but please, Nicholas – tell me what you know."

"Can't say I knows naught," he answered slowly. "Not proper knowing, as it were. I can repeat what I's been told. Tis about your mother, and if tis true or rotten cobwebs, I dunno. Here goes. There tis a fat old lady calling herself Elonza Caravidio. Well, no doubt she knows her own name, but says her husband went off years ago to work with horses in London. Reckons she found out he married, though never divorced, says it were a Bertha what called herself Lady Oswey, what stole her husband and then done killed him."

"I'm going mad," Illiana stuttered. "The whole world's gone

mad." She gasped, then sighed. "Perhaps I'm dreaming. Perhaps I should go back to bed."

Nicholas grinned. "Seeing as I reckons you be the smartest and bravest lady I ever met," he said, "tis you what decides now. I reckon there's my Sabs, she's waiting for you and for me. She knows tis you, only you, what can save her. Reckon your mum is feeling the same."

Illiana did not answer, but her thoughts, still jumbled, rejected the kind words. Her mother knew her as a fool and would expect nothing from her. Poor Sabine probably thought herself lost forever. The sweet words from Nicholas, and the even more surprisingly kind and almost affectionate words drifting lately from Marshall Charles, proved instead that both felt sorry for her. They did not think her strong. They thought her sad and stupid and lost, incapable, no doubt, of helping herself let alone anyone else.

She sighed. Self pity would, after all, be the worst decision to make now.

"Charles says he'll get me permission to see my mother. I'll try and find out if any of this weird jumble about the past is even partly true. If not, I have to swear the truth, and get her out. Otherwise, it's up to Charles. then we trace Sabine."

He was satisfied, even trusted her. She wished she could trust herself. "Right, Lady. What can I do for you now?"

"Are you any good at miracles, Nicholas?"

Nicholas sniggered.

Two slow sweating days drifted by, leaving nothing for Illiana to do except pray and hope, talk to her groom, and lie on the bed, trying to sleep. She used the fan that had been left to her, but while it helped the burning misery of her face, her wrist felt ready to snap.

When it happened at last, she felt no excitement and only fear.

Between two Alcazar guards, a priest between them, Illiana sat and watched her mother brought in to the tribunal office. Bertha seemed unrecognisable for one moment, her grey hair loose, uncombed, and with not even the pin of her normal neat head-dress. Her face appeared more haggard, thinner and utterly bleak. Her eyes were smears under heavy, swollen lids. She wore a tunic of woven flax, rough and colourless, seamless from its tight neck to an unravelling hem now dragging on the floor. Her wrists were bound and her hands hung rigid as though in pain.

Shuffling in, slow and held between two large guards, she barely seemed to notice her daughter. Illiana, horrified, jumped up to embrace her but was stopped by those guarding her.

At the far end of the room stood Charles. He did not come closer, but his voice was loud, even imperious. "You have no motive for refusing the recognition of a daughter for her mother, since that relationship is not in question."

The guards stepped back. Now Illiana knelt at Bertha's feet, clutching at her two bound hands. Purposefully she spoke in English. "Mamma, I promise we'll get you free. It may take time, but your arrest here is unlawful."

It was the priest, not her mother, who answered. "Mistress, I do not sit in judgement, but as you do not normally reside in this country, I shall explain why this accusation of heresy against your mother is lawful and undeniable under the Tribunal of the Holy Office of the Inquisition. She has twice been interrogated by the inquisitor here, Miguel de Morilio, appointed by the crown and therefore without any accepted contradiction permitted in any form. It is stated that this woman committed sexual sins with a Spanish senor of bigamous status, knowing full well the sin she committed, but claimed to be his wife and refused to acknowledge the sin of bigamy. It is said that later she killed him. The murder is not within our jurisdiction, but the Holy Church is here to bring sinners to confess and humble themselves before Holy God the Lord Farther."

Illiana, standing now, stared at the priest in his dark robes, then looked over to Charles who remained in the shadows, and then at her mother. Still holding her mother's hands, she whispered, again in English, "mamma, whatever the truth, you'll not be subject to this wickedness. Can you tell me, is this true?"

Bertha's eyes were tear filled but swollen with more than tears. Her face, in the candlelight, now shone with the darkening discolouration of bruises and cuts. She did not look at her daughter, but whispered. "A little true. A lot is lies. Child, get me out. Get me out of here."

Staring back at the priest, Illiana said, "My lord, I think I understand although some of this is undoubtedly untrue. I protest. If, as you claim, my mother was never married to Senor Diego Caravidio, then she is not liable to any Spanish tribunal. Senor Caravidio may have been guilty of bigamy but if he was, my mother is therefore unmarried, is of English birth and residence and therefore has no obligation under the law or inquisition of Spain."

Now she felt the strength of Charles at her back. He continued, "With the authority of the Marshall of the English Crown, I demand to speak with the official inquisitor, de Morilio. I declare that this procedure is improper, illegal and without justification. It must be ended immediately and Lady Bertha of Oswey, England, shall therefor be released forthwith into my custardy."

A variety of expressions sprang, fury from the priest, who sat straight and glared, and both anger and frustration from the standing guards. Illiana abruptly gained confidence. Bertha showed no expression and was slumped beneath her pain.

"Senor Marshall," the priest said, speaking through tight lipped restraint, "you may return here tomorrow to speak with the official authority in this matter. Until then, without proof or any decision possible, this woman – Lady Oswey, if that is her true identity, will remain in custardy at the tribunal. I make neither judgement nor decision and the General Inquisitor you wish to speak with on this matter, will not be present here until tomorrow morning. You may now leave."

Illiana was accustomed to dismissal but Charles was not. He remained where he stood. "My lord, may I point out that no man, even within the church, holds authority over me in this country. I shall return tomorrow at ten of the clock, and expect immediate audience with the tribunal, as I demand. In the meantime, although I accept the inevitable continued imprisonment of this noble Englishwoman, I must point out that no man shall touch her person until jurisdiction is proven."

While everyone stared at everyone else, the two guards holding Bertha upright, quickly dragged her, her feet barely touching the tiles, and disappeared through the archway and into invisibility. Illiana lost the warmth of her mother's fingers, and stepped back. Charles still spoke. "The solution, my lord, is simple. If the complaint against this lady is accepted as true, then she is unmarried and thus under no jurisdiction of any Spanish court. If the accusation is untrue, then the lady has committed no sin and is truly married, and now widowed. There is therefore no possible claim of Spanish authority of any manner. Should you speak with Inquisitor de Morilio before I see him, I trust you will make this clear."

He then turned, and marched, followed quickly by Illiana, from the chamber of the Tribunal.

Once outside, she breathed deeply, the sun's heat once more blasting down. More incontrovertible, she knew, even than the Spanish Inquisition. Charles nodded to his waiting men, and he helped Illiana into the saddle, saying softly, "My lady, your courage is impressive. So is your instant insight and understanding. You are about to win your mother's freedom."

She peered down at him, now flushed. "I have to."

"You will," he told her, thrusting the reigns against her palm. "Unfortunately, I have no idea as to the truth of these accusations. Nor does your mother seem capable of explaining. She has been badly treated, and I shall insist on the justification both of freedom and of apology. Perhaps compensation, though that's less likely. Once free, she'll need considerable care and help."

"And there's still Sabine to find."

Charles stepped away. "Also my orders to return to Seville."

Illiana did not sleep that night. She knew that her mother would collapse, but would not dare to dream.

It was the sick squeeze of humidity that swelled the heat on the following day. Clouds hung heavy across the sky, although without signs of rain. The tribunal chamber was busy, but Bertha was not there. A dark flutter of Dominican priests sat forwards, peering, while guards darkened every shadow from grey to black. Before her, on a high mounted chair, sat a man in deep livery, others alike on either side. The Inquisitor remained sitting in the high set chair, looking down as though claiming royalty.

Charles, with Illiana beside him, was followed by his liveried troop, every man now unarmed, but standing to attention in the light beaming through tall windows.

The Inquisitor squinted, stared and spoke as though he had little interest in the interruption.

"I am Miguel de Morilio, Inquisitor General Of Cordoba, Spain, by authority of His Majesty King Ferdinand of Aragorn and Her Majesty Queen Isabella of Castille, the royal monarchs of all Spain. Speak your case, sir."

Charles looked directly forward, as though speaking to the seated man's gold chain and cross, hanging against his black coated chest.

"I believe you already are well acquainted with the case, sir," he said. "I am Lord Charles, Viscount of Valdar, Second Marshall to his Majesty, King Richard of England, and on the king's orders."

Fearing that Charles had made a mistake since after King

Edward IV's death, it would be his son Edward who would inherit the throne, Illiana knew herself blushing but kept her silence.

De Morilio, coldly, spoke down to the top of Charles' head. "Sir, since you are claiming that Spain holds no jurisdiction over the female now in custardy, you will no doubt also realise that no English monarch holds power over me. However, I have agreed, condescended, let us say, to listen to your claim."

The vast row of seated priests, hands tucked within their sleeves, shifted, nodding or shaking their heads, but continued to stare. Illiana felt that most of the stares were in her direction. The guards stared only ahead.

Charles, without any chair offered, began to speak. He spoke clearly, loudly, with the words of authority, and quite briefly stated the case.

"There is, indeed, no need for any man to judge on the authenticity of this claim of bigamy made upon Senor Diego Caravidio. The gentleman is deceased, may the Lord take his soul in peace. The further claim is perfectly impossible to disprove for either Lady Oswey is legally married, and has therefore committed no sin in the eyes of the Holy Church, or she remains unmarried and is therefore answerable purely and exclusively to English authority, being the unwed daughter of the Earl of Oswey. I therefore demand that the lady be released from your illegal captivity immediately."

"On the contrary, sir," the inquisitor replied. "Since the prisoner in question claims to be wedded to a Spaniard known to have committed sinful bigamy, and has given her name as Señora Caravidio, she therefore accepts compliance within the sin of bigamy, and compliance to the justice of the Spanish Inquisition.."

Illiana shivered.

"She may have mistakenly claimed to be a Spanish citizen by marriage, sir," Charles answered immediately. "However, you deny that claim. Since bigamy cannot be accepted as legal marriage, you yourself state that she is neither married nor therefore under

Spanish jurisdiction. I ask you to be clear, sir. Is the Lady Bertha Oswey legally married to a Spanish gentleman?" He paused briefly. "Or is she not?"

The following silence was not silent, for several of the priests and one guard clustered around the inquisitor's high throne for some minutes, whispering and arguing. Eventually it was one of the dark robed priests who stepped forward and addressed Charles, crossing his hands as though in prayer, saying, "My lord, I regret to say that more contemplation on this subject is needed within the privacy of the tribunal. I should also, perhaps, point out that the young female standing beside you, sir, claiming to be the daughter of Senor Diego Caravidio, although illegitimate, is of Spanish lineage, and is therefore also legally answerable to this inquisition, should she cause or speak of any act deemed heretical."

"Naturally, sir," and Charles bowed as though he suffered a backache, "you may think and speak as you wish. I shall however point out that should your heretical claim against the Lady Oswey prove correct, this young female, being illegitimate, is of no provable parentage, which reduces her simply to stand only as English, and therefore most certainly *not* under your legal jurisdiction. On the other hand, should your claims against her lady mother be proved inaccurate, you shall have no jurisdiction over a young woman of legal birth and of unarguable innocence, simply seeking, as would be entirely proper, to gain the release of her innocent mother."

CHAPTER FOURTEEN

Bertha, huddled in utter darkness, could not think clearly, nor force her thoughts onto any chosen path.

The cell was small and against the stone wall lay a bed of straw covered by one woollen blanket, stained but thick. There was a chamber pot which had been poorly cleaned and the smell would soon be greater. There were no washing facilities, nor anything in the tiny room. The only door was padlocked from the outside and there was no window. No light entered and while those outside were baked, Bertha was cold and sat or lay with the blanket wrapped around her. They had taken her clothes. She wore the rough smock which had been given to her, and nothing beneath it.

A guard, a man as thick as he was tall, his boots wooden soled, had been ordered by the inquisitor to beat her and he had obeyed with obvious delight. The inquisitor had watched, then nodded.

"And again. This wicked wretch must confess her sins and beg for The Holy Lord's forgiveness."

Her face had been punched many times and the rest of her

body kicked. She had not been raped but suspected this might happen once the inquisitor was no longer present.

"Now confess, heretical sinner. First your name. The man you think you married, and you are married, is that true? Yet you know that sinner to have been bigamous? That is also true, is it not?"

Now she could barely remember how she had confessed. Yes, she was married. She had loved the man and he had taught her Spanish. She was distraught when he had died, but naturally she had not killed him. She loved him. She knew nothing of Bigamy. He had simply told her that he had sailed to England to find more work. He loved horses and they all loved him.

Because they had taken her boots from her, she was barefoot. The guard, holding the long handled whip, had pushed her back and grabbed one ankle, then had swung the whip once again, slashing the thin rope across the sole of her foot. This had been repeated again and again until the blood had spread across the floor beneath her.

Once alone again, without bandage, or willow bark for pain relief, without even food or water, Bertha lay on the straw, trying to keep scratches away from the screaming agony throbbing across the sole of her right foot. Finally the bleeding stopped, although no one came to clean away the threads of dark sticky patterns left on the ground. Gradually, very gradually, the wounds closed and the pains subsided.

When Bertha heard that she was again required to meet someone sent from England to inquire concerning the treatment of English citizens, she had quivered with both fear and hope. Seeing her daughter waiting for her, she had wondered if she was hallucinating, or was indeed about to be freed. Neither had proved true, although Illiana's attempt to embrace her had brought momentary comfort. Since she understood nothing and could barely speak for hunger and misery, Bertha had finally hobbled away, half carried, when the guards pushed and pulled her once more, one foot still horribly tender, and without knowing what had happened, let alone what might happen next. Finally thrown back into her cell, she fell onto the heaped straw and was immediately unconscious.

Unconsciousness slipped into the sleep of exhaustion and puzzlement and when she awoke, without knowing if it was day or night, she found the inquisitor staring down at her. Behind him stood two guards, and behind them the prison door was open. Bertha glimpsed a passageway, and another guard waited there, holding the flare of a tiny torch. Now accustomed to black being all that existed, Bertha found that the sudden light made her blind.

"Bring her," the Inquisitor told his guards, "carefully, however. We may be required – perhaps not – yet care is needed. Has this woman been fed?"

"Two days back, my lord. Well fed."

The inquisitor pursed his lips. "Have food prepared for when I have finished. It may not be long."

She was dragged to the tribunal chamber, the space virtually empty as was usual, although not always. The inquisitor sat before her on the raised dais, and guards surrounded her. Staring around and hopeful to see the liveried Englishman who had spoken for her, and possibly once more her daughter, Bertha was quickly disappointed. Neither was present within the hall. She now saw only the hated figure who had already ordered her torture. It was a creature without compassion. One who claimed to serve the Lord God, but instead satisfied the cruelty in his own soul and obeyed the Devil.

It was the inquisitor who spoke.

"Madam, you claim to have legally wed the Spanish citizen, now dead, the Lord rest his soul, in England some years gone?" Bertha grunted, saying that was true. "How can you prove to me, beyond question, mistress, that you did not know that Diego Caravidio was thus committing heinous and sinful bigamy?"

Now Bertha gulped. She struggled to think. "My lord, forgive me, how can I prove this? I had never travelled to Spain. Diego was the groom in the great house where I lived. My father was angry that I could marry a lowly servant, since I was the daughter of a baron. He – disowned me. It was sad, but I loved my husband. No one, not even my father the baron, said that my husband would be a bigamist. Diego never uttered a word of such things. We lived happily for many years. He never returned to Spain. Now I am here for the first time. Who is it who says she was married to my beloved husband before I married him myself? He was young and already working some years in England. I do not believe he could be already wed to some other woman. Ask my daughter. She has never heard even a whisper of such an unnatural past. She cannot be baseborn, for only last year Illiana was legally wed to the Earl of Birstall, a noble gentleman of England."

It had been more of a speech than she had intended, indeed, it surprised Bertha that she'd been able to say so much. Now she drooped, panting and trying to catch her breath. Her back ached. Her foot felt raw. Her eyes were swollen and they hurt. One ear, often used by a guard when wanting her attention, or to pull her from one place to another, now permanently stung and hurt. She squinted in the light and the heat. She did not hear the inquisitor sigh deeply.

"That ain't no truth, my lord," objected the principal guard, watching his master's reluctant relaxation of both shoulders. It seemed that the inquisitor had acquiesced.

"Not surrender, fool," spat the inquisitor. "I need time. Get that woman back to her cell. Feed her. Give her clean water."

Those were the words Bertha repeated to herself. Food and clean water were all she dreamed of in that moment, and behind them, the glimmer of hope for something even more amazing. Freedom.

˜

"Senora Caravidio? I am, I trust, speaking to Elonza, by birth Mistress Elonza Piero?"

The woman was small, swarthy, her shoulders hunched a little, her dark eyes small and just a little close together, seemingly aggressive. It was her feet, unusually large for her tiny size, which pattered impatient, bare and grubby on the baked earth. It seemed the glare was habitual. Naturally in Spanish, that questions sounded more like accusations. "You're no Spanish soldier, not in that strange costume. Are you a Moor? Or a Jew? How do you know my name, you a foreigner with no name given."

She stood, a little bent, in contrast to high laced neckline of the gentleman which she faced, the top of her covered head tipping the first ribbon of Charle's doublet below the neck. Her own clothes were sad, a loose brown smock over an unbleached linen shift, both hems frayed over her bare feet and the long hair sprigged toes beneath. Her hair was invisible under the white tucked covering, simply a linen cloth spread, loose at either side, and down over her forehead.

Charles did not smile although the tuck at the corner of his mouth had deepened a little. "Madam, I am a foreigner indeed. I am Lord Charles, Viscount Valdar, Marshall to His Royal Highness, King Richard of England. I trust that I have introduced myself sufficiently, senora." Only a friend already knowing Charles well, would recognise that he smiled, and that his smile was sardonic.

The woman, a few black wisps peeping now beneath her head cover, seemed somewhat startled. "So, what does a foreign nobleman want with me, then? I'll have you know I'm not for sale. I'm a decent woman, I am Elonza Caravadio and I do not speak to strangers, even when they show off their titles, and especially when they're foreigners."

"You speak of a matter I find both interesting and relevant for several reasons, madam." Charles spoke slowly, still in Spanish. "You claim to be married. Do you know the present whereabouts of this husband, madam?"

They stood facing one to the other within the tribunal chamber, where Charles had ordered the woman be brought. Although she had immediately been frightened, Elonza was equally angry. On one side, seated, but shifting and murmuring, six of the clergy sat watching. On the other side, having relinquished his podium chair, stood the inquisitor. He remained silent but also watched, barely blinking.

Now trembling but still angry, Elonza glared up at Charles but avoided the watchful eyes of the priests.

"I should not be here. I have done nothing wrong, and never have. I am a good Christian, a widow, and unless you wrongly accuse me of some sin, which is impossible since I have committed none, I demand to walk free."

"The man you claim to have married, senora? How do you know this?" It was Charles who spoke but it was the inquisitor who took a step forwards.

The woman, now staring sideways, shook her head. "I was told."

"Therefore, you also know where he died?"

Now Elonza stammered. "England, was it? I never went there. It was such a long time - ."

The knew voice interrupted. "Senora, since you have never been to England and do not speak their language, who was it who managed to inform you that Senor Diego Caravadio had remarried and then passed from this world, the Lord rest his soul?"

Now Elonza stared only at the inquisitor. Her stammer increased. "I do not remember, my lord. So long ago, you see, and a personal message. Years past, my lord."

"A total stranger, to whom you do not speak, nor understand, knew your personal address and was able to afford a personal messenger across the sea?"

She was flustered. "An old friend of mine, sir. Spanish, a neighbour, who travelled to England many years back, searched for my husband but discovered the sad truth. I cannot remember her name, Maria perhaps, sailed to England and returned after some months, and came to tell me. No messenger. No address."

"Yet, although you could not possibly know it, she knew Diego Caravadio's new English address, it seems?" Charles added.

Again Elonza trembled and seemed ready to sink to her knees. "My lord, so many years have gone by. I am not a young woman, my lord."

Charles now turned to the inquisitor. "My lord, may I suggest that this unfortunate woman be released immediately? She can give us no help, and is clearly troubled. Whoever the messenger, we cannot question her, nor prove the accuracy of such a message. There is no motive to restrain her here." He paused, gazing directly at the man standing to his right. "I have a second suggestion, my lord. It is, perhaps, a little more than merely a suggestion. It is a request, should your lordship be so inclined, to release Mistress Bertha Caravadio immediately. If no delay in her release complicates the situation, I shall take her into my care and ensure that she be well treated once entirely absolved of all cause to face this tribunal, and I will pay for a doctor to treat the wounds she has clearly, and clearly improperly, suffered. I also ask that her original clothes be returned to her."

The inquisitor sighed. "I shall need to consider this, sir."

"Then I shall wait until your considerations have been – let us say – accomplished." Charles did not move.

It was Elonza, no longer angry, who stared, terrified, and pleaded, "My lords, may I – has this – may I leave? I swear I have done nothing wrong. In the Lord's holy sight, I swear it."

Miguel de Morilio sank back to the only chair and closed his eyes. Some silent moments encouraged the priests to cluster around him, whispering. Elonza gazed from one to the other, unsure what she might do. She wanted to run. Then Charles raised one finger and turned to her.

"Madam, you are entirely free. The court here has no cause to delay you. However, may I ask you to wait for just some moments, safe and under my protection." Not having entirely understood, she hovered. Charles once more addressed the inquisitor. "My lord,

I request the immediate release of the English dowager countess now under my protection. I am waiting. She must be brought here and returned to me forthwith, with the apologies of the tribunal, and with the return of her clothes and other belongings which were in her possession when she was improperly taken by the guards."

De Morilio did not reply, but nodded to the guard at his back. His face was flushed and his fury sparked dark in his eyes. "Get her. Get whatever is hers. Bring her here."

The shuffle of sandalled feet on the tiles echoed with the faint mutter of grumbles, until, slowly the silence returned. The inquisitor turned back to Charles. "I bid you good day, sir," a brief nod, and with a swirl of black, he was gone.

Charles stood facing Elonza, who stooped, still nervous, with two guards, expressionless, remaining behind them. The huge chamber was now otherwise empty. The long minutes dragged. Where the priests had sat, now the chairs stood unused, and eventually Elonza crept to one, and after looking around as though frightened that one of the guards might arrest her, she collapsed, breathing in the waft of incense. Charles remained standing, straight backed. What he was thinking, which included words the priests might not have known but the guards certainly would have, was not evident in his face.

It was later that other guards carefully helped the released woman enter the chamber, still dressed in the frayed smock, but clutching a sack of her own belongings. Bertha seemed more terrified and perhaps confused, than relieved at the freedom she did not yet recognise.

Immediately Charles strode to her side, taking the bag of clothes from her fingers while supporting her, one arm strong beneath her own.

"My lady," he spoke quietly, "you have suffered so much, you may not be able now to recognise me." He spoke in English. "But I am here to help you in every manner possible, and to assure you that your freedom is now without argument. I will take you to your daughter, and you will stay with her in peace and comfort, well fed and with every right restored." He paused, then added, "The elderly woman now sitting close, is here simply to see you. You are free to speak with her, or not, entirely as you wish. She is the Spanish woman, Elonza, who claims to have previously married your husband. If you prefer neither to speak with her nor to see her, I shall dismiss her at once."

The slow and careful speech brought Bertha's comprehension flooding into new force. Now she turned, staring at the woman sitting before her. Her voice seemed more croak than speech but she spoke in Spanish, and loudly. "You call yourself Senora Caravadio?"

"You?" Elonza stared up, curious at first, and then abruptly afraid once more. Her small thin face was flushed. "I think I realise, and is this what I've done?"

The tiny wrinkled and poverty-stricken woman gazed up at the taller but equally wrinkled woman before her, the clothes similar in their stark destruction. Bertha's face was marked with scars and bruises, and Elonza's was not. The two women stared with growing animosity.

Then Bertha said, "You think you married my husband. You're the cause, then, of my torture in this place."

There was no possible answer as Elonza bent over in loud tears.

Charles led Bertha to a chair facing the Spanish woman. "You will need to talk with her," Charles suggested very softly, "And I should not be standing so close. I have no right to hear whatever you choose to say, my lady. I shall remain by the door, ready to lead you out to freedom and a safe return to your daughter whenever you wish. In the meantime, it may help you afterwards to know the truth, whatever that truth may be." He smiled and began to walk into the far shadows, but called back, "If you want me, my lady, remember, I am here at your command."

And so Bertha stared across at the tiny woman slumped in the opposite chair. "You knew Diego Caravadio, senorita, many many years ago, it seems. Will you tell me the truth? I won't ever repeat your words to this tribunal. Whatever you have done, I will never be the cause of another woman suffering as I did."

Elonza stared into her lap, wiping both her eyes and her nose on the sleeve of her smock. She spoke Spanish with the same accent and patois that Bertha recognised from the years with her husband.

Each continued to stare at the other, Elonza also continued to cry, although now her sobs did not distort her story.

.

CHAPTER FIFTEEN

"I knew him. He knew me. Diego." Elonza tried to speak more slowly and more softly, but her words still seemed to echo."

"You must have been -," Bertha was whispering, "young. Very young. I think Diego would have been older."

"He was some years my senior, but I don't know how much." She hiccupped and pressed one hand over her mouth. "I was just turned thirteen. My mother was sick and my father was strict. He hurt me. He used to hit my mother but he stopped when she got sick. He hit me instead. Then I met Diego. He was handsome. You know that."

"I loved him," Bertha said at once, "and I didn't care if he was handsome or not. He was wonderful."

"I thought so too," Elonza gulped. "My Papa wasn't kind but Diego was. He made me feel happy. It was such a long time since I'd been happy."

Pausing only a minute, Bertha's voice changed. "So, he took advantage of you."

The other woman nodded, but without looking up. "I never said no. I didn't think I was allowed to say no. And besides, I thought I loved him. My Mamma died, poor Maria, she died in bed and I was heartbroken but Diego helped me so much. He held me and comforted me and told me that God would look after her. Then," and she sobbed harder," he told my father that if he ever hit me again, he would tell the priest. Papa shrank back. Diego was strong and he challenged my horrid father. Then Diego gave me money. He held me close. He bought me shoes. I still have them but I dare not wear them too often, they might fall apart. And everyone in the town here walks barefoot unless they are rich and important."

Both women were barefoot, toes dark with sandy earth. Bertha's also oozed blood. She said, "I understand. I do. I'm sorry. It sounds very sad. At least Diego helped you."

"I was scared and I didn't know things, you understand, no one taught me what anything meant back then. I thought I must be expecting babies. I was very young and very ignorant and very frightened. I asked Diego if he wanted to marry me. He laughed in my face."

Bertha flinched. "You had a child?"

"No." Elonza wept more loudly but shook her head. "I had none. I still have none. Diego ran away. He left me."

"So that's when he came to England."

Again Elonza nodded between tears. "All the neighbours knew what had been happening and I thought I'd have a baby any moment. So I told folk we were wed. I said Diego went away to work, but would come back soon. Except I had no baby and Diego never came back. I said he had died, perhaps been killed. But he had been my husband so now I was a widow. I could never deny that story. Even without any babies, I had admitted to giving myself to the man I have loved. My father would have killed me if he'd ever discovered the truth. Instead, he treated me well until he died too. So for all these years, everyone here has accepted that I was legally married, happily until Diego disappeared."

For the first time she looked up, gazing, the wet tears striping her face, "I never told the Tribunal when the church got angry and began to punish us all. The church was kind, like Diego, until just a few years ago. I never said anything and just pretended to be a widow. It was an old man who lives across the street who went running to the inquisition when you said you were Diego's wife, and the man knew I was his wife as well." The woman's tears reflected the candlelight across her face, yet hid her swollen eyes. "He was a horrid man. His wife was horrid too. They liked gossip and carrying dirty stories. They loved seeing me upset. Solomino. Now I'll never speak to either of them ever, ever again." She fell, kneeling at Bertha's feet. "Forgive me lady. I never meant harm to anyone."

"So, it wasn't you who said I killed him?"

"Never." The tears now blinded her.

Bertha leaned over and took the tiny woman by her shaking shoulders. "It was Diego who was wrong." Bertha also seemed close to tears. "I found out – after we were wed – that he liked little girls. I tried to pretend I didn't know. He was wicked, but I still loved him. How can a man be wicked and kind at the same time?" She kissed Elonza's cheek, then called Charles. She now cried as well. "My lord, it's not this woman's fault. I have no money on me to give, but once I see my daughter, she'll pay you back. Can you give this poor woman some help?"

∼

From the litter, Bertha climbed slowly, staring at the long low building that Charles had told her was the barracks. Her face remained tear streaked, the bruises and cuts bright within their swellings, but the joy of freedom had wedged the smile between the scars.

"Illiana does not know you are coming," Charles told her, helping her down from the hired litter. "I'll take you to her, madam. Then I must leave."

Outside the building had seemed ramshackle, yet inside it was sturdy and comfortable. The heat beamed through the thin walls, but inner chambers remained cool, even beneath a flat wooden roof. It was neither heat nor cold that mattered anymore.

Illiana, bored, had been sitting in the dining hall for some hours, although without eating. She thought of herself, of Sabine, of Charles, and of her mother. Vaguely and without direction, her wandering thoughts of Charles seemed to dart upwards from the curves of ankle to the more strident curve of calf, past a flat knee and up to the powerful muscles of his thighs, yet his strength turned dark beneath the knitted silk hose, the unpronounced black codpiece and upwards to the doublet. This was black silk, clipped it's entire length by patterned silver clasps, overtaken by the leather baldrick and its long sheathed sword. The doublet was belted, also in dark leather, the purse tucked within. Below the belt, the hem lay flat, undecorated. Yet the silk glowed, and the sleeves were cuffed in heavy gold brocade. The small flat hat was also of gold brocade, which contrasted with Charles' rich dark hair, straight cut below the ears.

As a child, Illiana had known her father as her protector, but he had died. Difficult years had been followed by another saviour, but Benedict had also died. Now there was someone alive, kind, protective, handsome and fascinating. Her saviour. She imagined the strange thrill of – perhaps one day – saving him.

Yet the slurred and almost unwelcome visions of Charles floated into a sense of loneliness, and thus a reminder of both Sabine and her mother. She knew how dreadfully she missed Sabine. It was, largely, why she had risked travelling. And now, against her denials, she knew that she missed her mother. The stupid child wanted her angry mother to hold her again, as once long ago she had.

Then she did. It seemed not only miraculous but somehow absurd, as though her own thoughts had conjured the impossible. To the long empty table where she sat, Charles appeared, smiling, and helping beside him a woman who was at first unrecognisable. Then Illiana leapt up, her chair clattered back, and she sprang to embrace her mother as though this was fulfilling the greatest dream of her life. Her mother sobbed against Illiana's shoulder, they clung one to the other, and very quietly Charles disappeared back to the darkened doorway.

"You need wine. You need food." Illiana saw her mother's bruises, scars, wizened loose skin and the wrinkles where once there had been flesh.

The bag of belongings lay disregarded on the table. Bertha sank to the long bench while Illiana raced to the kitchen and begged for everything possible to be brought to the table. Mother and daughter sat watching each other over platters of meat and bread in milk, whipped eggs with sliced fish and roots fried within, of minced lamb held tight within pastry, and a huge jug of dark wine surrounded by cups, spoons and small knives.

Illiana drank. Bertha ate and drank. Chewing and sipping did not interrupt the talking. They talked over each other, repeated, then said it again. They hugged with their elbows resting in milk, and they told the other what had happened, what had not happened, what should have happened, and what they wished had never happened.

"It was as wicked as it looks."

"You mean the black swellings against pale skin?" Bertha reluctantly touched her wounds and winced. "It's the Holy Church in the name of the Holy Lord our Saviour. Yet it was wicked. It was cruel and I saw pleasure on the face of the brute who whipped me."

"I saw the Inquisitor myself. He always seemed blank. As if he couldn't feel a single thing, not good, not bad, not anything."

"He kept saying, '*Do it again.*' and the guard did, over and over again. Always something horrible."

Drinking heavily, Illiana sank back on her chair. "It's hideous cruelty. Our Great God preaches love, not cruelty. I pray the church in England never does any such thing. You know what we saw in Seville when we arrived. The smoke. The screams from the crowd."

"I thank every blessed saint in the Heavens above," Bertha croaked, "that it didn't happen to me. I expected it. That was what drove me mad. Whenever I closed my eyes, I watched my body crawl into flames. I smelled the smoke."

Illiana reached over and hugged her mother. "Can you tell me why? Do they just hate foreigners here? I heard the story of bigamy, but that isn't true, is it? Mamma, tell me you've never sinned."

Bertha paused, pulled roughly away from Illiana's grasp, frowning while slowly chewing on the pastry and bread. She swallowed and drank her cup dry. Then she looked up. "You think me a sinner? Tell me that you didn't, Illiana. Tell me first that you never sinned. Tell me – swear to me – that you didn't kill your ` father."

Her face already flushed with wine, Illiana felt herself bathed in guilt and flushed more deeply, yet the accusation was the shock that made her feel more sick. "I thought you said that once before, but I thought it was – well – you just being angry. Mamma, look at me. No! No, absolutely not and never ever wished to. I loved Papa and I missed him so horribly for years." Then, swallowing back bile, she said, "What makes you think such a vile thing,?"

"I thought perhaps – and I thought it was my fault because I should have warned you."

"Of what?" Illiana demanded.

Having misread the following silence, Charles had again marched close. He addressed Illiana, slightly bowing. "My lady, I trust the result now seems satisfactory. The Holy Inquisition has entirely relinquished all its accusations against the dowager countess your mother, and has accepted that it's information was irregular and untrue. There is no remaining motivation of any kind that puts your mother at risk." He then bowed to Bertha, saying, "My lady, I believe you need nourishment, considerable rest, and possibly medical attention. I have therefore requested a brief visit from the local medick often used to help the military on these premises. He has not been advised of what has happened, simply told that the lady requires some medication."

His gaze returned to Illiana. "My lady, unfortunately I must now say goodbye since I am required to return immediately to Seville, to await the arrival, officially, of his and her majesties. Both King Ferdinand and Queen Isabella are due to arrive there within the next days and I am obliged to attend them, and for specific reasons."

Now Illiana surprised herself with feelings of sudden even dismal loneliness. Abruptly, she was again alone and unprotected.

"But Nicholas?"

Charles paused. "I have informed your groom of your mother's return. He wished to come directly to welcome her safety and offer help, but I suggested he wait, allowing time for mother and daughter in privacy. No doubt he will turn up shortly. But now,"

"Seville. And then?"

"I have already delayed – and at my own wish. I shall leave within the hour. I will then await further orders, my lady." Charles nodded yet showed little emotion. "I believe you will need to remain here for some days at the least, with regard to your mother. I am assured that the Spanish military who normally reside here, will not be turning up for some time, being too busy with the Moors further south. Once you choose to leave here, should you return to Seville, I will gladly help with the further search, which I believe still needs fulfilling, regarding your friend Sabine."

Saying yes a dozen times, Illiana jumped up. "I can't leave until we know – whatever's possible. But Mamma first. If," she blushed, but this merged with the blush of wine and heat, "you're no longer needed in Seville, if you are going to sail home, I was wondering -,"

"Exactly as you wish," and the tuck at the corner of his mouth turned to smile, his eyes suddenly alight. "Either I shall find you, and stay to help as required, or you will find me still in Seville, and ready to do as you require."

Now they smiled at each other, dark eyes bright, to dark eyes brightening. Illiana was sorry as he disappeared yet again into the far shadows beyond the open doorway, but dutifully returned to Bertha. She sat opposite again, and grabbed up the wine jug, refilling both cups.

"You were saying about Papa. I like remembering him."

Now it was Bertha who blushed, merging the bruises. "Not a sweet memory, I'm afraid, but I loved him. I still do. So, I pretended, I ignored the truth." Although hard to say the words, Bertha drank, then blurted, "He liked little girls. Men have these odd desires, you know. Men have more thoughts of bed than most women or it could be the Spanish, though I'm simply making excuses. And some women as well, but that's another story and anyway, I never met one. Although it has nothing whatsoever, as nothing ever has or ever will, to do with the inquisition, but it is a sin according to the church, you know."

"More sins and Spain and churches? I don't understand. What has this to do with Papa?"

"You know because I taught you every proper thing a good girl has to know," Bertha continued, although not looking directly at her daughter. "Yes, no man can touch a girl until she has begun her bleedings. Between man and woman, of course, there must be children – or – well, just desire isn't proper. It can be called wicked. Quite a lot of priests, of course, also being men, but never mind about that. I never knew one of them either. Not everyone will ever find a man without desires, but it's procreation being the only holy motive. I have to admit that your dear Papa was not a saint in that regard."

Illiana winced. "I have a vague idea of what you might mean, Mamma, a horrible, ghastly thought. No, it can't be true and he never touched me either. I loved him and he loved me. He died of a heart failure. He worked so hard."

Bertha shook her head. "No, we all told you that it was a heart attack. You found him yourself, so that was why I thought – you and him. He died of a knife – a stab - to the heart. There was terrible blood. You didn't see that."

"Papa was lying face down. And I ran. I was so upset."

"At the Tribunal as I was given back my freedom, I spoke to the woman who had claimed to have married Diego. So, they thought I was the bigamous wife, but she admitted they had never married. She had been so young, and so ignorant, and when he hauled her off to bed, and then left her, she thought she had to pretend marriage or she herself would be the sinner."

Leaning back, Illiana felt her own tears now hot against her cheeks. She had her mother back in her arms, with an explanation of why that motherly love had failed in the past. Yet now her father was no longer the glorious saint as she remembered him. Love stayed, but shrank. She had still lost Sabine. Now she had lost Charles. Life tipped south, then up to the heavens – and then down into the abyss, the unknown and the nightmare. Illiana remembered what another woman, many weeks back, had told her – indeed, that it was like facing huge thorns from all directions. So many might stab, and anyone could be caught in the centre of total confusion.

Now it was Nicholas's arrival which brought back the smiles and laughs, each hugging the others, and the wine cups raised again.

Still drinking, still laughing, they watched the sudden change of blue sky into darkness which buried the sun and opened windows instead to the stars. It was even later as Illiana tripped, quite tipsy, back to her own little bedchamber, that she also remembered that at least she could no longer wonder if she had been illegitimate. Benedict would surely have been glad to know that. Her mother had been legally married. Yet wed to a sinner, if indeed she had correctly understood her mother's withering ramble, a seemingly kind and generous man who secretly grabbed young girls.

Bertha woke late, deep in the comfort of a genuine bed, although small, and a room which still resembled a cell, but a far warmer and more acceptable one. She also woke to a visit from the medick, who offered little help.

It was time, dancing bright and predictable, which once again brought health, and gradually Bertha's feet healed, the bruises faded, her eyes brightened and her skin softened, smooth again over rising flesh, the wrinkles disappearing as her body recovered.

She, Illiana and Nicholas often walked in the sunshine, delighted to wander the stalls, discover the fruit that grew here which they had never tasted before, and even to risk darkening their pale cheeks beneath the harsh and improper tanning of the heat. They rarely bothered to count days, and when Bertha chose to doze in the warmth, Illiana invariably rode, Nicholas beside her, exercising the horses and exploring further around the city.

They avoided Alcazar, and even a busy priest, his walking stick tapping along the lanes, would convince Illiana to turn in the opposite direction.

Some people living nearby became familiar, folk nodded, wished them a good morning, a bon dia, and overloaded donkeys would totter by with a gruff acknowledgement. Illiana often bought apples and turnips to offer the donkeys and horses she saw wilting under the sun. Discovering more interesting stalls tucked in shaded lanes, Illiana bought so much for her mother that Bertha stopped her.

Laughing, "I'm not so poor, my dear. There's no need to treat me every single moment as though it's my saint's day or the Christmas feast." Bertha did not once call her daughter stupid, foolish, ignorant or snail-witted. They often leaned together, kissed before separating for bed, wished each other blessings and golden dreams.

However, it was not until they smelled the insidious breeze blown stink of dark smoke, that they once more rushed into each other's arms.

Nicholas had waited outside the barracks with the two horses saddled and impatient, when the stench rose from the dark cloud in the distance. He shook his head. "Ladies, tisn't naught nasty. Autumn be approaching and folks is burning their rubbish from the land, farmers ready for the new ploughing. I reckon there ain't naught to fear."

Uncounted days drifted into weeks. And so, it was Septiembre, a Spanish melting of the summer heat into the more bearable balm and the lull of swelter, a mellow warmth that the more fragile English bodies adored. Then, as Illiana had hoped, Bertha woke one bright morning, sat at the long dining table awaiting breakfast, and said, "It's time to leave. I feel so much better. There's real energy hoping to crawl out beneath these clothes."

Longing to move again, to search for Sabine again, both Nicholas and Illiana now jumped up to hug Bertha.

"Tis a great new beginning," Nicholas said, filling her cup from the water jug. "I reckon we sets off tomorrow morning. I'll get the litter set up again today, and will get them kitchen folk to prepare food fer us to take with us. What does you reckon, we goes north or we goes south?"

"We return to Seville," Illiana said quickly. "I can't believe Sabine was taken so far, and if Charles is still there, he can help." She looked up at Nicholas. "That's what I think, but Nicholas, you should choose."

He frowned. "Trouble is, I've no notion, lady. My girl could be in that China Country fer all I knows, but I'd like to meet up with them Delgardos, for that's one thing I does know. T'was them as took her from her home and her family and her safety, and I want to kill every one of them. They kills me at the end? Well, I doesn't care. If my Sabs has gone to a Holy Place, then I'll join her, glad as not."

"I just can't believe she's gone – I mean really gone," Illiana said. "I keep thinking she's somewhere praying for us to come and find her."

"Then we goes to Seville," Nicholas told her.

Bertha shook her head. "The last time we were in that city, we saw the worst horrors of our lives."

It was as they left Cordoba and saw the smoke rising from the main square, that the horses became skittish, and Bertha peered from the litter.

Illiana immediately reassured her mother. "It's the time for farmers to burn old grazing, and prepare for new crops. It's the end of harvest time in England too. There's always bonfires after harvest."

The horses snorted, but Nicholas led the way to the principal road which would take them south west towards Seville. They did not enter the plaza, but they passed close, and there Illiana stopped, her eyes drawn to the smoke. This land was not rural. Did the church permit bonfires outside the cathedral, she wondered and then stopped herself. Only one kind of bonfire was encouraged by the priests here.

Not entering, but still watching, she stilled the impatient mount and stared from the lane into the light of the square beyond.

"It isn't only grass they're burning," she said. "There's the twigs and the undergrowth but there's something far worse as well."

Illiana knew her mother would be horrified, terrified, too scared to move and would never watch what she had long feared being done to herself. But again Bertha did the opposite, doing what amazed her daughter, and raced into fury. Now cured from her scabs and miseries, Bertha smelled the reek of torture, leaned from the litter's heavy curtains, and without bothering to hobble down the two steps, she jumped and began to run towards the open square.

At once Nicholas dismounted, briefly calmed every horse, tied the reigns to the gate nearby, and raced behind Bertha, grabbing her as they entered the frontage to the cathedral.

In shock, Illiana turned, turned again, then dismounted, tied her horse's reigns to the same gate, and followed her mother.

In Seville there had been crowds watching. Some had approved, cheered and waved, watching the judicial burning alive of strangers. Many in the same crowds had sobbed, covered their eyes, attempted to call for comfort, and had then slunk away.

Here there was no crowd. A small group of folk watched on one side, a smaller group on the principal side. The smaller group sobbed, men holding to the women. The other group was silent.

"Conversers," one man informed Bertha. "Made to convert to our church, but then caught transgressing. Caught cooking meat on Friday. Celebrating their own prayers, like them Jews does."

"Heresy then," the woman next to him muttered.

The man, brow deeply furrowed, spoke again. "That first fellow, I knew him. Was kind, always was. Was good to me when my wife died. He sold tiles, beautiful they was, he were a craftsman I admired."

It seemed that the woman was the sad man's daughter, and she was crying. "When Mamma passed on, God rest her soul, dear Samuel, he made a slab with her name in colours. Now he suffers for being such a nice man."

Bertha made the sign of the cross and pushed forwards. She began to hurry across the square, and both Nicholas and Illiana struggled to hold her back. She called, "I have to tell the priest. It's wrong, so wrong. They wanted to do this to me and then they found I was innocent. They kill the innocent. The innocent don't deserve that pain."

It was impossible to ignore the flames. Now too close, they were too brilliant and too aggressive. Streaming towards the smoke hazed sky, they engulfed the man caught chained and trapped within their greed. The smell was no longer of burning twigs, bark and leaf. It was the filth of death in terror, of cooking flesh and the agony suffered by the victim and his desperate family.

Behind the bursting flare of scarlet and gold, the figure of a small man was melting. The pain, at least, was over.

On the other side of the square another pyre was burning to its base and whoever had been staked there, was now a memory, and the retching reminder within the fetid fumes as thick as the smoke.

At the embers of the far stake, a woman was huddled, screaming. Her shrieks echoed. No priest came close to her although several stood watching from the steps into the cathedral. Shaking off both Nicholas's tentative grasp and her daughter's grip, Bertha ran to the woman, knelt beside her, and pulled her close. The woman's tears soaked Bertha's grand saffron silk gown. Now both women, wrapped together, hid their faces in the other's neck.

Behind them, Illiana stooped. "It is wickedness. I cannot understand such wicked cruelty, but you are both at risk. Please come away."

The other woman grabbed at Illiana's knees and Bertha stood, angry. "Don't stop me child. Someone must have the courage to tell the church they are wrong. The Lord God preaches love."

Now Illiana and the other woman both lunged, Illiana to her mother's shoulders and the other woman to her ankles. Bertha stumbled and stopped. "They believe they are right," the woman croaked, her voice almost lost in the crackle and hiss of the last sparks amongst the dying flames. "I begged them. I promised money. I swore to convert. They say your God wants to punish sin, then take the dead to live in the clouds. I don't understand."

"It's wrong," Bertha screamed.

"Mamma, they believe they have the Pope's blessing. The king and the queen give their permission. You want to be arrested again? They will, I promise they will if you run to them."

As the two stakes tumbled and the fires became embers, Nicholas and Illiana carried Bertha back to the litter, and Illiana climbed in with her. They did not see what happened to the dead man's wife, nor the other family watching their father's hideous departure.

CHAPTER SIXTEEN

Seville flaunted its autumn beauty beneath the sun, and no smoke, no reek of torture nor the sound of murder spoiled the dancing breezes.

The journey from Cordoba and its last horror, and then the escape back to Seville, had been slow by choice. Along the way, much of the scenery was so beautiful, they stayed wherever was convenient, adored the food, and relaxed in the sweet warmth.

Where the country was ragged and as dry as a desert, they kept riding until they came to a village more welcoming. Mosquitoes still rose avid from the streams, but the women were well enough covered to avoid attack, and Nicholas simply brushed the buzzing insects aside since it seemed his skin was too tough to penetrate.

Cicadas called so loudly in the long evenings that Illiana could not hear her mother talk, and laughed, asking her to shout over the background chitter. Birds continued to sing, eating their way into autumn, lunging towards mosquitoes, midges and fireflies, but the butterflies were waning and they passed some trees where leaves were losing their lush green youth. The sun still blazed, yet small white clouds hovered ready to quieten the approach to winter.

Entering the city at first Bertha feared the stink of burning bodies, but instead the air was fresh and welcoming, and the square was full of chattering folk, no smoke nor flame, and only cheerful friendship. Illiana, Bertha and Nicholas had little knowledge of what else was happening in the Spanish south, nor of the Inquisition, and not even of Charles and the troop of English men, sent on a mission still never entirely explained.

"Charles said they'd make camp above the port," nodded Illiana. "But that was so long ago, we might have to search."

"I reckon I should admit," Nicholas admitted, "how I hopes how he ain't left yet. I bin thinking on the way down here as how he'll be the best to know about them Delgardos, and where we gotta go now for my little girl."

Nodding, Illiana agreed with him. She did not admit that she had another reason, a reason as yet pale and tentative, to hope that Charles had not yet returned to England.

From the saddle, she looked across at Nicholas. "Do we aim for the port first? Ride around the entire city borders looking for camps? Or first find ourselves a place to sleep? I don't suppose we can stay at a military camp, even if we find it."

"Tisn't likely," Nicholas said, turning to the rumble of the horse drawn litter clattering behind them. "Being as how sick was yer Ma, best put her somewhere mighty comfy."

"Where we stayed before, then," Illiana suggested. "Too near the square perhaps, but it was very comfortable there. I loved it until – well, you know, but Seville isn't full of taverns and inns the way London is."

"Then I reckon we goes there now," Nicholas said, "and leave yer Ma in peace whilst we goes looking fer the camp."

"If the camp still exists," Illiana agreed, "everyone will know where it is. It must be big enough and unusual enough for everyone to see."

"If they ever leaves their houses," nodded Nicholas, "cos I

reckons there be most matrons what never go out at all lest they ain't got no husbands nor sons to do the shopping."

"It seems," Illiana sniffed, "that respectable ladies, and sometimes even the peasant women won't be seen in the markets. Whether they refuse, or their husbands stop them, I can't know. I thought we were all too modest in London but they're far worse here, and the men just sit on their doorsteps chatting to the men next door and even more men sitting on the doorsteps opposite."

"Only when the sun shrinks, they does," Nicholas pointed. "No fool sits outside when the heat burns worse than fires."

"Is it the real fires everyone is frightened of?" Illiana muttered. "Or just the sun? I like to see the men talking and chortling. When the whole of a village is so empty and silent, it's scary."

"Tis the trouble o' travelling to them foreign countries," Nicholas agreed. "Best stay home and see what you knows you're gonna see."

"It sounds horribly chaotic at home too," Illiana sighed. "Since the king died and the Woodvilles went wild."

"With luck, and with my daughter aside us, reckon when we gets home," Nicholas muttered, "t'will all be over and home will be home."

The folk on their doorsteps made it easier for Illiana to ask about a small military camp of foreigners wearing black and gold livery, somewhere on the outskirts of the city. After five fingers pointed in the same direction, they were confident that the camp still existed.

Paying once more for the hostel rooms which they had occupied some months before, was easy enough, since all remained vacant. It seemed that visitors from afar were avoiding the threat of new feverish church activity.

Stiff and sore backed after miles in a bumpy litter, Bertha needed help both from the litter's steps and into the hotel, then up the stairs and into the bedchamber assigned to her. The wide bed, uncurtained, lay snug and waiting, clean sheeted and cool beneath the shuttered window. Thanking them, Bertha lay down. The jug of water sat on the little table and within reach. Illiana kissed her cheek.

"Sleep, Mamma. Nicholas will ride with me as we go to find Charles and start the search for Sabine. If you get too hot or too cold, if you get hungry or want some wine, just ring that bell. It sounds downstairs and you'll get good service I think. We did last time."

"I'll sleep," Bertha sighed. "That's all I need."

After hours in the saddle, Illiana could have slept as well, but the turgid excitement, although she denied it, of seeing Charles again and the camp of laughing men, was a more attractive contemplation. She remounted, and with Nicholas riding at her side, they encircled the city, riding south, to where they believed the camp should be.

Tents stretched across the open scrub just beyond the reach of the city before the sea swallowed the land. A slight wind had swept in from the sea, although no tide threatened the port. The flagged tips of the dark blue canopies, and the openings into each shelter flapped and slapped against the hemp and flaxen canvas, but the men were out, lazing beneath the last warmth of the sun before twilight.

A cooking fire, central to the camp, sizzled with perfumes of bark and undergrowth, smells of apple, ceder, pine, and a mixture of everything which had been cooking. The smoke drifting up into the sky's orange tinge of sunset, was colourless yet aromatic. This was no fire set to stink of murder.

The men, lying stretched, others sitting, half dreaming, were grouped around the high dazzling sparkle of the flames. Many talked, many laughed, many lay quiet staring up as the sky's colours drifted into royal purple, gold and scarlet. One man snored.

Dismounting quickly, Illiana recognised Charles. He lay on his back, but was not the one snoring. His dark eyes were open and reflected the first glints of the stars as they gathered like tiny lit candles in the deepening blackness above.

Once she had dismounted, leaving Nicholas to tether the horses, and walked softly across to the singing heat, Charles neither moved nor altered the direction of his eyes, but he said softly, "The Lady of Birstall joins us. How are you feeling now, little one?"

Surprised, Illiana stopped, hesitating, then smiled. The rising twists of the fire's sparks and the increasing night's closure, was mesmerising, but she thought Charles' words were echoing the blur. He was drunk.

"Yes, I'm here, my lord. My mother has recovered. Now she's asleep. I want to make plans for finding my friend."

"We can talk in the morning," Charles said, slowly slurred again, but softly sweet. "My men have had little rest today and I doubt you have, crossing hill and valley both. Perhaps I could tell you that my tent is large enough for two."

Illiana paused. She hoped Charles had not heard her gulp. He was pissed, after all, and so she could forgive him. "I simply wanted to be sure to find you, my lord. Then I'll return with Nicholas to the alojamiento."

"Stay here instead," breathed the murmur under the rising moon. "I'll escort you back to your mother in the morning."

She suppressed the giggle. "You know I won't do that." And to keep her respectable distance, she said softly, "So no, my lord."

"I'm not your lord," he replied. "At least, not yet. Do you not desire a gentle night of sweet dreaming, little one?"

She stepped back. Illiana heard her mind whisper to her that she should agree. Her voice obeyed a different thought. "Hush. You know I can't, Charles, and when you wake sober in the morning, you'll be shocked at yourself for what you remember."

He did not look around but, lying still, he shook his head, the dust pale amongst his dark hair. "Not at all, my dear. I shall laugh at myself, unless indeed I wake with your body's perfume wrapped in my arms."

Now she almost also laughed at herself. "I smell of sweat and horse hair and hot earth."

"It's a smell I love. No doubt that's how I pass each day. And night." His whisper was as warm as the singed earth beneath him.

"Of course not." Yet the intoxicated mumble had been so deliciously unexpected, and Illiana now knew exactly what she would dream of that might. "However, if you come to the hotel in the morning, then I'll be so glad to see you. Now, sleep well, sir."

His drifting last words echoed her own as she moved away. "I would sleep better, little one, with your cheek against my naked shoulder, and your hand against my thigh."

Illiana walked back to Nicholas and the horses, where they waited further from the fire, too far, she hoped, for him to have heard Charles and his tipsy invitation into seduction. As she remounted, she looked across to where Charles still lay, silhouetted like a fallen statue against the crimson flare of flame and the rising, softly spiralling smoke. With his legs outstretched, she saw the length, the muscled thighs and the strength of them, almost seeing them in her own bed and without their dark silken cover. Quickly blinking, she snapped her mind shut.

Then she pulled on one rein, turned the horse, and followed Nicholas back towards the city. The sky hung in moon glow now, centred by silver shimmer, and a sense of excitement with magical possibilities. For the first mile, she could still smell the waft of the scented but dying flames, the heady pungency of burning ceder, and heard the faint crackle of fire turning to ember.

Back in the hotel and in her own allotted bedchamber, and within the cool toss of sheet on mattress, Illiana dreamed of the words that now haunted her, and, although ashamed, welcomed the redolence of the seduction, almost as though having accepted it. Or having, at least, wanted to accept it.

With a moment's reminder of the husband she had missed for

so long, now she imagined the touch of her finger tips against the curve of a man's belly, the tight hardness of his nipples and the caress of that man's fingertips exploring her own nakedness. Yet it was not Bendict's body, nor his fingers.

She woke with a dreaming smile and the echo of Charles' face hovering beside her. Immediately she pushed back her hair, shook her head, and sat up, dreams denied. She dressed, hurried down the stairs to the breakfast parlour, and stumbled into the girl holding the tray of eggs beaten into cakes, and jugs of milk, wine and water.

Charles, with no indication of any headache, sat at the table where Nicholas already sat, eating and grinning, mouth full.

Illiana hesitated, apologised to the waitress, who curtsied without spilling the tray, and watched as Charles raised his cup to her. Clearly, he was drinking neither milk nor water, and the wine dripped a little over the wooden brim. "Good morning, my lady," he greeted her, both the smile and the mouthful of breakfast quite obvious.

Where the sheen of his dark hair had, last night, reflected the silver moonlight, now it reflected the golden flare of the candle beside is platter.

Carefully without showing any risk of embarrassment, Illiana nodded, "I had hoped you would come, my lord. So now we ignore the inquisition and instead search for the Delgardos."

His reply did not help, as Charles said, "Last night, my dear, instead of agreeing to my heartfelt suggestions, you simply wished me to speak with you today. I am come as you asked, naturally."

She hoped she wasn't blushing. "My mother sleeps late now, but when she's ready, we can leave. Meanwhile, I'm hoping you have some ideas."

"A large number of them," Charles smiled.

Ignoring Nicholas, although she wondered what the hell he was busy guessing, Illiana stared into the shadowed tunnels of those heavy lidded eyes. "My lord Charles," she said, sitting herself on the chair opposite, "You clearly know that I heard your inebriated remarks last evening, and have decided to make a joke of them. I understand the justice. However, I am far more interested in discovering where my friend Sabine has been hidden, and I'd like to discuss that and ignore the other discussion, which most definitely requires forgetting."

Without blinking nor bothering to disguise the tuck which had deepened at the corner of his mouth, Charles replied with a nod, then spoke. "My dear Illiana, I forget very little, and am instead enjoying the relief of my own work virtually completed. I shall now gladly concentrate on the discovery of your friend, now I understand she's also the daughter of your friend Nicholas beside me. I myself have a particular interest in discovering the vile Delgardo games. I would cheerfully set about destroying that family and rescuing whoever has been abducted by them.".

"You says you went to the valley," Nicholas now felt safe to speak, "what you said was their village. There was none o' them, and seeming naught else. Not my little girl."

"I doubt they keep abducted slaves so close to their own homes," Charles said at once. "And they're invariably off travelling and indulging their crimes. I know where I would begin to search, and not so far from here."

"By the Port?" Illiana interrupted. "That's what I thought. If they sailed off, they'd leave her somewhere close by."

"You echo my thoughts, madam." Charles nodded, as though in congratulation.

Illiana said at once, "Or you echo mine, sir."

He raised a hand as though in surrender. "I have two suggestions. One is to begin asking, questions at the larger homes where a slave girl might be taken in. I would then suggest that you accompany me, should I have no success in those first days. Together we shall seem, I might say, more official, or even parental.

Finally, should all else fail, I would suggest a genuinely more official task, being to speak with the Spanish king, and his wife. They have both taken up residence in Seville. I spoke with them recently, the final task on my list of duties here since the beginning of the Holy inquisition."

"I don't think it's holy at all," Illiana scowled.

"Since it was their majesties who directly asked His Holiness the Pope to instigate the church's legislation," Charles continued, "those are not the sentiments you should ever state in the royal presence. Besides," and his smile softened, "you need their compliance. We are not in a position to begin a battle. Nor would the new English king defend us."

Nicholas and Illiana spoke together. "We have a new king at home?"

"You told me that his highness had died, God rest his soul," Illiana mumbled, "so the young prince had been crowned at the Abbey?"

"Not exactly," said Charles softly, "but that is quite a different story. In the meantime, destroying the Delgardos and discovering your friend are the tasks which matter." He was refilling his cup, and without asking, also refilled hers. "I intend starting the business within the hour. I imagine you will need to speak with your mother. However, on my return, whether with answer, or with the silence of well accustomed failure, I shall immediately tell you which."

"You want to start alone?" She lifted her brimming cup.

"A man alone may discover the secrets which no one would admit to a woman."

"Alright," She knew the sense of it. "But Nicholas could go with you."

Nicholas was leaning over, his empty cup and platter no longer of interest, he felt himself too involved to stay quiet. "I knows I might be too eager," he told Charles. "I might spoil them questions, you might say, but reckon I can stand back with the horses, and swear not to say a word lest you calls to me"

They left together as Illiana climbed the hotel stairs to her mother's small bedchamber.

CHAPTER SEVENTEEN

"I'll not deal with them bastards," the first man said, slamming his door immediately.

"Now that," Charles told Nicholas, remounting, "is the most difficult of responses, since it could mean truth, or a disguise of the opposite."

Yet the response was repeated and then repeated many times. Whether with hatred for the Delgardos, or because of secret attachment, this was a reply with which Charles soon became familiar. Once, when a somewhat deaf and elderly peasant opened his door, Charles sighed and answered for him.

It was a small consolation for Nicholas when Charles told him, "You see the Delgardo fame, if you call it fame. Notoriety, perhaps. But we are some considerable distance from the Degardo village, and from Granada, the place where most of their vile trade would be practised. Yet in such a situation, we know everything is possible."

"But not probable," Nicholas sighed.

"Probabilities are hard to qualify," Charles nodded. "Yet I would guess that the pirates would have no reason to dock here, nor anywhere along the river. I would assume Cadiz as the more likely port."

After almost three days had passed, Illiana even admitted to herself that she hoped constant failure would mean that the following day would bring Charles back to her side, suggesting they start again together. This time the magic wand worked.

Bertha, belligerent concerning Spain in general, tired of the heat and expecting shortly to complain of the cold, sat in her own room, munching on a cold supper of gazpacho which included a couple of moscas. Illiana sat on the floor, leaning back against the dipping side of the mattress, her eyes closed. Having finished her soup and the flavourless cocido, she now waited until she might claim to be tired and creep off to her own bed. It was as she was deciding never to return to that hotel again, or better still, simply to sleep all day and night in future, when Nicholas knocked on the door.

"My lady, is you in there?"

Both Bertha and Illiana admitted to it.

It was Charles who pushed open the door and stood in the pale diminishing light of the doorway. "A situation which I consider unjust, and an account of my own utter uninteresting failure are both due for explanation." He leaned against the lintel, watching Illiana but speaking to both women. "Which, I wonder, would you like first?"

"Please come in, both of you," Illiana, abruptly awake, hopped up and ran to open the door. Bertha continued to slurp her soup.

"In which case," Charles said, leaning back against the door lintel, "I shall answer both together."

He removed his hat and brushed back his hair. "During my last dreary and pointless wanderings from door to door of any home I considered might house an owner with either brain or knowledge, unlikely as it seemed, one woman, narrow eyed, asked me if I was attached to the business of the inquisition. Gossip spreads and this woman's brother is evidently resident in Cordoba. She informed me of something that troubles me. I told her that I did not condone many of those beliefs, and that I was English, but looking for the Delgardo gang. She told me of something else. I considered that particular something else to be distinctly disturbing. I therefore, with your faithful friend here as aid, rode immediately to the cathedral, visible from your window."

Since it remained shuttered, Charles merely waved one disinterested hand. "The story was troubling and I have made my opinion known to the bishop, without, unfortunately, the slightest expectation of being heard. I am not Spanish but the woman now under arrest, is."

Illiana, now sitting beside her mother on the bed, mumbled, "The suspense,"

Bertha looked up and said, "Elonza. It's her you speak of, isn't it. Referred by the same man who originally declared me adulterous in marrying a bigamous husband."

"Accurate, as always, Madam," Charles nodded. "She is being held back in Cordoba, and my suggestion is this." He now looked directly at Illiana. "I believe that you and I, my lady, should officially visit their majesties, at present comfy in their new palace here in Seville. The Alcazar is perhaps three breaths away, so you'll not be exhausted on arrival, and Isabella and Ferdinand, royalty sublime, have tidied it up somewhat, just for themselves."

Illiana wondered if Charles was ever entirely serious beneath the cold gaze. She said, "Yes, I would. I mean, of course I'll come, but it's not going to help find Sabine."

"Helping someone," said Charles without any noticeable smile, "is better than helping nobody."

She sniffed, as though admonished. "Yes, of course, but I'll have to change first."

There was still no noticeable smile but the tuck at the corner of his mouth seemed more tightly ingrained. "Since I believe you are only wearing your shift beneath your bed robe, my admirable lady, I would imagine so." He bowed. "I shall wait outside."

For a moment she wanted to tell him to go and wait in London's Tower, but instead she swept past him, hurried into her own bedchamber, and struggled to find something sufficiently grand to wear while addressing a queen and her king.

Bertha had followed her and was muttering. "That little woman may not be a saint, Illiana, but I do feel sorry for her. She never intended me to get pulled in. All she did, first as a simple child, was lie about being legally married in order to protect herself from the gossip and insults of the village. It was the man who lived on the other side of the road, he knew her and her past, but how did he know me? I'd only just arrived and I wasn't even in Cordoba yet. She needs rescuing and he needs arresting." She paused, stared at the rich green robe in Illiana's arms, and said, "Not that one, my dear. It's too tight."

At which she turned and flounced back to her own room.

Illiana dropped the green gown and flopped onto the bed. It was some time before she was satisfied with how she looked. Nor was there the aid of a mirror in her bedchamber nor elsewhere that she knew of in the hotel.

The Alcazar screamed beauty in its mixture of religious adoration, both as the Christian palace, which it now was, and as the glorious Moorish temple which it had originally been. There had been many changes but the wonder remained in both.

Charles, followed by five of his men, entered the great gardens, Illiana at his side. The sky was grey and a tinge of drizzle hung low, but the beauty shone its own sunshine. The great doors opened and Illiana followed Charles inside into the abrupt darkness. Then more doors were opened and the brightness returned.

They entered a huge and palatial room, its ceiling of marble so high and so pillared but reflecting the rich colours of the floor tiles in the hundred candle flames. They were expected, but neither sovereign was yet present. Two chairs, padded and golden tipped, sat facing the empty thrones, and here Illiana sat, but Charles stood behind his chair, leaning forward onto its high sculptured back. The five liveried men of the troop stood further back. They had left their weapons with the Spanish guards, but remained on guard themselves.

Charles also wore his livery and the black silk and gold thread glimmered even more deliciously in the flare of the lights.

In her own favourite gown of pure white, embroidered neck, hem and wide sleeves in silver flowers, Illiana felt hopeful and wished herself as grand as her companion. Her own dark hair was pearl pinned in a curled crown with only two tiny curls loose at her ears. Under the wide white and silver sleeves, the tight under sleeves were black satin. So was the drift of underskirt showing a tiny sliver beneath the elaborate white and silver hem. The neck line was far lower than she normally permitted herself and she tried very hard to forget this.

As Illiana wished she might feel and look more regal, Charles was wishing they sat in private together, where he might behave in an entirely different manner. Yet both remained still, and waited. It was approaching a delay of one hour when finally, the opposite doors swung wide, and the queen entered, her husband behind her. They both glittered more than the hundred candles, and the vast layers of their jewellery shone more beautifully than the sculptures, the maze of tiles and the golden thrones.

Charles immediately walked forwards and bowed elaborately, Illiana stood in a rush, eyes squinting in the luminescence, and curtsied, having practised many times. She then sat and Charles remained standing.

"Your almighty, glorious and gracious majesties," he said, without any sign of either awe, or subjection, apart from the low bow, "I am, as I stand before you, the humble lord marshal to his highness King Richard of England, and I am here only to represent his wishes and obey his orders, as before."

It was Queen Isabella, small and plain, who answered. She rattled as she leaned forwards and the rubies, diamonds, pearls and golden strings chimed as she moved.

"Sir, we do not forget the past so easily. We are perfectly aware of who you are and who you represent, and have not yet forgotten the long discussion we shared on your initial visit here only one week and one day past."

"So, what now, sir?" demanded the king, deep voiced.

It was doubtful that anyone present noticed the deepening tuck at the corner of Charles' lips. His hands were clasped behind his back but he nodded. "I am flattered that you remember my first visit, your majesties," he said. "However, the reason I come today is a matter entirely new, involving the lady, Countess Birstall, who now sits beside me. May we explain, your majesties?"

Both nodded. The king yawned. The small flat faced queen behaved somewhat more regally. Charles gazed down at Illiana and nodded.

She was prepared, and stood, curtsying a second time from nervous reaction. "Your gracious majesties, I believe you are aware that my mother was recently arrested by the Holy Inquisition for the sin of being married to a bigamist. She was recently released on his lordship's, the marshal's, request since the accusation was shown to be entirely untrue. However, we are now informed that the woman of Cordoba, who originally thought herself married to my father before he travelled to England, has been arrested by the same branch of the Holy Inquisition in Cordoba, for the sin of fornication before marriage. However, she imagined herself wedded, and is entirely innocent of all except ignorance. She is quite saintly and has both dressed and acted as a widow for almost her entire life. I now beg your majesties to intercede on her behalf."

Clearly this was a surprise to both Isabella and Ferdinand, now both leaning forwards.

The king said abruptly, "We do not interfere in matters of the church, my lady. The Holy Inquisition now in action in Cordoba is under Papal authority and acts as our Holy Lord God demands."

"Our Holy Lord God makes no mistakes," Charles said without bowing. "Yet mistakes have been made by the Inquisitor, Miguel de Morillo, and this even he cannot deny. I do not come today to beg for your royal judgement in this case which has never been properly presented to you, does not concern you and surely does not interest you. I simply ask that you award me specific written and royally sealed permission to attend the tribunal, and speak on behalf of whoever I believe should receive justice."

King Ferdinand shouted. "Such a royal prerogative would give the impression - ,"

The queen added, "Most definitely not, my lord. The woman you speak of, is clearly not English and I will not enter into any judgement concerning the Holy Spanish Inquisition."

"Nor do I ask that," Charles said softly. "Kindly reconsider, majesties. Remembering, perhaps, who I represent. Allies, I believe, would prefer not to make battles concerning disagreements of no importance whatsoever."

"But," the king stood, angry, and summoned his guard.

"I think - ," the queen, although she was glaring and seemed equally furious, was careful to speak with civility, "what you ask, my lord, is a royal intercedence without precedence, and without the smallest motive."

"I do not ask your royal majesties to intercede on behalf of the accused," Charles continued, chin raised but without any expression of anger, "the action I ask of your majesties, is for myself, as representative of English royalty. This regards my right to speak. It does not in any manner reflect on the rights of the Holy Inquisition. It reflects only on the rights of King Richard of England, your official ally."

"Yet during a case of which we know nothing and do not wish to know anything," Ferdinand protested "Although it would appear," and he leaned forward, his eyes threatening, "that since this heretical suspect is purely a citizen born within our jurisdiction, it is you, sir, who have no rights within the case."

Charles spoke without smile or frown. "Except that accusation against her, your grace, comes directly from the case against the Lady Bertha, of English birth and citizenship. A case in which the lady was proven entirely innocent."

The king snorted. "You elaborate too far, sir," he told Charles, and turned away.

The guards stood close, hands to their sword hilts. Charles, however, ignored them entirely. His own sword holder was empty and there was no hilt to hold. This did not appear to be his priority. "Your majesty, I ask you to consider a somewhat different, and as yet non-existent possibility, and I ask what you might feel inclined to say in such a situation. For instance, should his Royal Majesty, King Richard of all England and its dominions, and should he request a moment to speak during a meeting of the Holy Inquisition in Cordoba, would you deny him this request?"

"Ludicrous," muttered the king.

Queen Isabella raised one hand, palm outwards. "The situation you describe, sir, is not only absurd, but the provenance under the sovereignty of his majesty King Richard of England, has never yet instigated the power of the Holy Inquisition."

Now Charles smiled. "Very true, your majesty. What I suggested was not a probability, simply a consideration of what your highnesses would say should such a remote possibility occur."

"Naturally," the king snorted, "the case under review would be entirely different, and his majesty would be our guest. We would comply with any innocent request from our royal friend and ally."

The false smile spread beneath the cold stare. "Then I thank you, your majesty. It seems you have complied with my own request." And Charles bowed, as though in gratitude. Still facing the great thrones which now appeared to vibrate with the vehemence of royal incandescence, he began to pace backwards, taking Illiana's arm.

King Ferdinand roared. "You are not such a fool, sir, and know full well that no such compliance has been offered you. Return at once, or I shall be forced to order your arrest."

Pausing, Charles bowed but with only a slight bend of the head. "On the contrary, your majesty. Since I represent King Richard of England himself, and on his orders, your reactions to my humble self, shall be as to my lord and master. Nor do I imagine you would threaten the English king with arrest. Indeed, I am now puzzled, your majesty."

Illiana, stolidly unmoving, had been warned of this exact probability by Charles in his initial discussion with her, and so managed to keep her terror invisible.

The queen spluttered. "Your manipulations are unfounded, sir. We have made no such acceptance.'

'Yet," Charles spoke more softly again, "I have presented my written authorisation, the signature and royal seal for thorough examination, your highness. Your gracious majesties have both, on the previous occasion of our meeting, officially authorised the thorough examination of these declarations, and accepted them, also officially, as entirely authentic and therefore the outstanding and irrefutable proof that I am, symbolically, the figure of his majesty, king of all English dominions."

Charles paused, though not sufficient to encourage any reply. He then said, the smile in place again, "Thus, your majesties, you have appeared to accept the right of English royalty to be present and to speak during one deliberation of the Holy Tribunal as it sits in judgement during one specific trial. This does not include any royal prerogative on the judgement itself, only the right to speak, and to be attended during that speech. Should the final judgement rule against whatever I might say, this approval would give me no right to complain. I cannot believe you would deny this simple authority, your majesties."

Isabella stood, her small flat face inflamed, but for the first time the king abruptly stood, stamped irritably, and over-ruled his angry wife.

"I endorse this," he roared. "But only as the right to speak without any further inference involved, and in the parchment I shall sign, this shall be made clear. The final judgement is the business only and utterly of the Holy Inquisition and the inquisitor it endorses." He sat so defiantly that the landing of his royal seat upon the cushioned royal seat, resounded throughout the great chamber.

Both Spanish sovereigns, velvet, silk, golden thread and abundant severely aflame, stood with elaborate royalty and without any further acknowledgement, marched from the candlelit finery.

Once they had completely disappeared, the great doors crashing behind them, their chief guard stood before Charles, and bowed with a perfunctory stoop. "Your lordship and ladyship, you have their gracious majesties permission to leave."

It was back in the shadowed corridor when Illiana, noticeably trembling, stuttered towards Charles, then changed her mind. Finally, she said, "You still haven't explained why England has a King Richard and not a young King Edward."

With a sudden glint, Charles' smile seemed to rebirth as genuine. He said, low voiced, "Well, little one, that's something I promise to explain sometime very soon. Meanwhile, before these flustered religious monarchs have time to readjust their agreement, we must return, you, my dear lady, to the hotel, and myself to the camp where I expect the royal scroll to be delivered very soon. In the morning, I intend taking half the troop and return to Cordoba. I would suggest that while I am gone, you and your groom Nicholas begin to patrol the streets where any householder might possibly have seen your friend Sabine taken forcefully from the port by the Delgardo gang." He paused while Illiana absorbed the idea, but then added, "Not that I'd suggest you wear the same gown, my dear. It is, incidentally, quite beautiful and you outshone her majesty. I must humbly admit my considerable approval for that glorious gown," his smile inched wider, "and for the delicious lack of it."

Blushing, at first confused, Illiana remembered and blinked downwards at her low neckline and the half finger-length tuck of rising cleavage exposed. Her blush outshone the shadows but she said nothing. The troop of liveried men behind her were too close, and the Spanish guards strode immediately before them.

Once deposited at the hotel, Charles briefly promised to see her in the morning before he rode to Cordoba, and Illiana stood, still blushing, without having had a moment's opportunity to tell him never to speak to her like that again. Having thought it over, she decided he had not been sufficiently explicit. She would ignore the entire nonsense, as though she had not understood.

She was still blushing as she bumped into her mother coming down the stairs as she climbed up.

"Humph," said Bertha, noticing both blush and neckline. "You'll want to change first, I'm sure. Then I'll meet you in the breakfast room. Yes, yes, not for breakfast, but it's quiet there. I want to hear what happened."

Packing away her favourite gown, which she had only ever worn twice, and only previously with a high necked lacey shift that she had not brought with her, Illiana quickly changed and hurried back downstairs.

"Where's Nicholas? I should tell him too."

"Out exercising the horses,' Bertha said. "Now, I need to hear the good parts first."

The jug of wine was encouraging. Illiana sighed, stretched and poured the wine into the two awaiting pewter tankards. "Charles has royal permission to go and save Elonza. We'd only complicate matters if we went, so off he goes to Cordoba in the morning with his men. Meanwhile, we stay in Seville and carry on searching for

Sabine. That's you, Nicholas and me. Charles will probably be gone ages." She bit her lip. "I don't know actually. More than a week I suppose. Could be three. So, we pay a fortune in these rented rooms, hope they don't do anything horrible to anyone in that Plaza with no clouds of smoke, and we enjoy ourselves finding the disgusting Delgardos."

Bertha drank her wine and grabbed the jug, pouring the remaining dribbles into her own cup. "And, hope that vile gang doesn't find us first. Remember my dear, we search for Sabine, not for a family of criminals."

"Same thing." Illiana regarded her now empty cup next to the empty jug. "Sadly I can't believe we'll find her here. I think we lost her back in the Alhambra and all the Moorish towns, but we can't be sure of anything and I'm not stopping. We can afford it, and there's good markets here, and beautiful clothes and we have good horses, with the best groom in the world."

Bertha drained her cup. "Go and order more wine," she smiled, "there's a good girl."

It was at the same table in the same breakfast room, but early the following morning, when Charles strode to where Illiana, Bertha and Nicholas now sat. He faced Illiana but spoke to them all.

"We leave within the hour. If we succeed in freeing the woman Elonza, we shall either return her to her own home in Cordoba, or bring her here if her home has been sold off, which happens frequently on church authority, I'm told. I expect to be away for twenty days or more. Naturally I wish you considerable success regarding your own, objectives."

It was Bertha who leaned forwards, offering him her brimming cup of wine. "I'd prefer her not brought here," she said softly. "But success is more important, and you'll do as you must, my lord. I thank you most sincerely for giving such amazing help."

Charles smiled openly and shook his head at the wine. "I've

drunk sufficient over last night and this morning, although I thank you, my lady. I was thinking of other matters at the time." His smile grew and his eyes shifted to Illiana. "Other matters indeed, and particularly pleasant ones I should add. I should also admit that I have my own motives for everything I choose to do, and altruism is rarely my only reason."

She watched him leave. He pushed between the other two tables, both of which were entirely empty, but at the doorway he turned, grinned, bowed, twisted and disappeared into the shadows of the corridor. "Everyone leaves," she whispered to her stale bread and the small bowl of olive oil, her breakfast.

Bertha raised an eyebrow yet resisted telling her daughter how stupidly she was behaving. "That gentleman is on royal orders, so he could please himself and sail off home, but now he's off to help us. Well, for justice, rather than just us. You can hardly criticise the poor man."

"Not him. I was simply missing Benedict," lied Illiana.

CHAPTER EIGHTEEN

"Mamma, I think we've tried almost every house in Seville."

"Twice for those wretched stone boxes near the port."

"At least we're not in England," Illiana said, the blanket over her mouth although this did not stop her yawning. "It would be freezing and wet. Here it's sort of shiny with sun half the time."

"It rained yesterday," Bertha pointed out. "Which is good for the amazing fruit they have growing here."

Illiana yawned again. "I'm just bored, I admit it. I really, really, really hope we can find Sabine. That's all we came for, and look what's happened. I can't believe this inquisition. Well, of course I can, and you know best of all, but can our church be so cruel?"

"Not our church," said Bertha briskly. "It may rain in England but the church preaches love." She sat beside the window, shutters down, watching the return of the hotel's two assistant chefs, weighted with baskets from the market. "And we have more to do here, my child, than we would at home."

"It's Sunday tomorrow. I won't go to this church."

"I'm going to tell you a story," Bertha turned abruptly, smiling at her daughter. "Not one I've ever wished to tell you before, but I've changed my mind about a lot of things."

"The Bible preaching kindness?" Illiana guessed, still bored.

"Not in the least," frowned Bertha.

"Alright, the Bible teaching the inquisition?"

"Stupid girl," Bertha sniffed, a remark that Illiana had fully expected. She had not, however, expected what came next. "You grew up without any grandparents, nor aunts nor uncles. No cousins. Well, on your father's side, that was only reasonable. Whoever existed, and I'm not at all sure myself, they were in Spain and Diego never spoke of them." Looking down, flush faced, Bertha sighed, then sniffed. "If that pathetic woman Elonza actually turns up here, then I'll ask her. She must know Diego's family."

"An interesting thought." Equally boring, Illiana thought to herself, since they would surely be the sort of folk she'd already met in the poor little winding lanes of Cordoba.

"What I never told you," Bertha now sat on the one comfy chair, facing her daughter, "was anything concerning my own family. Both my parents were still alive, and I had a brother I thought very dull, and three sisters I loved."

Illiana sat up. "So why - ?"

"I had two reasons for never telling you, my dear, and I deeply apologise for both. The first reason, a confession and I'm so sorry, I was angry with you when darling Diego died. Now you know he was killed. Two knife stabs. I assumed it was you. That was more because I secretly distrusted Diego, but it was you I blamed. Yes, you know a little about this already. Thank the Good Lord, who would never agree with this inquisition, now I know, I am quite, quite sure, this was never your wickedness. For me to have thought it was you – my own stupidity and my own wickedness. You see, I knew of Diego's great weakness. At least, I called it a weakness and avoided ever speaking to him of what I'd seen. He liked to play very private games with little girls. A terrible sin, but he appeared to believe it a natural desire, simply a game, and never understood what it could do to the girl. it didn't stop me loving my husband."

"That's not the reason I need to talk about," Illiana gulped. "It makes me sick, and you've told me enough about it already. Tell me the other reason, the one I know nothing about."

Bertha's voice had blurred, sinking into murmurs. Now she looked up and spoke clearly and louder. "Still it's my fault, to be so angry with you, when I wasn't even sure, but just thinking it. So I never wanted to talk to you about anything private. Nothing that might be nice. I was just angry the whole time."

"Yes, and I just thought you never loved me at all." Illiana bit her lip, but shook her head. "Not your fault. Papa's fault. What he did sounds disgusting and I'm even sorry that I know about it. At least you love me now, but you're not telling me the other reason."

"I always loved you, my darling." Bertha's face was flushed and tear streaked. "I just felt so sorry for loving Diego and my anger – well, yes. The other reason was about your father too. You see, my wretched Papa was grand. Or at least he thought he was. He stood aloof when I was young. Not just to me, to all of us. Too grand to speak to little children." The sniffs grew louder. "I suppose he thought we were boring and no longer his business when we had nurses he was horrified when I told him about wanting to marry our chief groom, and he forbade it of course and locked me in my bedchamber for a month."

"You had an important father? A rich father?" Something was beginning to bring the drifting past threads together.

"He was a baron," Bertha sighed. "His daughter marrying a stable worker must have seemed so terrible to him, but after he locked me up, I wanted Diego even more. I ran off to marry him and that's when we joined the Birstall household, and of course that's where you were born. My father never, ever spoke to me again."

"You tried?"

"A hundred times. I took my baby to see him. That was you. He came to the door, refused to look at you, and slammed the door in my face. Our steward had already been ordered never to allow me into the house."

"A grand house?" Illiana was open mouthed.

"A vast building in The Strand. It's well night four years since curiosity crept me back there. My wretched Papa died at that time. I suppose my brother is the baron now. I can't be sure of anything."

"I'm sorry – no, I'm sure you don't want pity," Illiana said in a rush. "But what a cruel man. I loved mine and I think he loved me.. That's both sides of the family. What about your sisters?"

"Twice I tried very hard to find out anything about them," Bertha assured Illiana. "But on my own, I had no idea, still have no idea, who they are now. Who they married. If they married? Are they even alive?"

The pause swirled.

Finally, Illiana said, "Now perhaps Charles -,"

"I know," Bertha interrupted. "I told him. I asked him. Then everything else happened. Perhaps, when he comes back?"

"That's still almost a week away."

Bertha shook her head, reached out both arms, wrapped herself around Illiana, and, her tear wet cheek rubbed dry against her daughter's shoulder, whispered in her ear, "I will, one day, my darling. I promise, but only, please, if you never mention either of these two horrid things to me ever again.'

Illiana kissed her mother's forehead. She didn't think she had ever been hugged so close since she was a small child. "Mamma, I understand about Papa. I promise. I'll never say a word to anyone and especially never to you, but to talk about your family – I mean, truly a baron? And you're a real lady?"

"As you are, with more right," Bertha now spoke in a quivering voice of defiance. "You married an earl. I was just the daughter of one and no one wanted me. It hurts. I want to find my sisters, though it seems they never bothered to find me, but I'll do whatever I want to do, and do it quietly, and maybe never. Next year.

Tomorrow I mean it, Illiana. I won't do anything except cry if you ever mention this to me again." She pulled back. Sitting straight again, she clasped her hands in her lap. "Perhaps now is a good time to call for some wine."

Illiana risked saying, "You're brave, Mamma. Telling me all this. Telling me things you never wanted even to think about. No, I'll never mention it to you or ask you if you found out anything, but thank you. Thanks so much. And," she hesitated, then blurted, "if you find out anything, will you tell me?"

"I might." Bertha stood and rang the bell. "Depending on what I find out. Now, when that girl runs in, order some decent wine, Illiana. Until you bring me a very full cup of something strong, I intend to lie down and forget the past."

"So, I can't ask about your sisters. My aunts?"

"Very well, but these are my last words before I drink as much as I can and forget I ever spoke about it." Her eyes darted between sparking anger and tear-filled misery. "All three were my friends, two older, one younger. I spent many hours as a small child in bed with the new baby swaddled in my arms. Dear little Avis. She was bald for more than a year and then sprouted little white curls. I was extremely hurt when none of them came to help me. Not even to find me. I was never permitted to enter the house. I sneaked around to the kitchens, but even the staff were frightened to talk to me. I asked if any of my sisters had married, and the cook said no. Well, I knew that surely had to be a lie. So I gave up." Bertha blew her nose. "And that's that. Not a word more."

Their wine was brought and Illiana did as was asked. Retiring to her own bedchamber, she clasped her own brimming cup. She had no intention whatsoever of forgetting anything she'd been shocked, and fascinated to hear.

She also now realised, from past words which had puzzled her, that Charles already knew every detail, and assumed simply that most lords would be aware of the existence of other lords, however dull. No interest resurfaced. A family of wealth entirely lost. Yet the rich and the poor seemed equally kind, equally unpleasant, and inevitably, equally ignorant. Indeed, she had inherited wealth herself. In Spain, she had been spending a fortune but had never felt like a countess. Yet she was a lady indeed. But now she simply wished for Charles to hurry back from Cordoba.

When he came, it was raining. Illiana watched his arrival late one evening after an absence, even longer than she had hoped. Longer than he had predicted. As the great clatter through the pounding rain called her to the dining hall's vast front windows, she saw the parade as Charles, dripping and soaked but seemingly unconcerned, led his men, each half hidden beneath massive hooded rainproof capes, and tightly surrounded, a large litter pulled by two horses and driven by one of the men.

Unless one of his men, she couldn't count them as they swung, shouting, and reigning in their horses, was injured, Illiana could guess only one reason for requiring a litter. She was sure that Charles had first rescued and then brought the woman Elonza back with him.

Firstly, however, the troop disappeared in the direction of the stables and driven by curiosity, Illiana bounced outside, wished it wasn't raining, but dodged to the back of the hotel, pretending, should she be asked, to be complaining that the kitchen was closed and she needed more wine. Which was now also the truth.

The noise from the stables across the paved yard, was continuous. Horses stamped, neighed and snorted as they were brought the water buckets, mostly rain water now, and fresh piles of hay. They were brushed, blanket dried, and generally petted. The sounds of the unloaded litter were also clear, but no female voices joined the horses. Finally, Illiana peeped.

She was expecting to see the men too busy to notice her, Charles at least, accompanied by a woman. Illiana was therefore surprised to see two women, both cloaked, both glaring at the other.

Illiana quickly ran back to the dining hall, held up the wine jug when her mother asked why on earth she wanted to trot about in the rain, and settled back to catch her breath.

It was only Charles who came to the door. As she heard the imperious knocking, she looked across towards the window, and was forced to turn in a hurry when she heard the voice.

"What a patient young lady indeed," said the voice. "Were you waiting for me? I believe I'm a few days late, but you have the wine ready, I see. Most obliging."

Charles did not mention the drips of rain still falling from her high bunched hairstyle.

"Humph," said Bertha, tapping the side of the jug and pushing an empty cup towards him. "Half an hour back, Nicholas said as he heard you all arriving. I assume he's still out in the stables with all your horses?"

"And if you've stabled the horses," Illiana said, gripping her own cup, "I presume you all intend staying the night at the hotel."

"Not entirely." Charles flung off the soaked cape, sat on a nearby chair and pulled off his boots. Everything dripped both rain and mud. "My men are taking a rest and need food. The same applies to the horses. Afterwards, they'll be off back to the camp, but," and in his shoeless hose, he marched to Illiana's side, "I have arranged one night staying here, and for a particular reason."

"Of course you must be extremely tired," Bertha nodded as Charles filled the cup she had offered him.

"Oh, not too tired for some specific activities," he grinned at Illiana. "But I have another motive. Under necessity, I've brought back two women in need of more rest than myself. One is the woman I went to save. Elonza Piero. She has been treated by two doctors, but needs considerable rest and more friendship without any church involved." He paused, still smiling. "There is another female, of questionable heritage," he continued, "who calls herself

Josefa Martin, wife of the now deceased Santiago Martin, but who, before marriage, was indeed Josefa Delgado."

"You mean she knows about Sabine?" Illiana smiled hopefully at the answering smile.

"I must admit," Charles said, nose in the cup, "the story is rather long and has its unexpected moments. Nor has the woman in question yet answered a single question. She is not overly gracious at finding herself a widow. Yet there are many questions needing answers."

Everybody paused. When Charles made no further explanation, Illiana mumbled, "You mean? Well, perhaps you don't mean, she's going to be staying here? In this building? And so are you?"

"Not in the same bedchamber, as it happens," Charles told her. "Hers is not the bedchamber I'd prefer to share. However, her questioning needs to be officially witnessed. There's a good deal to arrange. Meanwhile, I have arranged three bedchambers, and it's Elonza who hopes the lady she so admires and wishes to thank," and Charles nodded at Bertha, "will visit her in the morning. The other woman's bedchamber will be locked against all comers, but," and again he grinned at Illiana, "my own bedchamber will remain open to all."

The bustle beyond the hall increased, but unseen since the hall's doors were shut. Illiana imagined the women taken to their rooms, food taken out to the stables, and the hotel staff puzzled at being told to lock the doors of one female visitor. Most of the staff, previously having only three quiet folk staying, sleeping and eating, had taken the opportunity to drift back to their families. Now everything was busy once again. Illiana could imagine the hotel's Chief Housekeeper rushing off in the rain to recall the malingering cooks, waiters and cleaners.

However, principally, Illiana was imagining something else, for Charles had seated himself on the opposite bench, and had raised his feet to the next table, while leaning back against the wall, raising his cup, and stretching his shoulders. Illiana therefore regarded the soles of the two feet facing her, ten toes neatly tucked in black silk hose, and the longmuscled legs before her eyes, elongated in a manner she had not expected. She knew Charles was a very tall man. Now the explanation of his height was explorable.

She tried not to stare. "It's Nicholas who should talk to that prisoner, if she really is a prisoner."

"Not in the usual sense of the word," Charles yawned. His hair, uncombed since the removal of the cape's wet hood, was a pigsty of rich black, seemingly as silken as his clothes. One long fingered hand pushed the hair from his eyes. "The woman has not been arrested. Indeed, since Spain here has neither sheriff nor constable, I assume it will be part of the royal guard which visits here tomorrow."

"To arrest the Delgardo woman?"

"Possibly to arrest me," Charles told her, though seemingly unconcerned. "We shall see in the morning." He swept both legs back to the wet puddled wooden floor, grabbed up his boots and soaked cape, and bowed to the two women gazing back at him. "Now I shall wish my men goodnight, and stumble to my own bedchamber. Buenas noches, señoras." He pulled open the doors, and allowed them to fall shut behind him as he disappeared into the darkness.

Bertha dumped her empty cup on the table, blew out the solitary candle and sighed. "Come along, my dear. The sooner we sleep, the better. I'd swear tomorrow is going to be a day of hectic surprises."

"I'd sooner wait for Nicholas," Illiana said. "He'll know a lot more than us, won't he, after being out in the stables with all the men."

"And equally exhausted." Bertha insisted. "We'll have a great deal to talk about in the morning."

Shortly before dawn, the rain, also exhausted, faded into drizzle and then stopped. The sun awoke and found its way to the horizon. For one blazing hour, the streets and flat rooftops basked in warmth, drying quickly. As Bertha and Illiana awoke, it once again appeared to be summer.

The weather seemed to improve even more and the sun shone with more enthusiasm when, once dressed, Illiana entered the small breakfast room, for Charles, Nicholas, and one other of Charles' men already sat at the larger table. Indeed, Illiana was accustomed to Charles, unless considerably cupshotten, appearing cold eyed and imperious. Indeed, even bad tempered until one noticed the increasing tuck at the corner of his mouth. Now, however, with only a cup of ale in his hands he smiled openly.

"I'm delighted you've come to share our good morning." he nodded to Illiana. "Allow me to introduce my second in command, my deputy, let us say, which is what he always says himself. This is Allan Reed."

She wondered what exactly she was supposed to say in reply and decided to nod and smile and say nothing. Meanwhile Nicholas was also beaming. He said, "My lady, tis a pleasure indeed. Tis nigh on two days I've not been seen, being mighty busy, but today, I reckon, will be a day o' celebration."

Illiana was not sure why Nicholas thought this, since Charles' return might please her, but was unlikely to excite Nicholas. "Well, it's so nice to see you looking so happy, Nicholas. But I admit I'm not sure - ,"

"Tis my Sabine," Nicholas said at once. "Now tis most likely, could be mighty quick - ,"

This time Charles interrupted. "Our friend here believes, and I am in agreement, that the Delgardo woman who remains in her bedchamber upstairs, will almost certainly bring some insight into his daughter's situation." Nicholas nodded, grinned, and clapped. "However," Charles continued, "I believe it equally probable that I shall first be host to a party of the Royal Guard. I expect them within the next hour and sooner rather than later. Once I manage to entertain that imminent group of visitors, Nicholas and I will question the woman upstairs."

"You don't mean Elonza?"

"Not at all," Charles smiled. "I believe she's already speaking with your mother upstairs."

Illiana paused. It seemed everything was happening without her. "And the guards? Royal guards? Is that concerning Elonza's freedom?"

"That might be a subject that trots into the general discussion," Charles admitted. "But their principal target will be somewhat more complicated. Simply, myself."

The sudden noises were loud, drowning out other voices. Illiana lost the opportunity of inquiring what was so complicated concerning Charles, and simply sat, gazing towards the doorway.

There was the tramp of many feet, shouts demanding order, and the subsequent bustle. Only the sound of any horses was missing.

The doors to the breakfast room were then flung open and eight armed guards marched behind their leader. In a brown and cream livery, the men stood to attention, their hands openly resting on the hilts of their swords. Their leader, however, wore a scarlet doublet over rich yellow hose, and was unlikely ever to remain unnoticed.

He marched to the occupied table, and faced Charles, managed a cursory bow, and immediately began to speak. Charles seemed unimpressed but did not interrupt.

"As Chief of the Royal Guard to His majesty King Edmund and Her Majesty Queen Isabel, I herewith inform you, my lord, that you are required to accompany us immediately."

Charles, still sitting, raised one eyebrow. "A pleasant request," he said. "Yet you have not fully explained such an imperious necessity. Are you implying that I am under arrest?"

The guard frowned. "Not as yet, sir. The questioning which must immediately take place will be the decisive factor. I advise you to accompany us now, sir."

"Certainly not." Charles still sat, cup in hand, and leaned back against the wall behind the bench. "I'll cheerfully discuss any business with you here and now, but I'll not be leaving this building, where I now pay for my legal accommodation, unless by royal command, - personally voiced."

He smiled into the pause that followed. The dark liveried guards remained blank. Their chief, however, took some time to answer.

Finally, he spoke, half growl. "Sir, I must point out that those other persons now present, have no place in this important business of propriety and the law of the land. I must therefore insist on a private room in which to carry out this business."

Charles chuckled. "Apart from the occasional waiter, who will certainly scuttle away if told, there are only three folk present now, apart from myself and your own bored but dutiful followers. These are my second in command, Master Reed, my loyal groom Nicholas and her ladyship, Illiana, Countess of Birstall, to whom I am much obliged, and was the instigator of my errand to Cordoba, which I believe is the reason for your – delightful – visit, sir. You therefore have my full permission to speak here and now, as you wish."

Being offered permission, brought the Chief of the Guard to a quiver of fury. "Sir," he announced, "I therefore shall demand your immediate compliance and my questions shall begin here and now." He breathed in loudly and straightened his shoulders. "Firstly, do you admit that nine days past, in Cordoba, you took the life of Master Rodrigo Solomino during a situation instigated only by yourself?"

Illiana was fascinated, shivered, and managed to keep her gaze on her empty platter. Her cup held wine, and she silently gasped, gulped it, and hoped that more would come.

Charles remained cheerful. "Oh, most certainly yes to the first part," he said. "That I was the sole instigator and entirely culpable is, however, quite absurd. Perhaps I should leave the explanation to the single witness." He smiled at Allan, who sat at his side.

Allan had clearly been expecting something of the sort. "With pleasure, my lord." He turned to the vibrant Spanish guard. "Sir, Viscount Valdar and myself had, at some length, been attending the tribunal of the Holy Inquisition in Cordoba, regarding Senorita Elonza Piero, who had been mistakenly suspected of sins of the – er, - flesh. Indeed, the young woman was eventually released as, let us say, quite innocent. On release, Elonza Piero wished to exchange words with a local peasant who lived in the hut opposite her own. This was one Rodrigo Solomino who had denounced Miss Piero to the inquisitor. "

The Spanish chief of guards sniffed. "Yet, I understand that the woman you mention was not present during the male's death."

"If you're implying that his recent history is irrelevant," Charles smiled, "then you lack both logic and imagination, sir. Now, Allan, please continue."

Allan did.

"Following the altercation between the man and woman now mentioned," he said, "I led Senorita Piero away, since, having been held for almost two weeks incarcerated by the inquisition, she was in dire need of medical treatment. I am quite sure you understand, sir. The creature Rodrigo Solomino rushed forwards, a dagger waving in his hand, and began to swear at his lordship."

"Is this corroborated?" frowned the guard.

"By myself," Charles said. "And before you choose to claim that such a witness to a witness is not sufficiently convincing, may I remind you that I, and indeed my second in charge, are both sworn by oath to the English Crown, to speak the truth before God while serving his majesty's wishes."

"Humph," said the guard.

"I fought the man Solomino," Charles continued, "without any noticeable advantage. I am a trained warrior, whereas the fool was not. He, however, was a long term and well known adversary, and exponent of gang war, attack on the vulnerable and with the desire to kill, and I am not. I am tall and have physical strength, but Solomino was taller, thicker, and older in years of experience without being past the age of, let us call it, active practise. He fought with a dagger, and fists. I did the same, since my sword remained in the Alcazar depository. An equality of advantage, I believe and Solomino, as my partner here will substantiate, was the first to attack."

"Yet, in spite of the equal footing you claim," the guard snorted, "you are almost unmarked, sir, whereas the other man lies dead with knife wounds to the skull, face, belly and groin, with the final stabbing which caused his death, to his heart."

With an unchanging smile, Charles nodded and raised his cup, although now almost empty. "So, it would seem that I was the victor, sir."

The guard turned, instructing his men that it was time to leave, but he spoke again to Charles. "This matter is not concluded, my lord. You will be hearing more from me over the next days. Should you attempt to escape justice by returning to England, let me warn you that guards will also be stationed at the port."

CHAPTER NINTEEN

As the doors slammed, the waiter thumped in with a very tall pitcher of wine, and Illiana slumped, it was Nicholas who leaned forward, eager for explanations.

"My lord, tis proper unexpected, and mighty impressive too. I reckons you must be a fighter o' brilliance."

"I'm not quite as untouched as the guard would have you believe. "He chuckled softly, holding out his cup while Nicholas refilled it.

Illiana promptly held out her own. "I knew nothing of this. Please tell us everything."

"The one who should tell us everything, is the widow we have locked upstairs," Charles told her. He turned to Nicholas. "The key remains in the keyhole on the outside," he continued. "Nicholas, would you accompany two of my men and unlock that woman, and bring her here. I may even offer her breakfast if she talks."

As Charles appeared pleasantly comfortable without the least concern for his possible arrest, Allan went to call in two of his men, who were lounging in the main hall. Nicholas, eager, accompanied them up the hotel stairs. Illiana remained sitting and watched Charles.

"So, you rode all the way to Cordoba, argued through the tribunal, managed to free that poor little woman Elonza, then found the man who had both her and my mother arrested with his spiteful lies, fought him and killed him, then dragged his widow all the way back here in Seville. Then shut her up safely for Nicholas to question about the Delgardos, and even managed to argue yourself out of a murder charge from the royal guards." She seemed more puzzled than impressed.

Charles nodded and laughed. "I am indeed a creature of amazing talents, my dear. I must also remind you that I have the huge advantage of being able to hide beneath the English king's upraised standard. Even though," and he laughed, "this latest escapade had nothing whatsoever to do with his highness,, and was simply a matter of justice." He waved one arm, while holding his cup in the other hand. "I should also add that I didn't escape injury from that vile barrel of a man, even though I then killed the brute. I have a slash from shoulder to wrist, but it is healing and wasn't deep enough to incapacitate. I also had the advantage of the Spanish royal permission to enter the tribunal, meaning that I was likely to return to the palace with full notification of any injustice."

"You planned the lot?" Now she was impressed.

"I did not, I assure you, plan to have my arm almost cut in two. However, yes, much of the remainder came through my own planning."

"And was it you who arranged this new English king you keep not explaining?"

This time his laugh was sudden and loud. Charles was definitely amused. "Lord forgive me," he chuckled then, "not in the least. I wasn't even in England. That's a very different matter, though. Most of the entire country is pleased not to have an underage child of a king, who would undoubtedly have been ruled by his vile mother's corrupt Woodville family, but the explanation is irrelevant for the moment. It's your groom's questioning regarding his daughter which will govern the next few hours, or more."

The heated complaints and stumbling footsteps could already be heard and within two breaths, the woman was pushed into the breakfast room. It would have been strange not to watch her entrance, but Illiana was staring in amazement. She had expected someone impressive and instead she saw a tiny woman, even smaller than Elonza, stick thin with a small puffy mouth. Three parts of Josefa Solomino were, however, unexpectantly large, her feet, her hands and her big brown eyes under thick black eyebrows and within another two breaths of arrival, one large palmed hand grabbed a spoon from the table and threw it at Charles.

Charles grinned, and caught it. Josefa glared at him. "Murderer. Bastard English filth. Murdering shit." She grabbed an empty cup, but Allan snatched it from her and pulled her further from the table. Charles continued to laugh. It was Nicholas, so large that he towered over the woman as though he was the oak tree and she was the peeping weed at his roots.

It was Allan who translated as Nicholas began to question her, and although this slowed progress, it forced Josefa to wait in silence.

"I knows naught about your family, mistress," Nicholas said, "but I heard as how one or more o' them snatched away my poor little daughter. Such an angel she be, but now is gone. Safe, she were, doing the shopping , being helpful and kind as always, and all of a shocking sudden, she were gone. T'was early this year, being months and months gone, and I come here to find her. I won't leave without her, and I hopes, and I prays, mistress, you might have some titchy little trickle o' idea where she might be gone."

Once the translation was complete, the woman pulled a face and spat on the floor at her own very large bare toes. "I don't know you, old fool, nor your daughter. How can you think I know such silly stories?"

She was now held firm by Allan, when Nicholas, which amazed Illiana, leaned abruptly down at her and fiercely slapped her face. Illiana had not even heard him shout before, let alone hit out at a woman. She was, however, delighted, and beamed at him.

Charles, still sitting, called, "Madam Solomino, be careful. We know your situation, we know your family stole away this man's innocent daughter, and we know your family will have mistreated her. You are, by birth, a Delgardo, and that is a name both hated and held in contempt by most folk in both Spain and England. The young woman's name is Sabine Farrier, and your cooperation in finding her is your only hope of staying alive. If you refuse to help, then you will quickly re-join your husband." This did not need any translation.

The small woman stared and clenched her fists. "Why should I know anything of this? Why should I know everything my brothers do?"

Nicholas said, "Cos you be in the gang yerself, and so were your husband. We knows it. No point lying."

Charles was less polite. "Your husband was known as a liar, a thief, a killer, and a man who enjoyed handing over the innocent to the inquisition. He enjoyed imagining their torture, and so did you. I gather that both you and your husband were much reviled and loathed by everyone living in your neighbourhood, and even the remainder of the Solomino family. Now I shall warn you just once more. You speak, you voice every detail of your knowledge, your suspicions, and the local heresay, and I will order food and drink for you to sit here, eat, drink and continue to talk. Should you choose to take the opposite path and pretend ignorance, you shall first be encouraged without pity, and eventually killed. Make your choice, madam."

She twitched, paused, pulled away from Allan, then mumbled, "T'were not me nor my sweet Rodrigo."

Allan grabbed both her upper arms and hauled her back. "Next time," he told her, "I need to pull you back, I'll be grabbing your neck. And as for sweet Rodrigo, how often did he beat you?" There was another pause, and Allan roared, "Answer, or lose both hands."

The woman shivered, muttering, "Often enough. Like all men. You, pig arse, and every other pig arse I ever met."

Illiana was about to deny this opinion of all men, but Charles grinned and held up one hand. "And knowing our pig-arse behaviour so well, madam, you will now believe it when I tell you there are no more warnings to come. You speak now, and satisfy the questions of these brutal men surrounding you. Begin now."

Josefa began to jabber like an angry water wigeon. "I dunno," she squawked quickly, "but yes, I heard a bit. Only way I heard, it was a mighty pain for my brother. Took some English trollop to sell to a hare-em in Granada, but there were half those Moors packing up, leaving or being hounded out. Soldiers everywhere and shouting their bloody heads off at the Muslims, and no way to trade nor get decent bargains. So poor Pablo, he couldn't get the cash he wanted."

"Pablo Delgardo?" Nicholas demanded. "Your brother had my daughter?"

"If you want to put it that way," Josefa yelped as Nicholas raised one fist. "It's neither my fault, mister, nor my poor husbands. If you'd seen that bastard slashing his wicked knife in my Rodrigo's face, with blood flying into the gutters,"

Nicholas interrupted. "Tis naught to do with my Sabine. Tell me what your filth of a brother did with her."

"My Pablo's a kind man," Josefa shrieked. "He ain't never hit me. Nor would he hit your girl. Just wanted to sell her. We all need money. We can't eat unless we got money. Trade is a fair business. You don't go killing folk in the markets that sell their wares."

"Where is the girl now," Charles demanded, standing abruptly. "I need an immediate answer."

"Dunno." Now Josefa wailed. Her voice was more vibrant than her height. "I lived with my husband, not my brother, but I heard as how when he couldn't get no coin for the trollop, he gave the girl to another of our brothers. For scrubbing and cooking, and the usual stuff. Dunno which brother. Lives down in the valley village. Dunno what street."

Charles and Nicholas stared at her, disbelieving. Then Allan hooked his fingers around Josefa's throat, muttering, "Finish your story, wolf bitch, or I squeeze tighter."

Again, she whimpered yet her face puckered in fury and Illiana was sure that she was planning a trick rather than telling the truth. "I told you, I dunno," she said. Could be Juan. Could be Lucas. Lucas has a wife that likes to have a slave. Could be any of them. I never care. I ain't involved."

Charles accepted this, and told her, "Since I accept your word, and cannot yet prove otherwise, I'll order food, but you remain under arrest. The royal guard, I'm quite sure, will appreciate you standing witness against me."

"You murdered my innocent husband," snapped Josefa. "I saw that knife go in. I heard Rodrigo scream. You English bastard, you'll hang."

It was Illiana who hissed, "You deserve to hang after what you did to my mother. It really was you, wasn't it, you and your husband, who liked to lie about folk and denounced an innocent woman who'd never hurt either of you. You deserve to burn. Why lie to get other women tortured by the inquisition?"

"Since this Delgardo woman does not understand the amazing dexterity involved in telling the truth, I'll answer for her," Charles remained ice cold, staring at the tiny woman whose large hands were fisted, and whose huge flat feet rapped against the stone floor. "Her motives, as with others who do the same thing, are principally for spite. The poor who resent being poor, wish others to suffer more. The sick who resent being sick, wish others to know the pain. Some are paid by the church to spy, and that makes for an easy lie. Lies can bring dinner and wine casks. Such lies can also persuade the inquisitor that the liars themselves are friends to the clergy."

Nodding, Illiana turned away from the small ragged woman while Charles rang the bell and ordered food and English beer, more wine and a visit from whoever claimed leadership within the hotel. Exhausted, Josefa crouched on the floor and stared at her large grubby toes.

Everything arrived at once. With the scent of hot bread rolls and burned bacon, Josefa jumped up. Charles took the wine.

"My lord," the man who followed the waiter, bowed and stood rigid. "I am Garcio Siodera, son of the owner, Senor Siodera, who resides at some distance. How may I serve your lordship?"

"By taking this woman to the local gaol, sir," Charles told him. "I have the authority to demand this, as you know, and should I discover that she has been released, or escaped, then the consequences will be severe. I trust you understand, my man?"

"I do indeed, my lord," he bowed again. "And I understand the situation, knowing the reasons, sir. The female will not escape." He grabbed Josefa's arm and she was hauled away from the table, frantically clutching both the bread already soaked in oil, and the almost empty cup of beer. Her mouth was full of bacon and she spluttered a complaint which proved impossible to hear clearly. Allan, after a nod from Charles, followed them.

Illiana sighed, but Nicholas turned to Charles, eyes alight. "You trust what she says, my lord?"

"Within reason," Charles told him. "The valley of the Delgardos is not so far distant, but when we visited that collection of slums, we gained no help. The principal hierarchy was at sea, but might now have returned. As for trusting that woman, no, I do not entirely. And as for returning to the village if the men are back at home there, it seems unwise. News of Solomino's death at my hand will not help matters. I intend visiting that prison within the hour. When I arrive back here after further investigations, I'll tell you my decision. Meanwhile, you've waited too long but need to wait again."

Nicholas hung his head, and as Charles marched from the breakfast room, leaving an empty cup and platter, Nicholas sat quickly beside Illiana.

"Well, my lady, reckon we still ain't no closer."

Illiana eyed the oily bread remaining on Josefa's platter, paused, then helped herself, one bread roll with bacon nestled between crusts. She munched. "I think we are, Nicholas. Honestly, Charles or whoever he is, seems to have a fair amount of authority. I'd swear he has a very good idea where darling Sabs is being kept, and now he intends to prove it."

"Tis been a hard time," Nicholas said, "fer you, little one, and for your lady mother. I reckon we all deserves a trickle o' what we might call – well, you knows what I mean, being what we wants."

"We won't leave without her. Not unless I die myself, and I won't. It's my mother and poor Sabine who keep suffering. Not me." Illiana swallowed, and pointed to the crumb and puddle decorated table. "Help yourself, Nicholas, we all need what we can get. Who knows, we might have to ride for a day without food, or get locked up ourselves. Now I have to go and see my mother."

"Reckon tis either her room or that lass Elonza's." Nicholas remained positive, wiped his nose on a napkin from the table, and tried to smile. "Bertha will want to talk with her, I reckons."

It was Elonza's bedchamber, one of the hotel's smallest, but cosy enough, and private since it was on the upper floor beneath the attic beams. Illiana could hear her mother's voice as she climbed the last steps.

"No more crying, my dear. What you suffered from Diego, brought me benefit, and we both suffered the same in those disgusting dungeons. They call that Christianity? I call it Satan's work."

"Oh, pity, pity," was Elonza's voice, "or you'll be dragged back by the priests again."

"No she won't," Illiana pushed open the door. "Because Charles won't allow it. We'll have Sabine in a few days, and then we can all sail back home."

Looking up, her face still tear stained, and slick, Elonza clasped both hands. "You mean I may travel to your country and escape my own?"

"Yes, why not," said Bertha at once. "I'm not sure what you'll do there but working, I mean, well, we can see. My dear daughter lives in a very large house."

"I can sweep and clean," then Elonza turned back to Illiana, "and your mighty friend, he killed that foul liar Rodrigo. He's the one, and that nasty little wife of his, who accused both of us to the inquisition."

"Charles isn't exactly my friend," said Illiana, and then paused. "Or perhaps he is, but he's at risk of being charged with murder."

"Oh, he was wonderful," Elonza enthused. "I saw some of it as the men dragged me away. I hope the wound in his arm isn't too serious, but he was so quick, so clever, ducking and dodging, swearing and thrusting. Oh, it was magic. I saw, over my shoulder, as his knife went straight into that monster's eye."

"Really."

"Such a lot of blood." She sniffed. "I never liked to see blood. It made me sick, even when I cut up the meat from the butchers. However, when it came tumbling out of that pig-monster's nasty dirty fat flesh, well, I confess, I was delighted. Seeing him clatter to the ground, I wanted to clap and cheer."

"I can imagine," said Bertha quickly, "and I know nothing of his own wounds, but that man Charles can certainly look after himself."

"I just hope he can look after Sabine," said Illiana.

CHAPTER TWENTY

In a space far less comfortable than her previous hotel room, Josefa lay on the bundle of uncovered straw and buried her frozen toes deep into the chaff, while staring up in hatred at the broken plaster over her head.

Two visions switched within her mind, each momentarily more important than the other. Other thoughts refused to ferment. Thoughts of her own future, how to escape and what would happen if she did not, were pushed by a strangling fear, into hidden depths where her thoughts could not reach.

Her two repeated memories brought the mouthfuls of hot breakfast back into her gullet. She remembered the burning, which she had felt obliged to watch, of the man she had disliked, and had then falsely incriminated, finally denouncing him to the inquisition. Only three months later, the brash Antonio had burned.

The mighty Miguel de Morillio, Cordoba's principal inquisitor, had thanked her and told her, softly, that the Holy Christ would never forget her dutiful service to the dignity of religious righteousness. She remembered grinning. It was what she'd wanted.

Antonio, the richest man in her own Cordoban street, had

attempted to speak out against her family, claiming the Delgardos as thieves and killers. Josefa had quickly run to the Alcazar, pleaded to make her accusation, and informed De Marillio that this man had attempted to rape her, an act of utter and iniquity against the laws of the church.

She had expected to enjoy his death and hated herself for hating what she saw. Especially for what she smelled. Having seen the man's hair in flames, then seeing his nose melt like a spoonful of fat in the pan. She had smelled the sickening reek, first hinting of the luxury of roast pork on the spit, but then the faced with the reek of burning flesh, the slap of flame on a dissolving belly and the old food within it, the rotting and rolling of falling brains from a dissolving skull, and the fading screams of a torture, even she had never before imagined.

The overlap of the alternative memory seemed both worse, and then easier. Now she saw endlessly repeated the killing of her husband, his heavy dance of expected victory as he thumped, kicked out into empty space, lolloped to face backwards and then forwards, brandishing the huge muscles for which he was renowned, and his pleasure in yelling the insults, swearwords and taunts which he shouted so often at everyone, including herself.

His adversary had been a stranger to her, tall and muscled yet not as muscled as Rodrigo, and although clearly determined, seemed almost to mock and taunt with humorous movements, darting, ducking and twisting.

Rodrigo, with fists as large as the holes in the street of beaten earth on which they fought, landed punches which bent the other man over, once making him fall. Yet most of those punches were missed, and thumped air, as the stranger simply moved aside, or bent his head while lunging at Rodrigo's belly and groin. Most of the stranger's punches arrived on target, and with unexpected force. Five times Rodrigo was winded, wincing or even howling in pain, and needed to pause while regaining his breath, and as Rodrigo paused, so the stranger stood back smiling, and waited.

When, finally, Rodrigo slashed at the other man's forward swinging arm, a seeming success as the blood splashed out and down. It was suddenly obvious this had been a trick and, head down, the man ignored his bleeding arm, ducked beneath it and pounded, his knife to Rodrigo's face. The blade cut from ear to eye and as Rodrigo screeched, so the blade entered his eyes, thrust deep into the welling blood and gore. Rodrigo tottered, raised both hands to the wounded eye, leaving his body unprotected. Now the stranger's short knife entered deep into Rodrigo's chest, directly into his heart. He fell, tumbling and rolling, wheezing as his screeches faded, and finally lay dead in pools of his own vomit and his own blood.

Cringing back against the wall, Josefa had sobbed, was grabbed both by the victorious stranger and his friend, and dragged away.

Now she hated that memory, and desperately missed the protection her husband had long given her. She could not believe, had he still lived, that anyone could have risked arresting her.

And yet, she had hated Rodrigo. From the day before their wedding to the day of his death, she had despised and loathed him, feared his frequent beatings, his continuously hurled insults, his tantrums as he smashed what tiny amount of crockery they had ever owned, and his determination to eat and drink almost the entirety of whatever they could afford.

She would be happier now without him, she knew. Not, however, while she remained in prison, facing possible torture. Her husband had, if nothing else, been her face of outward power.

Then the barred door swung open and she forgot the past miseries and abruptly faced the future. The man who had danced into her husband's life and killed him, was no longer a stranger. Josefa faced Charles and ignored the two men who stood behind, watching but remaining silent.

Without moving, she shouted, "You think you got the better of me and my innocent beloved. Well, think again, piss-pig. You wait till the inquisition burns you at the stake, when I tell them you tried to rape me, and cursed on the Cross."

Charles smiled. "An interesting prospect," he nodded. "Yet spoiled a little by the presence of two armed witnesses."

"I'll say they raped me too. Armed as they are, I had no way to defend myself."

A gruff voice echoed from behind Allan and Degal. "There ain't any of that happening with me here, stupid woman. I'm your door keeper, guard of the tribunal. Now answer what this lord asks you and answer true and quick."

"I told you every damn whisper I knew," Josefa shouted back.

Charles spoke softly, watching her as he leaned, arms crossed, against the cold stone wall and its ragged falling steaks of dirty plaster.

"I can hardly blame you for your – let us call it – displeasure, Delgardo widow as you are, but it would seem logical to now speak only the truth, with the hope that it would aid your release."

"That's no promise." The small woman wriggled deeper into the straw.

"I could promise you a blanket," Charles suggested. Outside the sun swept over a dry country. The summer heat was gone, but the autumnal heat remained. However, within a stone built square without window, where the original plaster had now flaked into tiny scraps, the space echoed only chill, airless but cold. No coverings warmed the lump of a bed.

"Get it then," Josefa sulked. "I told you the truth. I told you everything. Get me two blankets. I deserve two after you slaughtered my man."

"Your man was never a kind one," Charles pointed out. "Neighbours report your screams and shouts occurring every day without fail, and even now I see the grazes and dark bruising on your arms and legs. A red scar across your neck suggests a past strangulation, even a cut. Two old scars on one side of your face prove worse abuse. Now," and once again he smiled, "what you have told me is undoubtedly partially true, but the exact position of the abducted woman is entirely ridiculous. You suggest one of the most infamously vile of your brothers, who is known to use his wife as an archery target, and therefore the least likely to pay for a servant."

"I told you. I dunno."

"You would, however, know that that vile brother lives further south in the Delgardo village itself, which is not so far from the coast. Such facts shout against yout claims."

"I made no stupid claims, I said as I know nothing."

"You are therefore disinterested in either release, or at least additional comfort and warmth while you wait."

"It's you what should be in here, and you what should be scared of whatever's coming." Josefa buried her head, making her next words difficult to understand. "Might not be Pablo."

"Nor your eldest brother Juan, who leads the murderous gang you were born into. Tell me another, and give enough information for me to believe it. Don't pretend. Your lies are stupid and stupidly told. I'll believe the truth if you add details."

Sitting up, and shivering while wrapping both arms around her breasts, Josefa muttered beneath her breath, as though telling the truth might chill her the more.

"It was my little brother Lucas."

"I need a good deal more convincing than simply a name," Charles replied. "Where does he live? Does he have a wife and children?"

Josefa stared back and continued to mumble. The mumble resembled a grumble. "Did have. He was wed. Maria. Stupid little tart she was. She died. Was killed by Juan, and I'll not be saying more on that, but Lucas has two little girls, one not much more than a baby. He don't live in the valley. He moved after Maria died. He lives in Osuna, and still got no living wife. So he took the English harlot to look after the brats. Paid too. Tis Don Pedro who runs the town and it was him who paid for the servant girl. Osuna ain't pretty. On a hill it is, where the hills run higher. My Lucas is friend o' Don Pedro. Well, maybe not a proper friend, but works for him. I've not seen him for months. He don't like Rodrigo."

"I am finally interested," Charles admitted. "Without admitting trust, I might admit the possibility of some belief." He turned abruptly, and followed by Allan and Degl, he marched back into the corridor. The disinterested guard quickly slammed and locked the door.

Josefa returned to her cold straw and began to cry. One hour later, two thick blankets flew through the opened door, and landed on Josefa's head as the door was once more loudly locked.

The ride to the small town of Osuna was long and demanded fast riding, yet uncomfortable through the ragged crags, sudden tips and rising hills, and two days in the saddle were exhausting. Then before arrival, the night had fallen into sudden pitch like the locking of a windowless cell's door.

With the moon obscured by cloud, rooftops low and flat, the village was quiet. The tiny streets wound between small cottages, and the only visible life was a donkey rummaging between stones for a taste of grass. A tiny spire rose crooked from a drab stone church and here the open plaza, not much larger than the width of three narrow lanes, led to a palace of sorts, neither grand nor drab, neither huge nor cottage.

"Don Pedro," Charles muttered. "Either him or this is the priest's quarters. I shall see who has heard of Lucas Delgardo, who hopefully lives nearby, and the captured Sabine with him."

Dismounting, Charles slammed heavily on the high door's knocker, shaped as a copper winged eagle. Both Allan and Degal remained mounted, as Charles flung them his reins.

Almost immediately the door opened and a bent woman stood peering out. "Yes? You fellows want some help?"

"Madam, I apologise for the interruption. I am looking for a specific address, that of a man who works for Don Pedro. Would you have that information? Would anyone here?"

The elderly woman sniffed. "Wait a moment, sir. I shall ask

Father Augustin if he might help. Those who attend his services are always well known to him."

She tottered off, and although Charles had not the remotest knowledge of whether this Delgardo brother ever attended church, he thought it worth the wait. It was not a long wait. The priest, apparently older than his aged housekeeper, bent and bald, shuffled to the open door, attempting to avoid tripping over the trailing hem of his robe.

"His lordship Don Pedro's employees are generally known to me, sir. Might I ask your reason for asking?" he asked, peering up, since Charles was close to twice his height.

"I carry a message from Lady Osway, dowager Countess of Birstall, of England, and I personally also carry the authority of His Royal Highness, King Richard of England," Charles spoke with some exaggeration, "which will interest a Master Lucas Delgardo and his housekeeper and child minder, sir. So, I need to discover where to find the man."

"Ah," smiled the priest. "You speak of a good man, sir, one that works hard and helps others. Walk this street, known as the Saints' Lane, which leads directly over a bridge to a smaller rather winding lane, known as Little Street. At the very end, another wider street crosses to both sides. Turn left, sir, and enter the Grand Lane, and the cottage where senor Delgardo resides with his family is the very first you see."

Degal, listening from horseback, doubted if Charles would remember every twist and turn, so promptly pressed the directions to his own memory. "Yes, I know," he told Charles as he handed back the reins. Charles understood immediately and smiled, nodded, and they began the short ride to the long journey's end.

"Turn left, and it's the first house," Degal said, yet paused.

The three riders reined in their horses at the end of Little Street, and grinned at each other. The disruption which halted them was raucous. Several voices shouted, the thumps of fist to body and foot to laneway were indicative of riot, battle, or simply family squabbles.

"Well," Charles murmured, "we are visiting one of an infamous brood. This little brother may be the most saintly but he is still a Delgardo."

"One of them is shouting words I don't know,' Degal grinned. "And I can curse fairly well in Spanish, so this is interesting."

Allan sniggered. "Learn what you can, I'm more interested in how many voices. Best not be outnumbered."

"I'll take two," Charles grinned.

"Depends on which one it is," Allan said. "I think I'll stick to one."

"Don't stick too hard," Degal sniggered. "I'm happy with one. Though who knows – is this Lucas fellow on our side, or his brother's?"

"We count him out," Charles decided. "So, four Delgardos is the maximum we want to dance with."

The voices rose, a voice yelling was difficult to link with the same man mumbling. Finally, Allan said, "There's only three. If we're patient, there might only be two."

"Or we lose the saintly Lucas. Possibly even the girl."

Charles was impatient. "There's six brothers in total. I refuse to believe the entire family visits this town together,to cancel out the tiresome Lucas. I doubt we have more than four, so follow me, swords in hand."

"Charge," grinned Degal, digging in his heels past the stirrups.

The shouting and swearing continued, and two men in Little Street were on their doorsteps, intrigued yet simply listening. Both disappeared indoors as Charles, Allan and Degal unsheathed their swords and cantered to the left turning, "Cargo, velocidad máxima." The shouting and swearing abruptly faded.

Into the sudden staring silence, Charles pulled the reins, his mount stopped, snorted and reared. In front of him were five men, standing amazed, and in the open doorway of a white stone cottage stood a young woman, frowning but beautiful, blue eyed, her fair hair tousled, her body painfully thin and her nose bleeding.

"Which one of you is Lucas?" demanded Charles.

The shorter of the men, also seemingly the younger, neither announced himself nor stayed unmoved. He jumped to the side of the woman in the doorway. The four remaining men glared, gripping long knives, two of them blood stained, but stood still, watching.

Their livery was impressive in early darkness, with the courageous streaks of moonlight now struggling through the clouds. The gold threaded lines against black silk shone, and their identical hats, although not helmets, marked them as officers or warders, even guards of some kind.

"Four against three," Charles laughed. "Easy pickings."

It was Allan who called, "You thieves and cut-throats disturb the peace, and frighten the locals. You aim to kill your brother. Which of you claim the name of Delgardo?"

Snarling, wolf-like, one said, "You dare to confront the most fearsome men in southern Iberia? I am Mateo Delgardo, and will kill both you and your ragged donkey."

Allan's horse, a rich black gelding, disliked the creature Mateo as much as his master appeared to, and kicked out. Mateo dodged, and Allan jumped from the saddled directly onto the man's shoulders, his sword outstretched.

At the same moment and without a word, Charles dismounted and faced the taller man in the group. "Juan?" he asked. "Or one of his feeble-minded followers?"

Without offering a name, the man slashed back, and the third man stabbed at Charles from the back.

Degal was already entwined with the fourth, a muscular beast with black curls past his dirty red collar. They fought as they had predicted, Charles thrust his sword into one man's back, as he danced past the shorter man, twisted again, and found the first man's hands around his neck, gripping him from the back, roaring as the blood streamed from his ribs. "Yeah, Sancho, hold the bastard. Strangle the shit while I bash his head in."

Charles dislodged both as abruptly he sank to his knees, then sprang up and faced them again, grinning, his sword catching the moonlight.

An owl hooted, white wings above, as Degal fell, but he rolled as Antonie leapt onto him, and both entwined, rolling together towards the cottage doorway where both Lucas and the girl hesitated, now Lucas further back into the lightless house and the girl further forward. Now Degal was at the girl's feet, still hand to hand struggling with the man on top, but as Degal smashed up hard with one knee to the other's groin, the girl reached out, one step forwards and thrust a long serrated knife into the Delgardo's neck.

The man screamed twice, the girl stepped back, her knife dripping scarlet, shouting, "*Antonio, care-chimba, y ora agaste y saltaste en la caca,*" and as the Spaniard toppled, the girl moved forward once more and kicked him in the ribs. The man's arms twitched, he gurgled and then remained without movement, his eyes open and staring up at the white owl in the branches of a tree above.

It hooted once more, and the sound echoed in the stillness. Then it was gone. Antonio had also gone, but the other three, either noticing nothing or uncaring, continued to fight. Charles was bleeding heavily from a deep cut that had opened his lower lip, but the taller of his assailants bled more profusely from the back of his neck, his belly and both legs. The smaller Delgardo seemed unhurt.

Now Degal jumped over the dead body and hurtled onto the taller of Charles' attackers, his weight forcing the other flat to the earth. Charles was left with the most ferocious fighter, and Allan continued to fight Mateo. Both Lucas and the young woman now kept within the cottage shadows. Half the neighbours, men, women, even children, were watching either from their open doors, their windows, or the street itself.

Some yelled, other cheered and two men shouted advice. "Stick the bastard. That's Sancho, he's a filthy mean bugger."

It was into Sancho's mouth that Charles had rammed his final blow, first with the knife point and then with the hilt. The man, gargling blood, his teeth scattering as they tumbled, now fought Degl, spitting his last teeth and the point of his blood streamed tongue into Degal's face.

Although taller, Charles now struggled against the third man, each tricking one while the other tricked in the opposite direction and it was Charles who was bleeding more.

Mateo Delgardo fell, wrapped in blood as he curled around the spillage of his guts, the violent slash across his belly leaking more than blood. Allan, exhausted and white faced, struggled to stand by Degal as both now staggered to Charles and the last fighting Delgardo. Already Charles had caught the man as he pretended to duck, then leapt, and Charles had slashed against his left ear and that side of his head which bled heavily, and the man toppled back against the wall, panting, hoarse and guttural, gathering his breath for the next move. His long knife, point outwards, waved, grasped now by both hands.

He played for time. "I'm Pablo, you stinking bolsa de mierda. I'm the youngest, the toughest and the prince of the Delgardos. I'll outclass Juan if I want. You chose the wrong hero to fight, fucking imbecil. You got no mouth, no shoulder, no leg, you can't stand. How can you fight?" Charles appeared to be staggering, limping on one leg as blood streamed from his mouth, already soaking his right shoulder. In spite of his own suffering, Pablo laughed, a chuckle that sounded like an avalanche of pebbles, saying, "Give in, pathetic corpse that you are, or show me how you can try to protect your miserable self."

Immediately, his breath now recovered, Charles straightened without limp or stagger, although the streams of blood continued to pour, and immediately he hurled one small knife, and danced forward holding a knife far larger.

"I think I've shown you well enough," Charles muttered, yet no longer breathless.

For the first time, and the last, Pablo tried and failed to dodge, caught by shock, surprise and his own weakness. The knife Charles had hurled pierced Pablo's neck just below the chin, and as he jerked back against the wall, his head hitting the stone, Charles thrust his longer knife through the side of the head where the Delgardo's ear was already hanging, and his head bleeding. The knife point entered where th ear had been, and continued to pierce, entering deep into both scull and brain, until the hilt hit the cheek, the blade threatening to protrude from the other side.

Behind Charles, now Allan and Degal stood over the mess spread across the laneway. Had any of the Delgardoes still breathed, they would have been stabbed within less than that last breath, but all, except the cringing Lucas, were now already dead. It was the running girl who now joined them. She darted like a ragged shadow from the cottage and stood, staring, then turned to Charles.

"Lord God bless you and keep you," she said, wide eyed, and in perfect English. "You need help, and your friends. Come inside. I swear, Lucas will help and so will I."

Even in the cloud striped moonlight, her own swelling and discoloured bruises showed, but it was Allan who fell, drowning in blood. Charles and Degal, although badly wounded themselves, lifted Allan and followed the girl into the cottage.

Briskly pushing the girl aside, another two men came behind, one in uniform, the other thickly vibrant in velvet. The velvet gowned man stamped into the small flat room, one side taken in steep stone steps, the other with the dying flickers of a fire on slate. He turned and faced the others.

"I am Don Pedro, duke to be and owner of this town. Now . You'll listen to me and do exactly as I say. First," he pointed to Lucas, "you know me and I know you, so you get water fresh from the well, you get bandages or you rip a sheet, and then you run to the church residence and tell Father Augustin that we need him here."

Lucas, quite unlike his brothers, rushed to obey. Charles nodded to Don Pedro. "I'm much obliged, sir. I am Charles, Viscount of Valdar, in service to his majesty of England. I was sent to Iberia by royal orders, but this partial destruction of the vile Delgardo family has been concluded partially as my own choice, and partially as a service to Lady Osway, the dowager Countess of Birstall. I gather, sir, you know the crimes of the Delgardo clan."

"I do, sir." The Spanish lord nodded, then frowned. "I applaud your actions and your success. I can see there's a knife wound to your chest, more blood soaking that arm, and a torrent of blood from your thigh. You need immediate doctoring, my lord. I can begin, but when Father Augustin arrives, he'll take over."

Lucas had brought a bucket of water and a pile of muslin and linen beneath one arm. Allan, wheezing and about to vomit, lay stretched on the one settle, and Degal, spluttering and oozing blood down his entire right side from neck to foot, had collapsed on the floorboards.

Charles sat heavily on the stool, now bloodstained, Don Pedro bending over him, and the young woman running to help. Pedro's uniformed companion turned to Degal while Lucas began to rip to clothes from Allan, staunching the blood and testing for broken bones.

Looking up, Charles regarded the young woman, and said, "You must be Sabine, I think."

Although she spoke a ragged form of Spanish, the girl was quite clearly English, and although desperately thin, still showing the obvious wounds and mistreatment of the recent past, she helped with everything she could. Now she paused, almost smiling.

"I must, and I am," Sabine said, winding the first bandage around Charles's leg, over the knitted silk hose, no longer black but dark red, and still wet.

CHAPTER TWENTY ONE

Charles smiled. "Do you know, senorita, that your father, your friend Illiana and her mother are all in this country, at present in Seville, risking their lives and sanity purely, and, let us say gallantly, to discover and save you?"

With a change so remarkable that Sabine turned once more into herself, she stepped back as though hit, but then stood straighter, taller, and her face lit as though a torch shone, her eyes became wide, bright blue, and her mouth blossomed and spread into a smile of wonderment and delight.

In excited English, "They're here? You mean it? They came after me? That's incredible, unbelievable, wonderful. Oh, thank you so much for telling me. Where? Let me go to them now."

"The city is some distance from here, but sadly," Charles reminded her, "for you to travel across difficult terrain, and entirely alone, would be utterly foolish. I willingly undertake to escort you, but as you can see, not only is it night, but I am a little handicapped, and so are my men. In the meantime, I promise to protect you, and will take you to Seville as soon as I'm able."

She watched the blood still oozing from his arm and leg. "It might take a week."

"For my recovery, I would imagine the day after tomorrow. Not that I have the slightest idea what day of the week that is. Life has been somewhat bilious lately, but two nights and one day will undoubtedly be sufficient for my recovery. The cut down my arm is two days old, and comparatively shallow. It simply needs a tight bandage, which I'm unable to do for myself." Charles laughed. "I have one or two broken ribs, but they'll heal. It's not the first time. The only problem seems to be a deeper cut through my thigh. That's likely to limit my riding ability, and walking even more. Meanwhile, both my men need deeper and more serious help."

Sabine was dancing. "I'll help. And the priest - ,"

Lucas and the priest, a heavily covered woman beside them, had arrived and Father Augustin took charge. Immediately he bent over Allan Reed, lying on the settle and barely able to speak or keep his eyes open. The woman helped, bringing cloths and water, and offering a long thin needle threaded with a pale twine. Lucas was ordered to help Degal, while leaving Sabine to bandage Charles, although without any attempt to first remove the ripped black silk of his hose. Charles did not object. The skin tight hose served as an additional although torn bandage.

Sabine ran to the buckets, ran to the little waning fire, ran to fill cups with wine, ran to assure Charles that the slash down his arm was partially healing and only the upper inches still bled, but did not tell him that the leg wound seemed terrifying. "There's a rather nasty red mark, a sort of uneven stripe, around your neck, sir."

"Someone attempted to strangle me," Charles told her. "Deep finger marks perhaps, but nothing serious."

"You do seem able to talk quite clearly," Sabine admitted.

"Ah," Charles sighed. "I need more than a pinch or two to stop me talking, madam. I've been informed even by royalty that I talk too much."

She giggled. "I wish you'd talk a bit more. I want to hear all about my father. About Illiana too."

"Illiana," Charles grinned through his split lip, "is a rather remarkable young woman, I believe." He limited describing the details which remained etched in his memory. "With immense courage, although not entirely wise, which inspired her to travel here to save you. Your father, meanwhile, is a man of amazing determination, courage and kindness. You've been lucky."

"I have." Sabine was still excited, and could barely stand still, hopping from one foot to another even while tying the bandage. "It hasn't been fun until now. It was a nightmare for months. Now it's a wonderful dream."

"Lucas Delgardo?"

She whispered, "A little dim. A bit of a child." Now speaking louder, "Lucas is a gentleman, a good father, and tries to behave the proper way. Nor has he ever hurt me. He hates his brothers."

"And his sister?" Charles asked abruptly.

Sabine frowned. "I've never met her but she sounds nasty, and I think her husband is even nastier."

"Perhaps, although no more," Charles smiled. "I killed him. Josefa Delgardo, however, needs a home. She has now lost everything including her husband, and rests in the inquisition's dungeons. They will release her soon, since they have no religious charge to make, but she'll need collecting from Seville. You will be leaving here. The sister may agree to look after the children in your place."

"The children are sweet. One can't even walk yet. She's sleeping even with all that noise. The other's three years old. She's in the back room where everyone sleeps and she's yelling her throat dry. I checked. She's not hurt."

"Sleeping, throat dry or otherwise," Charles said, "sounds like an exceedingly pleasant prospect. I'm accustomed to sleeping on the floor. Nor do I need a blanket. My blood will keep me warm. The other two men need far more attendance."

Don Pedro had returned on the following morning and Lucas had relit the fire while Sabine attended to the children. It was when the priest and his silent female attendant returned, that Charles was more easily able to speak with Lucas Delgardo. Don Pedro had brought four attendants, a bowl of salve, and a good measure of willow-bark pain-killer with him, and now both Allan and Degal were awake and sitting up.

"It seems you've been unfortunate with the family you were born into," Charles told Lucas, as the small man carefully removed both the bandage and the hose beneath from his upper leg.

"I had a different mother," Lucas muttered, rinsing the blood from the long linen bandage. "Reckon you've not been mighty lucky neither."

Charles assumed that his helpful nurse was not referring to his unknown English family, but to the present circumstances with the Delgardos. "You don't sob for their loss?"

Lucas looked up. "They wanted to kill me when you turned up. I'm mighty glad to see them gone." He snorted, then pointed at the unbandaged leg. "Mighty deep," he added. "Needs sewing up."

"I thought it likely," Charles said, "on both counts. Stitch away and ignore me should I faint. Meanwhile, tell me about your sister."

"Same mother as me," Lucas said, threading an already blood dripping needle. "Pablo too, but he was a pig shit. Josefa," the needle plunged into Charle's naked thigh, "wed another pig shit. Not a Delgardo, but part of the gang."

Charles caught his breath, waited for the third plunge of the needle, breathed again and said, "She needs a new home. You need a children's nurse, but you're under no obligation, should you loath the woman." He paused, then asked casually, "How many stitches do you imagine this wound will require, master Delgardo?"

"Um, well, I ain't no doctor," Lucas muttered, "but I reckon about ten. Maybe eleven. Tis a long cut and a deep cut. Still bleeding a lot."

"Carry on," Charles sighed, "And as for your sister, I assume that a good deal of her less attractive behaviour was due to her living with a violent fury-filled husband, rather than her own character. Will you take her in?"

"She'll do. She always wanted kids," Lucas said, plunging the needle into the flesh, the leg now hoisted up over an adjacent stool. "Shame you're taking Sabine. She was good, but that was why my brothers got nasty. When they found it was the grand lord Don Pedro who paid for me to take poor Sabine, they came roaring back and wanted to double the price. Once they knew how rich Don Pedro was, they thought tripled, I reckon. For months they couldn't get rid of the girl themselves, told me how no Moors wanted even to speak with them no more, and they'd tried others with no luck. So, they were lucky to put her onto me anyway and still get paid the cheap price, being all they thought I could afford."

"A sweet thought," Charles greeted the seventh piercing of the needle with a small gulp. "Is there someone you can send to Seville to collect your dear sister?"

"Without Sabine, I'll need the silly bitch," Lucas admitted. "I'll get a neighbour's wife to mind the girls whilst I go to get her." Number nine stitch sank deep. "At least you got rid of that filth Pablo. Same mother as me, but took after his bloody father."

Charles watched the immediate penetration of the tenth stitch, but saw clearly that twelve would be needed in total, and sighed. Once healed, he noted, the scar would be even more raggedly obvious than the wound had been. Indeed, the stitches were coarse, some puckered, and the thread was dirty. He reached over into the bucket with his own kerchief, bringing back a wet sponge to wash the final results. The pain remained considerable, but the fate of living with one interestingly decorated thigh, did not trouble him in the least.

"However ," Charles added, "we do not seem to have met your gang leader. Big brother Juan, I believe, was not here."

"Juan's the eldest,' Lucas agreed, finishing off the twelve stitches with a large protruding knot. "He wasn't here, thank all the saints. Not the same mother as me. His old lady was Mathilda. My dad killed her. My mother came later. Oriana. Dad killed her later. I never met the old witch. I was only a few weeks born when she was chucked off."

"A delightful family," Charles nodded, washing out his kerchief for the third time. "You, my friend, seem to be the miracle of the mob. I presume your father was also eventually killed. By the law, or simply another of the family?"

"Was a fellow living over the street," Lucas nodded cheerfully. "No one ever missed my father, not even us children, but now, Juan's never alone. He'll know nothing of the brothers being dead now." He chuckled with delight. "Sure to be a nasty shock to him, it will. Only little me left in the family, but there's another six or so in the gang, cousins or hangers-on."

"I look forward to meeting some of them," Charles smiled.

It was the morning of November the first, and Sabine gasped, thrilled, when Charles told her that he felt capable of riding back to Seville, and asked if she could ride, or needed a litter. "There will be a litter," he nodded, "since poor Allan is hardly ready to leap fences."

Allan was sitting, poking at the fire's ashes. "I'm not facing the others if they see me climbing from a litter."

"Better than seeing you fall off your horse."

November had sunk into colder evenings and grey skies fought every day to outlast the sun. Neither Charles nor Sabine was complaining. In England they would have expected frequent rain, stronger winds and colder days.

"The evenings ain't so long here," Degal reminded himself. "It's a good place as the Lord God made it, but no way I'll stay. It's the church that's spoiled what Holy God made."

"Don't speak too loud," Sabine warned him. "It was after being dragged around Granada, Juan took me to some of the villages and then Cordoba. There was a burning. A woman. I didn't see it but I smelled it. I was sick before I even knew what it was, the stink was so vile. At least, I was sick on Juan's feet and that was the only good thing that happened for months. The church here is terrifying, but Father Augustin is a wonderful kind man, well, you've met him and you know it, but the inquisition is taking over more and more."

"It's stronger in Seville," Charles said. "But that's where we're going. After sweet Seville, the Lord willing, it's time to sail home."

"Oh, first to see my father, and Illiana." Sabine was quickly flushed, but smiled back at Lucas. "You've been good to me, but freedom, that's different, and I'll never, ever forget what your brothers did to me."

Charles raised an eyebrow. "Forgetting can be the hardest challenge, harder than submitting," he said. "But we need to move quickly, or sailing home in winter storms might challenge us further."

Having left Lucas with a heap of silver Spanish jeral coins, a fortune as Lucas stated, falling to his knees, Charles had virtually nothing to pack, nor had his men. They left at once.

The troop was accustomed to moving fast but the litter once more slowed them. Sabine, still wearing her rags since she owned nothing else and had no wish to waste time visiting markets, shared the litter's dubious comfort with Allan, who half slept but never complained. The wheels rolled and discovered every stone, every dip, hole and edge, and downhill it threatened to overtake the two horses that pulled it. Charles and Degal rode, and Allan's mount, reigns attached to the litter, trotted cheerfully behind.

The days proved tedious and longer than expected, but they arrived at Seville on the third night, two nights at hostels and the third seeing the wide glimmer of the great river, finally knowing themselves in Seville. So late that the morning approached, they rode into the back courtyard of the Hotel Grande, overlooking the Plaza. One of the grooms, was asleep on the straw above the many empty booths, and on waking fed and watered the horses. Charles, Degal, Sabine and the limping Allan knocked heavily on the locked doors. The sleepy eyed janitor, robed in half a cape, bare legged, peeped out in reluctance, turning to amazement. He opened the doors.

He stuttered, as he carefully pulled the dark cape tighter across his thighs. "My lord, indeed, I remember you well and welcome you back to us. The bedchamber you used before is vacant, should you wish to retire there. Two bedchambers on the upper floor are also vacant, and your two companions will be welcome to use them, separately or together as they wish. As for the young woman - ?" Certainly Sabine, wide awake and hopping, bright eyed and grinning, wore only a bedraggled smock and was bare foot. Although the janitor was equally bare foot, the impression was quite different.

"The young woman," Charles nodded, "will also need a separate bedchamber, paid for by myself as always. However, she has family to greet first." He turned to Allan. "Take the lower room. I'll take the upper story. Degal, help him. You both need to sleep for a fortnight." Now, as the janitor hovered, he smiled at Sabine. "Shall I deliver you to your father? Or first to Illiana?"

Now she was skipping. "Both. I mean, it's far too late. They'll be fast asleep."

"I doubt they'd forgive you for leaving them asleep while you stand less than a foot's length from their beds."

"Really, do you think so?"

Charles snorted. "It is the solitary motive for them having travelled here, and their somewhat prolonged visit has not been the most enjoyable. Whilst keeping the inquisition in mind, ensuring a rabid departure would also be appreciated, I imagine."

"You're going to barge in and wake them up from dreams?" Sabine was open mouthed.

"Certainly not,' Charles told her. "You are."'

The hovering Janitor interrupted with an incoherent mumble. "Sir, the staff being all fast asleep, no cooked supper is possible, but if you ask, I could open the pantry for wine."

Charles shook his head. "You presumably need your own bed more than I need wine."

Leaving the Janitor attempting to scribble room numbers with a quill and virtually no ink, Charles led Sabine up the hotel's wide stairs to the first floor. Here Five bedchambers sat, their doors tightly closed, three adjoining on the opposing side of the corridor, with one more on the left of the staircase, and another on the right. The rooms beside the steps, being by far the largest, were occupied by Illiana, the other by her mother. Opposite and central, slept Nicholas Farrier. To the left side, Charles had previously slept, and now Allan was staggering into the wide shadows, and immediately collapsed on the bed. "This," Charles pointed to the other end of the corridor, "will be your room, my dear, but I see no point in entering there first. The bed might tempt you."

"It wouldn't. Not if I hear Papa snoring."

"No doubt he is," Charles said. Degal waved from the staircase as he climbed to his room above. Charles returned the wave. "Your father is the central door which you stand facing now. I suggest you wake him."

"I just hope he wants to see me as much as I'm dying to be back with him."

"Since he risked his life to come and rescue you," Charles admitted, "your father will be more than thrilled to see you at this or any hour. Now I am following Degal to bed, and I see no good reason for you to delay what has been almost the entire year's endeavour."

Without waiting for any answer, Charles turned and briskly disappeared up the steps. Sabine was left alone, shivering with the accumulation of excitement, delight, and panic.

Almost fearful, Sabine knocked on the door of Nicholas's bedchamber. She heard the guttural choke of a snore interrupted. After a pause, the noise began again. Nicholas was deeply asleep. Sabine knocked again, and tried the door handle, pulling it gently downwards. Nicholas never locked doors. The door opened. She crept in.

Across the far wall and beneath a tightly shuttered window, a wide bedstead lay in crumpled warmth. Beneath the three blankets, two of them partially fallen, was the mountainous lump of a body, no particle visible, as it curled, yet still stretched from bolster to the final tuck, and the entire spectacle vibrated as the covered display snored sufficiently loudly to cause the window shutters to creak.

Very slowly and carefully, almost crying but not daring to risk more than a sniff, Sabine sat on the side of the bed. Immediately she could feel her father's body warmth, a heaving mountain of humanity. It was as if she could already feel the love, and knew what would happen next if she dared to wake him.

Since she had to, Sabine leaned over him and gently pulled the big brown woolly blanket from the face she adored and had missed so desperately.

She watched the wisps of his breath rise, the ruffle of his diminishing hair tufts, and the tightly closed creases of his eyelids. His pale lashes rested on the rise of his cheeks. His mouth was slightly open, facilitating the noise that rumbled from his throat. So, then she kissed his cheek. Still Nicholas did not wake, but the snore turned to croon, sensing the affection.

For some time, Sabine watched Nicholas, enjoying the pure thrill of seeing her father again, and knowing that he had come all this way to save her. It also seemed unfair to wait too long. With gentle fingertips, she stroked one pale fuzz of eyebrow, and whispered in his ear.

"Papa my absolute angel, this is Sabine. I'm here. I'm safe. I'm free. We can go home."

Not believing, knowing this was a dream, but a dream which he cherished, Nicholas smiled, blinked, and inched one eyelid open for less than the thickness of a feather. The eye did not close again. Slowly, both eyes dared to flicker wide.

Then, with a roar that woke the entire hotel including the staff, Nicholas leapt from his covers and threw himself literally at his daughter, grasping her with both arms wrapped so tightly around her, that she wheezed and could not speak. He was still draped with the second blanket and so not entirely naked, but this seemed of less importance to him, and he squeezed harder, kissing every tiny scrap of her, skin, hair and tunic, that he could reach.

Illiana woke to the bellow from the room opposite, and, still confused and partially wrapped in the fading dream, she grabbed her bedrobe and dashed into the corridor. She expected murder, fire, or the inquisition. Instead, she saw Nicholas's open door before her, feared something even worse, and dashed in.

Bliss was something she had stopped expecting, and now could hardly believe.

CHAPTER TWENTY TWO

The footsteps, as Charles strode down from his new upper storey bedchamber, alerted Illiana as she rushed from her own bed the next morning, aiming directly for the room where Sabine was now sleeping. She turned, paused, and nodded to Charles.

"You should now be sainted, you do know that now, don't you, sir. What you've done for us is, absolutely, saintly. Amazing! I totally love you."

Charles was not smiling, but his mouth twitched at both corners. "It is," he decided, "just faintly possible, that I love you too."

Illiana laughed. "Having Sabine back, it's just holy and miraculous and wonderful. Of course, it's what we came for,. Nicholas just keeps crying. He's so happy he doesn't know what to say, and you did it for us. Poor Degal and even worse for Allan. I think you have the odd bandage too."

"Odd indeed," Charles nodded. "But useful."

Too excited to understand him, Illiana pointed to the opposite door. "She's in there. She wouldn't talk about what horrible things happened, but there must have been – too dreadful – but she's just so happy and we all are, even my mother. She's sharing with Elonza now. Goodness knows how that will end, but at least Sab's not sick. She'll be alright on a ship. She says so, said it about twenty times last night. Perhaps she needs a day for resting and eating, but then tomorrow we could sail home. Not just hotels, not just Spain. Real England. Real London."

"It's not every day that ships sail from here to England, little one," Charles reminded her, the smile now more obvious. "But within the week it's probable, depending on the weather."

Startled, Illiana stared back. "But it's only October, or just turned November perhaps, but still Autumn. The weather's lovely."

"In southern Spain," Charles agreed. "But not into the northern seas."

She hiccupped. "True. I have to remind myself, England's not like here. Not always, but November in England isn't always horrible."

"I hope the climate proves you right, since I hope to return to England shortly myself, and the troop with me. Indeed, I have my own future to ensure, to arrange and to discover. We shall see." His smile crept into clarity. "Meanwhile, I'm keeping you from visiting your long lost friend, and I must see how Allan is recovering before galloping off to the palace."

"To see the king and queen? I don't want to see either of them again. They should stop that holy torture that's going on."

"I doubt they'll stop it," Charles told her, "since they started it. They have political motives as well as religious, but their beliefs are genuine, it would seem."

"That's worse," Illiana sniffed.

"Forget the misery," Charles said, turning away, "and concentrate on the changes that bring happiness." He pressed on the hotel door to the bedchamber which had originally been his own, and quietly entered where Allan lay.

Sometime later, having left the hotel, Charles returned to the camp close to the city port on the Guadlequivir River, where his men lounged, enjoying the midday sunshine and the illusion that they remained unwatched and unneeded. Charles arrived with a loud call to arms that shot every man into action. Charles was, however, laughing. He sat with them over a brief dinner cooked over the central fire, explaining everything which had happened, what had not happened, and what he intended would happen shortly.

"I need to see this damned royalty first," he said, nose in his cup. "I need what they'll probably call clearance, before leaving. Then we leave. The murder charge against my name may be nonsense, but for the moment it remains inconvenient. Should our king ever require us to return here over the years, I might find an immediate arrest as something of a problem. Meanwhile, we need our shipping arranged. The last English traders should be ready to leave over the next week or two. I can't get a message to his highness in time for him to send an official craft, so we take what we can get. It might necessitate two ships, and we need to wait until I return from the palace." He paused, and drained his cup. "Our unexpected English friends are also hoping to sail home, now four of them, or even five, depending on what your mother wishes to do with the Spanish woman. They can either sail with us, or with some of us. Meantime, I'm off to the tedious business of once again facing these royals."

"What about the royals back home?" one man asked.

Charles nodded. "I doubt I know much more than you do. It happened after we'd sailed."

"But you knew the duke already," another man said, taking Charles' empty cup and chucking it in the water bucket. "Not that we reckoned on him being king back then."

"I met his royal highness a number of times," Charles nodded. "As Duke of Gloucester, naturally. He was vastly different than his brothers, not that I ever met Clarence, but kings are not required to behave as do dukes."

"You only knew him on business?" the first man asked.

"No. King Edward was my business," Charles said, "and Richard was a friend, but he was too rarely in London for a close friendship. I am hopeful for our future, but since our leader was the previous monarch, the Holy Lord God rest his soul, officially we are now unemployed. That remains to be fixed, and we haven't finished duty here yet, so first, John, and you, Harold, you too, Paul, if you've finished with the bucket. I'll take three backing me this time. I'm taking no risks at this late stage."

"Then we should all come," Paul stood, brushing the gravel from his hose.

"Any problems arise, then one of you ride back here to collect the entire troop," Charles nodded. "But for now, the rest of you find out what you can about what shipping's due, clean up here, and get your livery straightened."

John Newton, Harold Griffiths and Paul Thomas, three of the troop's tallest, ran for their horses.

Within less than an hour they were waiting at the palace gates, an audience with King Ferdinand and Queen Isabella having been requested at short notice. No seating was offered, but their mounts were taken to the stables and the four men were taken to the place of royal audience. Here they waited once more, standing or leaning against the open doors. Time, a sunlit time, stretched and the slanting heat through the vast glass Ventana seemed to boil without the freshness of accompanying air.

Three hours later, an intentional delay as Charles was perfectly aware, two guards announced their royal majesties, and Charles with his men bowed as King Ferdinand and Queen Isabella entered, reflections of sunlight surrounding them, dazzling onto every jewel and every polished golden trim.

"My lord," the first guard spoke as the king said, still standing while the queen sank onto her throne, "his majesty wishes to know why, once more, you seek an audience."

Facing the glitter, Charles stared, eyes cold and without any noticeable expression. "Inform their majesties that I and my troop have finished the tasks and completed the orders for which we were sent here by his majesty, the King of England, Ireland and Scotland, Wales and Calais. We therefore, request your majesties' permission to depart from your great sovereign domain within the week. I have no further duties here." He paused briefly, then turned directly to speak to the king. "However, sire, I am aware that, having been forced as a matter of self-defence, to kill a member of the Delgardo gang, and have been unjustly warned that a warrant of arrest remains with my name until further investigations are carried out. I therefore need your majesty's assurance that this warrant will immediately be dissolved."

The king glared and the guard stepped forward, facing Charles. "My lord, I trust you are aware that you must not address his royal majesty unless you are directly requested to do so."

"I have been requested to do so by His Royal Majesty King Richard of England," Charles said, flat voiced, knowing full well and without embarrassment, that he was now strongly disliked.

His majesty relented. Still standing atop the dais which held up the two thrones, he had the advantage of gazing down at the unmajestic Englishman below. "I accept your request to speak," he said with regal condensation, "and I have no objection to your departure," he continued. "However, sir, as concerns your warrant for arrest on the charge of unlawful killing, I have not yet seen the full details and will not refute the right of law regarding this."

"Although," Charles said rather briskly, "I cannot argue with your royal decisions, sire, I must insist on leaving your domain only once this brazen and unjust accusation against me is repealed. Since I come on the direct command of English royalty, sire, I doubt that arrest for the killing, in self-defence, of an infamous gang lout, known for theft and murder across the whole of Andalusia, can be lawfully sustained."

At some distance although at precisely that moment, Illiana, Sabine and Nicholas arrived at the Port of Seville, dismounted and tethered their horses. There were two horses since Sabine had rode sitting in front of her large father, who held her so comfortingly that she almost felt herself in bed.

The port was a race of citizens hurrying to the small taberna, its benches still ranging outside where the noise over brimming cups was excessive. At the piers, and the stands where weighing and customs checks were in full swing. Crowds quarrelled, and objected. The sheds where trading goods were stored, gazed out at two ships still on anchor, waiting to row in once space was available for them to lower their gangplanks. Waiting cranes, their ropes already swinging from deck to shore, or to the waiting carters with their barrows, horses snorting, men ready to load.

Sabine, now permanently excited, clung to her father's arm as she stared around. Illiana wanted to ask her what had happened, when she had originally been brought here. She thought better of it. Instead Illiana approached the beaming crane driver who had dismounted from his high stepped loader, had stretched his shoulders, and was quickly aiming for the taberna.

"Sorry," Illiana stood in front of him. "Can you tell me if there's any ships due to sail to England today? Or tomorrow?"

"Not my business, lady," the man told her, too impatient to hover.

As he pushed past, she stepped once more into his way. "Sorry," she repeated, "but can you point to someone who might know these things."

The man sighed. "Try him over there. The fellow in black with a beard he's not combed nor washed in a year. He's the Jefe del Puerto. Doesn't know much but knows more than me."

Illiana avoiding those who rushed past, bumping into her and almost knocking her over, arrived beside the man indicated, his beard, bristling as far as his chest and his official cap perched on a head of hair too thickly wayward for any normal hat.

"Sir," she began again, "I'm sorry to interrupt you and I'm sure you're dreadfully busy, but my group and I, there being four of us, are looking for a way to sail home to England, preferably to the Port of London, one day over the next week, sooner if possible. Can you tell me what craft are expected over the next few days?"

Clearly the port chief did not mind being interrupted and smiled down at Illiana. The sun, glittering across the calm sea beyond the pier, was blinding her and she tried to change direction.

"Well, my fine lady," said the boss, "there's bad weather predicted, they say. High waves out in the Middle Sea, and winds howling like wolves. Shipping is slowing, being on the verge of winter, but there's trading craft still due, and there's one in port right now." He pointed to the massive carrack tied to the pier, unloading a hundred huge crates, enormous bundles of untreated wool, and a number of large wooden barrels rolling from deck to the hooks of the two cranes still working.

"That one?"

"She's *The Wind Victor*. One of the biggest. Won't be leaving again for a couple of days, but depending on the expected gales, she'll be off by Friday."

Illiana thanked him and set off towards the ship's high shadow. It was considerably larger than the carrack that had first brought her to Spain. She wondered if this gigantic vessel would roll more, or tip less. Whether size and weight would make sailing less comfortable, she did not know, but imagined it surely would.

Now dodging more ropes, crates and running men, she stood within the spread of the ship's shadow itself. The vast weight of the carrack heaved against the high stone quay, its wooden side, still brine wet, cracking and bumping, fighting against its own imprisonment, wood against stone. The smell of brine was making her feel slightly bilious but Illiana still stared up, and up further, and finally gazed at the poop deck, looming high, where three men stood, shouting orders and cursing those hauling up the stores.

Even higher above, a cloud of gulls screeched, swooping and diving as they searched for any fishing vessel arriving with food to steal. Even their great wings swept the wind into squalls and their calls were like a storm that drowned out the less impressive human voices.

Illiana was wondering if any of those men would hear her if she called her questions, or even bother to pause in their work, when she heard a high and frantic scream which made her turn at once.

Immediately she forgot about questions and even ships. For a moment seeing nothing, she hesitated, but the scream was repeated and Illiana ran. Any woman screaming needed help, and it might be Sabine, even though well protected by her father. Nicholas would never have left her even a finger's length beyond his guardianship.

Now it was Illiana pushing, shoving and running, until directly before her Nicholas stood, one arm, hand fisted, raised. It was certainly not her that he was threatening, and his other hand clutched at the hilt of the sword on his belt. The man he faced stood close, the muzzle of his gun just a foot's length from Nicholas's face. Sabine pummelled, screaming, at the man with the gun, and around them a milling crowd stopped, stared, and whistled, but did not interfere.

Sabine was wearing one of Illiana's gowns and had started to regain her courage, yet now it seemed the past was back in her life, and she pummelled the arm of the armed stranger, who was clearly no stranger at all.

"He's the most evil bastard in Spain," she was screaming. "It's Juan Delgardo. Kill this evil monster."

No one from the growing crowd seemed ready to interrupt.

"Which is the wrong 'un?" one voice asked in English.

"Which is the worst bastard?" another said in Spanish.

Illiana, unarmed except for the tiny knife hidden in her boot, ran to the creature she had never seen before and pushed him violently from one side. Too heavy, too accustomed and too angry, Juan Delgardo did not move, almost as though he had not even noticed the assault.

He spoke, between his teeth and without looking aside, "You touch me again, fucking bitch, and I'll fire first at this bugger and then at you." Then he spat and the saliva stuck to the toe of Nicholas's large riding boot. Without a breath of hesitation, Nicholas's fist reached over the gun's muzzle, and rammed hard into the man's broad nose. It spurted blood.

As the Delgardo lurched away, cursing, the gun fired, but the aim, which had previously been directed at Nicholas's head, had now flown high, its vehemence smoking with the stink of sulphur. Indeed, the mis-fired explosion also flung the Delgardo killer backwards, and he tumbled onto one of the onlookers behind him.

Nicholas kicked out but Delgardo was back on his feet, and darting forwards. He grabbed at Nicholas's leg and tipped him. Both Sabine and Illiana grabbed their hidden knives and ran to stab, but another stranger stepped between them.

"That's not proper," the man said, one hand held up to stop them. "Not right for three against one. Outnumbered. Not proper."

Illiana screeched, "That's a bastard Delgardo with a gun – against an honest man with just a sword. Is that right?"

Now Juan Delgardo roared, "That yellow haired puta belongs to me and I claim her back."

Although her Spanish was still limited, Sabine yelled in return, "I'm no puta and I belong to nobody but my Papa," and she pointed to where Nicholas was scrambling up. "This pig bastard stole me away and sold me to his brother, but the brother let me go. This is the Delgardo chief and ought to be in gaol."

As, startled, the interfering stranger stepped away, Delgardo grabbed at Sabine and Nicholas, back on his feet, swung his sword. With an echoing crack, it sliced directly through Juan's thick wrist, and the stump, bleeding profusely, dropped back while the hand twitched, and toppled to the red stained ground.

As though not feeling the immediate crushing pain, Juan lashed out with the gun in his other hand, smashing the barrel into Nicholas's face, and then firing it towards Illiana, but she had grabbed Sabine, and ran towards Nicholas, missing the explosion, which instead hammered into another stranger's foot. The man howled and his large wife stormed forwards.

"This filthy bastard is a Delgardo, and alone, so grab the filth and call the guards."

There had been a Delgardo companion, one of the gang, but younger, and at the first threat, this boy had run, disappearing into the sunlight. As the crowd, unsure, moved closer to the fight, so Juan swung with the still bleeding stump of his arm, snashing it into Sabine's face. Blood and dripping muscle, gore and broken bone stunned Sabine and she collapsed into the crimson puddled below. Then Illiana stabbed out with her small knife, and ripped into the bulging Delgardo cheek, and, with Nicholas now hurtling forwards with a blade far longer, Juan again fell back and fumbled unable to reload the gun with one hand.

The Port Chief, his beard of black crusted curls protruding as though a weapon itself, rattled forwards, and forcibly grabbed the gun from Delgardo's hand. He pointed it directly into Juan's face, the muzzle just an inch from Juan's furious black eyes.

Behind him, Nicholas scraped his sword point across the back of Delgardo's neck. Illiana helped Sabine from the ground and they stood together, shaking and watching.

Juan Delgardo roared, "Now tis not loaded, fucking idiot, and will not fire." Nicholas's great sword blade cracked against his neck, and he crumpled. Blood from his nose and cheek still covered the man's face as he lay still, flat on his back, two blood stained eyes staring up into the glare of the sun. Bending over the body, both Nicholas and the chief stared, then kicked delicately, each checking whether the body was man or corpse. Sabine collapsed in Illiana's arms as she hugged her, Nicholas heaved one mighty breath and swung both his arms around Sabine and Illiana together, while the bearded chief, the gun held tight beneath one arm, shouted for his assistant.

The corpse, a mess of blood darkening in the sun's heat, lay like a heap of dung. The handless wrist had twisted beneath his head as he fell, but the hand itself, a filthy scarlet mess of rigid fingers, sat alone beside one foot. The eyes now shut, the mouth hanging wide, the face seemed strangely relaxed, as though finally at peace.

No one else moved, then the shock turned to curiosity and gossip became as loud as the chief's shout. Gossip turned to rumour, stories of the Delgardos ranged, one man began to insist that an innocent man had been slaughtered, and that Sabine was clearly the dead man's daughter.

"Bright yellow hair to a very dark Papa?"

"His wife, then."

The chief's assistant bounded into sight, shoving through the mill, and others in uniform followed him. The chief kicked again at the Delgardo corpse, "Get that heap out of here, and that," he pointed to the small bloody lump, once a hand, "and off for burial and no church ground needed. You," and now he turned to Nicholas, "reckon you're under arrest, fellow. The bugger you killed deserved to die, but who the hell are you?"

"I," said Nicholas in English, standing tall in spite of his broken ribs and bruises, "am the English servant of the Lady here, and was protecting both her and my own little daughter. There be plenty o' witnesses. I ain't guilty o' naught. I deserves praise, I reckons, fer doing the proper right thing."

As everyone stared, attempting to understand, so Illiana, still squashed, called out a translation in Spanish, and the port chief sniffed. "Maybe fair enough. Wasn't it you asking moments passed about a passage to England?"

Illiana disentangled herself. "Yes, that was why we came here, sir. This, my friend and groom, and of course his daughter, also my friend, were here on personal business when that foul criminal attacked. My groom was heroic, and has rid your land of one of the worst villains you've ever had.

The crowd roared agreement and some clapped. The chief nodded. "Truth is truth," he mumbled, "so fair enough. I mark you a free man, Master Groom, and you can leave in peace." He pointed at the great carrack, still bound to the quay, but at the other end of the port and barely seen past the crowd which grew thicker every moment. "That's the one to take you back to your own country, my lady, and if you sail with her, I shall put in a good word about what happened here. She'll be mooring out in the river once fully unloaded, but needs a scrub and the sailors need a rest and a drink before reloading. So, two days, you've got, and in a moment or two, the captain, he'll be in the taberna, and you can ask for the cabins you want."

Although feeling the need to collapse herself, she thanked him and faced Nicholas, Sabine still in his embrace. "So do we get passage, including my mother" I think we need to sit at that bar anyway. We need one of those benches and a good drink each. Nicholas, you're hurt. Sabs and I are almost dead too."

Nicholas's face was marked, raw patches of flesh, oozing blood, and Sabine's eyes were both bloodshot. "Too true," Nicholas croaked. "I'll bring my little one, and I'll never let her get hurt again. Never, I swears it."

"You already saved my life," she breathed. "First that man Charles, and now my wonderful heroic Pa."

It was a limping stagger across the port to the tavern, and there they collapsed onto the first outside bench, but they were followed by many of the crowd. Now they were again surrounded and voices cried out, "I'll buy you a beer, my man," "Tis my treat and honour to get wine and food for you all," and "You just say whatever you want, and I'll be getting it."

Someone else leaned over with two clean kerchiefs. "Here, wipe off the blood while I get four mugs of wine."

They sat, breathing hard into the briny air, thanking and

praising each other while also thanking the crowd for their offers, drinking the wine and waiting for the captain of *The Wind Victor*.

"I bin told all about you," said the captain as he arrived. "There's a whole port full o' folk ready to tell your tale. I reckon I's proud to call you English. You gets three cabins or more here and now, and more if you wants 'em. If the weather don't turn to shipwreck storms, then we'll be sailing outta here early on Saturday morning. Port o' London is waiting, I reckon. Not many more ships will dare sail this time o' year."

"I'll pay for three cabins," Illiana said at once. "And I know someone who may want some more."

CHAPTER TWENTY THREE

"I've got you some cabins," Illiana told Charles as they faced each other the following morning over the breakfast table. "But I haven't paid for them. You can always cancel if you'd like to stay here and chat to the Inquisitor instead."

"Bertha told me." Charles leaned forwards. "You and your friends are even more remarkable than I'd previously known. My opinion leaps so high, it leaves me exhausted."

Although she smiled, Illiana still didn't have the energy to laugh. "That's sweet, and from you - ."

"Since I am surely the most courageous creature in England, - ."

"I don't think I know how to judge courage, but I can judge a few other things. Like kindness, incredible, amazing kindness."

Charles was briefly surprised and raised one eyebrow. "You judge me, little one?"

Illiana thought herself criticised. "No. Well yes, but only to say what I said. I mean, I just wanted to thank you. What you've done for us is incredible. Of course I mean Sabine, but you've helped with so much as well."

He was smiling. "I don't object to being judged. It happens regularly. No man can work for royal security without being constantly answerable for his failures, but I doubt anyone before has given quite such a complimentary opinion."

Now she laughed. "I'd be surprised if you ever fail. I'd wager your father is so proud of you."

Now Charles also laughed. "I doubt it. I doubt he knows who I am. He lost my mother when I was a child, and now drifts invisible through life with his secrets. I have met him once or twice, but would never recognise him should he pass me in the street."

"Fathers are all odd." Illiana thought of her own, the hero she had adored until recently when discovering the wicked side which her mother had long kept hidden.

She looked up. "Kings too. You say we have a new one, but not the child I expected. When King Edward died so suddenly, well it sounded sudden when I heard about it from you, his heir was a boy. Twelve years old, I think, but you talk of King Richard, a warrior."

Charles settled back, still smiling. "This has been an entirely remarkable year, not only for you and your family, my dear, but for our entire country. You want me to explain the twists and turns of royalty? There are other things I'd far sooner talk about with you."

"Sailing home?"

He watched her quietly for a moment. He watched her embarrassment as her thick dark eyelashes blinked downwards, covering her concern. Nor could he resist being aware of the rise and fall of her breasts beneath her gown. Then he spoke softly. "I know rather more about you and your family than you seem to know about yourself, my dear. I assume, although assumptions can be invariably proved absurd, that you remain in mourning for the earl, particularly after only a month of marriage. Otherwise, what I should gladly discuss, is somewhat more than a shipboard cabin."

Puzzled, Illiana told him, "Yes, Benedict. He was wonderful. I think I loved him but, well, I hardly knew him. I couldn't stop thinking of him as my master. Me as a kitchen maid, him as the earl, and now, after everything that happened here, it's hard to remember that different life, just a month, being married and rich and so comfortable. It's all so strange."

"And not knowing that your own grandfather was a baron. I presume, your uncle is now the earl."

"It's really hard to believe. Once we get home, I'll have to find out, but curiosity usually leads to disappointment, doesn't it."

"My own curiosity," Charles grinned, "promises delight, should I ever be permitted to reveal it."

Liking the smile and the glint in his dark eyes, Illiana's own curiosity was aroused, no longer involving her grandparents, nor her uncle. She wondered if she was blushing and looked down at her platter, and the cup standing empty. Reaching for the jug, she filled her cup, then refilled the wooden tankard beside Charles. His grin remained, while watching her cheeks flush and her eyes blinking, not daring to face him.

He thanked her for the wine.

She said, "It's funny, how we met and even more strange ever since. Sabine's safe, which is the best of all, and you killed almost all that disgusting Delgardo gang. It's not just revenge, but, that's going to save so many more innocent people."

"More importantly, now the leading brother lies dead, the entire brood is destroyed." He chuckled, his lips shining with wine which made them appear abruptly thicker. Inviting. "I presume he died without knowing almost all his brothers were already slain. I envisage him arriving at heaven's gate, Saint Peter refusing him entry, his entire family there hammering on the doors, furious at being sent down to hell."

She giggled again, trying not to spurt her mouthful of red wine. "I think they'll be stuck in purgatory a bit longer than that. They can carry on fighting each other in there. What I wanted to say before, and I expect you won't care and you'll think I'm very boring, you see, I don't have many friends except Sabs, and I just wanted to say I think you're my friend now. I'd love to think you are."

His answer was immediate. "It is sometime now that I've considered you my friend, little one, and I admit that I've been thinking of you as, perhaps, something more."

The blush was now more prominent. "Oh. I mean, you're a lord. You do know I'm only a kitchen maid. Well, alright, I'm not but it's all I've ever been until that one month. If you mean what I think you mean, then I can't. I wouldn't. Not unless, no, not that."

Charles leaned back, chuckling. "Are men all so disreputable, my dear? Perhaps we are indeed. So, shall I speak more openly? Forgive me, but much as I should love to gather you into my arms and then into my bed, it was not exactly what I had in mind. Nor are you a kitchen maid, little one. You were born a lady, and are now a dowager countess. Grand enough, don't you think?"

She felt her face burning. "For jumping into a man's bed?"

His laugh faded. "Neither jumping nor pressured," he said, his eyes now fixed, the heavy lids only partially hiding their meaning.

The blush had faded but Illiana still didn't face him. "I'm beginning to understand you," she said. "You're someone who takes an awful lot of understanding. Your face never tells what you're thinking. Actually, your words don't either."

"How very tedious for you," he told her, the smile still caught in the tucks beside his lips. "Understanding myself is entirely dull, even for myself."

"Which is not -,"

The door across the room opened, and Nicholas marched in with Bertha beside him.

"My little Sabine, thanks to you my blessed lord, now be deep asleep, wrapped warm and comfy. Back with friends and family. I left my lass dreaming. She needs a good long time resting, I reckon."

Bertha's smile was in blossom. "What an amazing miracle, and Illiana, my dear, no Delgardos will ever capture poor girls again, no young girls trapped as slaves. Now I dream of my own wonderful bedchamber waiting for me across the water back at home."

"Reckon t'will be a month to get there, but Saturday morning the ship will be waiting for us." Nicholas grinned, wide eyed, at Charles, having no notion of what he had interrupted. "Reckon there be other cabins, my lord, mayhaps not fer the whole troop."

"Not all my men expect a cabin," Charles told him. "Most would sleep on deck. I, on the other hand, being a man of high expectations," and he nodded silently at Illiana, "may hire my own bedchamber." He smiled rather suddenly. "Unless anyone would like to share with me."

"Happy to do so," Nicholas said and Charles laughed.

"I've no objection to that, my friend. First, we'll discover how many cabins sit empty."

Nicholas, still grinning, was hovering instead of sitting. "Just going to trot up them stairs again," he mumbled, "see is my Sabs is awake."

Illiana stayed at the table as Nicholas disappeared again, and Charles left through the main doors. Although she'd drunk both beer and wine and needed nothing more, she accepted the serving of bread, oil, and soft cheese, and fiddled, soaking the bread in the oil, and munching small pieces. She nodded as her mother ate avidly.

"So, after I told you all about everything last night, you told Charles?"

Bertha looked up and nodded back. "Of course, my dear. "Such wonderful courage and I wanted to tell such a lovely story. You and Nicholas and Sabine, heroes every one, and now the worst Delgardo of them all is dead too. I'd happily tell your story over and over again. Besides, for someone like Charles, it was important to know."

"I'm not complaining," Illiana said quickly. "I was just wondering what you thought of him. Charles, I mean."

Her mother paused, bread half way to her mouth. "He's an

impressive man. Likeable enough although all that official behaviour makes him seem rather aloof. Why?"

"I think he likes me," Illiana hiccupped. "And I think I like him."

Her mother shrugged and continued eating. "He's a lord and he's friends with the king. So, marry him."

"He hasn't asked me."

"Then ask him." Bertha leaned forwards. "You're a heroic countess, my dear. You can do anything."

"There's things I'm definitely still a coward about." Illiana munched and swallowed, then pushed her platter away. "I'm not ready to be just a mistress. The man surely finds someone else next year and dumps me, or has three or four mistresses at the same time, or you get older and get wrinkles and the man tells you to get lost."

Bertha smiled slowly. "It seems you have little trust in men, my child. Does this wicked Charles refuse marriage, even with a countess?"

She had no answer, and was pleased when Nicholas reappeared. This time Sabine was with him and the conversation changed immediately. Though excited to talk with her dearest friend once more, Illiana continued to think of Charles. She wondered if he thought of her, or was no longer interested as he checked on his men and then rode to the port to arrange berths, and probably to the team's camp nearby where his men would need to prepare for sailing home within two days.

With the aged Lord Benedict, Illiana had discovered love, and what love meant in bed. She had feared it, then found it sweet and safe. A younger man might not have similar ideas, however, might not be as gentle. Yet her mother called her courageous. Charles himself had called her courageous. Did being seen as courageous mean that she would be expected to show courage in bed.

Sabine interrupted her. "Dearest Illiana, you have drifted far away. Will you agree with what your Mamma just said?"

She stared at her mother. "Did you say I was an idiot? Then I agree."

"I shall never, ever say such a thing again," Bertha insisted. "I was the fool, my dear, not you." She sighed heavily. "The trouble is, my dear, I wonder if I've been a fool again. I'm worried about Elonza."

"I can afford the extra cabin."

"Gracious no, she can share mine." Bertha gulped the last wine in her cup, as though taking medicine. "However, I'm wondering what I'll do with her in England."

"She's sweet, and she's not expecting to be another countess," Sabine interrupted. "She'll find work in some grand house, though not in yours, I hope. That would be most uncomfortable, but she's nice. She'll find a husband and be married at last."

Bertha shook her head, but then nodded. "Poor Elonza, that would be nice and she's excited about leaving here. But," and Bertha lowered her voice, "she's frightened of everything. She won't even come for a walk or join us for dinner. I have to order food sent up for her and she won't take anything special. Not even wine."

"Living a lifetime in a tiny village, pretending to be a widow – well, that keeps you safe, I suppose. But without knowing anything about real life." Illiana shook her head.

"She's never seen the sea," Bertha mumbled. "She can't read or write. She lived in permanent fear of the couple living opposite"

Now Sabine smiled. "So the poor little woman needs to discover what life is really like."

Hours sped by. Nicholas returned to the stables, but hurried back, longing to be close to his daughter. Bertha asked the waiter if dinner could now be served in the little breakfast room, since moving tables to the larger hall seemed pointless.

"Whatever you wish, my lady."

There were, after all, no other guests except for two injured men remaining in their bedchambers.

It was after the main meal of a humid day that the women rested once more, windows shuttered against the beating heat, their bedchambers dark and quiet. Nicholas, the smile now permanent, stayed in the stables and unable to hug his daughter, instead hugged the horses.

Waking in the abrupt increase of heat, Illiana forgot her dream of a bed of more excitement than her own, and rolled from her mattress to peer through her window shutters. Seeing nothing, and quickly tumbling back into bed, she dreamed again, but this time while awake.

Reuniting with Sabine had renewed the delight in closeness, arms holding warm and tight, the return of talking, talking endlessly, someone understanding and talking back, sharing favourite memories. It made Illiana wonder if any man could be as loving. Indeed, she had rarely talked much with Benedict, although she had listened as he talked to her.

Then something very different had become evident as the stench Illiana now understood too well, had begun to seep, oozing relentlessly, soaking the air around her.

They were memories to banish, but the present could be worse than the past and Illiana was abruptly terrified. She needed only her shoes, so thrust her toes into them, and ran from her room to the stairs and down to the great windows looking out over the plaza. Illiana knew what she would see, knew she'd be sick, but could not avoid seeing what was being done.

Across the open square, partially paved, she saw the smoke rise in dark muddy swirls, and the sizzling twisting flame tips birthing the smoke.

Running from the hotel's doors, she dodged into the street which led almost immediately to the square, and there joined the gathering crowd who chose, either with interest or with disgust, to watch the torture of the inquisition. She called up to the man standing directly in front of her.

"Sir, who is trapped there? What is happening?"

The man turned, pulling Illiana beside him and to see more clearly. "Tis them Jews," he explained flatly. "They get told to convert or leave. They don't want to leave. Fair enough. They got family here, homes, business, many been born here, so they pretend to convert. Makes sense, but in secret they practise their own stuff. Same as us but changes. Fridays not Sundays. What to eat and what you can't. I had a friend, told me a bit, but left two years back. I didn't want him to go. Now I reckon it's just as well."

Three fires had been lit. Ash, sparks and the sooty thick smoke flew in the wind. As the flames leapt up, devouring legs, arms and bodies, it was clear that all three men strapped to the high wooden stakes over piled twigs, cut bark and boughs, seemed already drugged or dead, their eyes shut, heads unmoving, cheeks lying on their shoulders.

"Did they die quietly before this vile murder?"

The man looked down at her again. "A sensible family arranges that," he said.

"Not a sympathetic priest?"

"Are there any?" the man asked.

The stench filled the sky and Illiana grabbed her stomach, bending, refusing to be sick. Now the sky was black although it was not yet evening. The man beside her, eyes glazed, shook his head and stepped back, then strode away. Illiana wanted to run across the plaza square to shout and scream against the inquisition, to tell others watching that this was not the work of Christianity, but the work of the devil. However, these three men were already dead, and the priest at the far edge of the square would soon have her staked alongside the three pyres, and she'd know the horror of burning alive, and seeing her legs aflame beneath her. There would be no one to kill her first, nor to save her while still alive.

Then someone grabbed her arm and the long fingered hand was firm and inescapable.

Having imagined burning herself, now she screamed and

another hand clamped hard over her mouth. Then she thought it was the man who had spoken with her, but, turning, she saw only shadows, eyes behind smoke, and hats drawn low.

"Come away. Now." the voice thrummed directly into her ear, and she knew who had grabbed her after all.

Leaning backwards against the black silk and the muscular solidity beneath it, Illiana allowed Charles to help her, almost lifting her back through the other folk watching, until once more she stood at the doors of the hotel, her body as limp as her will.

She whispered, "I want to run away."

Charles told her, "Tomorrow you sail far away. You'll see no more of this sickening cruelty. Our church is not always kind generosity, but no inquisition will come to England."

"They say King Henry the Fifth burned the Lollards alive. "

"Well nigh seventy years gone, and neither of us alive to remember it. No man, woman or child will ever burn alive in England ever again, not under this king nor any future king."

She was in his arms now, ready to fall had Charles released her. She stretched out one arm, reaching to open the doors, although she would sooner have collapsed to the steps.

Instead, sweeter still, Charles lifted her and she realised that she sat before him on the saddle of his Spanish gelding, his strength supporting her, both arms cradling her, his hands grasping the reins at her waist. Both remained silent, wrapped like lovers, and only the horse neighed as it trotted forwards, directly away from the reek of the plaza.

They rode slowly, the trot soon fading to walk, the hooves a faint plod on the beaten earth. They skirted the city streets, winding to the soft earth of the outer lanes, now heading directly towards the river.

The intense comfort and sense of utter security allowed Illiana to lean back against the steady heartbeat and the itch of golden embroidery on soft silk, but finally, whispering, Illiana asked,

"Isn't it too soon for the port? That ship will still be moored out in the river."

"No port, no ship yet, my little one." The warmth of his breath floated down against her forehead, a more gentle smell.

She wriggled, trying to look up at him, but was not permitted to move. Instead of pushing against the hard restriction, Illiana rested, loving to be cradled. "Then where?"

"Another home to welcome you," he murmured.

Darkness now enclosed them. No longer the rank smoke of murder, this was a cool night and above them the first glimmer of star specks peeped out. The only smell was of old dried grass, hot earth, and distant water. Nestled in beauty, she wished such a dream might continue forever.

Abruptly, as the ride seemed to slow even more, she heard the murmur of voices, then the tiny clink of cup against cup, and finally saw the dither of golden specks, not high silver stars, but the tips of flames and the scarlet spit of heat rising, dancing sparks red and gold.

Yet before she could think of pain and terror, Charles said, "A small camp fire, and it invites you, as I do, to sit and talk and drink until the stars grow larger and the fire sinks to embers." Charles dismounted and lifted Illiana down to the small crowd of liveried men, the troop sitting around the cooking fire, some laid out on the soft dry grass, each with his own gentle gaze up at the stars now creaming in the glitter of unbelievable magic.

One man stood, took the reins and strode off to unsaddle and feed the horse, while Charles brought Illiana close and sat with her beside the crackling brilliance. Another man razed his cup, Charles nodded, and at once two brimming cups of wine were brought. A third man called, "Greetings to the lady and you too, my lord. How's Allan now?"

Charles nodded. "Better than before but less than tomorrow. We'll not be sailing home just yet, my friends. Degal might manage the voyage but Allan needs a week of doctoring."

Now Illiana whispered, "Then you won't travel with us on Saturday?"

"I cannot," he told her very softly. "It was my wish and my intention, but I'll not leave Allan to die alone, nor bring him to die at sea. Only if my friend dies first, or recovers sufficiently to travel, will I take sail. Will you remember me, little one?" He lay back, resting on both elbows, Illiana resting gently, her head against his chest. Continuing to whisper, he said, "I will never forget you, as long as my own life lasts. Can you imagine what I dream?"

The fire sparks were hot and dizzy golden, the stars behind were cold silver, buried in utter blackness, but Illiana was deeply asleep.

Only a little later, she woke and believed herself still dreaming. She barely felt the narrow bed beneath her, simply the strength of the arms around her and the steady heart beat beneath her ear. Then, realising herself awake, she did not dare move, and gradually judged where she must be. Above, now the shadow of the tent moved silently in the wind. Her bed, she told herself, was not the man, but a narrow base heaped with softness spread beneath her. Beside her, sharing the softness and adding his own warmth, Charles lay and held her against him. Still fully dressed except for boots, her toes remained comfortable in their stockings, and her hair was tangled around his long fingers.

Because her breathing had changed and her eyes had blinked, Charles whispered, "Awake, little one? Stay here tonight, and forget trouble, pain, fear and death. Here you are so safe, not even memory can hurt you, and I will not touch you further, I promise it, although the temptation is as beautiful as the stars."

She stayed curled against him, smelling the warm wine on his breath, knowing her own breath would smell the same, but said, "If you had come to me on the ship home, my cabin or yours - ,"

"Promise me nothing, little one," he told her. "or I might ask for proof tonight. I cannot sail with you, much as I wish I could."

"Your life takes you to strange places. Will I ever see you again?"

"Do you distrust me, my love? My plans already live in my mind." Although it was his clothes that cradled her, she felt the muscled thighs across her own legs beyond the cloth of her skirts, the finger tip caresses of his hands, and the delicious imprisonment of his arms. Over her brow, his chin enclosed her, moving softly as he spoke. "I doubt you realise how beautiful you are, I doubt you know your own courage, but it's not your virtues I adore, it's the gentle inner truth of you, the woman you are. Trust me, little one."

"So one day you'll hold me like this again?"

"When I marry you, my dear, when our bed is soft and curtained, and when I unclothe you, piece by piece, and discover what I already imagine, but will not touch."

CHAPTER TWENTY FOUR

Confined to a tiny cabin with the heaving, creaking, tipping and the rolling of the ship, was the custom at sea and Illiana was comfortable with what she had already experienced before. She wandered the decks when permitted, and spoke with the crew. This was an English trader and its sailors, when not too busy, were pleased to sit beneath the sun's blaze and talk of home.

The first three days of ease smelled not of brine, but of the fresh river water as they sailed the Guadalquivir towards the port of Sanluca and the entrance into the great waves of the northern sea.

Bertha also accepted the mounting pleasure of those first days when the rolling of the hull was a reminder of what she had become accustomed to on the first journey. She had another reason for leaving her cabin as often as the weather permitted, which was to escape the tiny space she shared with Elonza.

Elonza had never travelled the oceans before. She had never trudged the coasts and had never seen the mighty waves. Even her stubby toes had never felt the warm incoming ripples of the Middle Sea. Safely tucked away in a sunny laneway, unconcerned, since she had always been known as a respectably wedded young woman, now a gentle widow, no threat had ever troubled her except the one pair of horrid pig-neighbours across the road. Others liked her. She helped pot shrubs, grow and sell spinach and lemons, she swept paths and cooked when some friend proclaimed a birthday. She ate, pottered, slept, chatted, and saw no life beyond the bleached stone walls, the beaten earth below and the bright blue sky above.

It was her own minute house, left by her parents, in which she had a bed, a cooking pot, one room and even a window. She knew the priest, she knew the church, she knew the market. She had never known anything else of any description, nor wished to.

Now having climbed aboard the carrack as a newly blossoming almond bud, excited to begin a new life, the small Spanish woman shivered, worried the new life which awaited her, might not love her as she had hoped. The crew were busy preparing to sail, yet men smiled as she boarded, and her new friend Bertha, the woman she had almost brought to death, was close at her side, helping her. The promise was sweet, kind and welcoming.

Yet the first day at sea had abruptly turned to threat. The cabin's size had not troubled her and the bed was no smaller nor less comfortable than she had used at home. The sense of belonging which had cuddled her all the long years in the house where she'd been born, had now whistled far, far away and what remained was proving violently unhospitable. From the tiny window above her bed, all she could see was wild blue water. Having only ever known the solidity of land, the lurching risks of waves had been beyond her imagination. Beneath her, everything rolled and jolted, sank and swayed, churning her stomach and turning her excitement to terror.

Bertha had helped her, brought her a breakfast she could not eat, brought her ale which she could not drink, and had then left her alone. She had been repeatedly bilious, filling the chamber pot with vomit and then smelling it, which made her sick again, not knowing how to empty it. Alone in bed, Elonza cried. She missed the little hot streets of home, the safety of her tiny house, the candle she could afford to light for an hour each evening, and the safe pleasure of her own cooked food. Now life was too strange to stomach, and those she had believed her new friends, were rarely beside her.

Now November, there were more dangerous waters as they sailed from the river and winter's waves knocked against the sides. They span against the prow and jolted suddenly, until The Wind's Victor lurched violently and quickly sent the other unaccustomed traveller, Sabine, scurrying to her bed.

Sabine and Illiana had chosen to share a cabin. Illiana did not speak of who she had dreamed to share her bed, and instead had chosen to keep close to Sabine. It was all she had come for, although not all she had found.

Almost one year past, when on the journey to Spain, she had accustomed herself to the habits of sailing and had been too excited to complain. Again, now, Illiana was excited. To have succeeded and now to dream of home with her friend beside her, was as exciting, perhaps more so. However, she discovered the difference of an angry winter ocean, and the dreary reminders of what she felt she had now lost.

Sabine's memories of her trip out, were hideous from the beginning, and nothing had ever helped her learn the sweetness of wind in the white sails above her head. She did not know the joy of their stark outline against a vivid blue sky in a world of reflections and the fresh tingle of brine, the leap of the fish and the sweep of an endless horizon. She had never discovered the ocean's beauty. She had been raped on the second day, and by three strange and brutal men who had formed a queue, waiting and watching. She had known only the beginning of the nightmare.

Now as Sabine rolled and vomited, she knew this was the start of a glorious dream. However, Elonza's dream was fading into the nightmare she feared.

At first the gulls flew over the sails, screeching into the rush of the tide. Then each day seemed longer. Often the glimmer of the sun brought the astounding leap of the dark finned creatures hurtling, protruding lipped faces appearing, then splashing back into the deep blue. The strum of sudden heavy rain, water pelting onto water, and finally the rich serenity of the night.

When the moon shone high, it reflected like another sea beast, a silver crescent rippling over the dark waters. Once, Illiana, leaning over the gunnels, saw her own reflection gazing back at her, but when the lurching and tipping increased, the waves rose as high as the crow's nest and the wooden prow sounded as though broken, so she hurried to the cabin and curled with Sabine.

Otherwise, it was Nicholas who sat and talked to his daughter, helping her on deck in the sun's warming bask, or next to her, sitting on the edge of the bed where she lay.

"Sailing out, all them months ago," Nicholas chuckled, "I sat with the crew to try and speak a bit o' Spanish. When I were proud to practise them foreign words with them foreign fellows, there weren't hardly none as understood me no how."

Bertha now had no need of hearing Spanish words to remind herself, and found the English sailors less interesting. She no longer called her daughter a fool, and was happy to stroll beside her, yet when the angry weather sent her back to her bed, she attempted to cheer Elonza, but found only a miserable woman vomiting, which forced her to vomit as well.

Then, gradually as the erratic autumn seas turned to winter fury and the weeks brought them away from the Iberian coast, into the wild challenge of the northern tides, so storm followed storm. Winds lashed through deep waters and lightening split a sky as dark during day, as at night. The explosion of storm over water seemed to divide threat from safety.

Bertha was sick over the side of the ship, Elonza sobbed and ate nothing, Illiana fell, missing her footing down the steps to her cabin, and Sabine curled deeper into her blanket. Only Nicholas still smiled, either bringing water to Sabine, or chatting to the sailors on deck.

The sails were brought down, legs straddling the rigging, and the men rushed to the oars. Sabine felt sorry for herself and even more sorry for the sailors. On the next mild day when she tottered across the deck from left hand gunnels to the right hand gunnels, she sighed to one of the men. You're having a difficult voyage, she sympathised. "What terrible weather." She still felt bilious but smiled. "It's dreadfully hard work for you."

The man looked startled. "Sorry you feel so sick, miss," he told her, "but we reckon the weather's pretty good for this time of year. We expected worse. Only another twelve days or so, and you'll be back on dry land, for the wintery gales blow us on faster. Once we've unloaded, I'll be off for Christmas with the wife. Perhaps you'd best have a cup of wine."

Sabine thanked him and dashed downstairs to be sick again.

Five long days swam by, calm with a mild sun turning the sea a glittering blue, and even Sabine began to eat. She also had that cup of wine.

Elonza, helped by Bertha, struggled onto the deck for her first glimpse of the ocean's magic. For one moment, a blink of delight, she wondered if she had discovered beauty. The sailors, lazing on deck with mugs of ale, were talking together, and Elonza listened. It was a strange and ugly language which she disliked and could not understand a single word. She realised, and called herself a fool for not realising before, that her new life and her new world would not even include her. She had chosen to leave safe familiarity, only to enter the abrasive rejection of any true friendship. There would be voices gabbling, she would hear only ugly noises, and ears turning away from her own words. She suddenly realised that she now journeyed into alienation, bitter cold, and utter loneliness.

On the sixth day, a storm blew down from the north, sweeping them off course. Waves threatened to break the main mast as the men scurried to bring down the sails. The ship twirled like a dancing queen, and it was late that night before they managed to regain control and point in the right direction. By morning the waves had subsided, the sun returned, and Nicholas sat rigidly on the narrow bed beside his daughter, holding the chamber pot for her while she vomited, wiping her shivering face with his own shirt.

On calm days, Bertha, Nicholas and Illiana sat crammed around a small table, its legs firmly screwed tight to the floor planks on the lower deck, next to the kitchen fires. They squeezed onto the benches, also immovable, and took the same food served to the sailors. Not all the crew ate at the same time, but some faces soon became familiar. The captain, however, did not appear. He took his meals on the forecastle deck.

"Well, we done good by them Delgardos at least," Nicholas said into his beer cup.

A sailor at the next table, hearing that one hateful word, looked over. "You ain't friends with them pig filth Spaniards?" he demanded.

"That's hardly what he meant," Bertha glared back. "This brave gentleman killed one of them, in self defence, I may add, the leader of the gang, one Juan Delgardo. Previously, another friend of ours killed the other brothers. Now only a few of the gang remain, and I imagine the gang is now fallen apart. No one of the name Delgardo still parades those hills and lanes."

The same man dropped his wooden spoon onto the table, stood and clapped. "Hooray," he called. "Them bastards have robbed us blind over past years."

Two more of the sailors cheered. "Well done, mate, them Spanish should be giving you a prize."

"I got me prize," Nicholas grinned back. "I got me precious daughter back, what them shitty turds stole away. I wish I'd made that slime-ball suffer the more."

A mug of simmering hippocras was thumped onto the table at Nicholas's elbow as the sailor grinned over his shoulder before returning to deck. The tankard was a hot perfume of cloves, cinnamon and roast chestnuts. Illiana stared, then stood and marched to the kitchens from where aromatic steam jostled with buckets of discarded rubbish.

"More hippocras, please," she called. "Enough for three, no, make that six." She took her second hot refill down to Sabine. "Your dad's being called a hero. The crew clapped when they heard about the Delgardos."

Sipping, her face flushed and smiling, Sabine said, "Well, he is, and so are you for bringing me this. Better than any willow bark."

"You deserve something twice as good." Illiana sat on the edge of the mattress, then moved to her own bed which stood against the opposite wall. "You deserve a whole wonderful new life."

Within moments, the door was again flung open and Nicholas marched in with more cups of smouldering spiced wine. "Reckon you needs it more'n me," he said, handing them over.

Sabine grasped two cups and sipped from both, grinning through wet scarlet lips.

"One day," Illiana said, "you'll tell us what happened to you. I know I'll cry, but you must say it, dear, get it out of your mind and not let it fester in secret."

Her eyes fixed down on the crimson sizzle, Sabine told her, "I don't want to talk about it. I'll be sick again. I feel too ashamed."

Nicholas grabbed her, nearly spilling both hot tankards. "You doesn't never say that again, Sabs," he said, gruff voiced. "It ain't shame, tis only anger wot you can feels. You's brave and clever and none of it ain't your fault. Don't you never feel shame. The shame is on them buggers what did it to you."

Once again the door flew open, Bertha appearing with another cup in her hand, the steam rising.

"I thought," she said, gazing, puzzled, at the others, "that it's you, my dear, needing the hippocras more than I do."

Sabine had no spare hand. She gulped at the remains of her first cup.

"Reckon I best go and get some more," decided Nicholas.

Now sipping at the second cup, Sabine grasped the third cup with a grin even more deeply flushed. "You're all gorgeous," she told them. "And so is this. When I'm back at home in London with the church bells ringing outside, then I promise I'll make myself tell what happened. You're right, I should tell, but you won't like it."

Bertha was wondering whether she should also be describing her own torture at the hands of the inquisition, but at least she had not been dragged to the stake and burned. She sat beside her daughter on the bed, and accepted the next cup of hot wine brought in by Nicholas.

She had already taken such a drink into the next cabin, her own bed warmly comforting, where the ever more distressed Elonza lay curled, clutching her belly, but one blink at the steaming cup had been enough. "Oh, no, lady, no. Not spices not anything to swallow," and had struggled to sit. "Lady Bertha, forgive my stupidity, but don't the folk of your country speak my language?"

Surprised, Bertha had frowned, sipped the hippocras herself, and answered, "No, my dear. What could you think? The English speak English."

"Then who will employ me, if no person understands me, nor I them?"

Standing to leave, Bertha had smiled. "You'll be safe, dear. I shall look after you. We all will."

The northern weather hovered, changing direction, changing its mind. Calm days slipped slow, then the winds whipped new fury and the storms followed.

Sometimes on milder days, Bertha took Elonza's hand and led her onto the deck, sitting with her, speaking in Spanish. But Elonza heard Illiana and Sabine, instead of the Spanish she had heard and spoken with them before, now chattering in the new strangeness. Once, even with Bertha, Elonza having smiled and wished her *'Bon dia,'* heard the one friend she trusted answering her in gruff foreign growls, saying, *'Good morning, my dear. The sun is shining. Will you eat breakfast with me?'* So not only would all the inhabitants of the new home she had chosen, speak a jumble of language she could not grasp, even her own few friends would be strangers to her.

Again Elonza had cried. Everyone in this strangely terrifying and unintelligible country of rain and freeze, would now know she had never been legally wed. She would only be known as the raped peasant child who had lied all her life.

Finally the days were improving, some days there were gulls screeching overhead and the ship, said the crew, was on target. One seaman said, as cheerful as the sun above, that they should arrive in three days, perhaps four, perhaps even two.

Food was getting more scarce but dried meat, looking rather thin and tired, still sat on platters, bread was still baked , and the ale still flowed. Then as the ship sailed closer to the horizon, now some fresh fish appeared, newly caught from the deeps, flesh glowing, fins broken off, each platter with two fresh clams beside the thick white slices.

Sabine had started eating more, invariably sitting with her father and friends at the wedged table amongst the ravenous and whooping crew, enjoying whatever scraps of food arrived, but Elonza rarely ate anything, and had sat glumly and silently with them only twice. Bertha duly took her food to the cabin, or at least, took whatever was left after everyone else had eaten yet invariably Elonza would peer up from the bed, take just a crust of stale bread, or refuse the food entirely.

It was midday, and not even Friday, when the bo'son yelled, "Tis a day fer feasting, my friends. Hurry for dinner or we shall all be bewitched by the smell of newly caught fish and clams so mighty alluring, t'will be snatched up by our lads before you visitors get a wiff." The wiff was strong, and everyone ran, grabbing platters and what food they were permitted.

Bertha finished her own share, grabbed another plate, and jumped up.

"I must be the decent nurse, the kind friend," and laughed. She heaped what pieces of fish were left, grabbed a clean spoon and some bread, and chugged from the enclosed eating deck, trudging up to her own cabin.

Pushing open the door, she was already greeting Elonza in Spanish, when she realised that Elonza was not there. Indeed, the cabin was empty. Bertha deposited the platter and hurried to the cabin next door, usually occupied by Illiana and Sabine, although at that moment both were still enjoying their midday dinner.

That was also an empty cabin, and Bertha was puzzled. To imagine Elonza up walking the decks in the sunshine, peering over the gunnals and watching the waves slap against the sides, was an idea as unlikely as seeing the fish themselves gathering on deck.

Back to her daughter and Nicholas, though merely smiling at Sabine, Bertha said, "It's a bit of a puzzle, but I can't find the woman. Elonza, that is. She's had such a wretched few weeks at sea, and I'd like the think she's up in the fresh air and enjoying using those forgotten legs of hers, but it seems so odd. I'm up to try and see her. Would anyone come to help?"

They did, even Sabine, belly comfortably full, so the three women following Nicholas, marched the steaming decks, climbed the stairs both up and down, and although not expecting to discover Elonza wrapped happily by the tiller, also explored from for'sail to forecastle, prow to stern, but found nothing. Some of the crew, running past, or relaxing by the gunnals, stared with interest and called, "You lost summint, Lady?" or, "By your leave, lady, you seem mighty lost. Can I help?"

The tall sailor who called to Nicholas, received the first answer. "Mate, tis a little old Spanish woman, what come sailing with us, and has gone. Not gone as such, but not to be found. Can you look on the lower decks fer me, in case the female be hiding around your cargo for some daft reason. Even have a peep in them bilges?"

The sailor was shocked. "A respectable passenger disappeared?"

"Afraid so. Spanish, name Elonza."

"A sweet little woman, but easily frightened," Bertha came running up. "And speaks no English, but can surely scream loud enough if she trips and falls."

"And has been sick day after day," called Illiana. "She's been so sick and eaten almost nothing, perhaps she lost her direction and could have fallen in the Hold. Even maybe starving and fainted."

Several others of the men joined them. "A female gone proper missing. It won't do, no way, and search we will."

Now everyone was shouting, yelling to the captain, feet slamming deep into the bilges, the captain appearing, red faced. "This is impossible. We look after all our passengers."

"Them bilges is leaking again, dirty enough for drowning the rats."

"There be a leak after o' the Hold too," another sailor shouted. "I done clamped it wiv a swodge o' tar, but there ain't no woman."

The minutes passed in hope, then of denial, and the rush of half the crew peering in every deep shadowed corner. Staring at barnacles, sweeping downwards as they spied sea-worms self-burying, then into the galley where the three cooks were busy preparing for supper and wiping off the mould from the meat they would serve that evening, every sailor now shouting, swearing and unbelieving.

Finally, one man climbed part of the rigging on the main mast, stopped, hand pointed into the wind. He yelled, "Reckon you can stop searching. Reckon I found her."

Everyone rushed, deck vibrating, to the gunnels where the boy on the mast was pointing. Peering, shouting, and the ship tipped, too much weight on the left.

The figure was distant now. Yet the floating body of Elonza

could not be mistaken. As yet no hungry sea monster had taken her deeper, and the woman lay half on the surface, floating as though serene and enjoying the sun over her eyes. Her face stared upwards. Her arms lay loose at her sides and even the little pointed toes of both feet, brown leather, peeped above water.

Bertha screamed, every man yelled, Illiana sank down on the deck and wept, Sabine embracing her. Nicholas was calling, "Tis terrible, a disaster, but it ain't time to stop. Oars, I reckon, get closer, has any man got a net, a hook to pull the lass up. We must move mighty quick."

The wind sang, blowing them in the right direction, the long hook was swung out and the limp soaked corpse was hauled up like a fish for supper.

Now Elonza lay on the deck, streaming water. The sunshine reflected its vibrant golden colours across the small peaceful face, down the drenched mess of her clothes, the heavy dark water-logged drifts of her hair, pins and sedate cap gone, the flood of water swimming out from her and beneath her. Her eyes were shut, but her mouth was now a golden smile.

As the chaplain was called urgently from his bed and came running, the captain gave the orders, and the plans for burial began. The body would be blessed, well wrapped in a small square canvas sail, and kissed by her friends who spoke softly, saying their goodbyes in Spanish, and apologies added.

"Tis a mighty shame," one crew member sniffed, "but all our burials at sea be back in the water. Our Lord God don't approve of suicide, but reckon we can pretend it were a slip o' mistake. So, bless the corpse, and back she goes into the mighty waves."

The hidden and bloated memory was weighted beneath and all around with stone and rock tied with broken rigging, and then carried to the gunnels where it was carefully tipped over the side, and so returned to the water from where they had rescued her.

CHAPTER TWENTY FIVE

Nicholas, Bertha, Sabine, Illiana, the chaplain, the captain and the entire crew, had bent over, watching, praying, crossing themselves and whispering goodbye. The splash was almighty, echoing into the sunlight and into their minds.

"What a terrible thing to happen on such a happy journey," Illiana whispered.

For the crew, the dispersal was quick, followed by an abrupt return to work. For Illiana, Sabine, Bertha and Nicholas, it was almost incomprehensible and they gathered, staring at each other, wanting to rest but unable to relax or think of sleep. Nicholas had pitied the woman, had been glad to see her saved, but had only been, and was still, transfixed entirely with the safety of his daughter. Sabine, thrilled with her own rescue, banishing memories, and clinging to both Nicholas and Illiana, sniffed, Illiana was distraught and cried, but again, it was saving Sabine that lit her dreams.

Bertha had known far more of Elonza than the others, and was the one who had invited her to share a new life in England. Now she understood more, and knew she should have shared her time more often, cared more, and explained more. She felt both guilt, and yet, told herself, perhaps the death was the righteous spinning of the Wheel of Fortune. It was the years of lying from Elonza, about a marriage that had never existed, which had caused her own imprisonment, her foul torture, and almost her death in flames. Yet she had been saved, and so she had imagined that Elonza had also been saved.

"She was innocent after all," Bertha sighed to Illiana. "It had never been her who'd spoken to the inquisition, or accused me of bigamy. That was the Delgardo vermin."

Illiana stared at her feet. "No blame to her. No blame to you, Mamma. The blame is Papa's. My father abused her, then ran from Spain and deserted her."

Sabine, listening, had quickly turned away, hurrying to her own cabin. Bertha said, "It's true. Diego would have deserved the inquisition. No, I can't think of that, I'd have jumped onto the pyre with him, but the priests imagine themselves right, you know, cleansing sinners of their sins."

"How can a priest imagine he can watch torture and call is God's will?"

"And how can a woman," Bertha breathed, "think she loves a man capable of such torture and sin?"

"Tis what happens at sea," a large shouldered man interrupted, "done now, time to forget if she ain't no wife, no mother, no daughter. Might have tripped, not jumped, you won't never know. We all gotta die one day."

"Suicide is a sin," another man said, poking his nose towards Illiana.

"You want to join the inquisition too?" demanded the first man.

"We doesn't know, and we doesn't care," a passing sailor said. "Thinking on misery just makes you bloody miserable. It don't do no good to the lass what died."

It was the sight of the sodden, broken woman hauled up from the mighty ocean on a hook, and then the violent splash of the stone clad corpse later as she was returned to the water, that haunted both Bertha and Illiana for years.

On the seventh day of December, and already into the start of the Christmas season, *The Wind's Victor* berthed in the Thames estuary and waited its turn to row in to the quay, and unload. The weather here was glum but dry, winds bumped against the high built stern, but no storm shook the mast as the sails were brought down and folded tight on deck. Bobbing on anchor, the patient vessel waited, and after an hour it was rowed to shore, fastened, and the gang plank was lowered. As the crew began to prepare for unloading, so Illiana, Bertha, and Nicholas helping Sabine, climbed carefully and slowly to the steady dry land sitting solid beneath a grey sky,

"We's home," sighed Nicholas.

Shaking with excitement and relief, Sabine burst into tears. Nothing now lurched or rolled beneath her feet, and her father held her in both large strong arms.

For beginning the English season of snow and frost, the day, still early in the morning, was surprisingly mild. However, after adapting to the rich hot climate of the Southern Iberian peninsular, Sabine, Bertha and Illiana instantly shivered, pulling up the hoods of their cloaks. Even Nicholas pulled up his woollen collar to cover his ears.

"I expected the cold," complained Bertha, huddling inside her fur lining, "but not quite as bad as this."

Delight, however, out classed the weather. Illiana stared around, breathing deeply, grinning like a chef carrying in the roast goose for Christmas Day.

"I miss our horses," she said. "I hope they're all happy back in the sunshine at home. We'll have to hire a large litter. Nicholas dear, you'll have to ride the horse to pull it."

"Might take a few hours," Bertha said, "but we'll be home for supper. As long as it doesn't rain."

"Perhaps I should ride the horse," Illiana insisted. "Nicholas will want to stay with Sabs." She did not explain any further, nor admit that she loathed riding in any litter. She actually considered it far worse than sitting on a rolling deck in a storm. Nor was any road free of ditches, holes, , muddy patches, where the earthen road had sunk, and sudden meetings with large fallen stones.

Since any memory of lurching decks immediately brought the sodden body of Elonza back into her mind, Illiana quickly shook the waves from her imagination.

The larger litter waiting for hire, however, just within the port, included a driver.

"London," Nicholas said, handing over the coins that Illiana had given him. "Short drive down from Cripplegate. Long as we gets there before them gates close. Closes early in winter."

"I promise I'll make it," the driver assured him. "Climb in. Tis well cushioned."

The rattle, bump and fears of overturning continued for many hours, but the litter pelted onwards. Pulled by three horses and a driver who yelled his head off and did not bother avoiding the holes, nor the ditches, they hurtled through the iron bars of Cripplegate just as the Gateman decided he should lock up as soon as the church bell rang.

The dark December night was promising rain when, finally, the litter lurched to a halt outside the Latymer Mansion. Candles were lit in the ground floor windows, and the great hall was singing with light, the shutters not yet raised.

Simply climbing from the litter took some time. So many hours shaken and cramped meant considerable fatigue and soreness, with swollen ankles, headaches and bruising. Gradually, however, the four friends and relatives stood, grasping each other's arms and hands, sharing protection, affection and immense excitement, outside the huge shut doors of the building they had so long called home.

"It's nearly a whole year since he – and I've been a widow."

"Oh, Illiana," Bertha cried, "why think of that? We're all trying to forget that awful tragedy on the ship with Elonza, and now all you talk about is someone else being dead. Think of the fire in the hall, our beds with the hot bricks waiting for us, and a late supper made by the best cooks in England."

Illiana stepped forwards, raised one hand to the large metal door knocker, and was about to announce her return when the doors swung open and a beaming Manders, the Steward, stood to welcome them back. Illiana almost felt like hugging him. Although politely immovable, Manders wished he could hug them back.

Instead, he said, bowing, "My Lady Birstall, I am delighted to see you again. Come in, come in. You are all so heartily welcome back to the home that has been awaiting your return. I was serving beer in the hall, when I heard your voices, and so I came at once."

Already they could hear very different voices, a man shouting, a woman squealing in temper, and finally a woman whimpering.

Both Illiana and Bertha had guessed, while Sabine smiled at the old familiarity. Nicholas simply grasped Mander's hand and shook it. "And mighty glad we is to be here," he said loudly over the shouting within. "Tis been a long hard time, and reckon I'll not never be wanting back in Spain."

It was his deep voice that resonated and the entrance to the grand hall now burst wide as Olivia, hesitant, peeped from the candle flicker, then squealed, "Oh, Illiana, it's you, my dear. You didn't get burned at the stake after all. Come in, come in and get lovely and warm by the fire."

The fire was blazing. The new earl, fat calves stretched to the hearth, was almost setting his toes alight through his thick woolly hose, and clearly was not feeling too poor to stock up with huge dry logs. At the stomp of five pairs of boots entering, which included Manders, he turned in surprise and immediately scowled. "Oh, bothersome bodkins, you've all come back."

It was more affectionate a welcome than Illiana had expected from him. She kissed Olivia's cheek, and pondered as to whether to do the same to her sister-in-law, whom she disliked intensely. She simply smiled, and asked Manders to bring wine, preferably hot hippocras, and more chairs close to the fire. She had pulled off her cloak and so had Bertha, each handed them to Manders, who called for two pages, one to take the fur lined luxury to the cloakroom, and the other to order hippocras prepared immediately in the kitchen. Meanwhile, with a defiant nod to his master, Manders brought two chairs as close to the fire as would not interrupt the earl and his sister. When the first page returned, he helped the steward carry the wide settle to face the hearthside, and then bustled off to bring the drinks.

Neither Benjamin nor sister Beatrice smiled as both Sabine and Illiana sat together on the settle, shoving the cushions into comfort at their backs, while Bertha took one chair and Nicholas cheerfully took the other. Now the fire's glorious warmth was shared out between too many, although Olivia, the only one now wobbling on a stool at the inglenook's corner, smiled as though delighted.

The earl stared at the more distant flames, then at every newly arrived face, finally stopping with his gaze fixed on Nicholas. "I believe I am correct," he said coldly, "in remembering that you are a groom at this establishment?"

"Too right," nodded Nicholas, the grin intact. "I's mighty glad you still accept me as such, my lord. Tis been a mighty difficult year." It did not occur to him that the earl thought he should immediately move. It had been too many months now that he had been accepted as part of the family.

"A filthy year, sadly true," Bertha sighed.

Quickly Olivia asked, "Such a long time away, my lady, and it sounds dire. Tell us, please explain what's happened."

Beatrice scowled and opened her mouth in disgust, about to shout her complaint, but seeing this, the earl quickly tapped her hand and shook his head. Both reluctantly relaxed.

Bertha told her story in considerable detail. "Heresy," she began, "is a terrible sin, and we all fear and detest such wickedness, but in Spain it seems they believe anything and everything to be heresy, will torture and burn the poor soul who perhaps walked too fast or hiccupped in front of the priest. They call it the Inquisition, yes, we all know, that word has drifted around in the shadows in the past as well, but now it is positively new-born, and is more wicked than anything these poor victims might have done."

"It's the Holy Bible that demands punishment," the earl glowered. "And tells the way to redeem a sinner." The silence scowled back at him. He immediately added, "Those who attend church on a proper regularity, and those educated enough to read the Holy Book themselves in Latin, will know this, as I do of course."

"Spain is full of sin," Olivia frowned. "I believe it to be a Caliphate, whatever that is, and full of rich Jews."

Now able to spit her own complaints, Bertha said, "Not at all, my dear lady. Both Muslims and Jews are being tortured by the inquisition, and many have left. It's the Christian Church, led by some evil inquisitor, who cracks the whip. They accused me, can you believe such a thing, of having a child out of legal wedlock, since they claimed my dearest Diego was a bigamist." She put her kerchief to her face, dabbing at both eyes. "The most terrible things were done to me. I cannot say the words. I was imprisoned and tortured – yes, that is true – tortured – until my dearest daughter and Sabine's Papa Nicholas, saved me." Now she leaned to the side, patting Illiana's lap. "But," she continued with enthusiasm, "I had another saviour, and he is also dear little Sabine's saviour, and so the only reason we are back home, all safe and sound. This was a great lord, the son of the mighty Earl of Cleeves. Yes indeed. Charles, Viscount of Valdar, who directly serves the royal crown. He knew the injustice of the claim against me, and saved me, he did, making the inquisitor look quite foolish."

Even Illiana and Sabine were staring fascinated while Benjamin and Beatrice, who had both started to glower, were soon bright eyed in amazement.

"A proper Marshall? On direct king's orders?" Olivia asked.

"Yes indeed," Bertha told her. "Therefore, I might say it was King Edward himself who was my saviour, proving I am a perfectly innocent married woman, with a completely legitimate daughter."

"King Richard, dear," Olivia interrupted with a soft and hesitant murmur.

"Never heard of him," said Bertha.

"You have been away for rather a long time," Beatrice pointed out, the previous fascination returning to glare. "A great deal has happened and you've missed a lot while sitting in a dungeon." She sniggered faintly. "I'll not say, you can all find out for yourselves."

This was a subject which interested Illiana, having heard only small beginnings from Charles, and Sabine knew nothing of this at all, but Nicholas said, "All kings is good holy majesties in our country, thank the good Lord, but that there king in Spain, he were happy to have folk burned alive for naught."

"I knew about a child once, and heard him screaming. It was while I was held by the beasts, the Delgardos, in Cordoba." Then she stared into the fire, her eyes moist. "I can't talk about that either." When Illiana gripped her hand, Sabine leaned back and now her eyes were shut. "

With a finger pushing back her uncovered hair, Beatrice stood, still frowning. "All these horrid stories are of no interest to me," she said. "Except perhaps for this Lord Charles, a more interesting gentleman, maybe. I'll weep for no one except for myself, and you are all clearly safe now. You come back to an overcrowded house of great comfort and have nothing to complain of. I shall now retire from your tedious stories."

As she swept from the hall, both hands to her wide skirts,

ensuring that the heavy damask whipped against Illiana's stretched legs, everyone else slowly stood, knees still less than balanced, and Nicholas said, "Time I went to see me old friends in the stables, I reckon. Sabs," he turned to his daughter, "you's home now. I shall see you again in the morning." Leaning over, he kissed her cheeks and marched outside.

Illiana took Sabine's arm. "I think we all need our rest. I heard Manders call for the staff to prepare our beds, so hopefully they'll be clean and warm. Sabine will share mine. She won't go back to the servant's quarters."

"Whereas," said Bertha, "I shall now sleep sweet and forget my dreadful ordeals."

Abruptly left alone, the earl pouted, yawned, and pushed his chair back to the only, best and nearest place by the fire.

With Sabine's arm grasped tightly, Illiana hurried up the wide stairs leading to the quarters within the tower. Here one of the maids stood holding the door partially open, and pushed it wide. Both Illiana and Sabine followed her inside.

A small hearth was bright with eager flames, and the huge curtained bed was piled high with bolsters, pillows, blankets and a vivid velvet bedspread embroidered with fairies and unicorns.

"Thanks so much," Illiana said. "It's Leticia, isn't it. I remember you. This is excellent, thank you."

Blushing, the girl pointed. "Tis your baggage brought up too, my lady, and all your belongings already hang safe and well aired in the garderobe. Would you like me to unpack your bedrobe for the morning?"

Hot bricks, now back on the grate, had warmed the bed as both Illiana and Sabine climbed under the swathes of linen and wool, and the servant girl dashed out with whispered wishes of golden dreams.

"I'll have golden dreams when I'm sure you're all right," Illiana whispered into the pillow next to Sabine.

"I feel wonderful," Sabine told her, and then apologised. "It's living with those vile creatures in Spain," she shook her head. "They mostly spoke some English, but it was all swear words, and curses and ugly rude things. I must, forget it all."

"No." Illiana, although still officially a married widow, had taken off her small hair netting of pale lace, and the pearl pins which usually held it tight to her head. Now both she and Sabine wore the long loose curls of virgin women. "No," Illiana continued, "please darling, tell me everything. Of course you don't have to, but you should. Otherwise those sickening thoughts creep into the little dark corners of your mind and stick there so you can't ever forget them. They just stay stuck and make you feel sick for ever and ever."

"I don't feel sick," Sabine told her, smiling widely. "I'm home. I'm with my lovely very best only friend. My lovely pappy is close by, and all happy too. I honestly couldn't be happier. It's like getting back to heaven."

"I feel a bit like that too," Illiana giggled. "But I didn't have a horrible time in Spain, not really, only being frightened for you."

"I sort of guessed." She had. "It was that wonderful towering Charles, wasn't it. He's wild about you."

"I'm wild about him, but I don't even know if I'll ever see him again."

"I'd wager he'll make sure that you will."

"I pray he will." Now Illiana sighed. "Unless that horrid flirt Beatrice gets in first. She obviously likes the sound of him."

"Charles is far too intelligent to fall for that," Sabine said, stifling a yawn. "She's a conceited idiot."

Illiana snuggled closer to Sabine. "Now tell me all about everything. You know I'll be upset, but I'll hold you tight and make you feel better and buy you loads of new clothes and never ever let you go out on your own ever again. If I was a queen, I'd make you a duchess, and if I was a bishop, I'd make you a saint."

"I can't be a saint," Sabine said abruptly. "I'm not a virgin."

"I couldn't care less," said Illiana. "Nor am I, and I wish I could jump into bed with Charles and do it all again." She paused, "But that's not the thing we want to talk about. Tell me your whole terrible year-long story, and I promise I'll never repeat a word to anyone else."

"They're all dead now," Sabine whispered back, "so I'm safe. Even safer because I'm back home with you and my father. So, I'll try and say it all without making you even more sick than me."

CHAPTER TWENTY SIX

The king did not dream of gold, nor did he desire it. That barely interested him, unless cash was needed for matters of the country's security. He dreamed of peaceful worthiness as he rolled, still deeply asleep, and turned again, dislodging his wife.

The bed, sufficiently enormous to accommodate six folk or more, gave space for rolling and turning, but discovering herself on the edge of the mattress with half the velvet curtain in her eyes, Anne woke and giggled.

Richard woke at the sound of the laugh. "What have I done this time?"

"Nothing," she whispered back. "I'm not on the floor yet." And she snuggled herself back against the warmth of her husband's body.

Since two guards, a valet, two pages and a silent priest, the only one who never snored, also slept in the royal bedchamber, usually in somewhat cramped beds against the walls, their royal highnesses kept their voices low. Indeed, the queen invariably trotted off to her own separate bedchamber where she had a little more privacy and at least those who slept on the three separate tiny beds were all female.

Now sovereign for five long months, Richard rarely succeeded in sleeping the entire night through, since keeping the two thousand problems from his mind was entirely impossible.

Lord Hastings had not surprised him in the slightest. He had expected the secret plots to come to the fore. The Duke of Buckingham had, however, surprised him and saddened him a great deal. Buckingham had never been entirely capable of full understanding, whereas Hastings had been exceedingly clever, and liked to prove it on a monthly basis. From the first gathering in London after his dear brother's death, Richard had ordered one of his men to keep a close watch on Hastings.

The plot to take over the new king had been foreseen, and not only was Hastings arrested immediately, but so were the several of Hasting's compliant friends within the city.

Buckingham, rarely able to think for himself beyond arranging the next feast, had seemed the perfect officially supportive companion. Until, of course, John Morton, Bishop of Ely, a man incapable of thinking of anything except plots and treachery, was put too closely into Buckingham's care. Buckingham had at first felt proud at such an honour, but the bishop had quickly taken advantage. Richard, although disillusioned, was soon aware that the fault was his own. It was a mistake he would never make again. Trust had to be earned, not simply offered to the nearest smile.

Naturally Richard had never trusted the Woodville family. It had surprised him that brother Edward had succumbed. The Woodvilles had taken a good deal of weight from Edward's shoulders, and so had Richard. Edward had done his duty as a good king, but only by sharing out the more dreary parts of the job. For so many years during Edward IV's reign, Richard had been powerful, yet utterly loyal to his elder brother. Edward, had extended his trust beyond that faithful brother, including the eager in-laws, who trotted behind him whilst also getting their rewards.

The entire country knew the certainty of the Woodville's intentions. They had proven it, even without pretence, first by refusing to admit King Edward's death for several days until they had prepared themselves. Then by announcing their importance during the first gathering of the Royal Council when the widowed queen, who was not on the council at all, sat herself at its head. She conducted the meeting together with her son Thomas, and finally, during the journey of the new king to London, they avoided the agreed meeting with the late king's brother, Richard, now the Official Lord Protector, who, should have been the one to accompany the young heir to his palace at the great Tower.

The three actions formally announced, that the Woodvilles, family of the young heir , on his mother's side, would be the power of the realm, and the power behind the throne since the new king was only twelve years of age.

Although for all the years of Edward IV's reign, it had never even occurred to little brother Richard to turn against the rightful king, Richart had always been equally aware of his own position. Now that position had become of importance not only to himself and his family, but also to the entire country. He could not imagine a more destructive dynasty than a Woodville sovereign ship.

In the Last Testament of King Edward, he had officially named his brother as Royal Protector, almost giving the rights of the crown until the new king himself wore it.

Richard took control within the day.

He swore his loyalty to the future ruler, but held his own responsibilities intact. Already Royal Constable, and now Lord Protector, he did exactly what he knew his late brother, God rest his soul, would have wanted and expected.

Of course, not long after, the entire expectation of the country blew into fable and folly.

Having delayed the date set for the coronation, sensibly changing the one set by the Woodvilles during that improper council meeting, there was now time to call Parliament. Some of the designated Lords were no longer available since they had dashed off to order their robes for the coronation, but the vast majority were present and glad to gather.

That was when Lady Elizabeth Talbot, Duchess of Norfolk, walked into Westminster Hall and announced the long held secret, concerning her elder sister, now deceased, who, she claimed, had rightfully been Queen of England, and so proving the Woodvilles to be of no consequence.

Secret marriages, legally binding as handfasting was, had been a favourite pastime of the late monarch, and could not be doubted since the presumed Queen Elizabeth Woodville had also married the king in a secret hand-fasting. Indeed, it had been several months after that private ceremony, before his late majesty had even admitted it had taken place.

That had been an unexpected discovery at the time, making his people shrug and snigger. A king taking some months to admit the existence of his wedded queen, had seemed odd enough.

However, the first marriage to Lady Eleanor had never been admitted. It was a good way of getting a stubborn female into bed, but now it showed King Edward as a bigamous.

The Duchess of Norfolk answered questions, to prove her story. Then that Bishop Stillington, a member of the Lords within the upper house of parliament, stood and stated that the duchess spoke the truth, since he himself had been present, and had been called to stand witness.

Few doubted the facts as presented. The two witnesses were far too important to doubt, and few were sorry to see the Woodvilles revealed as of no consequence. Some, having known that Lady Eleanor had been the lusting kings great desire during that time long past, were not surprised.

Richard, sitting in contemplation, had never previously known the truth, although he knew of his brother's past indulgences, and when taking into account the delay on announcing his marriage to the Woodville widow, Richard had most certainly suspected something important was not being entirely admitted.

Elizabeth Woodville had been beautiful, passionate and, although known as greedy and unpleasant, was very much alive with personality and grace. Somewhat older than Edward and already having birthed a family, she would certainly have known how to play the game. The delay in announcing the marriage gave rise to two possibilities. Either he rejected the idea of having such a woman as his wife had attempted to find a way out of it, but failed due to Elizabeth's threats, or, perhaps more likely, he had delayed until positive that his previous secret wedding would not be divulged.

The Lady Eleanor Talbot had been even more outstanding with a beauty that had rushed Edward's breath up to the moon. Also older, also a widow yet without children, she had been desired as no other. A deeply religious woman, Edward had surely realised that she would not please him for long, but he had endowed her afterwards, and had certainly treated her well. When she had sadly died, God rest her soul, his highness had shown his sorrow, but was already officially wed to the mother of his children. He never admitted that these children were not legitimate.

Richard also had two illegitimate children, loved them both dearly, kept them safe and in comfort, but had never pretended their legitimacy. He had later married Anne, after rescuing her from his other brother. The situation had been both sorrowful and devious. The rescue had seemed to him essential, and he had taken her to Sanctuary. Later, partially from a sense of duty, he had suggested marriage. Even as a child they had been friends. Richard had been happy to live with her, and adored their son. Their married friendship had turned to love. A comfortable, easy love which united them in humour as well as in other delights.

Discovering the alarmingly dramatic situation, concerning the supposed heir to the throne being of illegitimate birth, Richard knew in his heart that the shiver down his back was fear, and the future was like a barrel of grapes waiting to be trodden into something quite different.

Now that period of shock, doubt and demand had slipped into memory. Richard's coronation had passed, the safety of the two illegitimate nephews had been securely arranged, keeping their new homes unknown, ensuring no Woodville attempts to take back the boys, and claim the elder as king after all. In spite of this success, there had been a couple of futile rebellions, quickly and easily stopped. There had even been an attempted invasion from across the Narrow Sea, a cross-eyed Lancastrian who claimed whatever his mother encouraged him to believe, and even though within the Lancastrian line, he was only twentieth in that line as heir.

Richard accepted the crown, shared his coronation with his dear wife, and as the king and queen attempted righting of wrongs of the past and the adding much needed new laws. Richard insisted on using the English language of his people instead of the long used royal French, he outlawed situations which had long troubled him, and he moved from the sweet friendship of the north into the rigorous elitism of royalty in Westminster.

He had always upheld duty, welcoming responsibility and relishing the improvements he dreamed of. There were other aspects of sitting the throne that he now enjoyed. The hard work suited him. Good food, good wine and good friends were always to be treasured. The problems were greater than those of a duke, but not so much.

Becoming king had been as much a shock to Richard himself as to his people, and the chaos and death surrounding the confusion had helped nothing. Yet those citizens struggling to improve their own lives, or those too poor to care who sat a golden throne, cared little who wore the crown as long as their taxes seemed fair, their laws were righteous, and the foreigners kept to their foreign lands.

The Tudor fool, claiming a right he had never held, and denying having inherited the original illegitimacy, seemingly a persistent difficulty of the years, had been blown back to his Burgundian mud strewn huddle.

The Lord God, it seemed, having anointed Richard at his Holy Coronation, had truly chosen the man He wished to be king. So, Richard accepted what could never be denied.

Now winter days grew ever shorter, the Christmas season had begun, the city squares were loud and busy with stages, puppet shows, miming's, nativity plays, dances and games of mob-feet ball. Groups gather at the churches singing the sweet songs of Noel. Other groups gathered in less holy places and sang the hilarious and entirely improper Noel songs which had been invented in the back streets, becoming as popular, if not more so, as those respectably religious

The Holy Bible, forbidden by the Vatican ever to be translated into ocal languages, had once been secretly translated into English. Although forbidden, Richard owned this, and loved it. Reading this was his consolation when the work of a king exhausted him, bored or annoyed him.

Yet what annoyed Richard was not always what another might have expected, and what delighted him could be equally unexpected.

"Your highness," the door had opened but the guard on duty remained standing in the hallway, "Viscount Valdar, leader of the Royal Contingent of Marshalls, has returned to England, sire, and is waiting at your highness's pleasure."

"I'll see him now," Richard, sitting at the long table, looked up from his documents. "Bring him in."

Richard's attention had returned to the papers when Charles knocked and entered. In full livery, he now also wore the golden collar of his allegiance. He bowed low, his head bent, until Richard said, "My Lord Valdar, Charles, I doubt your mission was in any manner comforting. So now tell me exactly what my brother intended when you left on his orders, and what, if anything, has been accomplished."

"Sire," Charles regarded his new king, a man he had met many times, yet only as the Duke of Gloucester. "His highness King Edward, may his soul rest in holy peace, was disturbed by news of the reawakening of the inquisition in the Iberian peninsula. Gossip had reported both motivation and intention, but his highness wished to know if any danger stood in secret behind this suspicious resurrection."

"And?"

"The new awakening of the Holy Inquisition, sire, is undoubtedly both religious and political. I can also state with certainty that the principal motive has been ignited with royal intention beyond that of the Vatican. King Edmund of Aragorn and Queen Eleanor of Castile are determined to unite the country as a Christian realm, gradually removing the Jewish population unless they convert to the Catholic beliefs, and eventually also to dispose of the Caliphate"

"I had imagined exactly that," Richard murmured. "An entirely Christian empire will please those above and those below, but the actions of inquisitors do not convince me of God's holy approval. Returning heretics to the judgement beyond is righteous but torture can be heretically cruel. Cruelty contradicts the teachings of the Holy Book itself."

Charles bowed, the tucked shadows at the corners of his mouth deepening.

"I was also required to ensure that no English, Welsh, Irish or Scottish citizens of your highness's blessed realm would ever be held accountable by such foreign judgements."

Ther king also smiled faintly. Naturally, my lord. I trust you were able to fulfil this requirement?"

"I was, sire." Charles bowed again. "I made the facts clear and unarguable. The situation was accepted by both their royal highnesses. I was also able to arrange the immediate release of the one

English woman held in Cordoba by the inquisitor there. She is now safely back in London, sire. She is, indeed, the daughter of his lordship, Baron Oswey."

"Really?" Richard frowned, then said, "No doubt, sir, you mean the sister of the new Baron Oswey.

"Interesting. It seems that more than one unexpected inheritance took place while I was otherwise busy abroad. Of interest to me, since I intend asking permission to marry the lady's daughter, widow of the late Earl of Birstall, may his soul rest in peace."

"Now I am equally interested," Richard told him, and the two wider smiles met. "I have never met the lady, but I knew Benedict over several years, and called him friend."

"His place is now taken by his brother, Benjamin, I believe. I would not call him friend."

"Another matter of interest." The king settled back in his high wooden chair, leaned his quill on the table, and faced Charles more intimately.

"We are not strangers, sir, and have no need to speak as such. As one of the most highly regarded of my late brother's Marshalls, you are now here to report all results, and discover whether the rumour, gossip and unbelievable notifications are indeed true, and whether this new king wishes to continue your status in his employ." The king was now chuckling. "My dear Charles, as always you have completed my dearest brother's past requirements. I also imagine you will have discovered that this strange new monster is indeed England's king."

Charles echoed the chuckle. "A shock, sire, but a happy one."

"I can most certainly confirm, Charles, that your position under my rule not only continues, but with increased gratitude from myself." His majesty's pause was brief, and he then continued. "I believe we should now speak on less official matters, Charles. If you'd like to ring the bell just behind you, I shall order refreshment."

It was over cups of wine, a better wine than Charles had tasted for some considerable time, that the conversation itself relaxed. "I imagine you gained some knowledge of the country beyond the matters of church?"

"The country is beautiful, sire." Charles sighed. "But it suffers from a lack of unification, and lawless gangs worse than our own, terrify certain areas. During the various problems that arose in Spain, sire, two of my men were seriously injured, one of whom was close to death for many days. Though now we have returned safely home I have disbanded the entire troop. Naturally we're open to any and all orders from your majesty and will re-band immediately if required."

"So a traumatic year for us both has now almost subsided." Richard laughed. "Christmas first, sir. Although once Epiphany is passed, I doubt I'll leave you long in peace."

"Christmas Day, yes indeed," Charles frowned into his cup. "A year then, since my intended bride was widowed."

Richard heard the second chime of the Westminster bell. "I have an important meeting scheduled for half gone this hour, but first I recommend marriage, Charles. Apart from the pleasure of children, the necessity of the heir to your title and property, children open your life in lighter ways, that is," and he grinned, "when you're permitted the time to spend with them. I'll send Jon Bannister to see to your two injured men. He's a doctor that I trust."

"Then I should leave you, sire." Charles stood. He bowed, smiled and added, "I respect you as the duke I once served. Now, I have the pleasure of looking up to you more."

A blink of pause was interrupted as Richard quite abruptly roared with laughter. "Charles, if you sit and I stand, perhaps you can look up to me. I shall keep that in mind."

Chuckling, Charles bowed again. "Is a king permitted such a sense of humour, sire?"

"Since you are a sword's length taller than me, my friend." and Richard drained the last of his wine. "Not that I care. I am an average height, perhaps and have long been accustomed to my brother as mountainous as you are. Or a little less? It's the trouble with my shoulder that has effected me seriously. Coordination of left to right was never exact, which made me a poor bowman, a shock to my father. Nor did I master the sword much past my apprenticeship. I prefer the axe, and have acquired a greater skill."

Charles raised an eyebrow. "Before the coronation, sire, you were known as the best warrior in the land."

"That's of no consequence, my friend. Dukes invariably get twice as many compliments as earls, and kings twice as many as dukes."

"Viscounts," Charles replied, "get very few, I assure you, sire."

Richard smiled, but as he spoke again, the humour dissolved. "Every anointed king has been chosen by our Lord God, although not for reasons we are ever permitted to know. Some in the past have been great men and have served their country well. Others have failed. Anger, greed, so many mortal sins aggravate our lives, even once raised to the responsibility of taking the throne." He stared, pausing again, and then stood. "I have a temper. I enjoy the blessings not always granted to other men, but I will be the king I was told to be. It was so unexpected, so unwanted, and I knew the urge to run. I was never a coward, even as a boy. Yet, faced with the throne, I understood cowardice. Then, I thank the Lord, I was permitted the courage to deny that cowardice."

Standing beside the door which remained tight closed, Charles faced his king and drew a deep breath. "I understand anger, sire, and have killed because of it. Without it, I would waver. When attacked, if we respond only with defence, then we will die, but if we respond with anger, and so attack the attacker, then we can enter a battle with optimism. I understand desire, I also know lust and the greed that brings, and I believe I understand what you mean, your highness. No man is perfect, but a King, if he accepts his position, must learn that perfection entrusted to him by God. Confidence comes when fear fails."

"Then you understand me very well, sir," Richard told him. "And I already know that as the Royal Marshall, you take that responsibility in the same manner. I trust you, Charles, and in spite of being unusually tall, you are, in affect, a little king. So, I hope you continue to give the help I need, and once the proscribed year is passed, you will most definitely receive my permission to marry as you choose."

The chuckle was sudden, and the king smiled as Charles said, "It is the lady's permission that I still hope for." He shook his head. "I've not had the courage to ask her yet. Oh, such simple cowardice, how unwanted you are."

"Cowardice, sir? Or doubt, perhaps? You suspect she may not be good enough for what you need? Or," and the grin enlarged once more, "you suspect you are not good enough for her?"

"Sire, the latter is undoubtedly the truth, but also the former. Cowardice dances like a family of wasps in my eyes, every time I consider commitment."

Now both laughing, Richard said, "Commitment simply brings a safe haven, Charles."

So, Charles stepped out into the passage, the guard immediately stood to attention, Charles nodded, still smiled to himself, and strode from the palace to the stables.

CHAPTER TWENTY SEVEN

Standing on the edge of the river's bank, Illiana had watched the water shiver, and with magical silver curls, begin to freeze. Ripples rose a little, as though playing, but curdled into solid white. The shadows of the fish disappeared.

As a spit of low wind snatched a tiny brown leaf, twisted and long dead, from the ground, it was carried, dithering, to the river, it then basked on the surface without moving. No current took it slowly downstream. No tide swept it back to shore. No wavelet dragged it beneath the squelch. It sat exposed and unmoving. Now the Thames had frozen.

Illiana turned. London's streets stood in mist, a shining paleness between the trees. She watched as her breath gusted like puffs of steam, their heat disappearing out into the bitter cold. The heat from her mouth burst against the freeze of the outside, and quarrelled, each attacking the other. It was the ice that won the display as the pale steam dissolved.

She and Sabine stood embraced, silent and gazing, when Illiana interrupted the dreams. "The weather seems to be getting much colder. When we were little, nothing ever froze. Christmas rained, but it didn't turn to ice."

"I'm not turning to ice," Sabine smiled, although still huddled close. "It's been a long walk and that warmed me up."

"A swooping huge contrast to Spain, though." Illiana began to trudge back into the city, pulling Sabine with her. "I wonder if they ever have cold winters with ice and snow."

Sabine muttered into her fur collar. "I never want to think of Spain again. It's blessed by the sun, but not by the church. Even that poor little woman Elonza,"

"I don't want to think about her either."

Within half of the hour, back past the soaring white pillars of Saint Paul's and through London's narrow streets, then crossing the Gold Row to the great house they had both once adored, Illiana and Sabine wandered home. The new earl had shattered the welcome, but the house and its grounds were still beautiful.

The first tree was the old oak, from where as a servant child she had stolen acorns to play with, and roll beneath her mother's tiny bed. Now it was huge, the largest tree on those grounds, branches stretching black and leafless, outwards, intermingling, curving up, then out again. Almost pushed aside was a tall thin fur, clutching still to the thin green foliage that seemed like neither leaves, nor spines. Bending across, as though trying to speak with those trees, was a willow. In summer it wept with trails of green beauty, but now it dragged its boughs, bare and lifeless, amongst the undergrowth.

Only the birch kept its beauty, its silver bark continuing to overtake the thin and leafless branches.

Yet the small pond did not glitter with reflection. The sky was grey and the clouds hid any sunshine. It was only midday, but a mockery of twilight seemed to have forced its path downwards.

Sabine giggled at Illiana. "Yes, it's all ice, shouldn't we hurry back indoors? The door's only just over there, or would you prefer to climb inside the chimney?"

"A sweet thought, Sabs. I'll try that tomorrow, but only after the fire goes out, and I'll still be covered in ashes."

"Don't, don't ever remind me."

"Our memories, so much of Spain, the inquisition, the Delgardos, and you hardly knew Elonza, but I felt so sad, we have mountains of bitter memories, Sabs dearest. We came through it remember." Illiana smiled. "We have to be proud of what we survived."

"My lovely completely crazy friend," Sabine snuggled beside Illiana, "I'll cheer up. Yes, I know the house is dismal nowadays, but it's not horrible. Dinner wasn't bad. Although you didn't eat a thing."

"I ate one nice thing. It was a thin slice of ham. The rest was mostly turnip which I didn't like. I hope they gave it to the horses."

"You keep trying to make jokes." Sabine sniffed. "I upset you, didn't I."

Illiana turned quickly, hugging her friend. *You* didn't upset me," Illiana sniffed into her friend's hair. "I was upset *for* you. I want to murder those Delgardos all over again. I almost wish it had happened to me instead of you. Darling, it's just too horrible. Why do people want to be so wicked? Why do so many folk choose hatred?"

Sabine kissed Illiana's cheek. "You know the one good thing about having a terrible time? It's like heaven when rescue comes. I didn't think I could ever feel so incredible. So happy. Like a sudden exciting bliss. I still feel that. I could dance."

"I felt like that too," Illiana sniffed, "when Charles brought you back safe. When I first saw you again, I just started crying, but it was an excited crying. You know what I mean."

Sabine giggled, "At least I know I'm never going back to Spain."

"None of us ever will," Illiana told her, "never would, never could. There are brutal gangs here too, especially up on the Scottish borders. People get killed all the time."

"I won't think about that," Sabine said, "but at least we don't have the inquisition. Your poor mother."

"You, yes, even my mother. Even that poor woman, you know who I mean, the good Lord rest her soul. I've been so terribly lucky." Illiana sat on the bottom doorstep, staring at her feet. "I almost feel guilty."

"You were so brave, my father says. You used a gun, and it worked, even though you'd never used one before."

"Never shall again." Suddenly Illiana laughed. "I almost blew my hand off."

Sabina sat on a higher step, her feet dangling just above the gravel path's surface. It was after a small pause when she said, "So now you want to get married again?"

With a gulp, Illiana looked up. "You're not supposed to know. And anyway, he hasn't ever asked me. He only talks about tossing me into bed."

"I bet you're tempted to say yest to that too."

She was remembering the hours they had spent tightly entwined, when she said, "Sabs, I almost did, but, well, nothing happened. Not the sort of thing we mean, anyway."

The silence shifted into dream. They watched a kestrel fly overhead, then swoop down on the other side of the frozen pond, then saw him rise again, something moving in his claws. Illiana didn't want to know what was now dying. It was Sabine who finally said, "The thing we're not talking about. It's horrible when some brute makes you. Truly utterly disgusting, but later, with Lucas, then I told him he could and he was sweet. Can I actually admit that I liked it. After ages, I even wanted it, but you already know all about that."

Illiana smiled. "Don't be embarrassed. I'm glad to hear you say it. It's not just the men who enjoy doing it! With Benedict, he was always so sweet. At first, I thought he couldn't be doing it properly because I thought it would hurt and be horrible, but it wasn't."

Sabine held out her hand. "Come along, Ills, one day, if you promise not to laugh at me, we can talk about it."

"When I was a kid, well, before I was a wise old married matron, I used to hear some of the staff talk about it, and giggle and say strange things, especially in the kitchen." Pausing at the back doorway, they began to pull of their gloves and hoods. "I never understood a word of it then. I pretended I did, but I didn't really want to listen. It's so different when, – but, Sabs dear, you didn't love Lucas."

"Of course I didn't, but I was stuck with him and he was sweet. Most women don't even love their husbands. It's all arranged with lords and ladies and rich people. They do their duty and don't have fun."

"Except for kings. They do their duty but they do everything else too."

"Hush now, someone may hear us."

The subject changed abruptly as they entered the wide back entrance, avoiding the kitchens which sounded extremely noisy as they passed. A page took their thick hooded cloaks and they moved on into the great hall where the fire was smouldering across the grate. Earl Benjamin lay back in his armchair, his nose in the air and his mouth open. He was snoring. Beatrice was attempting to embroider something, was clearly in difficulty, and sat by the dining table, two beeswax candles flaring beside her. Olivia was not present.

Since returning, rescued, renewed and valued, Sabine had not worked. "Nor will you, not ever," Illiana told her, "unless you want to go and marry a beggarly canter, you'll never be a cleaning girl, nor even a maid. You're my very, very special friend."

She shared Illiana's bed, and in the great Hall, they sat together as two ladies regarding the newly painted murals. Sometimes, although gradually no more, Nicholas had divided his time between the stables and the mansion. He had slowly absorbed the glares and remarks which made it obvious he was still considered a servant. Sabine had encountered the same reactions. Illiana had insisted that she disregard the insults. "You're my very, very best friend, and my guest."

She had said much the same to Nicholas but he had smiled and shaken his head. "I ain't no guest, lady. I reckon I's proud to be yer groom."

"Head groom, and friend."

"I shall remember that, my lady."

Illiana had insisted. "Stop calling me a lady. Sabs calls me Ills. I call you Nicholas. Not that I'm in love with the name '*Ills*', but call me Illiana and I don't care who's listening."

"Reckon I'll try," Nicholas had said, but didn't.

Illiana strolled to the fire, sitting on the settle which now stood to one side. As Sabine flopped, Benjamin grunted and sniffed, slowly waking.

"Tis you two again," he complained. "There's no peace in this house any more."

Illiana regarded him. "Where's my mother, do you know?"

"Why should I know?"

She sighed, leaned back, and closed her own eyes. The warmth was delicious but she had no intention of sleeping. Indeed, quietly she had to agree with her brother in law, that the companionship offered neither privacy nor friendly pleasure. No one snored now, but she heard Beatrice swearing under her breath. Her sister in law was evidently not a brilliant embroideress, even though she persisted. Since Illiana had never attempted such a maidenly hobby in her life, she silently sympathised.

Eventually, "Olivia? Your wife? I mean, where is she now?"

Illiana and Benjamin gazed into each other's eyes with irritated defiance, but it was the voice coming from behind her, that answered.

"Olivia," Bertha said, her entering footsteps unheard but her voice loud, "is in her bedchamber sobbing. Not an unusual situation. However, I am not suggesting rushing to her aid, Illiana my dear. I am about to go out, the litter stands ready outside, and I need you with me." She added, "Sabine, my dear, I cannot invite you on this occasion. Either enjoy the fire, or go up and tell Olivia that she should stop crying, and kick her husband instead."

With a shrug towards Sabine, Illiana followed her mother from the hall, allowed Manders to help her on with the enveloping cape and gloves which she had only just taken off, and reluctantly scurried back out into the white freeze. Nicholas was driving the litter. "My lovely lady," he greeted Illiana, "I shall try ever so hard not to get them wheels stuck in holes nor gutters."

"We'll just slide on the ice," Illiana nodded, climbing into the rattle, then quickly pulling the curtains.

"Tis a mighty good road coming soon and not so far," Nicholas's voice was muffled through the heavy wool shade as the horse began to trot.

Bertha was quickly snuggled within a heap of damask and velvet cushions. Her cloak, hood almost over her eyes, was as thick as the cushions. "Well, Mamma," Illiana said, trying to find her own woollen burial, "We're off to Saint Paul's? No, we've passed it. So, it's off to Westminster? Through the Ludgate? Yes, we did. I heard the gatekeeper shouting. Now I'm on the way to the Old Sludge Fleet. So, we crossed it, and now?" Having no idea where her mother was taking her, this puzzling journey seemed vaguely exciting.

The litter clattered and creaked to a stop in the wide glory of The Strand, where the houses followed the way of the river, joining London City to the great beauty of Westminster, passing the homes of the rich and those important enough to have bought one of the mansions lining it.

"We've stopped here?"

Since the litter stool silently on the cobbles, she could hardly doubt it. The horse looked bored. Nicholas did not move, but called, "We surely is, ladies. Right where you wants."

Clambering down, then helping her mother, Illiana was staring only at the house standing beside her. She promptly did as she had teased, and slipped on the frosted cobbles. Hands to the low stone wall, she steadied herself. This was one of the smallest houses, and the least pretty, but it remained powerful and clearly despised her, however well dressed she might consider herself, as she hugged herself within her fur lining.

"I'm guessing," she whispered to her mother. "Am I right?"

Bertha already stood straight, about to present herself as the daughter of a baron, the sister of a baron, and the mother of a countess. "Of course you're right, why would we be anywhere else? Now come along, and we shall do something I should have done years and years ago."

Slamming through the small iron gateway, Bertha approached the tall doors within a pillared archway. She rapped quickly as though summoning a page, and stood waiting on the top of the three shallow steps.

Answering the door, clearly the steward had no idea who he faced. "Madam, may I know your name and your business?"

"You may, once I give it," Bertha said, pushing directly past, and turning to Illiana. "Come in, come in, dear. This is the home I was born into, and is now the residence of my brother, Robert, now Baron of Oswey."

"My lady," stuttered the steward, "I shall inform his lordship and will return to you directly."

Illiana entered behind her mother, throwing back the rich emerald green velvet of her cloak, its lining of white winter fur still clinging to her. She did not, however, enter alone. Bertha, staring back and immediately delighted, simpered as she saw their unexpectedly arriving companion. Indeed, as Illiana had slipped on the cobbles beyond the Oswy Mansion, she had found a steady hand beneath her elbow, supporting her. The accompanying voice murmured, "A surprise, I admit, my little one, and an ambivalent surprise, since I imagine you're on your way to visit your uncle the baron, whereas, delighted as I am to see you, I would far rather now have you all to myself."

Looking up into the shadowed dark eyes, Illiana had wanted simply to fall into his arms. She sighed.

"You're home safely. I mean from Spain."

"You noticed."

" suppose all you lords live in this place of palaces? You, what? Next door?"

He grinned. "The one next to the one next."

"I should ask, I mean, Allan and Degal?"

"How polite of you, my dear. Yes, they are well, although devoid of the speed to gallop. How well do you know your uncle?"

"I wouldn't recognise him if he stood in front of me."

"Then," Charles had said, "although Robert is not my close friend, I will now steal the pleasure of leading you inside into his charming company."

Within moments, the fourth Baron Oswey stood in his own thickly carpeted corridor, staring at two women, flanked by the mighty Charles, Viscount Valdar, the tall man whom he knew disliked him.

The younger woman was probably no more than twenty years of age, black haired beneath a married woman's pearl pinned headdress, and was extremely beautiful. The older woman, a little shorter and a little less beautiful, seemed somehow slightly familiar.

Remaining polite, the baron said, "My lady, I am pleased to meet you, yet I admit I'm puzzled. Did my steward say your name was Bertha?"

"I certainly hope he did," Bertha scowled. "Since I am your poor ignored sister. Robert, you should instantly remember me. Once you threw a candle stick at me. I threw the candle back and set your hair on fire. Very pretty."

"Oh, vandals and thorn trees," he exclaimed at once. "How? Is it? Shit pots and bloody arsenic." He wilted, leaning heavily back against the wall, "Gutter piss and devil juice, is it really my wretched sister climbed back into the world?"

"Well," Bertha smiled, "we never got on."

With a grin as wide as Illiana's, Charles stepped forwards. You know me too, my delightful neighbour, so now is the time to be welcomed into one of your well warmed solars, where we can continue this greeting without frightening the staff."

"Hollyhocks and wet sawdust," growled the baron. "Come on, then." And led the way past the arched doorway into the grand hall, into a small chamber backing the hall. It was cosy and Bertha remembered it at once.

"My favourite room." She sank onto a high cushioned footstool, stretched her hands out to the small sizzle of flame in the hearth, and added, "Wine? I think refreshment must be in order."

There stood one solitary chair, un-cushioned, so Illiana curled on the Turkey rug before the fire, and Charles, gazing with condescending humour at the baron, leaned over the back of the wooden door frame. Unwilling to shake the glower, Robert of Oswey sat on the hard oak chair and after clapping his hands, without bothering to look back and check that someone had appeared to the call, ordered wine. "Get on with it. Doesn't have to be the best. Just find something."

"Not married yet?" Bertha asked him once the page had run off to the wine pantry.

"No," the baron growled. "Too many damned women in my life already."

Bertha brightened. "You mean Esther and Denise are still living here? Even Avis? With husbands and children?"

"None of the blasted females dared marry," he grunted. "After you married a foreign servant and Papa disowned you, we all stayed unwed. I don't want any moaning wife and I don't want those damned Moaning sisters either."

Illiana was laughing into her kerchief. Bertha was angry. Charles chuckled. Robert stared at the various faces around him and decided he liked none of them. He addressed Charles. "Don't know why you're here too," he objected. "What have you to do with this female dross, anyway?"

"I'm going to find my sisters," said Bertha at once, stool, brushed herself down, and trotted off without a backward glance.

Illiana quickly climbed onto the discarded footstool. "Well, what a charming family I have after all."

Charles now also walked forwards, standing beside the newly occupied footstool. "I knew your father for some years," he told the baron, "but we were never friends as he did not enjoy visitors. Nor did he seem to enjoy his miriad of daughters. I never knew your mother, and I heard that once she died, your father slipped quickly into growing irritability. You, sir, have neither lost a wife, nor gained one, but permanent irritability appears to have taken you also. This young lady, however, is your niece, Illiana."

"Humph," said the baron.

"Flints and fetlocks?" suggested Illiana.

"Just more females," Baron Oswy sighed. "You don't plan on moving in, do you?"

As Illiana grinned and shook her head, Charles interrupted. "Not at all," he said. "She plans on moving in with me." And as Illiana's head jerked upwards in amazement, Charles continued, "I shall now have the absolute pleasure of searching out your sisters, sir, and getting to know my future aunts."

CHAPTER TWENTY EIGHT

It was late, suppertime past, and Sabine had already fallen asleep on the settle, left entirely alone beside the fire, when the noise of invasion woke her and she blinked, looking up to see herself surrounded.

Illiana bent over her shoulder from behind the settle, and whispered, "Meet my exciting new aunts."

Apart from Illiana herself, now Sabine faced a bright smiling, bright eyed woman with a wide mouth, who giggled, stretched out a tiny spotted hand, large palmed and short fingered, and said in a rush, "I'm Esther, your new friend, my dear, and this is my sister Denise."

Startled, Sabine took Esther's hand, although not sure what to do with it, and then saw two more hands reaching for her.

"My darling, what a wonderful thrill to discover a new friend, and I'm Denise." Denise was pretty, her hair was greying but sleek silver streaks shone through like moon glow, her eyes were glittering blue, and her cheeks, quite round, were well powdered. She wore pale blue over dark blue, and clearly seemed as excited as she said she was.

The third hand came from a younger, hovering woman in vibrant red satin and silk, wafting a perfume of rosemary and lavender, a little too strong perhaps, with blue eyes so huge they dwarfed her little fat nose.

" I'm the youngest. Even younger than my sister Bertha. I'm Avis. The nicest of all."

The others laughed.

Bertha had slid onto the settle beside Sabine and was also chuckling. "My stupid brother," she said, "is more than an idiot. Nearly as bad as my father was. He thinks being a baron means he can sit by the fire and snore day in day out, except when he goes to bed at bedtime, and goes to sleep and snores all night."

"No, no, we mustn't be wicked ourselves," smiled the elder of the women. "Our brother is really rather sweet, but after a horrid childhood, and carrying the shocking scandal of his sister's reputation, sorry dear, but it did really echo the Halls and terraces back then and even seeing us, the high and mighty would raise their eyebrows and look away, so now he just wants to be left alone the entire time."

Illiana was also laughing, and Sabine joined in. Illiana said, "Charles is here somewhere, but I think he's probably being polite to our idiot lord and master. Are they all like that, then?"

"Charles isn't, and surely he won't be when his own odd father blunders off to Purgatory."

"I hope not," Illiana smiled to herself. There had been no private repetition of his hint at possible marriage, but this time the quickly dissolved words had seemed less like an invitation to becoming his mistress, and more like an attempt to be proper.

"That's three of them, isn't it," Bertha said, shaking her head. "My father was so stern, we all avoided him. Now my brother is just a lazy useless fool. The previous Earl Benedict was an amazing gentleman, but now, God rest his soul, he has left the earldom to a rat-like brother, and although I've never met dear Viscount Charles' father, it sounds as though Charles never has either."

"Never mind about them. For us, everything's new," Illiana grinned. "Even the king."

"We might even get to meet him."

"I met the previous one," Denise said. "Many years ago. That was King Edward, such a handsome man he was too. He invited me into bed. I would have done it if I could have, but my Papa suddenly appeared beside me, and nearly killed the king."

"I Haven't met the new king yet," Elser nodded cheerfully, "but I went to the coronation with Robert, since he didn't have anyone else to take with him. I did the curtsey thing and thanked him, but that's not meeting, is it. He's not as tall and handsome as his brother before him, but I think he's probably nicer. Look at those nice changes he announced, very decent changes."

"Like stopping anyone from grabbing the property as soon as a man is arrested, even if later they're proved innocent. Some gentleman could lose everything, be found not guilty, yet still couldn't ever get their property back. Well, now they don't lose a thing unless found guilty."

"The previous queen did that horrible grab in the past," Denise sighed. "The trial proved the wretched man innocent. The Woodville queen still kept her greedy little fingers on the property."

"So, now she's been proved not to be a queen, and never was, we had a bigamous king."

"And the new king has changed stopped anyone grabbing everything before you go to Gaol as guilty."

"I'm getting lost here," Bertha chuckled. "Never mind about kings and queens and laws being changed. Half the time I didn't know the old laws."

"Just as well you were never arrested then," sniggered Avis.

A short silence left everyone staring at everyone else ,when finally Illiana said, "Well, she was, poor absolutely innocent Mamma, in Spain. The inquisition."

"Oh, I've heard shocking stories," said Esther. "Yes, poor darling. Tell us what dreadful things they did to you."

Illiana expected her mother to blush and refuse to answer but instead, with a sigh, Bertha said, "I was asleep when they grabbed me. It was like a nightmare coming true. I couldn't understand it, but I was thrown, truly thrown, into this tiny dirty little cell, all cold stone and black as a moonless night. I screamed and cried, but no one came for so long, I think I fainted. No one fed me, didn't even bring water for more than a whole day, but I lost track of time."

Avis jumped over and hugged her big sister. "Poor darling."

Illiana shivered. Bertha continued. "After so long, two men came in. One was a priest and the other was a guard. The priest wasn't any nicer than the guard. They spoke Spanish of course, but I learned that from my husband, so I knew what they said. I couldn't answer their questions as I was crying too much."

Bertha had begun with a humorous relish, but now she had sunk back into the truth of it, and was crying genuinely and heavily. Every single woman wrapped their arms around her, half hugging each other, and now everybody was crying. Sabine, remembering her own different torture, heaved, clutching her throat and mouth, thinking she would vomit. Illiana now hugged Sabine.

She said, "It hasn't been easy. Not for any of us. Sabine perhaps even worse than my mother, then Nicholas too, he had to look after everyone and do the hardest work while at the same time he was worried really horribly for Sabine. She's his daughter, but he was still wonderful and helped us constantly. Even Charles, now where is he?"

Lord Benjamin, the third Earl of Birstall, had hidden in the tiny corridor chamber, usually used only for folk waiting patiently to see an earl, who was pretending to be too busy for the visit. There was a tiny brazier and the chair beneath this held the sleeping earl. Charles, following the drift of snoring echoes, had marched into the recess. Since the earl had wanted no candlelight, only the red glow of the brazier showed the smaller chair which Charles pulled out, sat down, and remarked loudly, "So how are you now, my lord, with your late brother's family restored to you? I'm sure you are absolutely delighted."

The earl squinted into the darkness. "I'm frankly tired, sir. I don't wish to be rude, but I'd just sooner be left alone."

"It's simply such a delight to see you, sir," Charles continued without moving. "I admired your brother, and knew him fairly well. I believe that you and he were never close, even as children."

"No doubt he told you that. It's true," the earl grunted. "Different characters. Different attitudes. Different desires. He got all of it, but, finally, at long last, I'm getting it too."

"Title and wealth, my lord, yes indeed." The tucks at the corners of Charles' mouth did not show in the dark. "The luck you deserve, no doubt, at long last, but," and his voice lowered, "I gather your marriage is not as happy as both your elder brother's marriages."

"Only fools marry expecting love," Benjamin said. His scowl was also invisible in the flicker of the red coals.

"Benedict, Benjamin and Beatrice," Charles mused. "I presume your parents were Archibald and Agnes? Yet no Catherine or Clair, Clement nor even a Charles seemed forthcoming."

"Not sure I get your point, Viscount," Benjamin hoisted himself upwards, stamped both feet, but remained sitting. "Not sure I care, either. Just what are you saying, sir?"

"I apologise for being aimless," Charles said, eyes now half closed. "Simply remarking on such interesting aspects now apparent within your family, sir." He also sat forwards. "Sadly, I believe your brother's first child was born too early and never breathed, God rest its young soul. Then some years later, his son died, God rest his soul also, at around the age of four. The yellow pox, I think, and horribly sad. Otherwise, my lord, you would not have gained the title."

"No children yet, true enough, not me nor Benedict before me, but there's time," Benjamin was gruff. Charles was considering whether it might be entertaining to goad the fool into anger by continuing the conversation.

Countess Olivia had not appeared, but Beatrice had heard voices, intentionally avoided the main hall, and then had heard the voice she knew as her brother, discussing the family with a stranger.

"Well, now, my lord," she said at once, sweeping into the tiny remaining space. "I am delighted to meet such a fascinating gentleman, and so handsome too, if you forgive me for saying so."

Charles blinked. "You have good eyesight, my lady." It was, after all, extremely dark.

"I see an interesting face and figure, sir, in the light of the brazier. May I introduce myself?" She did not wait for permission. "I am the Lady Beatrice, daughter to one earl, and sister of two others, and you, sir, are you Charles, Viscount Valdar. I have heard so much regarding your courage and virtue, my lord."

Having decided that this woman was most definitely unmarried, Charles leaned back and grinned. "A somewhat unexpected introduction, my lady. Thank you, but I confess, I am not here on a social basis, and simply need to speak with your brother."

Beatrice promptly balanced herself on the long wooden arm of the chair where Charles was sitting. The balance was precarious since the arm was narrow, but with one foot solid to the ground, Beatrice remained stable. "I'll not interrupt you, my lord." She smiled sideways.

Aware that she would tumble if he stood, Charles remained where he was. "I am here, my lord," and kept his gaze directly on Benjamin, "since I am already well acquainted with the dowager countess, your sister-in-law. You may remember that at the start of this year when your grace first took residence in the manor, I was able to inform you as to the actual identity of that lady, whom you had assumed was a servant, indeed only a kitchen maid before marrying your brother. Since I have all my life lived close to the Oswey Mansion, I have always been aware of the facts. While attending your brother's funeral, I realised that you were ignorant of those facts."

"Dammit, sir," Benjamin shifted uncomfortably. "I have a perfectly working memory. So, what now?"

"My acquaintanceship with the Ladies Bertha and Illiana has deepened since I met them in Spain. However, you may not yet be aware that we shall be married early in the coming year."

Beatrice interrupted first, screaming, "She never told me that."

"As yet, she does not know," said Charles. "But that alters nothing. You, sir, will not be bothered with plans, plots nor permissions regarding the wedding ceremony, since the lady is a widow. However, I thought it helpful to inform you of the immediate changes coming, and to assure you that the lady will then vacate this property. You will no longer be bothered with sharing your home. However, I also wished to add that I trust, most sincerely trust, that in the meantime, you will be treating my future bride with consideration, propriety, and the comfort to which she is entitled."

Benjamin stamped both feet, and swore under his breath. "Bastard interference, that's what this is, sir." He snorted the words. "As yet you've no right to tell me what to do, and I'll inform you now that I've never yet treated any woman with anything but kindness and decency."

Beatrice, who had left the arm of the small chair where Charles had sat, encircled the room with a swirl of shadows. Her glares, both at Charles and at her brother, were unseen. "Twaddle, sir," she addressed Charles. "Marching in here without invitation. And as for you," now to Benjamin, "You've never been nice to a woman in your life. Including me."

Ignoring his sister, the earl glowered. "I shall inform you now, sir, since you are uninvited, you have no place here. I ask you to leave."

Charles, however, remained seated, smiling up at the man spitting furiously down at him. "Nor does it seem you are what your wife might call a kind husband, sir. Does the Countess Olivia still sob in her bedchamber."

"She does," Beatrice flounced between her brother and the chair. "But it's usually her own fault."

Finally, Charles stood, staring back. "I simply wished, while in the vicinity," to make you aware of some minor matters. First concerning my friend Illiana. Secondly, allow me to mention my slight friendship with our admirable new king. His highness and I are frequently sharing news, and imparting information. You are not dependant on the sovereign's charity sir, and have no need of his good opinion, but should he hear of matters that might force a bad opinion, you might regret it, sir. I simply wished to advise you of the facts, and suggest that not only do you treat the Lady Illiana with civility, but perhaps you should attempt to forge a better relationship with your own dear wife."

"Not forgetting your own dear sister," added Beatrice although she seemed equally furious with Charles.

As Charles strode from the little colourless room, he heard the footsteps and looked up. Illiana was slowly descending the stairs, and looked glum. Charles moved to the last step, and Illiana discovered herself dissolving between his arms.

He whispered into the ear he now smothered, "If you scream for rescue, my little one, there is only me left who can do the rescue. He looked down into her neat little eyebrows, kissed lightly between them, and then kissed her on the mouth.

Neither screaming for rescue nor resisting at all, Illiana opened her lips to him and pressed forwards. She tasted the warmth, the gentle tinge of wine, and his sense of hunger. His tongue, burning hot, touched hers. She knew herself falling into him, even though she stood safe and entwined. She adored the strength of his arms, the long muscles of his legs, all of which seemed to be supporting the body which now she felt she no longer had. She was gasping when he pulled a little away, but remained between his arms, his one hand held to the back of her neck, the other to her shoulder. His tunnel eyes were so close to her, she felt she might walk in and cuddle tight below his lashes.

He whispered, "You know what I dream of, don't you, my love. What I want most of all."

She swallowed, whispering back, "I do, but,"

"I want you to marry me," he continued. "I may not replace your first husband, who was indeed a good man, but I am in love for the first time in my life, and want to prove it to you."

"A real marriage?"

Charles chuckled, stroking her cheek. "Not a king-like handfasting, never to be disclosed? No, my dearest, I can be secretive, but not sinister. I'll buy you a dress of rainbows and carry you off to church."

"I'll be a real wife?"

"If you tell me yes."

"Of course I'll tell you yes. I've almost surrendered to the other invitation. This one is what I've wanted for months."

"I always meant marriage, little one." He laughed, kissed the tip of her nose, and then kissed both her eyelids. "My words were never clear simply because I'm an idiot, because I doubted you'd want me after Benedict, and because my work might make commitment difficult, because I'm accustomed to flirtation, but mostly simply because I'm a ridiculous fool."

"And fools marry fools."

He kissed her again, pressing against her, his breath in her throat. And when they were interrupted, for a moment they did not even respond.

"I don't mind at all," said Bertha. "A good choice for both of you. I just wanted to squeeze in a slightly different subject before you disappear upstairs."

"We have no intention of disappearing upstairs," Charles murmured, still firmly attached to her daughter. "Instead, we'll shortly be on the road back to The Strand to discover whether my father still exists, or not."

Mother surveyed daughter. Bertha said, "I hate to delay you, but I have a fountain of explanations to soak you with before you can nip off to meet this strange stranger. I presume the reason is to inform him that his son is about to get married? Yes, that's been guessed already. But hold on. You see, I've never, ever had so many glorious friends, all my delicious sisters rediscovering me. I thought none of them wanted to know me after my shocking marriage, and I was somewhat peeved. It was Papa who was always a tyrant. He forced them to swear on the Holy Book, and locked them in their rooms without food until they did it. My brother too. In fact, he spent quite a lot of his youth locked in his very boring bedchamber."

Initially impatient, Illiana was now fascinated. "Go on. And I think they're all lovely, but your father sounds like Benjamin. How many pigs are there wearing ermine and velvet?"

"An enormous number," said Charles, cheerfully flashing his black satin doublet. "Look, no ermine and no velvet, but I've known plenty of unintelligible bastards who should never wear a title, but often received one for being a pugnacious and brutal fighter who helped win a war."

"The aristocracy sound very English," Illiana sighed.

"They're only vile because of being human," Charles did not release Illiana. "Lords, ladies, hard working traders, the rich, the poor, the poverty-stricken, the healthy and the sick, each divides between the blissful, the wicked, and those in the middle who have not decided yet."

"Benedict was a lord, and utterly wonderful. I loved my father, and he was wonderful as well. Benedict was lordly and rich, which was incredible. My Papa was hard working, clever, but just a groom." Illiana nodded vigorously into Charles' shoulder. "Both really seemed perfect."

She was about to add Charles to her list when Bertha added,

"Your father? No, you know the truth, my dear. Apart from his disgusting sins which I eventually knew, and refused to believe. I never admitted that Diego was so far from perfect, however much I loved him. He was a saint to me."

"And to me."

"But not to everyone," Bertha sighed. "He had a wicked, nasty side."

Charles said, "It seems we speak constantly of the dead, God rest their souls. My Lady Bertha, there was something more alive, which I believe you wanted to speak of."

"Yes, yes, and dearest Illiana, your perfect Benedict empowered you in his final testament. You own a home, perhaps a great mansion, which you've never even seen. I remember he named it Benedict House. It could possibly be a tiny one room cottage, but I don't think so. The grounds are farmed and certainly bring in an income. Besides, the Village of Benedictsbridge must tell its own story."

"He lived there with his first wife, poor lady," Illiana said, feeling abruptly sad to remember. "He said she was wonderful and worked so hard in this tiny farm, money invested, employing everyone from far and near, creating a whole village, with crops and milking sheds, and then, if I remember properly, a huge Smith's business, not just for horses, but for all weapons and armoury, for gold seals and metal pumps and everything a forge can produce. It makes a fortune and employs everyone who doesn't work on the farm lands."

"In Devonshire?" her mother reminded her. "Yes, just so. Well. Neither of us have ever been to Devon let alone Benedictsbridge and the house, whether a stable or a mansion."

"I doubt dear Benedict and his first wife, he told me that she was even more titled than he was, would ever have lived in a stable. They had something built and I expect it's glorious."

"Exactly," Bertha smiled widely, clasped her hands and nodded with satisfaction. "'Tis yours, my dear, and always will be, but, hopefully it could squeeze in your darling Mamma and her three glorious long lost sisters."

As they talked, Charles had opened another of the doors along the corridor near the stairs, entering a small annex. He had brought one of the two wooden chairs forward for Illiana to sit, and was busy closing the door, when the silence outside changed to a shrill delight of mixed voices, the door was clanked open once more and three women rushed in and collided with Bertha. The sweep and swish of silk, satin and damask, ruffles, coloured embroideries and dangling tassels, wide golden cuffs over tight white lace cuffs, and brilliant swirling hems over shifting white muslin ones, all sang their own colourful music while everyone hugged everyone. Finger rings clicked on thumb rings as hands clapped, and Charles abandoned his fiancé, moving back to the wall. Now five elated women all spoke at once,

"I haven't any doubts it's a mansion," Bertha said. "That house will be grand, I'm sure of it.

"I don't care if it's a chicken shed," Esther insisted.

"I'll sleep in the fields," declared Avis.

"I'll do all the cooking," Denise told them, "if there aren't any staff. I learned when I was little, but I've never been able to practise. I can build my own fire too, and then I'll buy a caldron."

"You can't afford a caldron," said Esther.

"Wel exactly, why do you think I'm still living with paddy-toes Robert?" Denise demanded.

"I always thought I should study a few things and join a convent," Avis sighed. "Then I could have left Robert and lived in a Nunnery. Had my own cosy little cell."

"You already have a cosy little cell," Esther reminded her.

"Indeed," Avis grunted. "Which is why I failed the Habit. Being penniless in a huge house with a very boring brother who dreams of being alone, is no holy delight."

Denise kissed Illiana five times, outdoing Charles who simply stood, watched and laughed. Illiana wrapped her arms again around Denise, and said, "All fascinating, and what wonderful women you all are."

"*We* all are."

"Yes, of course you can all live there, wherever it is, if you can find it. It'll be wonderfully comfy and we'll change things and get new things and do everything you want."

"I'll drive an ox and till the fields."

"You mean you'll plough the fields."

"I won't even need an ox," said Avis. "I'll do it all myself. Anyway, what does an ox look like. I've certainly never seen one. Does it eat people?"

"No dear, only weeds."

Illiana flopped on a cushion, sitting cross legged on the ground with her skirts bundled. "I just wonder," she was taking a risk, but the question disturbed her, "why none of you ever looked for my mother years ago. I mean, I suppose I sound horrid, but I know she got so lonely after Papa died. Yes, I know my grandfather threw her from the house for marrying a servant, and refused ever to speak a word to her after that, but she never missed him anyway. She says he was a tyrant."

"He was. He thought a father's only duty was discipline."

"And his idea of discipline was as strict as a viper."

Bertha shrugged. "I married Diego for love, but there was an extra reason, and that was to get away from our father."

"Our brother just hides and wants to be alone, father's affect on him was just as hideous."

"Worse, poor grumbling and moaning little Robbie."

"But you three," Illiana insisted. "Couldn't you have searched? Asked around? I think she kept hoping."

When Charles said, "Speaking of the wicked rich, the Baron Oswey always had somewhat of a reputation. I gather smiling was an effort reserved only for when he met the king."

"Which didn't happen often," nodded Bertha, "because even the king avoided him."

CHAPTER TWENTY NINE

"We were all huddled together," Esther told them, "when we knew about Bertha getting married to our head groom. Terrified. Not of Diego of course. Only of Papa."

"Bertha, and Diego were kicked from the house," Avis continued. "And kicked is the right word too. Then Papa locked each of us in our bedchambers and for two long dark days and we had no food and nothing to drink. Once my maid managed to squeeze bread crumbs under the door but that was it for two days."

Denise whispered, "I still remember curling on the floor nursing my stomach and feeling ill with hunger. Then I reminded my self that sometimes the poor did this anyway, because they couldn't buy food. That stopped me moaning about myself."

"The poor can be wicked too," Esther interrupted, "but it's the rich who have the power."

"Not if locked in their bedchambers by their father and starved,' interrupted Charles from the shadows.

"I had some water in a basin in the garderobe," Avis said. "It was for washing my hands of course, but I drank it. I don't think it helped."

"Probably dirty water from the Thames," decided Illiana.

"Then when he let us out," Esther said, "he dragged us downstairs, threw us to the ground in the Hall, and whipped us, each one."

"And we hadn't even done anything." mumbled Denise.

"Then," Denise announced, "he demanded we never, ever, not for any reason, make the slightest attempt to discover our darling sister or contact her. He slammed our hands on the Latin Bible, and made us kiss the Prayer Book, and we had to swear it by God Himself."

"And that was that," Avis sniffed. "We didn't. We couldn't."

"Even when Papa died, may his soul rest in peace, though I doubt it will," continued Esther, "we did nothing at first. Then, very slow and we started to look. Honestly, we looked and looked and looked. We just couldn't find any of you."

"I don't suppose you were exactly practised at searching the undergrowth," said Illiana.

Avis blushed. "We had no idea where. We discussed it in whispers for months. We thought you might have run away to Scotland or Cornwall."

"By then dear Diego had died too, Lord rest his soul, and his name had gone from stables all over London." Bertha smiled at her sisters. "So that would have made searching for us even harder. That was after nine years married, so I assumed none of my dear sisters ever wanted to see me again. I missed you so much and I thought you hated me for marrying a servant too, but now I know it wasn't your fault."

"It was our fault for being scared little idiots," sniffed Denise.

Esther was also blushing. "It seems so stupid, looking back, but the scandal was huge, you know. Friends wouldn't speak to us. We were of this wicked family of sluts and harlots. No man would come near and if they did, Papa howled and sent them away. He refused to enter into any marriage arrangements for us, even though we had sworn on the Holy Book."

"I was scared for years," said Bertha. "That's how I was brought up. I had to be a good girl even when I was in my thirties. Except," and she wiped her eyes, "to my daughter. I thought I had to try at least some discipline, and Diego certainly never did. He just laughed and rolled around and gave people gifts he couldn't afford and hugged everyone. Then," she blushed into the hovering candle flame, "I truly thought, because of the terrible secret I suspected, that my daughter had killed him. Killed her own father. I knew why, but I still blamed her. Secrets, secrets, and anger boiling under the surface. Self pity." She sniffed and avoided Illiana's stare. "It was the inquisition that taught me courage, and even common sense. Isn't that a terrible thing to say? It was such blatant cruelty, justified by a church that preached goodness and love, and they seemed to ignore whether I was innocent or guilty anyway. That made me pray for justice. So, if I want justice, then I have to practise it too."

"Horrid injustice isn't supposed to teach us kind hope," Esther whispered.

"It taught me courage," Bertha said, sitting straight. "it taught me not to assume I knew the truth when I didn't, and it taught me to make sure I was right, and then have confidence in it. Courage. Now I've got it and I'll never lose it again."

Yet instead of acknowledging the courage he had preached himself, Charles said, "Well, welcome, my lady. I presume you heard the voices and laughter and hoped to share the entertainment." Everyone whirled around and gazed with everything from sulk to smile, but principally disappointment, at Beatrice who had quietly stalked into the room.

"That house in Devonshire," said the vision, "does not belong, by right, to Illiana."

Illiana stared back and hoped she looked fierce. "It does legally," she said loudly as everyone else fell silent. "What is the right that differs from legality?"

"Poof, tis obvious," Beatrice now shouted. "The right of family."

"Which includes me," said Illiana. "I am most certainly of Benedict's family."

"Not the birth family," Beatrice sneered. "You may call yourself a lady and claim decency from Baron Oswey, which forced dear Benjamin to let you stay in our home, but you're still the daughter of a foreign groom and a housekeeper, disowned by her own family, who knew nothing but scrubbing kitchen floors."

The anger now sizzled like broth on the hob. It was Charles who said cheerfully, "What amazing new insights, my lady. I had imagined that Earl Benedict, your elder brother and first born child, the only member of your family expected to wear the title, was a gentleman who loved and admired his new wife, the wife he had chosen himself. He was legally entitled and had the integral right, , to give whatever he had created and bought personally himself, to whom he also chose. You offer an interesting alternative, madam. That being the right of a younger sister, never in fact a close friend, to inherit whatever she wishes to claim, even though what she claimed never had the faintest connection to her."

Having long known and so long enjoyed having a voice which few ever interrupted, Charles smiled, tapping his fingers on the sheath of his scabbard. The scabbard was, however, empty. His sword lay in the cloakroom just inside the main doors.

Beatrice seemed unexpectedly on the verge of tears. "I thought you were a nice man," she pouted at Charles.

"I am an excessively nice man," he told her with an accompanying very nice smiled. "But madam, I believe you suffer from having spent a lifetime being overlooked by your father, and after a fruitless attempt to arrange your marriage, being overlooked by your brother." He spread his smile to each one of the feminine company. "I should remind you, my lady, since I happen to know, that you are extremely lucky to have avoided marriage to Lord

Hamerling, who is deaf and simple minded, and not at all wealthy since he gambled away every penny, ending borrowing from everyone in the family, and never paying back a farthing of it. What is more, being ignored by your brother is far more peaceful and beneficial than being noticed by him."

Suddenly Illiana clapped. "I don't know any Lord Hamerling, but I agree with avoiding your brother. He's permanently angry."

"Unlucky," Denise added, "My brother is very sweet, but not very clever. After years of being tormented by his father, he just wants to live all alone and drink too much."

"But I," spat Beatrice, "am a Latymer by birth, family of the Earls of Birstall. Whereas you," and she pointed at Illiana, "are a kitchen scrubber with an old worn out claim as the granddaughter of a baron. I'll have you know that the great House of Birstall is far, far superior to the poky little House of Oswey."

Illiana sighed. "Just as well that I'm the dowager countess of Birstall, then. Which you are not, dear Beatrice."

"How shockingly true," Charles sighed, "though perhaps I should add that the great House of Valdar supersedes that of Birstall, and Illiana is about to join it, eventually becoming the Countess of Cleeve. When His majesty realises how indispensable I am, she might become the Duchess of all England." He paused, now only smiling at Beatrice. "Why does all this need to be recognised? A title can be useful, I admit it. Wealth can be damnably useful, even quite attractive. It offers scope. However, what matters is character, madam, and what you are yourself will gain you far more notice." He laughed. "Good or bad."

Being an apt moment for another interruption, the door flew open and Sabine stormed in, her arm around Olivia, who seemed to have shrunk, and was clearly reluctant to enter.

Sabine announced, "The earl has hurt his dear wife, and certainly not for the first time. How dare he!"

Standing firm in the flickering shadows, Sabine, wearing her friend's grand clothes, looked more the countess than the woman she supported. Olivia's face was swollen with tears. Beneath those tears, one of her eyes was closed and bruised. Tiny beads of blood were smeared across her upper lip, which was also greatly swollen, and beneath the protruding bones of her neck, the bodice of her gown was stained with dark, sticky blood, mixed with drips of gravy thrown from some past meal. She had grown scrawny and even her clothes, falling loose, showed how thin she was.

Illiana was the first to run and hug the small bruised woman.

"What did he do to you?"

"Humph," snorted Beatrice. "Simply tried teaching her to obey and behave."

Furious now, Illiana shouted back at Beatrice. "You've had a rotten life and you hate your brother. Can't you sympathise for someone with an even worse life, who has even more cause to hate your brother?"

Olivia's intervention was shrill and high pierced, then collapsing into tears once more. "Please, please, no more quarrels. I just want to,"

Avis rushed forwards with a kerchief. Bertha breathed deeply. "What idiots we all are. Illiana, if we are welcome to run off and live happily in your country mansion, can we take Olivia too?"

"Absolutely, definitely, any time you like. Right now, if you want to, but remember, Benjamin knows the address."

Olivia blew her nose in the now soaking wet kerchief. "I can escape? I can really run away?"

"He'll chase her," scowled Bertha. "He'll be even nastier if she leaves him. He'll feel humiliated."

"He'd have no one left to whip and punch."

"Except Beatrice." smiled Illiana.

Beatrice, stood shaking, whether with fear or with anger was unclear, but probably both.

Every other woman again hugged, kissed, thanked, promised prayers, and embraced again. Charles, having been caught in the centre of the group, was quickly included, and could not stop laughing. Now his eyes were also moist, although only from amusement.

Esther, her warm satins smothering her rubies as she tried to straighten her clothes now creased from a hundred hugs, managed to say, "Please, all my lovely darlings, can we run back to poor Robert, tell him he's about to be left in glorious peace. He can sing to himself without being laughed at. He can sleep and sleep, and for him, that will be the best of all. Meanwhile, we can steal litters and horses and pack our bags and scramble off to Devon before Christmas."

"The solstice has passed. The days are getting longer."

"Only by three blinks and a hurried cup of wine."

"Of course you can," waved Illiana.

"We'll take Olivia," shouted Bertha.

"I wish you'd take Beatrice," sighed Illiana, "but you certainly won't agree to that."

It was as the shrieks of delight echoed from most present, that Charles disappeared. It was during the second hoops of noise that he reappeared, and this time his scabbard was not empty at all.

Beatrice had slapped Illiana, and Bertha had immediately slapped Beatrice. Esther had then slapped Beatrice and cursed her for slapping her little sister. Olivia was howling, and her nose had once again begun to bleed as she tripped, falling against Sabine. Beatrice had grabbed Esther's loose virginal hair, and Sabine had darted forward, grabbing Beatrice by the neck. As Sabine ran forwards, Olivia stumbled without support and sank to the now grimed floor. The boards were streaked with blood, scratches and muddy wet footprints. It now seemed that every woman had at least one swollen red cheek.

Denise was on her knees, helping Olivia when the door was flung wide with a thunderous smash, and the earl marched in, waving a tiny sharpening knife in one hand, and a large quill pen, dripping ink, in the other.

He demanded, "What the devil is going on? Get the fucking

shit out of my house, all you damned stupid women." The quill nib pointed at Olivia. "What are you doing here, idiot slut? Get back to your bedchamber or I shall thrash you again and bare skinny arse naked this time."

The tiny knife clattered to the floorboards as Charles stepped directly to face him, his sword point hovering against Benjamin's mouth. It pricked his lower lip. The tiny spring of blood brought a roar of approval from Illiana, Bertha, Olivia, Esther, Denise, Avis and Sabine. Even Beatrice seemed silently to smile.

The earl spluttered and spat. Charles continued to grin as Illiana grabbed another kerchief and, resting one hand on Charles' shoulder, carefully removed the spit from his chin. "Most thoughtful, thank you," Charles said softly, and then raised his voice. "You do realise, sir, that I am entitled to use this sword in matters of self defence?"

"As shall I," Benjamin shouted, once again spraying saliva.

"The quill's nib may scratch," Charles remarked, "but I doubt it will kill me. I seem to have noticed that, at this moment, you are somewhat outnumbered, sir."

"Yes, by a squawking mass of tarts and idiot slatterns," Benjamin retorted. "Like my wife, useful for just one damned thing, and rarely even for that."

"Women can stab too, dear," Beatrice abruptly told her brother.

Within the very small annexe, very little light and even less space permitted movement. Now, whirling, unexpected and sudden, Benjamin moved from the sword point and launched at Beatrice with the pen. With the space crammed, Beatrice had been only a toe's length away from him. As both Illiana and Sabine jumped on him, the quill's nib slashed across Beatrice's face, pulling away only as it reached the curl of her lower eyelid. The long slit oozed blood, the eye, although uninjured, seemed to swell and Beatrice tumbled back as she burst into heavy sobbing tears.

"I've never seen her cry before," Illiana muttered, now with her hands around Benjamin's stubby neck.

Charles, the sword tip raised again to the earl's face, now pricking at his nose, spoke between his teeth. "Why, you fool? You hate the entire world? Or you know yourself so inferior it makes envy the only emotion you recognise?"

The earl yowled. "Hatred, and why should I not, when every fool I meet is scum? All women are whores or terrified little rats. They call themselves rich, just for opening their thighs to the elite. Most men, like you, whoever you claim to be, are conceited bastards."

"Envy indeed. I've no objection to you hating me," Charles told him, smiling, "and you have met me before over the years. Not as friends, and never will, but you know exactly who I am. What nonsense are you pretending, even to yourself?"

The room was crowded, without the space to stagger free. Long skirts, heavy legs, everything moved in a slow shuffle, until Illiana remembered the bell and reached, ringing it as loudly and for as long as she could. It rattled and pealed, echoing throughout the ground floor and up the stairs, startling every man and woman working in the kitchens, who stopped, whatever they had been doing, spoons and brushes in hand, while staring at each other.

The ringing chimes continued and Manders rushed to the little solar, pushed his presence into the dark alcove, bit his tongue and asked, as politely as possible, "Did someone call?"

The candle, guttering down to the wick, spluttered a pink glow and abruptly disappeared.

"Yes, I did," Illiana called back to Manders through the utter blackness, "Please, some wine. No, maybe wine is not such a good idea. How about a few kitchen knives? It's help we want, we need an interruption."

"Don't bother," Charles said pleasantly. "I believe the mighty Earl of Birstall is about to interrupt us himself."

With a fury that virtually blinded, and utterly confused him,

Benjamin was dizzy, searching out whichever woman infuriated him the most. Long hair slapped against his cheek as one woman turned. Blonde hair, black hair, gowns of swirling silks, pursed lips, glaring eyes, both blue and deep brown, tiny scrawny hands grabbing at him, and the scratching fingers and nails. The whispering and snickering, and men who sided with the women, Lord Charles, bastard that he was, so tall, so grand, so conceited, and now Manders taking the side of the worst bitch amongst them all.

Lady Beatrice, swirling in scarlet velvet, glared at him. Countess Olivia stumbled beside her, skirts in mahogany silk, then pushed past. Illiana in deep green damask and wool was between two ladies, Avis and Esther both wearing blue as blue as a summer sky. The old hag Bertha swirling in black and white chiffon, then Denise, another stranger, deep red from neck to toe. Jewellery clinked, catching reflections of light that stabbed the earl's eyes. The earl coughed, heaved, lunged at the kitchen scrubber Sabine, but was stopped by the black and gold livery of Lord Charles, and then the livery of his own steward.

His howl was loud as though in terrible burning pain. It rattled the roof beams, the shutters and the door frames. The earl grabbed the long blonde curls beside his ear, tugging, until Avis whimpered, kicked out with one leather boot, and then lunged with teeth and nails. Benjamin had already escaped, kicking out at Olivia. Illiana grabbed two long pearl headed pins from the tucks of her hair beneath the netting, and stabbed Benjamin, hard, through the back of his neck.

The earl howled again and hoisted Illiana upwards, her feet lifted from the ground. She also kicked out and the point of one boot found his groin. Denise was saving the fallen pearls and spun, pushing one metal point into Benjamin's hand. He released Illiana, but stamped on Denise, her ankle caught beneath his large foot, and kicked her with the other. He caught her shin with a boot almost enormous and she fell back, whimpering.

Charles was already facing Benjamin at one small breath's distance, and again the sword pointed directly into his face.

"This time," Charles warned, "I'll not be so careful. I tell you now, stop, think, be calm, and then I suggest you leave. Then, my lord, we also can leave. You will be neither harmed nor humiliated. You will have the peace of your home once again around you. Forget us, forget this day, it has no meaning nor importance. Leave this room, and we shall leave your home."

The command had been slow, cool, clear, and like the voice of prayer in a silent church. Benjamin panted, tried to clear his head, and began to wonder who he was. Everything stilled. Even the boards did not creek. The earl bled. From the two thin marks at the back of his neck, blood trailed like fragile trickles of water when the saucepan boils over. The back of his right hand had stung, one small red drop now dried into a dark and sticky smudge. He was not badly hurt but his groin throbbed, his neck ached and his hand smarted. Both his lower lip and the tip of his nose stung, and blood had oozed from scratches, now dried, but still sore.

More fiery and more painful than all else, his temper hurt him.

Then slowly, as he stood, bent over and panting, his temper died.

The earl felt the merging embarrassment more painful than the bleeding sores, his breath was a struggle, and he stepped back, panting and miserable. As the throbbing continued beneath the staring eyes of all those around him, the earl straightened, blazing, even more furious.

After one moment of wasted time, without the smallest idea of how to help, Manders had quietly left, but he did not head to the kitchens. He headed to the stables.

Bertha clutched Illiana. The other three sisters stood tightly together, ready and even eager. Sabine stood close to Bertha, her hand closed on Illiana's. Olivia, hunched on the ground, stared up into Beatrice's hesitancy.

The noiseless moment shivered for one quick blink and then

shattered. Olivia stood, climbing quietly onto her knees and then to her feet. Taking just three small steps, she stood directly behind Charles.

Charles kept his sword, pointing slightly upwards, at the earl's open, panting gape. The shining blade point almost tipped the edge of Benjamin's front teeth, its silver polish illuminating the wide crimson throat beyond.

Yet this was a threat, a proof of possibility, and Charles kept his arm unmoving.

Now Olivia lunged, pushing with both her hands behind the elbow of Charles' right arm, bent outwards, his sword steady, just inches from the earl's mouth. With the unexpected and abrupt force pushing behind him, Charles unaware and unprepared, saw his own blade's streak of gleaming silver steel stabbing in and up, entering unintended, but thrusting deep.

Instantly pulling backwards, Charles swept the steel away, and as a gushing flow of blood poured from Benjamin's mouth, he toppled at Charles' feet. Behind him, seeing what she had done, fully intended as it was, Olivia also toppled. With a shivering failure of both knees, the woman fainted. Charles stood still, staring. Then his blood dripping sword clattered to the ground and he knelt, examining the earl.

Benjamin lay flat on his back. His face had entirely disappeared beneath pools of scarlet, darkening slowly, the stink of dying breath, pierced brains, and the abrupt escape of urine. He lay still, in a puddle of sweat and stink, blood and piss.

Charles examined his victim quickly and efficiently, then stood over the corpse. "He's dead. How interesting. It seems I've killed him."

Olivia, eyes now fluttering, whispered, "I killed him, my lord. I wanted to."

Charles turned, leaned over, and helped Olivia stand, his arm around her waist. "My lady, I shall privately give you the credit for doing what was utterly right, courageous and justified, but in public I shall rightfully take the blame. When my sword causes death as my hand clasped the sword hilt, blame can hardly be disputed. You, my lady, were not even armed."

She was crying, but softly this time. Her already swollen eyes now puffed and closed. The final gurgle of blood had choked back into Benjamin's throat and the chug of it brought Esther to his side, her knees in the puddles, thinking him alive.

Charles said, "No, my lady. Although unintentional, I'm glad to call him gone."

No one chortled the usual 'May the good Lord rest his soul in peace.'

Again silence, and then Manders wading in, a hay pike tightly grasped, and Nicholas behind him, holding his own sword in one hand and a hammer in the other. Once more, every one stopped, and all were staring at each other.

Nicholas blurted, "If t'was any of my ladies, then it weren't them, it were me."

Charles smiled. "Relax my friend. I claim the right as culprit, but a culprit without sin, perhaps, since I can also claim self-defence."

"It was me," but Olivia's whisper was utterly exhausted and almost unheard.

"You don't want to lose your work for the royal house," Illiana's whisper was louder than Olivia's, "and I can take the blame. I wanted to. If I could have, I would have."

"And me too, my dear," Bertha said.

Stepping over his own sword, Charles led Illiana to the side wall, and leaned her back against the plastered stone. Then, both hands gently on her shoulders, he kissed her lightly on both cheeks and more slowly on her forehead. "You, my little one, should have killed the vile creature, but then would have taken the right of blame, from you. I do have justice behind me, and would never lose my position for killing in self defence. Had I killed this viper simply to save the women he attempted to violate and even kill, I would still be announced innocent of crime. There is no courageous heroism in what I do. I will not be charged, and no man shall say it should not have been done. I have killed before and the reputation does me no harm, whereas if you, or any other woman here, chooses to stand accused, she would be immediately exonerated, yet the reputation of a dangerous murdering woman would stick. I don't say that is fair or right in any manner or situation, but it is a fact we cannot easily change."

"I had every right to kill the pig," Olivia spluttered, "and should have before now."

"As a countess," Charles told her, "you would never be brought to public trial, but killing an earl is not an easy charge to suffer. For myself, and since it was my blade entered the fool's mouth, it is far, far easier for me."

With a heave, a rustle and many sighs, the women stood, straightened, nodding and whispering. Manders dropped the garden rake. Nicholas stood limp, unsure, then was hugging his breathless daughter. Bertha shook her head at Beatrice, and Beatrice stared, unmoving, down at her feet.

Denise said, "Well, my lord, should you ever need a witness, I believe you have several, all more than willing."

Charles thanked her, took Illiana's hand, and looked to Manders. "Knowing the sword and the hand holding the hilt were mine, please inform the entire household, arrange for the funeral, and help Lady Beatrice to rest, food, wine and privacy. Meanwhile Nicholas," and their eyes met, two men roughly the same height, "I suggest you make preparation and all billing shall be sent directly to me. Ladies Esther, Denise and Avis need to be transported in comfort to their previous home, where they may pack, and rest the night. I suggest that the Lady Bertha accompany them. Tomorrow morning, after they have bid their brother goodbye, they must be transported in the same comfort, to an address in Devon, and made comfortable there. I suggest you stay there a week, in company with your daughter. Illiana and I, on the other hand, shall first be visiting his highness, King Richard, and afterwards, the manor I call my home, which might, or might not, still contain my father."

"I'll travel with Papa," Sabine said abruptly, although still simply another shadow amongst the lightless jumble, "because he's wonderful, and I'll help everyone settle in the new house, whatever it's like, in Devon. Benedictsbridge or something, wherever all that is. South somewhere, I think, but when we get back, I want to live with Papa of course, and, just as important, with Illiana too. Illiana needs a maid and a friend, so I'm coming with you now, Papa, but," and she stared at Charles, "wherever she goes, I have to stay with Illiana too."

"I believe," Charles grinned, "you have made your intentions quite clear, young lady. On your return from Devon, which is indeed in the south, you will be extremely welcome, along with Nicholas, in my own home in The Strand, and on a permanent basis. Although I very much doubt you'll be awarded the title of serving maid."

CHAPTER THIRTY

"I believe, sir, you are just a little early for our Christmas feast," smiled the king.

"Under the circumstances," Charles grinned, "I might have forgotten what day we're in, sire, but I am not yet expecting, nor even hoping for a feast."

"Although no doubt wine would be acceptable, Charles?"

"Without doubt, your highness," and Charles bowed a second time. "And while your graciousness is in abundance," he grinned, "a young lady waits outside beside the guard of the door, sire. I should love to introduce you to my future bride."

Richard was already laughing, and now laughed loudly and more deeply. "Bring her in, sir, bring her in. This will be a considerable pleasure, and one I shall enjoy, before you both join me for the Christmas dinner at the palace."

She had been standing, arranging her face as she hoped would be acceptable. A smile, of course, but not so falsely brilliant, eyes wide and honest, not too openly ridiculous. Surely she would begin with hands clasped, although the immediate curtsey would demand they separate, so why clasp them at all! Illiana shook her head at herself. She decided she would probably seem an idiot anyway, should simply relax, and be whoever she actually was, whoever that might be, as she told herself with a smirk. Meeting a king, still feeling herself a kitchen maid, the great new monarch of the entire country - ? Charles opened the door and grinned at her, catching the smirk.

"His Royal Highness," Charles said, "would be delighted to meet you, little one, and that's a genuine repeat of his actual words. This isn't a king who bothers to be a royal speech-maker unless he's on duty."

Richard was not alone. Two guards stood, one at each doorway. This was, however, far less than would be present if he was holding audience.

Illiana's curtsey nearly tripped her over. "I'm delighted to make your acquaintance,"

Richard stepped forwards, watching in case she needed a hand up.

This was not expected nor intended to be a long meeting. His highness was intensely busy and only snatches of moments were peaceful, when he might squeeze in his own cheerful smiles, but Charles had one important matter to discuss. "Not that this will bother you overmuch, sire," Charles said, "but I feel you should have the full and truthful facts first, before I report myself to the law. Since you are ruler of the realm, sire, and also my personal master and leader now, I must report to you first and foremost."

"My dear Charles," said the king, "we can chat another day, but for now, my friend, please just get on with it."

The obedient statement followed abruptly. "I have killed the Lord Benjamin, 3rd Earl of Birstall, the title inherited from his elder brother Benedict almost exactly one year past."

So, the king nodded, only faintly frowning. "I know nothing of this, so will appreciate the facts, sir. I knew the previous earl fairly well, as you did, Charles. I do not, however, know anything of the brother. I am listening."

"First, sire, as no doubt you are aware, this lady is Lord Benedict's dowager countess. Their marriage, although sadly short, was a happy one without problems. Now, as you are aware, I benefit from this lady's widowhood. We plan to marry within the first months of the new year."

Richard smiled again. "The new year, I presume, as dated on the new calendar, beginning the first day of January, and not so far away.."

"Indeed, sire."

The king's smile hovered. "I shall gladly attend your marriage, unless I am compelled to be elsewhere on business at that time. Now, continue as to the new earl's death. Knowing and trusting you, Charles, I do not expect either scandal nor admission of actual murder, but I must know what has happened."

"I am not expecting difficulties regarding this," Charles shrugged, "since there are numerous witnesses, including Lady Birstall here. It is incontestable that Lord Benjamin, the 3rd earl, was a gentleman with difficulties. He was generally disliked and frequently hated. He mistreated his own family and in particular his wife, the Lady Olivia, daughter of Sir Winston, Baron Lymm. Indeed, at present the lady bears considerable injuries inflicted by her late husband. Yesterday afternoon, while in the 3rd earl's home and company, in presence also of his injured wife, of my own fiancé, and of several other persons, I was forced to defend myself and all others present, as Benjamin the earl had become excessively violent. I am entirely honest, sire, in adding that I had not intended my sword to intrude so far within the earl's head, but within seconds of it doing so, he lay dead and I am entirely responsible."

Nodding, Richard stood. "Very well, Charles. I trust you, I believe you, and now I know the facts. Thank you for the full explanation. I see no reason whatsoever for you to be charged as culpable of crime, sir. I shall ensure that you are neither arrested nor accused." He placed a firm hand on Charles' shoulder. "And with that, my time is gone, sir. No doubt I'm culpable and can be blamed for that. I have another appointment, but I thank you for your visit, for the charming introduction, for the clear facts which I'm bound to hear soon through inaccurate gossip, and hope to see you at Christmas, Charles."

ONCE THEY HAD LEFT, three steps backwards and then turning, they stood as their horses, ready saddled, were led to them. The groom helped Illiana to mount, and she leaned across to Charles and thanked him for everything. "And he really calls you friend."

"We had the advantage of knowing each other for some years previous to the late king's death, God rest his soul," Charles said. "Richard will be a great king, if not exhausted within the first five years. Even our King Edward, whatever he benefited, struggled for most of his life and fought hard for what he thought right. Folk so often crave wealth and power, but they don't anticipate the crashing responsibility. So many of us flounder beneath envy and jealousy without realising that no man or woman who has ever lived, has had a life without struggle and pain."

Illiana sighed. "It's true and I know it. I hated some of the folk in Spain and I know wickedness fruits here too, but perhaps the wicked suffer more. Everyone was envious of the last king. He was famed for greed."

"I find no fault with the late king. I also knew Edward. He lied, he cheated and laughed about religious rules, but he also cared and worked to help his country and nine times of each ten, he forced himself to do the right thing. He had difficulties, and eventually couldn't overcome the passion."

"Like drinking too much and eating too much?" Illiana was laughing. She had never met him but knew the gossip.

"Not a man in the country ever failed to know his king's overpowering passions." Charles laughed. "But it never made him unlikeable. He tried to smuggle every beautiful young woman he ever met into his bed. He ate from every dish and drank each jug dry. It was that same enthusiasm that made him generous, eloquent and charming. He was the man who originally sent me to Spain to ensure justice for the English, and before you ever met me, my adorable dearest, he sent me to Italy to ensure no problems with the Medici family."

"So King Edward was half wonderful and half a greedy pig."

Illiana rode close now to her future husband, past the towering cathedral and the glitter of its reflective windows, past the large square of huddled mansions, market, taverns and hostels of the great Westminster Sanctuary, where thieves and gamblers mixed in utter safety with those claiming sanctuary from the law. They rode slowly for the streets were crowded, crowds making their way towards the city and hurrying to avoid delay when entering at Ludgate. The hustle and bustle, the push of horses riding past, the rumble of barrows and litters, the sudden march of priests holding up their crosses and swishing past in a glory of white and scarlet, then the shove of a dozen sheep forced forwards towards the Shambles. Glitter shone, then disappeared, leaving the lurking shadows.

Echoes of the tumultuous year still left their stains, yet as the final days promised new prosperity, trade had burst huge and now budded even further across England, with new businesses evolving.Working families now enriched, ordinary folk chatting cheerfully with their lords, no sword in either hand, and the promise of more to come, was turning the desolation of chaotic rebellion and its memory into the safe wealth of a new life.

Charles rode slowly, enjoying Illiana at his side, only one guard riding close to their backs, for they aimed only for The Strand, and the mansion that Charles had always called his home.

Instead, the great magnificence of the Cleevesbrydge Mansion thrilled Illiana to such a breathless delight, that she stared, as though never before having seen anything like it. "You seem impressed, my love, but you have just seen the royal palace," Charles remarked as Illiana sat, as still as though stunned.

She said, "A palace is a place for kings and feasts and everything. This is simply a family house, but it's so, utterly beautiful."

"We're an old family." Charles nodded to the guard behind them, who trotted quickly past the gateway and into the grounds to inform the staff that both the Viscount and his special guest, were imminent arrivals. "It's an old house, built when there was more space, and less to pay. Could you ever call it home, do you think?"

Suddenly Illiana grinned at him. "I'd marry an octopus just to call this home. " she reached to his hand, "You only have two beautiful arms so you're not an octopus. " she asked. "It just looks so welcoming. What age are you, my lord? I have no idea."

He chuckled. "My dearest love, I may look older, but I'm twenty eight years past my birth, with a few months hanging to the year's tail. You, my little one, are little indeed at twenty one by nothing more than a month. Indeed, the new king is not much more than I am, at the proud age of thirty one.

"All babies then."

"Probably not so much the man you're about to meet," Charles added, "should I discover whether or not my dear father actually exists. If anyone can find him, I'll have the pleasure of introducing him to my future wife, and even of reminding him who I am."

Illiana was still excited and laughing as they entered, the great double doors flung wide by the steward, who bowed low. "My Lord Charles, and My Lady, the future Countess Illiana." Clearly the recent messages had arrived. "Enter, and I shall order refreshments immediately."

"Where's my father, Thatcher? Is he even at home? Even alive?" Charles helped Illiana shrug off the huge sky blue cloak in which she was swathed, and tossed it to Thatcher.

"Sir," now the steward clutched the mountain of outdoor

warmth, "the earl is most certainly at home, and I have informed him of your arrival and request to speak with him. He sits in the Grand Hall, sir, and has informed me that he awaits your appearance with delight, and with pleasure in abundance."

Charles asked, frowning, "Did he use those actual words, Thatcher? Do you quote the man?"

"He did indeed, sir," the steward replied. "I have quoted his lordship precisely."

"Good Lord above," Charles declared. "He must have gone completely mad. Either that or he's cupshotten. Well, my little one, let's see if I can recognise my own Papa."

At that precise moment, although considerably further south, Nicholas Farrier and his daughter arrived in the village of Benedictsbridge, and halted the following rattle of the two litters, one holding three tired but chattering women, and the other carrying two more ladies beside a mountain of luggage. Esther, Denise and Avis crawled to the curtains and pulled them wide, while Bertha and Olivia sat in the larger of the litters, both almost asleep. Wisely, Sabine had accepted her father's aid in making the journey on horseback.

The village actually sat in sunshine. It was the twenty third day of December and although not yet midday, official dinner time, the small church watched the queue spread west. The building alight with candles, shone and flickered, its short spire shimmering more gloriously beneath the pale sunshine. In London at the same moment, it was bitterly cold with frost rimed cobbles, windows and door steps. Yet in Devonshire, the sun had discovered a scrap of sky free of low cloud, and was peering down at the eager new arrivals.

"Except on those vile days of horror and flame," Sabine whispered to her father, "and you remember all that just as I do, the streets were always so pitifully quiet. A threatening silence hung across back lanes like the law of poverty and fear. Yet everyone should have been singing and dancing, it was so blazing hot and beautiful.

Bertha heard the faint words, leaned over and pulled back the curtains. "I shall never forget Spain," she murmured in her own whisper.

"Sometimes," Olivia said, her face sun warmed as she peeped towards the opening, "I wish I'd gone to Spain with you all."

"Never think that," interrupted Bertha at once. "You'd have escaped from your vile husband, but you'd have faced worse."

Sitting astride her horse and ahead, Sabine still grinned at her father. "Now here, it's freezing cold, but out there everyone's talking and smiling and laughing." Nicholas nodded, stroking his horse's neck, looking over her ears to the busyness of the streets. Folk carried flowers for the church. The flowers were hard to find, but sprigs of holly, large bunches of hellebore and tiny bunches of snowdrops were clasped by many. The echoes of music from the church organ spread beyond.

An open square was too small for games, but a sturdy thatched tavern flanked one side, and opposite the church was a little fenced garden of soft grass around one huge oak tree. Beneath the tree a Nativity scene had been spread, six candles fronting the careful display of tiny details. The village claimed just one square and three streets lined with cottages, but beyond were farms and huge farm houses, budding groves thick with apple trees and ploughed fields.

Beyond it all, and jutting like a monument on the horizon, was the many peaked roof of what was clearly a large house, although half hidden by tangles of ivy and the flowerless thorns of wild climbing roses.

"That's it," Denise screeched, pointing. "It must be."

In the other litter, Bertha murmured only to herself, staring up,

"Wild thorns, but not the threat of Spain, now the prettiness of home."

The churchgoers looked over, and most smiled and waved. "Tis such a tiny place, I reckon," Nicholas reckoned, "tis every man, woman and child will be friends with every other man, woman and child."

Waving from the litter, "Which is what I have always longed for," breathed Avis.

"And what I dream of," said Esther.

"And what we deserve," added Denise, "especially those other two in the other litter, poor Bertha and the even more unlucky Lady Olivia.".

Both Illiana and then Nicholas had sent messages ahead, but the second carrier had arrived only four hours previously, so the staff within the mansion were still creating the transformation they needed to welcome owners they had never met, the elite from London, folk with titles and polite distinction.

The four sisters rushed in with arms outflung, Nicholas trumpeted his own excitement and Sabine danced down the wide corridor, wishing Illiana could see this transformation of her mother, who had once been permanently stiff, scalding and drab. Even Olivia was smiling widely, hoping to grasp eager hands. Enthusiasm now burst where misgivings concerning everything had once ruled.

Already the fire was blazing, candles were lit high in sconces, and in tall silver brackets. Chairs were cushioned, a settle was long, deep, well armed, and swathed with blankets and a pillow. Floor boards were waxed, and three tapestry rugs were spread by the inglenook, for sitting to admire the bursting flames.

The Birstall Coat of Arms, blazoned almost as brightly as the blazing fire, was painted on the chimney breast above the hearth. Against the far wall was a long table of dark oak, stools on either side and the master chair at its head. The other wall was host to three enormous windows, each mullioned with real glass in the leaden frames, looking out onto the hedges of the grounds, and the banks of a small stream still running beyond. "Plenty o' fresh fish come a'visiting here, mistress," one woman smiled, pointing.

"And soon, miss, I reckon there'll be nesting doves in the willow," a younger woman pointed upwards.

"Never let that horrid Beatrice woman see that coat of arms," Bertha added, "or she'll start claiming the place as her own after all."

"And your names?" Denise begged. "This is going to be a household of friends, no bowing and plenty of hugging."

The younger woman looked terrified. "I'm Peg," she whispered, "and I'll does as I'm told, m'lady, but only me mum's ever hugged me afore."

Although dinner was not yet ready to serve, Nicholas and Sabine sat at the table, speaking softly and privately while the sisters were galloping upstairs to choose their bedchambers. "I gotter help this lot with that pile o' bags, sacks and baskets," Nicholas muttered. "But reckon we needs a bit o' quiet to ourselves and all. Tired, is you, lass, after all the riding?"

"A little." Sabine was exhausted and her back throbbed.

"Tis a mighty grand house. Lady Illiana don't know what lucky stuff she's got."

"She will soon," Sabine nodded. "Once she's married, she can come here with Charles for holidays. I'm not sure how many beds there are, but there's bound to be attic rooms or something."

"I reckon grand rooms under the beams," Nicholas grinned. "But not fer us, at least, not this time. Shortly we be on our way back to London and The Strand. Sadly, tis a mighty long ride, but we'll be back here too, when they comes fer getting away from them rich neighbours."

"Dinner first," Sabine said quickly. "Otherwise, I'll need one of those litters all to myself."

"You really is that tired out, then? Nicholas patted his daughter's knee. "Well, I don't reckon we'll be missed too bad, so you have a mighty good rest first, my love." He waved back towards the settle.

"There's something I thought you might know," Sabine slumped over the table, her arms as a cushion for her head. "I didn't want anyone else to hear, but Bertha said something about her dead husband's sins. I just wondered, do you know what she meant?"

"Sadly, we all got sins. I heard a priest once, telling me we was born with them. Not sure how that works, but tis the priests what knows best."

"Illiana's father, that man Diego, you worked for him back then so you knew him well. I know he was a brilliant groom, but not so good in other ways." Sabine gulped. "Illiana never knew, but Bertha did. She just never admitted it until very, very recently."

Nicholas sighed. "The Lady Bertha, she says as how she's changed since Spain. Tis a mighty hard thing, little one, as you knows full well, to know wickedness and cruelty. The lady, well, she says as how tis making her strong. She reckons she feels mighty different." He stared at his daughter's exhaustion. "I'd say as how weeks o' dreadful nightmare, well, you ain't gonna be unmoved. No one can. I'd have guessed t'would make any lass weak and more affrighted, but Lady Bertha says as how she's stronger and won't never be afraid again." He smiled gently. "But I don't reckon you changed, my little lass. You seems as perfect to me as you always was."

Looking up, Sabine sat silent for a moment. "Yes, I know what Bertha says, and it's true for her, but I never thought about that for myself." She paused again, then shook her head. "I think I'm the same as I've always been. Yes, it was horrible and terrifying but I wasn't tortured. Yes," she lowered both her eyes and her voice, "but it wasn't the first time I'd been raped. I mean," and once more she gazed directly at her father, "that was what I wanted to talk about. No, no, not rape. I promise not. At least, not really. It was Illiana's father I was thinking of."

"Was the best groom I reckon I've ever knowed," said, frowning. "Better n' me. There weren't a horse what didn't trust and love him, but me, well, I ain't no horse."

"You mean you didn't like the man? I thought you were friends."

Shaking his head, Nicholas raised a hand. "Summit I ain't never told you neither, sweetling. P'raps I should."

Two doors burst open at the same moment. The great Hall doors leading from the entrance and the kitchens was flung back as three aproned women marched, holding high the trays of food and wine they brought for dinner. At the same moment, the back door opened with a scurry of laughter and remarks on the glorious smells, the glorious house, and the glorious bedchambers.

"I have a bedchamber more beautiful than ever before," Denise announced. "And Denise and me, we're sharing. We'll talk all night together."

"And I shall be alone in peace, and my new room is the larger," grinned Esther.

The three large kitchen trays were unloaded and the platters spread across the table where Nicholas and Sabine sat, laden with roast chicken, their skins spread with oozing honey, fresh bream, with a burst of roast apples and herbs. Piled fresh baked bread and rosemary rolls, fried mushroom pancakes, turnip mash with cabbage and rhubarb dough balls, Apple tart with thick custard, and two enormous jugs of wine. Spoons rattled and cups jostled, an odd assortment, with one metal tankard, three wooden cups and a pretty silver grail shaped jug, recently polished.

"Has been a right proper pleasure," said one of the women. "We've not cooked for others than ourselves for a mighty long time. Now at last we can make a feast."

"Considering," interrupted another woman, "We ain't no high chef sort o' cooks, but I reckon you'll enjoy what we does."

Peg had joined them. "Though mayhaps you ladies is used to better back home."

Avis shook her head, the long curls still in disarray after the endless hours of bumps in the litter. "Never. This, my dear friends, is the best I could even imagine."

"And there's Peg," said Esther, "and two wise women I'd love to know better. Will you tell us your names?"

"Betty," one said, glowing.

The other's smile was even more of a beam, and she was twice the size, blissful in a generous width. "Me, well, I be Gladys, and in charge o' the kitchens. There be Tom too, scullery boy, he is, but we calls him a page. He be too shy to come out of the cupboard, but you'll all meet him soon enough when I tells him he's gotter empty the chamber pots."

"Now," said Bertha, as though addressing a banquet. "I've cooked for grand houses. A lady I may be, and certainly am, but I can cook, and I can tell you, this meal is impressive."

The food was good and everyone ate more than usual. The recent travelling also demanded more nutrition. The wine, home brewed, was less strong but more delicious than many.

"We got a weeny little row o' grapes out the back," Betty explained. "And there be five good lads that grow what we needs, grabs the fish from the stream when we asks for them, looks after the vines, and has enough skill for looking after the apple grove. Then there's the two sweet brown cows and the three little goats, Maisy, Daisy and Milly."

"Don't forget to name them cows," called Peg. "Milk, cream, and even cheese when we got time for all that frothing. Jilly and Lucy, out in the fields but comes to the shed when we calls."

"Tis not a proper big farm," admitted Gladys, but there be plenty o' them around and mighty close by too. They got a hundred hens up the lane, and Dolly, she's Roff's wife over the back, she got a big orchard with pears in season."

Nicholas was filling cups, and passed one to Esther, the elder sister. She raised it. "Come on, lovely friends. Help yourselves. No, no, not all so polite. Sit with us, eat and drink and let's all share stories.

Whispering to her father, Sabine said, "This is all very nice and friendly." She licked her fingers, now covered in honey. "Illiana wouldn't mind. I mean, when we were maids ourselves, she would have loved it, and Bertha is just another sister, so I hope she'll understand."

"Reckon the Lady Bertha looks mighty pleased. She surely ain't moaning about nothing."

Bertha was sniggering into her platter. "What about Charles when he comes? He's an important viscount. One day he'll be an earl himself."

"What I knows o' Lord Charles," Nicholas was also licking his fingers, "which be more than you lass, since I done spent many hours with the gent while searching, if you knows what I mean, he ain't no bossy lad. His troop o' Marshalls, mostly is peasants and country folk just like these 'uns, and he mixes with them the same, all brothers, as it were. No *yes, sir – no, sir.* Tis all, *'Allan, what about,* and, *Samuel, lad – if you got time to spare from biting your toe nails.'"*

Sabine laughed and helped herself to the last remaining rhubarb puff. "It's lovely having a tops o' turvey life. I was a poor little scrubber, friends with a cleaning maid. Then I was best friends with the countess. Then, it was Spain and that was vile, but now, I'm not sure what I am, but I know I'm happy."

"With you, and us back home, and all what's coming around, I reckon I be happier than ever." Nicholas was gulping from the large metal tankard and looked just a little flushed. "I reckon tis a fair time I don't miss your mother no more. I missed her fer years, lovely lass that she was but now tis well nigh seventeen years, sadly I reckon I can hardly remember her face."

Sabine had no memory at all of her mother. "You're my father and mother too," she told Nicholas. "I won't embarrass you by calling you Mamma in public." He chuckled. Everyone was laughing.

Since only two sharp knives had appeared on the table, although there were twelve bright spoons of both wood and tin, and of various sizes, every one at the table, now including the staff, was finger tipping, licking, and dripping apple juice and pickles.

"I want to stay overnight," Sabine said suddenly and loudly. "It's a long journey back to London and I can't ride all night again. I'd fall off the saddle. We'll stay overnight where there's the same inns as before, but here for a night or two first would be wonderful. I don't mind sleeping in the cow shed. Or I'll curl up here on the settle, or with all those wine barrels in the cellar."

Clearly Nicholas was also attracted to the idea, but muttered, "Will our Lady think we done fall'd in the river? There ain't no way we can send a message."

"There are plenty more bedchambers," called Gladys. "Apart from the master chamber, there's three more just one floor up and there's our staff rooms of course, up in the attic."

"Plenty of rooms, plenty of vacant bedchambers," and with a gulp , Sabine, complete with a mouthful of mushroom and onion, gasped, "Olivia. She came with us. She's going to live with us. Where is she?"

The very tired countess was standing shyly by the doorway, drinking in the rich smells of food and wondering if she could slip between the other women at the table.

Gladys hurtled to her feet. "You greatest lady of all," she stuttered. "You taken the bed for yourself, I hopes, my lady. Now come, bless you, to the head of the table and enjoy what dinner we's prepared."

Bertha stretched out her hand to Olivia, who sank gratefully onto the cushioned chair. "I found a lovely bedchamber with two windows," she smiled, picking up a spoon. "And now I'm starving."

"You're no ignored, mistreated lady in this house," Sabine called loudly from the other end of the table. "You're the grand Mistress. You can practise being bossy."

Bertha poured Olivia a cup of the wine, raised her own cup and stared back to Sabine. "It's nearly Christmas," she insisted, "Illiana will be jaunting off to the palace for the Yuletide feast, and besides, she's with Charles. She won't be thinking of us at all."

"Anyway," said Betty, "the cat needs company. He roams all over, frightening away the mice and rats. Not that he eats any of them, he's too fat already with what we feed him on left overs. He always sleeps alone in the small room by the top stairs. He'd love someone to cuddle him there."

Esther clapped her hands. "Please stay the night, my dears. This is Illiana's property, and you're her best friend. You've more right here than we have."

"We'll have a royal feast too," called Avis. "Stay for Christmas. It's only the day after tomorrow."

Although avid with her knife and an over full spoon, Olivia looked up. "This will be my happiest Christmas of my whole life. I know it will."

"Stay till St. Stephens," Denise said to Nicholas. "We'll all go to midnight Mass at that little church in the square tomorrow."

"Saint Winifred's in Winifred Square," muttered Betty.

"Then have the best Christmas feast in all England." He gazed down with a quick blush at his empty platter. "Even more fancy than this mighty good feast I just felled in love with."

"But I've only got riding boots with me," remembered Sabine. "I didn't pack for churches or sitting cosy by the fire."

"You can dance barefoot, Miss," giggled Peg, who was obviously already tipsy. "I always does, since I ain't got no shoes nor riding boots nor naught of that kind. Just stockings, and if tis warm, I keeps them safe and clean and all. I just wriggle me toes. I promise, tis always better to dance that way."

Olivia looked up again, one hand remembering to cover and hide her bruises. "I have three nice pairs of shoes," she said, "But I haven't danced a step since I was married."

At once Gladys said, "We have friends who are minstrels. So it's a blessing and a delight to look forward to, there'll be music and dancing for all of us this Christmas Day."

CHAPTER THIRTY ONE

The long slim elderly gentleman was already partially dozing in the high backed armchair.

He jerked upright, however, as the Steward announced the unexpected arrivals. "Goodly gracious heavens above," spluttered the earl, patting his chest as though searching for a kerchief, "what youngsters we have in the family."

Charles was grinning. "You must be my genuine father, sir. I imagine I may even have met you once before. Sir, please meet my future wife, the glorious Lady Illiana."

His lordship dragged the palm of one large quivering hand back across his forehead, seemingly to push his hair from his eyes. Since he was entirely bald, however, this would seem an old yet not forgotten habit. "Well, well," he said. "Yes, Papa I am. So dear Charles, it would surely be you. Don't think I have any other children. Don't remember any."

"You do not,' said Charles cheerfully. "I am clearly sufficient."

"How's the king?" the earl added. "Richard now, isn't it. I seem to remember Edward bowling off."

"It is the twenty third day of December, sir," Charles informed

CHAPTER THIRTY ONE

him. "Our charming but odd monarch, King Edward, died around the third day of April, some months past. Not that we can be sure of the exact day, thanks to the Woodville manipulations."

"Yes, yes, boy," the earl sniffed. "I know. Of course I know, and now it's Richard. That's right, isn't it." He scratched the bridge of his nose. "I must pop over and visit him one day, and you, pretty young lady. You want to marry my son. Are you sure? Might not be such a good idea, you know. Goodness only knows what the boys spends. He gads off all over the place. I never see him."

The grin remained. "This is Lady Illiana," Charles said, speaking loudly and bending over his father's ear. "Up until this moment, sir, she has agreed to our marriage. If she now changes her mind, the fault is yours."

"Not at all," sniffed the earl. "Would be your fault, my boy, for rollicking around all over the country. I keep forgetting your name."

"Charles, last time I looked," Charles told him. "And I assume you are Lord Tristram, Earl of Cleeves."

"Umm," decided Tristram. "Good boy. Quite correct. You've got a good memory."

"Not inherited, I believe, sir."

"Well, well, now I have a daughter," A sudden gleam lit the earl's dark eyes. "And very pretty at that. Not that you look much like my dear wife. Well, I suppose you wouldn't, really. Would have been nice, though."

"I'm sorry to hear of your wife's death, my lord," said Illiana politely.

"Why? Did I tell you?" The earl was puzzled. "A mighty long, long time back, it was, far as I can remember. You," the long finger pointed at Charles, "were just a bundle of fluff. Out of swaddling since you insisted on crawling all over the place. Wriggly little toes, quite a few of them too. Can't remember your name, though."

"I think, even at that age," he said, "I was still Charles."

"Didn't look much like you though." The earl peered at Charles.

CHAPTER THIRTY ONE

"A lot smaller than you. I picked the scrap up once. Kicked those funny bundles of legs all over the place, he did. Tiny feet too. Had lots of toes. Amazing how things grow."

Charles changed the subject. "It is indeed," he said with some care beneath the grin, "I've wandered abroad lately. I have been on his majesty's business. I'm home now, however, as you may have noticed. Back from Spain. No doubt you've heard of Spain, sir?"

"Umm." The earl glowered. "Hot place. On the Middle Sea."

"Most astute," appreciated Charles. "But now I have returned here, to my home, which I trust you accept, sir, as, um, acceptable."

"Here?" The earl stared around the enormous shadows, firelit, of the great hall.

"Unless cupshotten," Charles continued, "I'll no doubt sleep in my bedchamber."

"Good. Upstairs," nodded Tristram.

"What is more important, sir," Charles continued with patience, "Lady Illiana, my fiancé, in case you forget, also needs a bedchamber in this home of ours. Unless you have a number of new guests I know nothing of, we should have several possibilities. Unless you object, sir?"

"To what?"

"At some distance from your own rooms, father, I am aware of a large bedchamber furnished in gold and white velvet, complete with closet. I believe this would suit my fiancé, should Thatcher arrange for the room to be aired, warmed, and the bed linen refreshed. Shall I inform Thatcher on your behalf, my lord?"

"Yes, yes, call Thatcher," said the earl. "But damnit, not bedtime yet, is it?"

It was a room she loved before she had even explored. The sheen of the golden colours brought summer within, even when the large window proved that winter was without. Although there had not yet been time to change the bedding nor light the fire, Illiana flopped onto the bed, rolled four times across its width, therefore

CHAPTER THIRTY ONE

wide enough for four large people, and wondered if Charles would ever share it with her.

Men seemed to think that women should come to them. They called. It seemed like a summons.

Benedict had been very different and they had shared the same room as though it was equally theirs. Whether that would have continued into the future, she could not know, but she'd heard enough gossip concerning other lords and the elite, whereas even the gossip concerning the ordinary men sounded quite horribly bossy.

Imagining Charles like this just did not work. Only wild excitement rang true. Yet, she knew it possible, the excitement might be her own anticipation without any relevance to the facts.

Illiana climbed from the bed, and stared at herself in the mirror. It stood, facing her, from the corner of the shadows, fully leaded and covered at the back within a large oak frame, and so showed such a clear reflection, she felt she could even see the small black spot on her skin over one eyebrow, and the little missing corner of one tooth. Her mother had walloped her as a child, and that one tooth had taken the full force. She had loved seeing herself in mirrors. They were rare enough, and most were spotted yellow which transformed any reflection into a nightmare. Suddenly seeing her self, had always seemed like a sweet proof of her existence.

"I love the room," she told Charles, now having left it. "Thank you so much for choosing it. For having me stay here at all. It will be hundreds and hundreds of times more glorious than living with Benjamin."

"I assume you had a comfortable bedroom?" he looked up, grinning.

Charles now sat alone, legs spread to the fire, a large cup of steaming hippocras on the little stool pulled to the arm of his chair. Still wearing his outdoor clothes except for his boots and cape, his toes, within the black woollen hose, wriggling towards

CHAPTER THIRTY ONE

the hearth and its leaping flames, and so presumably had not yet returned to his own bedchamber to change back to indoor attire.

At first, she imagined Charles as a baby, with tiny plump toes, naked without those silken hose. Then she imagined his bed. Grand. Velvet hangings. Tassels. A vast window overlooking the river. Finally, she imagined climbing into it.

Attempting to keep her own wandering thoughts from repetitive beds, she said in a hurry, "For you now, really home again, that must feel, well, nice. Wonderful."

Abruptly he stretched out one arm, grabbing her, his arm around her waist and his hand to her wrist, then pulling her onto his lap. Her damask and woollen skirts flapped into a twist and she felt only the thin linen of her shift between herself and his thighs. She had no idea, however, as to whether this was an intentional move of long practise with endless women, or simply the luck of the lunge.

Illiana giggled. "What if your father comes in, or what about Thatcher – or any one?"

"No one will," he assured her. "My father forgets who I am and has no reason to visit such a tedious stranger, and no staff appear unless I call them. The fire will keep us sweating for at least two more hours before needing a prod, and there is another cup waiting here just for you, my love, tipped with steaming mulled hippocras. Sip slowly, or you'll burn your lip, and that lip, as full and soft, needs me, little one, without the injury of scalding first. It's my own body will burn you, my love." And he pulled her tighter.

Beneath the fold of her shift, she felt the muscles of his legs. She felt their length, their speed, and their heat. Now his arms enclosed her and her head was against his shoulder. She could hear his heart beat very softly, as though from a great distance, pounding, fast and powerful.

Whispering, since she was now unable to speak aloud, Illiana mumbled, "I thought,"

CHAPTER THIRTY ONE

"Best not to think," he told her as his fingers slipped warm from her neck to her shoulder. "Meanwhile your golden room is two steps from my own. Which, incidentally, is not golden. It is the sinister colour of old mustard and black. When I steal you from your golden haven, and drag you into my own quarters, you will shine, silver perhaps, and I shall have the delight of finding you."

"So your bedchamber smells of mouldy mustard?" It was an attempt to escape from thought of beds.

"Not that I've ever noticed. I shall ensure that it reeks of spice. Ginger, cinnamon, and saffron."

Illiana started to smell a drifting promise of ginger. Immediately she said, "And do I come to you?"

"It seems you are forgetting who I am, just as my father does." Charles grinned and the firelight glowed scarlet across his face.

"I could hardly forget. You have such bright eyes."

"No doubt they are blushing," he chuckled back at her, "ashamed of the lurid thoughts now in my head."

She was confident that her own blushes were genuine. "I'm worried in case someone comes in. I keep hearing footsteps and doors shutting, and I don't know, will your father be angry if he sees me like this? It's been so long, I can't remember, and my mind goes around and around."

With his face bent towards her, his breath hot on her cheek, he told her, "First, I kiss you. Then I explain all the matters that trouble you. Bedchambers indeed. Now I feel the rise of your ribs, each separate beneath this double layer of bodice. I also feel the heave of your breathing beneath your ribs, little one. You breathe quickly, as though expecting what is undoubtedly coming,," and he spread two warm fingers beneath her chin and moved her face towards him. Only for a brief moment the scarlet reflection stared directly into her eyes, and then he kissed her.

With his lips hard and is face hot, he pressed against her. His lips moved then, as though tasting her, and his tongue, slick with

CHAPTER THIRTY ONE

mulled wine, discovered her own throat, the inside of her cheeks, and the hovering impatience of her own tongue.

Illiana wanted more when he stopped, pulled away, and grinned down at her.

"Your mother now laughs with her long-lost sisters, wealthy and prepared for peace and pleasure. Your piteous Olivia," he told her, "will find all the peace beauty, delight and appreciation of personal choice that she has been denied during years of being bound to a man, who never understood the meaning of love. Your newly discovered aunts now live happily with their sisters in a country home where they can do precisely whatever they wish, and where you will visit whenever you want. As for Sabine, she will come here, but not as a maid or servant, but as a friend. Her father, although I shall most certainly put him in charge of the stables, will not be either groom nor gardener. He will live in this house and be as much a friend as he wishes. We have sufficient bed chambers here to start a rookery. But," and he smiled again, his mouth so close to hers that she knew he needed another drink, "all at a polite distance from us. There are six bedchambers in the tower, two on each floor, and a cellar below for the prisoners."

"You imprison people?"

"My memory, somewhat more efficient than my father's," he told her, "recalls no prisoners of any kind, only wine barrels. However, it lurks down there, waiting for the future."

"What a cosy thought." She laughed into the glow of his eyes. "Are you so accustomed to arresting the wicked, and riding into battles and killing strangers?"

Pausing a moment, then laughing, Charles nodded. "No doubt I am. A sweet life, but one I shall escape now, and dream of you, my love, not of swords and knives."

"You've made me think of Sabine," she whispered. "I wasn't close to my mother once Papa died. She never seemed to want me. Sabs was my one saviour, but," and she sniffed a little into the pause, "it's only recently, a few weeks gone, I found out my mother

CHAPTER THIRTY ONE

thought I'd killed Papa. It's a horrid story. I'm not going to repeat, but now I think, and I don't want to think, and I hope it's wrong, but perhaps it was Sabs herself."

His kiss silenced her. His mouth closed on hers, breathing out her breath so it merged with his, silencing her. When he eased away, the black tunnels of his eyes strengthened the magic, pulling her into his darkness.

"Listen little one, talk to me of whatever you wish, whenever you wish, and I will help, or simply listen, or ask to delve deeper. But your father's problems seem to be true enough, although I never knew him, and although he never inflicted his sins on you nor suffered you to know him beyond his love as a father."

"But he did with Sabine."

"I've spent many long miles in company with her father. Nicholas talked of many things. Of his daughter, of your father, and of a good deal else. He's a good man and I welcome him into my home, but you need the truth, always the truth whether sweet or cruel. Our lives will never be utterly kind. That happens for no one and we must help in times of cruelty as well as in kindness. So, I can tell you, no, Sabine did not kill your father. Nicholas did."

Now she was shivering. "That makes no sense."

"It does, and comes from love and kindness to his daughter. He saw her escape from him out in the grounds. Then Diego crawled, laughing, from beneath a bush. His hand was bleeding and he held it out to Nicholas, and laughed about what had happened. Sabine had tried to defend herself. Had tried to kill him, perhaps, but as a child, had no strength. So, Nicholas killed him."

"How old was Sabine?"

"A child. Eight, perhaps, as you were." Illiana was staring, pale faced, and Charles smiled. "No doubt Nicholas would have preferred I'd kept that private. He'll never wish you to hate him as the man who murdered your father, but," and he kissed both her eyelids, soothing their shock, "he did not swear me to silence when he admitted his story. So you now know the reason. He did

CHAPTER THIRTY ONE

what was right, and you will always understand the truth. As your husband, little one, I shall always tell you that truth." Charles kissed her again, his tongue across her lashes. "Now, my future wife, we trust, and must trust, and you must tell me anything and I will tell you everything. There will be far more love, happiness and joy, and that I promise." He sighed, his breath again on her tongue. "I endlessly imagine you naked, though I've never seen you naked, nor touched your secret beauty, only dreamed of you. I've felt the shape and the heat of your body, and I know the beauty of your face but to see the glorious truth of what now sits hopefully in my mind, that will be the best of all."

Her face was buried against that throbbing heartbeat. She mumbled into the dark velvet. "I've never ever seen myself like that," she said, her words entirely blurred. "I've never looked in a mirror or seen reflections in water, not without clothes. Never and I don't think I want to."

"You may want to," he grinned down at her, "when I tell you how exquisite and adorable you most bewitchingly appear to me."

"You may not think so when you see the horrible truth."

"My dearest," his hands were wandering, "I already know. I know because while clothed, I see you as utterly enticing. Whatever beauty I see, once you allow me to slowly undress you, will be what I love. It's you, little one, the whole of you, that I dream about. I love your voice, I love your ideas, I love the meaning inside your eyes, I love everything you say. I shall admire you and laugh at you and teach you and learn from you, and always desire you. That's how I am, my love, and that's how you are. If I invite you into my bed before our wedding night, would you come? If I creep into your golden comfort before our wedding night, will you throw me out?"

"I wouldn't have the strength." Her whisper was too soft for Charles to be sure he had heard her.

"Say that again, and we may retire a little early tonight."

CHAPTER THIRTY ONE

"What does your father do in the evenings?" which was a gulp of sorts.

The chuckle was equally as soft. "He often sits in the garden and watches the river creep by. When he shivers enough to remember it's winter, he'll sit with us, sometimes, talking, drinking, telling the stories of his own youth. Supper is served at around six of the clock. The cooks here are good, the kitchen staff excellent. I know every one, and sometimes tell them to search new ideas and experiment. They laugh and produce miracles. Thatcher, whose father was indeed a thatcher, sings, and keeps a viol hidden in his own chamber. Christmas this year will be spent with the king, and my father will forget where he is and fall asleep in the roast goose. Once every evening closes, we bid goodnight to a gleaming silver moon and the dancing silver glitter of the stars, we argue over which bed we will roll into, we snuff the candle, we undress each other very, very slowly, we ignore the long mirror which cannot ever do us credit, and then we pass the night embraced as tightly as dreaming allows."

It was just a little later when she looked up, and said, "You know what I love about you the most?"

He gazed back into her eyes, then said, "My left ear, perhaps?"

"I am very fond of that ear," she admitted.

He nodded. "You did kiss it quite recently."

"I had another answer in mind. I was going to say, everything. You burn with such confidence, so with you, finally I'll be wrapped in confidence too."

About the Author

My passion is for late English medieval history and this forms the background for my historical fiction. I also have a love of fantasy and the wild freedom of the imagination, with its haunting threads of sadness and the exploration of evil. Although all my books have romantic undertones, I would not class them purely as romances. We all wish to enjoy some romance in our lives, there is also a yearning for adventure, mystery, suspense, friendship and spontaneous experience. My books include all of this and more, but my greatest loves are the beauty of the written word, and the utter fascination of good characterisation. Bringing my characters to life is my principal aim.

For more information on this and other books, or to subscribe for updates, new releases and free downloads, please visit barbaragaskelldenvil.com

Printed in Great Britain
by Amazon